Teller

a novel

Frederick Weisel

Grateful acknowledgment is made to reprint portions of the following:

"What'll I Do?" by Irving Berlin
© Copyright 1924 by Irving Berlin
© Copyright Renewed. International Copyright Secured.
All Rights Reserved. Reprinted by Permission.

"The End of the World"
Words by Sylvia Dee
Music by Arthur Kent
Copyright © 1962 (Renewed) by Music Sales Corporation (ASCAP)
International Copyright Secured. All Rights Reserved.
Used by Permission.

"If I Fell" by John Lennon and Paul McCartney
© 1964 Sony/ATV Music Publishing LLC. All rights administered by Sony/ATV Music Publishing LLC, 8 Music Square West, Nashville, TN 37203. All rights reserved. Used by permission.

This book contains an excerpt from the forthcoming *Elise: A Novel* by Frederick Weisel. This excerpt has been set for this edition only and may not reflect the final content of the forthcoming edition.

Published by Dog Ear Publishing
4010 W. 86th Street, Ste H
Indianapolis, IN 46268
www.dogearpublishing.net

ISBN: 978-145750-637-6

This book is printed on acid-free paper.

Printed in the United States of America

For Meg and Chelsea

And my Mother and Father

Life can only be understood backwards; but it must be lived forwards.

— Kierkegaard

Acknowledgments

I would like to thank friends and family members, who inquired about my progress with this novel over the years and withheld their skepticism that I would ever finish.

A particular debt of gratitude is owed to early readers, including Loralee Denny, Marie Gewirtz, Paul Haase, Jeanne Hunsberger, Lee Lehrman, Carol and Robert Sanoff, and Chelsea Weisel. Any remaining errors are mine, not theirs.

Individuals who helped with research, include: Dr. Tom Crane, for explanation of the nature and treatment of gunshot wounds; Erica Dincalci, for background on feminist singer-songwriters; Steve Zahniser, for clarification of legal proceedings; and several acquaintances, nameless at their own request, for information on correct dosages of illicit drugs.

Thanks to Kelly McManus for photography that helped me create a smoking gun, and Lee Lehrman for the cover design and advice on page design and type fonts.

I write today with the voices of several teachers in my head, including Kay Zahn and Robert S. Fogarty.

And especially to my daughter, Chelsea Weisel, who taught me viola fingering and endured a coffee table at home piled high with books on guns and drugs . . .

. . . and to my wonderful wife, Meg McNees, who helped me find the right words, woke me with coffee at 5 am, drove with me to scout Sonoma County locales, accompanied me to lectures and workshops, and generally listened to me talk about the plot and characters for years—and always had something encouraging to say.

Contents

Part I

CHAPTER 1

IN MARCH OF that year, I saw a man named Paul Barkley shot to death. It happened late at night in the parking lot of a café in Santa Rosa called Galileo's.

I knew Barkley slightly. He'd done me a favor, and I'd been looking for a way to repay him. Barkley himself said he didn't want anything in return. He just hoped it would all work out. Later that's what I remembered—the hopefulness of his gesture.

My name's Charlie Teller. For most of my life I've made a living as a ghostwriter of celebrity autobiographies. Entertainers and sports figures. More than a dozen books in all. The most famous was on the doomed Olympic speed skater Tina Terrill.

At the time of this story I hadn't worked for several years. I'd come up from Los Angeles after the Christmas holidays, trailing my ex-wife and daughter, Jill and Lucy, to this small town. I found Galileo's on the second night, and was partway through my meal at the bar when I heard my name spoken behind me. Turning, I found a man with a round, boyish face and dressed in a silk shirt that billowed outside his trousers. He raised both hands, palms out, in a posture of mock surrender and apologized for the intrusion. He said that his name was Paul and that he owned the café and was with a group across the room. I was known to him from a photo in a magazine feature a few years before. He enjoyed my books, especially the one on Virginia Hardy—which is what most people say.

Barkley was polite enough that night not to mention my recent eclipse or to ask why I was in town. We spoke for a few minutes, and then he invited me to join his party. He was one of those people whose persuasion is founded on such perfect confidence in what they're urging you to do that my agreeing to have an after-dinner drink with his friends was like joining a winning team. We stood together while he introduced the people around the table. He put his hand on my shoulder. "This is my friend Charlie Teller," he said.

The conversation that night was about Bikram yoga (one of the party had just joined a class). In a lull, Barkley leaned close to me and said he knew someone locally who would make a perfect subject for me. Before I could say a word, he excused himself and made a call.

His subject turned out to be the developer Rajiv Patel, who had emigrated from India as a child and for the past forty years had made a national reputation for building thousands of multistory parking structures. "The Prince of Park," they called him. He lived in a valley east of Santa Rosa. I had heard of Patel, of course. He was rumored to be among the richest men in America. It wasn't really my type of project—my expertise is fragility. But I hadn't received many offers lately, and so I made no protest as Barkley arranged my meeting with the titan of capitalism.

Like so many things with Barkley, the arrangements were accomplished effortlessly. Within a week I had moved into my own apartment on the Patel estate—a sprawling compound called *Shanti Bhavan*—and accepted the task of what the old man referred to as "compiling my papers."

And so began my new life: During the day I interviewed Patel or wrote. Several nights a week, I drove into town to see Jill and Lucy, and to share a dinner with Barkley and his friends. If I had doubts about the enterprise, I recognized it as work I knew how to do. Suddenly employed again, as if the preceding years of idleness had never occurred, I felt grateful for the simple pleasures of the job.

On that night in March, two months after our first meeting, all the regulars were already at Galileo's when I arrived around ten. It was a clear spring night after weeks of rain, and the group had moved onto the garden patio. Old Motown hits played on the house sound system, and the tables had been spread apart to make a dance floor.

Sitting at one table was John Coffey, Barkley's business associate in another one of his ventures, a fitness center, and Molly Fryor, a lawyer who was training at the center as a distance runner. Next to them were Stephen Robb, who managed Galileo's, and Carl Drake, a waiter at the café and Stephen's lover. Nico Eden, a masseuse at the fitness center, was perched on a stool at the patio bar.

I took a stool beside Nico, who had opened a bottle of wine. I poured myself a glass, and watched Barkley pull Molly up to dance. They made a good team. Molly moved fluidly with the rhythm, while Barkley had a jerky, loose-limbed style of his own invention. From time to time he was urged to new eccentricities by the rest of us.

Between two songs Nico turned to me and kissed my cheek. Nico was a girl of the hour. Looking out from under a head of bleached spiky hair, she was continually trying out new weapons against the conformity of the world around her. As she viewed it, her role in life was to shake things up and, wherever possible, challenge conventions—conventions that seemed to have been invented for no other purpose than just to piss her off. But like many young rebels, she had not yet found her own signature, and so her assault varied. Tonight she wore a faded denim jacket over a minidress, red high-tops, and star-shaped earrings. She was married to a mysterious young man named Vincent, whom the rest of us had never met. Despite our differences in age and cultural mission, Nico and I were—in her own expression—tight. Several weeks earlier, when we first met, she told me I was an eternal friend because I had co-written the autobiography of one of the six people she admired most in the world—the British rocker, Nick White.

Barkley danced to us and, shouting above the music, said he had something to talk to me about. He handed me an envelope. "This is the beginning, pal," he said. "Hang on to it. I'll talk to you later." Then he smiled and danced away.

The envelope was unsealed. I looked inside and saw a sheet of paper and a computer memory stick. I slid the envelope into my jacket pocket.

"He looks happy tonight," I shouted to Nico.

Nico said something that sounded like "page."

"Pages?" I asked, touching the envelope in my pocket, but the music drowned out my voice. Nico reached into her woven handbag, drew out a plastic container, and began eating fruit salad with her fingers. Between bites she sang along with the music.

Aretha Franklin's "Respect" came on. Stephen and Carl got up to dance. I drank more wine and let the intoxication run through me. I was happy to be with these people, listening to this music.

During "How Sweet It Is," Stephen picked up a call on the phone at the opposite end of the bar. When he returned to the dance floor, his face was red with anger. He drew Barkley away from Molly and began to talk to him. Deserted by their partners, Carl and Molly joined together in a stylized version of a swing routine. My attention was on the dancing couple, when I noticed Barkley lean close to speak to Stephen, who shoved him backward into the wall, and walked out the service corridor toward the kitchen. It took a moment for the scene to register with the dancers, and then Carl left to follow Stephen.

Barkley shrugged at us, and resumed his dance with Molly. Percy Sledge began to sing "When a Man Loves a Woman," and Nico asked me to dance. I declined, but she said, "OK, just hold me while I do," and pulled me onto the dance floor.

We moved slowly between the tables. She pressed her head close to mine, and I felt her hair on my lips. Her hands were sticky from the fruit. Once when we passed Barkley, he put his arm around me and smiled.

We danced two more songs, and then I quit, dizzy from the drinks and my growing suspicion that Nico was not wearing anything under her dress. I went to the restroom and washed my face, and then feeling the envelope in my pocket, hurried back to the patio to find Barkley.

The music had stopped, and Barkley was gone. "You just missed him," Molly said. I ran outside, but by the time I reached the café parking lot, I couldn't see anyone. Knowing that Barkley liked to park his vintage Mercedes away from other cars to avoid scratches, I headed toward the back of the lot.

As I made my way between parked cars, I heard voices. A figure moved in the dark. Then came three loud claps, as if someone were dropping heavy books onto a table. A small pickup with a camper shell drove toward me. The truck roared past and disappeared up the street, through a red light, toward the freeway on-ramp.

The Mercedes sat at the end of the lot where the truck had come from. At a distance, I could see a figure in the front seat. I called Barkley's name and jogged toward the car. With a few steps, I could make out one side of his boyish face lit by the lot's orange lights. But there was something wrong, too. The head was tipped onto the seat back, and in the dim light, I saw a shadow spreading down the passenger window. As I reached the driver's side, I heard a sound pouring out of the open window of the dark car. Violins racing up the scale, and ahead of them, a woman's voice rising high and cold in the night sky.

CHAPTER 2

A BAND OF yellow plastic tape imprinted with the words CRIME SCENE DO NOT CROSS outlined the parking lot of Galileo's. Within it sat half a dozen police vehicles, their rooftop lights flaring yellow-blue and their radios emitting bursts of static. The officers stood taking statements from my friends. Barkley's beautiful cream Mercedes glowed under a ring of portable flood lamps. An EMT crew had already slid the body onto a stretcher and into the back of an ambulance. A police technician now probed the car's interior.

I sat drinking coffee with Molly on a low brick wall outside Galileo's. The sight of Paul in his car kept returning to me. I felt dizzy and nauseated and was struggling to stop my body from shaking in the chill morning air.

A uniformed officer had interviewed us, and now a detective, standing in front of us, was taking my story again. I tried to focus my attention on his questions.

"Was the truck already moving when you came into the parking lot?" he asked.

"No, first I heard the three shots," I said. "Then it went by me."

"What did you see?"

"An ordinary pickup truck. Nothing special."

The detective was a short, powerfully built man. He had close cropped hair and wore a turtleneck, golf jacket, jeans, and Adidas. He asked questions in a quick, impatient voice, and when I answered, made what looked like small ticks in a notepad. His name, he said, was Eddie Mahler.

"You told the officers it was a white Toyota," Mahler said. "Any unusual features on the truck or shell?"

"It was covered in red dirt, like it had been driven off road."

"Did you see the driver?"

"Just a glance. I think it was a male."

Mahler looked down at his notes. "Was there a passenger?" he asked.

"I didn't see one."

"Did you see anyone go from Barkley's car to the truck?"

"No."

"So we don't know there's a connection between the truck and the murder?"

The question surprised me. "I guess not," I said. "But the truck was back by Paul's car. The driver must have seen something."

Mahler ignored my comment. "You were coming out to the parking lot to speak to Mr. Barkley about this envelope?" He held up the envelope I had given the police officers.

"Yes."

"He'd given it to you earlier in the evening?"

"Yes. I didn't know he was going to leave." This now sounded doubtful.

"Did he leave abruptly?"

"No, it's just I didn't know he was leaving."

"Did he receive a phone call or a message that called him away?"

"I don't know. I was in the restroom."

Mahler turned the pages in his notebook. "In your statement to the officer, you said that earlier in the evening you observed Mr. Barkley fighting with Mr. Robb."

"I don't think I said 'fighting.'"

"What do you think you said?"

"I think I said 'disagreeing.' It was a disagreement."

"OK. What was this disagreement about?"

"I don't know. There was music playing, and they were on the other side of the room."

A new wave of dizziness washed over me, and I swallowed a foul taste in my mouth.

Mahler watched me. "Are you okay?" he asked.

I nodded.

"How did Mr. Barkley act this evening?" Mahler asked. "Was there anything bothering him?"

"Not that I could see."

"Would he have told you if there was?" The question had an edge to it.

"I don't know."

"Is there anyone who would have cause to do him harm?"

I paused. "I guess I didn't know him well enough to answer that," I said.

Molly coughed into her hand. A small woman in her early thirties, she had an aggressive, wired intensity that drove her as a trial attorney and competitive runner. An hour earlier, on first hearing of Paul's death, she had cried uncontrollably. Now she sat stiffly, listening to every word.

"Counselor, would you like to add something?" Mahler asked her.

"Not at this time, Detective Mahler," she said, meeting his eyes.

Mahler paused to regain his train of thought, and then turned back to me. "You're employed as a writer?" he asked.

I nodded and described my arrangement with Patel.

As I finished, recognition shone in Mahler's eyes. "Charles Teller," he said. "You had that . . . thing with Susan Sparrow?"

Mahler smiled. It was a wise-guy grin—one of those looks that express pleasure in seeing someone squirm.

"Yeah, the thing," I said.

"What was your relationship with Mr. Barkley?" Mahler asked.

"A friend. He made the arrangement for me to work with Patel."

Mahler made more ticks in his notebook. "When you got back to Mr. Barkley's car, what'd you see?" he asked.

"Watch your step here, Charlie," Molly said.

"Are you trying to hinder this investigation?" Mahler asked her.

"No, sir. Just advising a citizen."

Mahler turned back to me.

"Paul was sitting still," I said. "I thought he was just waiting for something. Then I saw the blood on the seat and the window."

"Is that all?"

"I said his name. I didn't think he could hear me. The engine was off, but the radio was playing loud music."

Mahler looked at his pad. "Actually a CD," he said. "An opera by Donizetti called *Lucia di Lammermoor*. Maria Callas 1953 recording in Florence. The recording quality's not great, but Callas' voice is worth it. Your friend had taste."

"Opera was Paul's hobby," I said.

"It's a hobby for Eddie, too," Molly said.

Mahler turned and stared at her.

"I mean, it's a hobby for *Detective Mahler*, too," she said.

Mahler turned back to me. "So you heard the music?" he said.

"It startled me."

"Startled you?"

"That's right. I wasn't expecting it."

"OK," Mahler continued. "You said his name, and when he didn't answer, you went back to the café and called 911 on your cell. Is that right?"

"Yes . . . no," I said.

"Which is it?"

I drank some coffee. It had turned cold.

"I touched him," I said. "I reached into the car and touched him." I looked at Molly. She was watching me carefully.

"You touched Mr. Barkley?" Mahler asked. "You didn't mention that before."

"I know. I forgot."

Still watching me, Molly drew a deep breath and let it go.

"Where'd you touch him?" Mahler asked.

"On the face," I said. "His cheek. With the back of my fingers."

"Why?"

"I don't know. I guess I wanted to know it was real."

Mahler watched me again. "Did you touch anything else?" he asked.

"No. I just touched his cheek, and then I went back to the café and called the police."

Mahler was silent.

I leaned back on the wall and put my hands in my jacket pockets. In my right hand, I felt the memory stick. It must have fallen out of the envelope before I gave the envelope to the uniformed officer. Revealing it now might seem as if I had been intentionally withholding it. Instinctively, I folded the stick tightly in my palm.

"Was Mr. Barkley drinking?" Mahler asked.

"He may have had a glass of wine."

"How about you?"

"I had several drinks. I wasn't drunk."

Mahler looked at me. "You own a gun?" he asked.

The question caught me off guard. I found myself smiling. "What're you kidding?" I said.

I turned to Molly. She wasn't looking at me anymore but was peering down into her cup of coffee that she slowly swirled. "Don't say any more, Charlie," she said quietly.

CHAPTER 3

The Ghostwriter

EVERY AMERICAN AUTOBIOGRAPHY, someone once said, is about one thing—escape. Look into the frightened heart of an American life, and you'll find a compulsion to flee—a seed planted in the national character at the start by those ships sailing out of Europe and landing on our shores.

The wealthy and famous who hired me were no exception. When they told me their life story, each had its moment of longing for the exit. "When I was nine, I swallowed my first bottle of pills," Skye Lurie told me, recalling one of the misadventures that would eventually land her the title of America's troubled celebrity teenager. Tina Terrill, the speed skater, said that after she got her driver's license, she had a recurring dream in which the windshield on her car turned into a rearview mirror, and the more she pressed the accelerator, the faster everything familiar disappeared.

This was the wellspring of their autobiographies, the dark center of their worlds, the part that propelled them through life and the place where they hid. Always, in that first week of our working together, my clients would say, "There's something you need to know, Charlie, if we're to write this story." After the first couple, I learned to expect it.

The impulse to autobiography is primal. Somewhere deep within us is the conviction that the comings and goings of one life can tell us something about human nature in general and maybe about ourselves. But what is it, after all, that makes us *want* to tell our story and read another's? What is it that we think we can learn from the story of someone else's life?

That was my job.

In some sense, my work was muddied from the start. If an autobiography is an intimate act—the telling of one's own story—my job was to tell someone else's own story. To write in the first person for another person.

Of course there were some who said that it wasn't really work at all. How hard can it be, a book reviewer once asked, to sit beside a film star on the deck of a $30 million home and write whatever she says?

He was partly right. There was much to ease my labors. At the actress Susan Sparrow's house, I swam in a pool built of Italian marble. With Nick White, the British rock singer, I ate twice a week at five-star restaurants in London. Tina Terrill loaned me her Porsche Carrera for six months, and then told me to keep it.

Nonetheless I did work. For Ms. Terrill, I tapped away at a keyboard while she paced restlessly around the room with training weights strapped to her legs. Over six months I nursed a manuscript from the shaky hand of the recovering Skye Lurie. Susan Sparrow paid me to listen to more than 200 hours of audiotapes of her paper-thin voice alone in a room recalling tales of ambition and betrayal.

My clients had different reasons for wanting to tell their stories. Jump-starting a career. Finding their feet. Remembering their roots. Or, redemption. Among that crowd, the need for redemption was huge. Whatever I have said or done, please, please forgive me.

And if it didn't come out right, that's why I was there. Make it sound sexy, they said. Don't use my words, use your words. Say that, only better. Can you make it sound better?

In one way or another, I did make it sound better. Their books—my books—sold in preposterously large numbers; all but one of them went into multiple printings. Two were turned into cable movies. Once asked by a reporter what he was reading, the President of the United States named a title of mine.

Serious readers, on the other hand—my wife Jill's professional musician friends, for instance—made a big show of their not reading my books. They spoke of them as if they were indulgences, to be read only if one were at loose ends. Likewise, the critics hated most of my work. *The New Yorker* referred to *White Nights*, Nick White's autobiography, as "stylish flatulence." An editor once confided to me that my books had their highest sales in a chain of airport bookstores; apparently their purchase required the desperation of travelers, at the end of a runway gate, with no other option to fill empty hours of air travel.

And yet?

In moments of reflection, as I floated in that Italian marble pool, the idea occurred to me. Aren't autobiographies born in a question we ask ourselves: how did I get to this point? Don't we look back over the path and tell ourselves a story? This is how it happened. This is who I am.

If this were so, then—in spite of the cascade of trivia—didn't the paths of my clients' lives constitute, in some measure, a truth?

Let me tell you a story. In the middle of my career, after Tina Terrill's book came out, I was approached by the agent of a well-known English actor to explore the idea of my helping him write his autobiography. It never came about for a variety of reasons, and it's best that I don't identify him here. Let's just say that he was a distinguished actor, who defined Lear for his generation, and then late in life made a fortune in advertising voiceovers, where that sonorous voice, bred over three hundred years of Anglo-Saxon lineage, was employed to convey the merits of a particular brand of fruit juice.

I met him, along with his agent, at Elaine's on the Upper East Side. He was small and frail, but his voice, even as it greeted our waitress, had a commanding tone. After the drinks had been ordered and I had paid homage to his talents, he leaned across the table and said, "I've already put a good deal of work into this." Reaching into the pocket of his tailored suit, he pulled out a sheet of paper and spread it out before me. On it was a single jagged line—a series of peaks and valleys—a kind of timeline of rising and falling personal fortunes. Speechless, staring down at the paper, I noticed several obvious erasures and redrawings, where the actor had revised the line, sharpening a peak, trimming a valley. Signs of his labors.

When I looked up at the actor, he was smiling. "There you have all the essential information," he said. "Of course, you'll need to write it up a bit. What's that marvelous American phrase—'flesh it out'?" He waved his hand in the air to indicate the insignificance of the effort. The drinks arrived, and he lifted his glass in ancient arthritic fingers and forgot me. For a moment I wondered if this were an English joke, or the opening gambit in the agent's contract negotiations. But something in both their faces told me it was genuine. As I say, I did not take the assignment. The actor found someone else to do his fleshing out, and the book became a bestseller.

Was he right? Is there really a line that holds the meaning? Is a person's autobiography nothing more than a succession of achievements and setbacks that can be represented in a line?

And what about those places where we would erase and redraw the line? Can any of us be trusted to say what's in our heart and tell our own story—or worse yet, to hire someone like me to tell it?

The problem with escaping is that we leave behind us, even among those we love, different versions of the truth and everything we couldn't bring ourselves to say.

CHAPTER 4

I LIVED THAT year on top of a wooden tower in an area east of Santa Rosa known as the Valley of the Moon.

The stocky, two-story tower had been built in the nineteenth century as a reservoir for the orchard that once surrounded it, and was of a type common in this agricultural landscape. In recent years, Rajiv Patel had remodeled the structure as a guesthouse. According to estate gossip, the occupant preceding me had been a beautiful female "guest," who disappeared one night, taking along a platinum silver Jaguar XJR that did not technically belong to her. She left behind a trim love nest—a neatly designed one-room apartment on the tower's top floor, with quadrants devoted to a sitting area, sleeping space, kitchen, and a walled bathroom. On the south side, off the sitting area, a glass door opened onto a narrow balcony, where I sat sometimes in the late afternoon to drink a beer and watch red-tailed hawks float on air thermals as they searched for prey.

The valley's unusual name originated with its earliest inhabitants, the Miwok tribes, who observed each month the way the full moon seems to rise and fall and rise again on a single evening behind the peaks of the Mayacamas Mountains that frame the valley's edge.

When Mahler's interrogation had ended, I headed home, driving out Highway 12, a narrow two-lane road, and in the bright starlit morning, didn't meet another car the whole way. I entered *Shanti Bhavan* via a gravel service road to avoid driving past the main house and waking anyone. The road wound through the fields and met the estate's blacktop drive near my tower.

As I climbed the stairs and walked into my apartment, with the scene at Galileo's still on my mind, I was surprised at the ordinariness of the room. The space was all just as I had left it twelve hours earlier—dishes stacked in the drainer, bed covers neatly tucked at the corners, work files piled on the desk.

My nausea had subsided. I found some cold water in the refrigerator and drank a full glass. I went to my computer and plugged in the memory stick.

There was just one file named "Robles." I opened it and found an untitled spreadsheet, seven pages long. Across the top of each page were column headings: location, date, condition. "This is the beginning, pal," Paul had said. The beginning of what? I looked at the screen. It was like looking at a magic box, waiting for it to open. Something seemed to lie on the edge of discovery. I watched the screen for a moment longer and then closed the file. I wondered at my decision not to turn over the memory stick to Mahler. But now something in its hidden meaning held me.

I knew sleep would be impossible, and I needed to move, so I took my swimsuit and headed down to the estate's indoor staff pool. *Shanti Bhavan* consisted of a dozen buildings spread out under ancient live oaks. In the center was the main house—Patel's own living quarters. The house had been modeled after a California hacienda: white stucco walls, red-tiled roof, and shaped in an open square around a courtyard. Beyond this were various office buildings, staff quarters, a separate residence for Patel's personal attorney, Whitman DeVries, a gym, tennis courts, private and staff pools, a garage enclosing half a dozen cars, a stable and riding track under cover, a clinic, and a miniature Hindu temple with seating for thirty.

The pool was dark, and there were no other swimmers. I turned on the underwater lights and swam a dozen laps. Then I showered, dressed, and walked through the enclosed corridor to the staff dining room. It was after seven, and the kitchen was serving breakfast. At a table by myself on the patio I had a croissant and a carafe of coffee and read the local morning paper.

In the small town, killings were uncommon, and Barkley's murder was the lead story under a banner, "Businessman Shot." A photo showed Barkley's car surrounded by investigators. The story, obviously written in haste, contained few details. The suspect or suspects were at large. The motive was unknown. Barkley was identified only as a local businessman. Chief investigator Eddie Mahler declined comment.

Realizing that Jill would see the story, I called her on my cell phone. She answered on the second ring. She said she had read the newspaper account.

"Were you there when it happened?" she asked.

"Actually I was in the parking lot when he was shot."

"My God, Charlie, are you all right?"

"I'm fine. Tell Lucy I'm okay."

"I'm sorry about Paul," Jill said. "I met him that one time we had dinner at Galileo's. I know he was a friend of yours."

The statement hung in the air for a moment. We had been divorced for years, but it still sounded strange for her to say a friend of *yours* instead of *ours*. It was a reminder of our separate lives.

I thanked her and said I'd meet her and Lucy on Sunday afternoon for a planned canoe trip down the Russian River.

* * *

When I finished the call, it was time to conduct my regular Friday morning interview session with Patel. I collected my recorder and notebook from the tower and went to the main house.

After two months the sessions were running thin on new information. I had already gathered the basic outline of Patel's life. He had been born and spent his early childhood in the Dharavi neighborhood of Mumbai, then called Bombay. At age five, he immigrated to America when his father's brother invited the family to help him run a hotel in New London, Connecticut. The young Patel's technical aptitude was spotted and nurtured by a sensitive middle school teacher. He won an engineering scholarship to Cornell.

On graduation he foresaw the West Coast building boom and started Torana Construction in California with loans from his extended family. One project led to another, each larger than the one before. He took risks, stretched his credit. His reach grew, first in southern California and then across the state. He flourished with the times: housing tracts in the San Fernando Valley, industrial parks in San Jose for the burgeoning computer chip industry, and everywhere parking structures. He built a vertical business structure and bought mills, trucking lines, pre-cast plants, and real estate franchises. By the eighties he started making the lists of the wealthiest men in the country.

All this, of course, I could have gleaned from published accounts. There were more interesting—darker—stories that I had heard before I began the project: a partner who disappeared in the Santa Inez Mountains in a company plane, dates with the suicidal country–western singer Dottie Wagoner, and a contract with NASA to send something that officials declined to identify into space. But, in an authorized autobiography, these tales would be off limits.

I met Patel in his study and set up my recorder. The study was a square, windowless room with a desk, sofa, and several soft chairs arranged on a Persian carpet. On one wall were bookshelves. The other three walls were covered with matching framed photographs, each showing Patel shaking hands with a different well-known actor, politician, or athlete.

Patel sat facing me in a black leather recliner. He was a short, soft, heavyset man, with legs that barely reached the floor. His hair was thinning, and his eyes were milky white. He was clothed in a silk dressing gown alive with bright amoebas. He had an air of soulful boredom, and on several previous occasions, he had laid his head back on the chair cushion and slept unself-consciously in my presence for an hour. When he spoke, his words were heavily accented and indistinct, and his voice trailed off like smoke rising in the air. On this day, like most others, two dun-colored Irish wolfhounds sprawled beside his chair.

We were joined for the session by the attorney, DeVries, and Patel's bodyguard, Shawn Lawrence. DeVries, dressed in his tailored suit and large round glasses, sat at a table beside Patel. He had the clockwork look of someone put together by a series of expensive tutors, boarding schools, and universities.

Shawn was a large man in his mid-twenties. He had a thick chest and shoulders, boyish pink cheeks, and shaved head. He wore a short leather jacket over a polo shirt, khaki trousers, and a pair of sunglasses tucked into the top of his shirt. He sat upright in a chair by the door, with his hands folded in his lap. Like a communicant, he stood when Patel stood and sat when Patel sat.

Patel's watery eyes studied me. "You look pale, Charlie," he said. "Are you well?"

"I'm fine," I said. "Little trouble sleeping."

"Perhaps you saw the news of the death of our friend, Paul Barkley," he said. "Sad news. Paul was a gifted businessman and still young. It's distressing, wouldn't you agree, when our society's violence comes so close." He raised a hand and fluttered his fingers to express the proximity.

As our session started, Patel repeated several dreamlike parables, which I had already recorded at least once before, of his early years as a poor child in Bombay—a favorite involved his walking in the street with his mother and seeing, taped to the inside of an apartment window, a picture postcard of the Brooklyn Bridge.

When he finished, I opened my notebook to the questions I had prepared about his adult life and business. He answered several of these, but soon the strength seemed to go out of him, and he gazed at me with vacant, milky eyes and smiled sadly. He could tell me, the look seemed to say, but to explain to one so far down the chain of existence would require an effort capable only of Lord Vishnu.

After half a dozen more questions, he puffed out his cheeks and narrowed his eyes as if in deep thought. Then abruptly he exhaled and said, "Any ideas, Whit?"

My heart sank. Ideas were not likely the province of Whitman DeVries. DeVries cleared his throat. "I believe," he said, "I can prepare some . . ." His mind searched for the right word. "Materials," he finally said. The word had an ominous sound.

"May I ask, Mr. Teller," DeVries added, "if we might see a sample of what you've completed to date?"

"A sample?" I asked.

"Yes, whatever you have. Naturally we're not familiar with your methods, but for the purposes of due diligence, we ought to inquire. Draft chapters, an outline, perhaps. Can I suggest a week from today?"

"Sure," I said. "I'll pull something together."

At ten-thirty Patel signaled an end to the proceedings, and—led by Shawn—took his dogs for a walk through the eucalyptus to the private pool where he swam. As he walked away, the animals moved powerfully on either side, their giant backs rising to the little man's waist like the symbols of the land of his birth, the proud ancient lions of Uttar Pradesh.

CHAPTER 5

RETURNING TO MY room, I found a message from Nico on my answering machine. I called her number at the fitness club.

"Stephen was arrested this morning, and charged with Paul's murder," she said.

"You're kidding," I said. "How do you know?"

"Molly called me. She has a friend who works for Eddie Mahler. The cops found the gun that was used, and it belongs to Stephen."

"Where is he?"

"County lockup. Molly's trying to arrange for his release, but in the meantime somebody should go see him. I called Carl, but he's not in, and I have to work here the rest of the afternoon."

I agreed to go.

"Come by the club afterwards, and let me know how he is," Nico said. "If you want to follow me home, I'll cook dinner and you can meet Vincent."

The county jail is a thick, fortresslike building along the freeway on the northern edge of town. Its red brick walls rise in a massive block, with narrow windows cut like slits in its facing.

A guard escorted me to the visitors' room. It was a dark, enclosed space. On the right were half a dozen partitioned windows for speaking to prisoners. The guard pointed to a chair in front of one of the windows and walked away. On the other side, I saw Stephen in an orange jumpsuit come toward me. He slumped in the chair and leaned toward the speakerbox.

"I wish you didn't have to come here," he said.

His face was white. Under his eyes were dark shadows. "My hair's standing up," he said. He reached up and smoothed it down. "For some reason, we're not allowed a comb."

"It's okay."

Behind Stephen lay a large open space. A workstation stood in the center, where two guards stared at computer screens. Around the workstation, inmates sat at a dozen small tables, reading newspapers, playing cards, or sleeping with their heads on the tabletops. The room's far perimeter was lined with cells. Except for the bars, it might have been an airport lounge.

"He's really dead, isn't he?" Stephen said. He looked frightened.

I nodded.

"They told me when they brought me here. But I still can't believe it. It just doesn't seem real."

"I know," I said. "Tell me what happened last night between the two of you."

"Paul and I had a . . . misunderstanding."

"A misunderstanding? You looked pretty upset."

"It was a scheduling thing. Not a big deal. It just pissed me off. I had to get out of there."

"What'd you do?"

"I left. I went home."

"With Carl?"

"No, we came earlier in separate cars. Carl followed me out to the parking lot, and we talked for a few minutes. I said I wanted to be alone, and I went to my place and Carl went to his."

"What time was that?"

"About eleven-thirty."

"You went straight home?"

"Yeah. Takes about twenty minutes."

"Anyone see you?"

"I don't think so. People in my complex were asleep."

"Did Carl leave at the same time?"

Stephen shrugged. "I guess so. I saw him get in his car. I assumed he left. I didn't see."

"Either of you drive a white Toyota pickup?"

"No. I have a Subaru. Carl has a Volvo wagon. Why?"

"I saw one drive out of the lot right after Paul was shot. You know anyone who drives one?"

"No, but white pickups are pretty common around here."

"What about the gun that the police say is yours?"

Stephen sighed and shook his head. "It was stupid. It's a little .22 caliber. I only had it because of those gay bashings in Guerneville last year. A couple of nights when we were closing Galileo's, we saw skinheads at the Club Raz across the street. Carl thought we should have some protection. I never even fired it."

"Where'd you keep it?"

"Under the bar in a cabinet. It wasn't locked."

"Anyone besides Carl know you had it?"

"Some of the other waiters probably, I don't know," Stephen said. "This is all so strange. I didn't shoot Paul. I mean he could be a pain in the neck. But it wasn't like I'd kill him."

"What'd the police say when they arrested you?"

Stephen shook his head wearily. "They're not saying much. But I get the impression they think it was a gay triangle thing."

"What's that mean? Paul wasn't gay."

Stephen looked down. "He experimented," he said. "Couple of years ago. But it was ancient history—way before Carl. And Carl knew about it."

"Maybe someone else was jealous," I suggested.

"Could be. Last few years we traveled in different social circles. Paul was a real party animal. But he moved into the posh set, out of my league."

A guard approached Stephen.

"You know anyone angry with Paul?" I asked.

Stephen smiled faintly. "Some of our suppliers. I think we were behind in payments on a couple of them."

He stood to leave. "Tell Carl I'm okay," he said before he turned to follow the guard.

* * *

In the parking lot outside the jail, I called Carl and reached him on his cell phone. As gently as possible, I told him about my visit. He had a lot of questions that I couldn't answer, and I promised to have Molly contact him. He asked if I'd go with him to the jail on Sunday to visit Stephen. He didn't want to go alone the first time. I agreed on the condition that we go early, because I was planning to spend the afternoon with Jill and Lucy. As he hung up, I realized how little I knew about the small circle of people at the café. I'd been included because Paul introduced me, but I wasn't part of any of the business enterprises like the others.

I drove to the Redwood Fitness Center in a renovated section of downtown. I parked out front and climbed the stairs to the second floor. The center's massage rooms were at the back of the building, down a wide corridor with a glass-walled classroom on either side, where exercise classes were under way.

Across from the massage rooms, I saw Nico sitting in John Coffey's office. She jumped up and hugged me. Coffey sat behind a cluttered desk, wearing sweats and a Lakers cap. He was a tall, thin black man who had been a member of a legendary relay team at USC in the 1990s. He stood and shook my hand, and I sat in one of two director's chairs beside Nico.

I told them about my meeting with Stephen.

"There was a lot of tension between Paul and Stephen before this," Nico said. "Stephen might say it wasn't a big deal Thursday night, but he's talked for weeks about how crazy it's been."

"Crazy in what way?" I asked.

"I'll let Stephen tell you. I think Paul couldn't let go of managing the catering business."

When I recounted Stephen's comment about Paul being late on payments at the restaurant, Coffey nodded in agreement.

"The police were here this morning asking questions about our accounts," he said. "Apparently Paul had $8,000 in cash on him when he was killed. They asked if I knew why."

"Did you?" I asked.

Coffey shook his head. "I'm a trainer, not a businessman. That's why I went into partnership with Paul. He took care of the money side. I'll know more in a few days. I've hired a forensic accountant to look at the books for the club, the restaurant, and the catering business."

Nico put her hand on my shoulder and headed for the door. "Come on Charlie," she said. "Follow me home. I'll cook some pasta and introduce you to Vincent."

Coffey snorted, and Nico looked back at him. "Vincent's reclusive," she said in explanation.

While I waited for Nico to fill her small daypack, I stared at one of the exercise classes in session. Twenty young women and men were punching the air and kicking in time with the Stones' "Start Me Up." Facing the class, calling commands into a headset was a tall woman in a silver leotard and skirt. Her shoulder-length red hair had yellow streaks running through it, and it flew about her as she danced. She was darkly tanned, and her face and neck ran with sweat. She wore orange lipstick, and as she danced, she threw back her head and sang along with the song.

"Put your tongue back in your mouth, cowboy," Nico whispered in my ear.

I hadn't heard her rejoin me, and I blushed. "She's a . . . striking woman," I said.

"Striking? Is that even a real word? What is it about you guys and women who look like that?"

For a moment the two of us stood watching the class.

"Her name's Page Salinger," Nico said. "She was Paul's girlfriend. They were going to be married."

"Really?" I said. "She looks like she's taking his death pretty well."

"Page is Page. She does things her own way."

"Isn't it odd that Paul never brought her to the café or mentioned her to me?"

"Separate worlds. Paul had a few of them." She guided me away from the exercise rooms and down the hallway to the exit.

"You know, you could help figure this out, Charlie," she said. "You'd be good at this."

"At what?"

"Clues. Finding out who killed Paul. The police aren't going to do it."

"I'm a writer. I don't know anything about murder investigations."

"You ask questions. Same thing."

"My job was to sit in the background and take notes," I said.

"Maybe that's not your job anymore," Nico said.

I looked at her.

"Paul helped you get that gig with Patel, didn't he?" she said. "Maybe this is how you're supposed to pay him back. One of those universe things. Right the balance."

I wondered how much Nico knew about my fall from grace. "I think it might take more than asking questions about Paul's murder to right the balance," I said.

"Hey come on," she said. "It's not over until it's over."

I walked Nico to her car—a 10-year-old, faded red Saab. She threw her pack on the passenger side and climbed in the driver's seat. "Paul loved you, you know," she said.

"I hardly knew him," I said. "What was it, two months? We had dinner together and talked. I never really knew much about him, his business, where he came from. I didn't know about his fiancée until just now."

"He talked about you to me," Nico said, ignoring me. "He said you were a 'luminous talent.' He said you saw into the hearts of the people you wrote about."

I reached for my keys. "Separate worlds," I said. "That was a long time ago."

CHAPTER 6

Virginia Hardy

I CO-WROTE MY first book when I was twenty-two. It sold well for a small autobiography, and in one of the exceptions of my career, the critics liked it. The *New York Times* called it a jewel.

My subject was the novelist Virginia Hardy, a woman who knew something about youthful dreams. In 1924, she published a novel called *St. Mark's Place*. A year before *Gatsby*, the book created a sensation. It told the story of Elizabeth Thurston and her rise through New York society. The book contained the distinctive voice of a new kind of American woman. The novel and its author were taken up by the smart set, and Virginia Hardy joined that bright coterie of New York writers and artists in the 1920s. For a few years, photos of her were everywhere, her face caught in the lights of a Broadway opening or framed by the rich and famous at an exclusive party.

Then gradually she faded from the scene. She wrote two more novels in a Thurston trilogy, but neither of them caught on. She went to Hollywood, married the English screenwriter Gabriel Lake, who was killed four years later in an automobile accident in Palm Springs. She took a university teaching assignment for a year, and then another, and another. She disappeared below the surface of public notice, only to appear every ten years or so with news of a failed marriage or a DUI arrest. For much of that time, she wrote—novels that were published in small printings and hundreds of occasional pieces, reviews, columns, and introductions to other writers' books.

I met her in the mid-1970s at Kit's Books in Santa Monica, where I was clerking. At first, she was just another regular customer. A trim, small woman with white hair, dressed in jeans and a flannel shirt. She came in several times a week and browsed in the back stock. Once she bought a copy of *The Golden Bowl.* "I woke up this morning thinking about Maggie Verver," she said. "I have to go back and see if she's still the same cunning young woman." When she left, I noticed the name on her credit card and remembered *St. Mark's Place* from a senior seminar at Princeton.

After that, we chatted whenever she came in. I knew her favorites—James and Wharton—and her disdain for Lewis and Dreiser.

I fancied myself a budding fiction writer. I woke up every morning at 4:30, and for a few hours sat at my typewriter pecking out tales of my generation. Two were published in literary journals, and I was shopping a collection of stories with New York publishers.

Several months after Virginia and I had met, I asked her to read a story called "Glass" about newlyweds whose relationship was coming apart. She returned it the next day. "It's fun" was all she said. Watching her walk away, her thin frame stiffly upright, I decided to write a literary portrait of her as a forgotten novelist.

It was a respectful essay. Full of admiration for the early writing, it urged a re-examination of her work. When I screwed up my courage, I showed it to her. This time she read on the spot, sitting in one of the book-store's stuffed chairs, holding the pages at the edges as if to avoid being soiled. When she finished, she handed the essay back to me with a tight smile. "There are several errors," she said and left.

I assumed I had insulted her. But a week later she was back. She asked what I intended to do with the essay. When I hesitated, she handed me the name of an editor at the *Atlantic Monthly* "who isn't as stupid as the others."

The profile appeared in the *Atlantic* and caused a buzz. There were appreciative Letters to the Editor, and several newspapers did "Where Is She Now?" pieces. Then a book publisher proposed that I approach Virginia about a memoir.

She dismissed the idea, but I could see in her eyes excitement at the prospect. Her reluctance stemmed, I learned later, from the knowledge of the pain the remembrances would bring her, and from the hints she was already having of the presence of liver cancer. When she finally agreed, it was with her characteristic bluntness. "OK, Charlie," she said. "But for heaven's sake, let's not make it your usual piece of crap."

· · ·

We began working together in her apartment off Wilshire in the evenings and on weekends when I could get away from my job. But the odd hours allowed little continuity, and the apartment, with its walls of old books and memorabilia served not to open her memory but to stifle it with contradictions. It was not long before she proposed we move to a cabin on the Mendocino Coast that she had bought years before in one of her resolutions to restart her creative life. She offered to pay me so I could quit my job.

Initially I was reluctant to live with Virginia while we worked on the book, but in the end the proximity enabled us to be so productive that I required it in all my later contracts.

We drove up the coast together in my Volvo laden with cartons of letters and unpublished manuscripts. The cabin sat two miles outside the town of Mendocino in a grove of redwoods. There were two bedrooms, a living room, and a rustic kitchen. Virginia hired a local woman to cook dinner for us every night, and we set up a work space before a large window with a view of the ocean.

Our work routine soon developed its own grim pattern. Virginia awoke late each morning, pale and weak. She sat in a chair by the front window and endured long spasms of coughing. Spurning food, she drank black coffee and smoked her way through a dozen Pall Malls. She required that she not be spoken to. By noon, she began answering my questions or dictating into a tape recorder. She spoke slowly and carefully for two to three hours, pausing only long enough to change tapes or light a cigarette.

At three, she stopped work and took a nap. When she awoke, she began drinking, filling a coffee mug with Dewars. As the afternoon wore on, the alcohol made her meaner, and by evening her mood was nasty. She picked at her dinner and moved back to her chair, where she sat for several hours, correcting my drafts from the day before, the manuscript balanced on a breadboard on her lap. From my bedroom, where I sat typing, I could hear her pencil slashing at the pages. In the margins she scrawled the words "idiotic" or "pure shit." Sometimes she called across the cabin, "Why can't you write what I tell you?" Then came the increasingly deprecating comparisons: "My auto mechanic is a better writer." Or, "The man who cleans my septic tank would not have written this!"

· · ·

Even so, day after day, she told stories, remembered in detail across decades.

The model for Elizabeth Thurston had been a young woman whose face Virginia had seen for an instant one night in 1922 as the woman entered a party on 84th Street. With her escort behind her, she stood in the doorway, no different from a thousand other beautiful women of the time. Then she paused and scanned the room. For a moment the façade of sophistication fell, and the girl's hungry spirit peered through, searching for something in the multitude of faces. Then, just as quickly, the expression disappeared. Someone called to her, the girl laughed, and the room swallowed her.

From that single image, a snapshot, Virginia created a lifetime. She wrote *St. Mark's Place* in 18 months, the story spilling out as fast as she could type. It was if she knew everything about the young woman—her childhood in Pennsylvania, the train ride to New York City, the apartment in the Village, her first sight of James Crain, and the Richardsons' glittering party.

Later, when Virginia struggled to finish the third novel of the trilogy, she searched for the true identity of the young woman in the doorway. After a year, she found her—now a housewife married to a commercial real estate agent in a Connecticut suburb. The woman easily accepted Virginia's pretense for their meeting, and they drank tea in her kitchen. In an hour, Virginia lost everything that might have connected the woman before her with the girl she had invented, and Virginia felt the story in her mind slip away like a forgotten song.

She wrote two-thirds of a novel about a socialite running for public office, and left it unfinished. Out of money, she took a job teaching English literature at Barnard College. At a weekend party on Long Island, she met Gabriel Lake, who was visiting from California. Lake borrowed a Stutz Black Hawk sitting in the driveway and drove Virginia to a roadside diner in Montauk. After Christmas, she followed him back to Los Angeles, and they were married.

Lake wrote popular screwball comedies in Hollywood during the thirties. Despite his adopted home in southern California, he never lost his English manners. He dressed in corduroy suits and woolen ties, whatever the season, and kept an office in one of the studios. He sat at a desk for six hours a day, typing his scripts, with the simple industry of a civil servant. By his side was an alarm clock set for four o'clock. When the alarm went off, he stopped writing, even if in the middle of a sentence, collected his hat and coat, and drove home. On the weekends he took Virginia to the Bel Air hills to play tennis with the stars of his acquaintance—Gable, Lombard, Dunne—luminaries Lake treated without deference. "Chaps rowing together in the same boat," he called them. He was solicitous toward Virginia, but made clear his disdain for fathering children. His one indulgence was for fast American cars, which in the end killed him.

Lake's estate paid Virginia's way for two years. She wrote a thin novel about Hollywood called *Sunset Palace* and had trouble finding a publisher.

She went back east. In the forties, she accepted a position as lecturer and writer-in-residence at Smith. Her teaching load was light, but the position required that she develop a work of fiction. With her classes scheduled in the late afternoon, she wrote mornings in the downstairs study of a rented house in Northampton.

By October, she was having an affair with John Fenton, a professor of Jacobean drama and a Smith legend. Fenton had written the first authoritative study of the bloody plays of Ford and Webster, and his lectures, full of frank discussions of sex, drew capacity audiences. He was handsome and careless. With his depressive wife living two hours away in Boston, Fenton was able to make himself a guest at Virginia's house three times a week. His habit was to arrive in the afternoon, while Virginia was teaching and prepare dinner.

Once when Virginia was delayed in returning, Fenton read her manuscript. In an hour, he re-typed the last two pages, changing a scene and adding a character. He meant it as a one-time joke and thought it might be more amusing if he didn't mention it. The next morning she saw the changes and knew, of course, that it had been Fenton. But she decided to play along, and—in those days before computers—she began typing where Fenton had ended. She expanded Fenton's scene and accepted the new character as a central figure in the unfolding drama.

They made it a silent game. Three times a week, they wrote in tandem—one in the morning, the other in the afternoon—neither ever speaking of it. Each evening they ate dinner and made love—the story playing mutely in their heads. At times, their love making was mirrored in their writing, with Virginia describing the awkward first meeting between Margaret Allen and Tom Preston, and Fenton describing their first kiss. Other times, they wrote as if settling a score. Fenton allowed Virginia's beloved Beth Emerson to die in childbirth, and Virginia ended the affair of Tom and Emma, which Fenton had so carefully arranged.

It went on like that for two years. When *Homefront* was published in 1948, Virginia dedicated it to JF, "for showing me the way." In his *Times* review, Fenton challenged the logic of the New York scenes, which only the two of them knew Fenton had written.

Homefront was a failure with the public and the critics, and Virginia's publisher dropped her. The following year Fenton's wife made a serious suicide attempt, and he moved to Boston. Virginia never saw him again.

Her imagination stalled. The voice in her head disappeared as if it had finished its work. For hours at a time, she stared at the same lines of type. She kept notebooks of false starts in case she might find a way to make them work. She knew what it was like for something to take flight. Now everything she tried was second rate.

· · ·

One evening after Virginia read that day's manuscript, she called to my bedroom. "I need something else to read to clear my head."

I showed her the books from my nightstand, but she waved them away. "Did you bring any of your stories?" she asked.

I handed her a binder of my collection. "You don't have to read them all," I said, but she scowled at me until I returned to my room.

After a few days, noticing the binder on the floor, I said, "So what did you think?"

She stared at me. "Why did you write them?" she asked.

"To tell a story."

"No, seriously, what were you trying to do?"

"I guess I was trying to describe a moment or a scene in a character's life that expresses his or her inner reality."

"Inner reality?"

"What's unique about them. What the characters themselves can't say."

"Can't say? They're characters in fiction. You can make them say anything."

"No. That's just it. Not if they stay true to themselves. I guess it sounds pretentious. But when it works, I think the short story is like a moment of revelation about the character. Like, I don't know, Chekhov."

"Chekhov?"

"You know what I mean."

"How old are you?"

"Twenty-two."

"It's kind of a small ambition for someone so young, isn't it?"

"I don't think so."

"No? Even if you succeed, it's not much of an achievement—like sticking a pin through an insect."

"If it's a good story, it uncovers something about who we are."

She smiled. "You're afraid, aren't you?" she said.

"No," I said. "I'm trying to learn the craft."

"Speaking of moments, do you have trouble getting an erection?"

"For god's sake, Virginia."

"Surely you've thought of it."

"It's none of your business."

She laughed out loud. "I spend six weeks describing every intimate detail of my life, and you won't answer a simple question?"

"It's not the same," I said.

She looked at me. "Your stories are unreadable, Charlie," she said. "I couldn't finish them. They're not revelatory. They're redundant, regurgitated, repetitive, reptilian, . . . "

"OK. That's enough," I said, turning to leave.

"Did we just have a moment of revelation?" she called after me. "Like, I don't know, Chekhov?"

. . .

She suffered waves of depression. In the late fifties, she was hired to teach at the University of Chicago. A colleague introduced her to an administrator in the medical school named Warren Stapleton, who was ten years her senior. They spent a season attending parties together to meet his family and business associates, and when that was done, they married and moved into Stapleton's home in Lake Forrest. It was a huge castle of a place, built with Midwestern heaviness and enough strength, Virginia later said, to withstand aerial bombardment. There were 19 rooms for the two of them. On her first visit, Virginia walked through the house, bewildered by its foreignness, until she discovered there was not a single book in any room. Stapleton traveled much of the time, leaving Virginia alone in the house. She wrote at an oak table in the dining room, built to seat twenty, the sound of her typewriter keys echoing in the empty space like hammer strokes.

On dark winter mornings, she overslept her lectures. She taught herself to drink—first bourbon and later scotch. At the end of the second semester, the university dismissed her. She tried to take her life with pills: twice she swallowed a bottle of seconal and threw up before it had a chance to work. She drank half a bottle of window cleaner, which left scar tissue on her esophagus.

One day, when Stapleton was in New York, Virginia climbed into one of his cars and left with only her purse. She drove south until she grew tired near the Missouri border, where she moved into a boarding house and wired Stapleton for money. She returned to writing, working on her own in the town's public library. The product of her labors was a study of three women novelists: Austen, Emily Brontë, and Eliot. It sold only modestly but arrived in the first wave of a new awakening to female writers and was enough to qualify her for another teaching job.

The arc of her teaching career could be measured, Virginia told me, by the increasing number of words in the names of the institutions willing to hire her. She had started at Barnard and Smith, and by the sixties was teaching women's studies at Southeast Illinois University at Edwardsville.

She lived in town and rented half a Victorian near campus. She taught three classes a week and avoided the other faculty. One night she awoke in the emergency room of the local hospital. She was seated on an examining table, wearing a hospital gown. In the mirror across the room, she could see her own face. There was a cut over her left eye and a line of dried blood running down to her ear. She had no memory of it. Treating her was a young Indian doctor, whose name, R. Manisnuvani, was stitched on his lab coat. He greeted her, calling her Missus HarDEE. He looked at her chart and face and said, "The young woman had been seated in the station an hour before the train was to arrive." It was the first line of *St. Mark's Place*. "My mother made me read it," the doctor said with a shrug. "But I loved the character of Miss Elizabeth Thurston. She won my heart."

He readied a cotton pad to clean the blood from her face. The palms of his hands were white against the brown of the rest of his skin. So close to her, he smelled sweetly of something she couldn't name. "Missus HarDEE, you must take care of yourself," he said. "When you fall down like this, you can cause serious injury." When he touched her chin to raise her face, he saw the tears running down her cheeks. Without pausing, he stopped them with his pad and then dried the paths to her eyes.

"Do you ever think," he said, concentrating again on her wound, "what happens to your characters when they go into the heads of your readers? They live there. In so many heads around the world. They take up residence in the memory. Is that not a most remarkable thing?"

The blackout scared her. She stopped drinking for a few years, but replaced the habit with long, unfiltered Pall Malls that she chain smoked, and kept in the pocket of her cardigans. She wrote poetry—dry, brittle poems published in a thin volume called *February Morning*.

In the late sixties, Virginia's third husband passed away and left her a settlement large enough to allow her to retire. She moved back to California and took the apartment in Santa Monica where I found her.

. . .

In our three months together, the writing of Virginia's book had a tidal rhythm. In one phase, she held drafts tightly, arguing for an hour over a word, writing six drafts of a scene. In the next phase, a day later, she sat silently while I wrote, letting the text unfold, surprised by what she read as if it were new.

As the chapters took shape, a change came over her. It was the double-sided recognition that this book, the last that she would write, might achieve esteem and success equal to her great novel, but that its emotional heart would lie in her own unhappiness for having failed to find the one thing she wanted. For the first time she was a character in her own writing, and her frailties and mistakes were trapped on the page by the beauty and unsparing focus of her prose. Towards the end it was a battle to finish a page. The story was the story she had told herself for decades, deep within her own mind, and now as it grew, line by line, on the paper before her, she wrestled with each turn in the path all over again, as if it were still possible to change its course with the power of her words.

One night she came to the doorway of my room. "Who do you think will read this book?" she asked. She had not bothered to dress and wore a man's bathrobe over a flannel nightgown.

"The *Atlantic* article showed there's an audience," I said.

"That's not an answer."

"I just meant it was a popular issue. A lot of people wanted to read about you."

"A lot? Where'd you learn English? Who are these *lot* of people?"

"Readers of your novels."

"Oh, for god's sake, my books are out of print. My readers are in nursing homes, or they're little untalented literature students like you, beating off in library basements."

"You've lived an interesting life," I said, although I knew there was no persuading her. "People will respond to that, even if they're not familiar with your novels."

"Interesting? You mean fucked up, don't you?"

I looked away from her, and she leaned back against the doorframe.

"What do you suppose these readers will say?" she asked. "Too bad the poor woman drank? How unlucky in her marriages?"

"It's not like that. The book's a picture of a creative writer."

"Yes, a picture."

Several minutes passed before she went on. "What do you want, Charlie?" she asked. "What's in it for you? This isn't your writing—it's mine. Do you think this will elevate you and help you publish those stupid stories of yours?"

"You know that's not true," I said.

"Do I? Did you find, what did you call it, the moment of my revelation? What I couldn't express myself?"

"That's not what this is."

"You thought this would be a fucking piece of cake, didn't you? When you couldn't write your stories, you thought I'll help this old woman write her book."

I didn't say anything.

"Maybe you just like having your name on the cover. Isn't that the fetishism of serial killers?"

I took a deep breath. "It's been a privilege to have worked with you," I said.

"Good for you, Charlie," she said. "Christ, I should have done this myself."

We stood looking at each other.

"Just finish the goddam book," she said and went back to her room.

. . .

During the final six weeks we worked together, Virginia grew increasingly ill, some days too weak to leave her bed. She hired a home nurse to care for her. Once the writing was finished, I drove her back to Los Angeles. She was unable to look at the book proofs and yielded corrections to me. Her acknowledgment of me in the preface was generous. She even arranged for a photograph of me to appear below hers on the dust jacket flap—which set a precedent for the rest of my books.

She died in the fall, three months after our return from Mendocino. The book—*Virginia Hardy: A Life in Letters*—was released the following spring. It was a handsome, serious-looking book. On the front cover was a black-and-white photograph of Virginia Hardy and Gabriel Lake from the 1930s. The reviews, which were mainly favorable, treated it as if it were a contribution to American literary study, and several colleges asked me to give a talk on Virginia's life. Sales of the paperback edition were higher than expected and prompted a reassessment of Virginia's novels, which were reprinted in a boxed set.

After Virginia's death, her lawyer sent me a letter that she had left with him for me. It was single sheet of paper, with her writing in the familiar crooked scrawl. It said, "The first one's easy."

CHAPTER 7

NICO AND VINCENT lived in the countryside, about fifteen miles west of Santa Rosa. I followed Nico on the Bodega Highway, through Sebastopol, and onto a two-lane road that snaked up and down gentle hills.

A few miles outside town, the houses gave way to a rural landscape of vineyards, apple orchards, and small sheep farms. As we made our way further west, the cultivated hills were replaced by stands of towering redwoods and eucalyptus, and a broad gray band of coastal fog spread across the horizon and darkened the sky.

The "West County" nurtured a unique lifestyle and political attitude. The residents were small farmers, craftspeople, and artists known for political activism. They were vocal in opposition to new housing developments, wireless networks, and the conservative national agenda. Roadside signs protested chemical spraying of the vineyards and the war in Afghanistan.

Nico and Vincent's house lay a mile off the main road, down a rutted lane that led into a dark redwood grove. The rustic cabin was built of redwood shakes, grayed by age. It sprawled oddly in several directions, as if built by different architects in a contest of wills. Rusted farm equipment lay in the yard amid waist-high grass, and ahead in the drive sat a VW bus on blocks. A golden retriever trotted toward us.

"Welcome to the end of the earth," Nico said, joining me beside my car. "This is Verlaine," she added, reaching down to the retriever, and the two of us followed the happy dog, named after the nineteenth-century French symbolist poet and drug addict, to the front door.

The interior had the low-ceilinged snugness of a ship's quarters. The entranceway opened into a cluttered kitchen and adjoining dining area. Beyond that was a living room with a wood stove and two walls of crammed bookshelves. The unmatched sofa and chairs were covered with Central American blankets.

In a chair next to a reading lamp sat Vincent. He was a thin, muscular man dressed in a red T-shirt, overalls, and work boots. His gray hair was pulled back in a ponytail. A pair of wire-rim reading glasses rested on the end of his nose, and he held an open book. As he raised his head, the lamp showed a scar curving down his left cheek.

Nico introduced us. "Vincent works for the post office," she said, leaning close to kiss him.

"Letter carrier?" I asked. He looked unlike any mailman I had ever seen.

"I drive a truck," he said. His voice was flat and toneless.

I asked him what he was reading.

"Keegan's History of the First World War," he said.

"Isn't he the one who thinks the war could have been avoided?" I asked.

"Something like that," Vincent said.

"Vincent's hobby is military history," Nico explained. "He was in Special Forces."

"Where'd you serve?" I asked and then remembered the secrecy surrounding the group.

Vincent looked at me for a moment. "I did some work in the first Gulf War," he said. Another subject opened and closed.

I asked for the bathroom. Following Nico's directions, I walked along a dark corridor, but I took a wrong turn and opened a door into the garage. An old convertible occupied half the garage. The other half was filled with spools of irrigation tubing stacked in a pyramid.

After finding the bathroom, I returned to the living room, where Vincent handed me a beer, and invited me to follow him outside to see their wind turbine. Nico was already busy with dinner.

The turbine sat several hundred yards from the house, on a bare bluff. Its tower rose thirty feet, and the three blades were whirling through the air and making a low humming sound.

I looked across the meadow below. There wasn't another house in sight. "You're pretty secluded out here," I said.

"We like it that way," Vincent said.

For dinner Nico made pasta in a homemade pesto sauce and a salad. When I complimented the meal, Nico said, "Last year, Vincent and I were on the Mendocino Tuber Diet. You probably heard about it. For a while, it was a real big deal. All the movie stars were on it. It's where you eat only vegetables that grow underground—potatoes, beets, carrots, turnips, parsnips, taro."

"Taro?" I asked.

"Tastes like sweet potato," Nico said. "The idea is focusing on tubers makes you more grounded. They're feminine plants, growing in the earth's womb. Not all that macho above-ground, erectile stuff."

I nodded as if I knew all of this.

Vincent ate with his head lowered. To encourage him to join the conversation, Nico reminded him of my renown as a writer. Turning to me, she said, "Vincent didn't like your book on Nick White."

"I hear that from a lot of his fans," I said.

"Nick White was a good musician," Vincent said, "but I would've liked more about his music and less about his religious awakening, or whatever that was."

"As a matter of fact, I agree with you. But Nick felt he couldn't tell his story without discussing religion."

"So you did what he wanted."

"I'm a hired co-author. I can offer my advice, but in the end, it's my client's autobiography."

I could see that Vincent had expected this equivocation and was losing interest. "Nick had me join him on stage in Munich," I said.

"Cool," Nico said, her eyes widening. "What'd you do?"

"Sang backup on 'Stages of Love.' It was wild. The fans were throwing things at us the whole time."

Nico laughed. "That's what I miss about Paul," she said. "He always told stories. He knew so many people, actors, and musicians. He was exciting to be around. We'd be at Galileo's one night, and Bill Reed would walk in. Or, Julia English, who was on that TV show. It was like that all the time."

"He was a name dropper," Vincent said. "Whenever Barkley was describing something, he'd use famous people's names. It was some sort of code for him. Like it was supposed to mean something to the rest of us."

"Charlie and I were talking about Paul's murder," Nico told Vincent. "We think the police are on the wrong track."

Vincent shrugged. "I'm sure they have some good evidence," he said.

"Charlie's going to investigate the murder on his own," Nico announced, smiling at me.

"Am I?" I said.

"Come on, Charlie," Nico said. "Didn't Paul come to you the night he was killed to tell you something? I was sitting next to you. I saw him. People are always confiding in you. They can't help it. It's who you are. It's like what you do."

"People hired me to write their books," I said.

"You're not curious what Paul wanted to say?" Nico asked. "Do you think it was a coincidence that he came to you?"

I thought of Paul's memory stick sitting now in my computer.

"Maybe this is supposed to be your next project or something," Nico said.

At that moment I must have flushed, and Nico backed off.

Vincent had been watching us without speaking.

Nico made a face at him and then said, "Vincent didn't like Paul."

"Why was that?" I asked.

"He was devoted to making money," Vincent said.

"He was a businessman."

"It was more than that." Vincent looked across the table at Nico.

"What do you mean?"

"He wasn't what he pretended to be."

"He always seemed laid back to me. Like he was doing it with one hand."

Vincent stared at me. "Let's forget it," he said. "The guy's dead. It's not important now."

After dinner, Nico disappeared into the kitchen to make coffee, while Vincent and I went out on the deck. The hillside behind the house dropped steeply through thirty feet of rocky forest floor toward a dry streambed below. Large redwood pilings supported the deck over the precipice.

For a moment we stood silently looking out at the forest and the fog that was slowly filling it.

Then I turned to Vincent and said, "Listen, I never told Nico I'd investigate Paul's murder, and I don't know much about Paul—or Nico and you, for that matter. I only moved here three months ago. But I don't think Stephen was the one who killed Paul. That last part is just a guess. Even so, it makes me a curious about a few things."

"Like what?"

"Like what you said in there about Paul being devoted to making money. If Paul had a fault, it's that he was overly generous. He was always helping somebody."

"But as you say, you don't really know much about him."

"I do know when someone is full of crap. In my work I've learned to listen to a lot of bullshit and sort through it to see what's true."

"I'm sure that's what makes your books so distinctive."

I ignored the sarcasm. "You don't want to tell me, do you?"

"It's none of your business."

"I think it is. I'm the one who saw him after he was shot."

"How's that qualify you? You were there. So what?"

I stared at Vincent's lean face, his dark eyes, and the scar that now seemed like a badge of defiance. From somewhere within me, I suddenly felt a new equal measure of energy. We all have moments when we're given a chance to change course, to start a new direction. The occasion is rarely momentous.

Many people don't even notice it. But it's there, like a line at our feet. If we cross it, we're changed, and everything from then on is new. As I stood on that deck in the dark forest evening, one of those times presented itself to me. I thought of Nico's comment a few minutes earlier that Paul Barkley might be my next project. And so, staring at Vincent's face, I took a step.

"Okay, how about this." I heard myself saying. "You tell me what you know about Paul, and I won't be curious about why you have so much drip irrigation in your garage and where you grow your marijuana."

Vincent smiled. "You're new at this, aren't you," he said. He looked straight ahead for a few seconds without a word. "How much do you weigh?" he finally asked.

"Hundred fifty. Why?"

"I learned some things in my work, too," he said. "And I'm just wondering how much trouble it's going to be to throw you over this railing."

CHAPTER 8

I DROVE HOME from Nico and Vincent's house, and it was nearly midnight by the time I arrived at the base of my tower. When my headlights shone on the drive, I saw a black Mustang parked beside my house and a figure climbing out of the front seat. It was Eddie Mahler.

Mahler leaned against the front fender, waiting for me to join him. "Hey, Teller," he said. "Is our local Boswell working late tonight?"

"Sure," I said. "A writer's always at work. What can I do for you?"

"A few questions. All right if we talk inside? I'd like to see your water tower."

Inside, I offered him some sparkling water and filled two glasses. He walked slowly around the room. He picked up a copy of Thomas Hardy's *Return of the Native* from the coffee table. "You reading this?" he asked.

"Yeah," I said. "I thought I'd read them all again in order."

"Kind of an odd choice for someone like you, isn't it? Wouldn't that stuff about fortune's false wheel preclude the need to chronicle a person's life?"

"I don't have anything against fate. If it's true, it just makes the details of our lives that much more ironic."

"Speaking of ironic, you see the latest therapeutic studies are confirming what Skye Lurie said in her book about recovery treatments? Or, is it *your* book, I've never been sure."

"You read that?"

"Surprised that cops read?"

"No. I just didn't think you'd be interested in a book like that."

"I worked gang task force. Spent a lot of time with kids in trouble. Lower on the social tree than Skye Lurie. But same problems. You did a nice job of showing how tough recovery is."

I nodded in acknowledgment of the compliment. Mahler sat in one of my two matching leather chairs with his feet on the ottoman and sipped his drink. I sat on the sofa and put my glass and the bottle on the coffee table between us.

I tried to remember what I had left in view. On the desk my laptop lay closed, with the memory stick beside it.

"Of course, some of the other books were pop trash," Mahler said. "Tina Terrill was a spoiled kid. Susan Sparrow was a T&A book. It's an uneven body of work." He smiled cheerfully.

"Let's say 'eclectic.' The books were aimed at different audiences."

"How does this latest book with Patel fit in? Seems a bit out of your line. Not your usual troubled subject."

"Patel's an interesting case. He's an American story. He came here with nothing, worked hard, and . . . "

"Gave us a thousand parking lots." Mahler sat back in his chair and drank his water. He smiled his wise-guy grin. He was having a good time. "I don't know. It sounds panegyric. I don't see you breaking a lot of new literary ground here."

"I'm glad to have the work," I said.

"Yeah, I guess you are. One thing I've been trying to figure out is why the famous hotshot writer Charlie Teller would come to our little backwater."

"I moved here to be closer to my ex-wife and daughter."

"Really? I mean no offense, but from what I've read, your life's been a train wreck the last few years. You've had a couple —what would you call them— missteps?"

I nodded in concession.

"Ten years ago, you're writing the autobiographies of Nick White and Susan Sparrow, and now you're here," Mahler said, looking around the small room, "writing the life story of the king of parking garages."

"Maybe Hardy was right," I said. "It's all about fate."

"Maybe. I just want to be sure there's not another reason you arrive here the same time we have what looks like a drug buy gone sour and someone gets killed. As an observer of lives, what can you tell me about Paul Barkley?"

"Did you say drug buy?"

"We'll come to that. What about Barkley?"

"I hadn't known him long. We met socially. Just a casual relationship."

"What'd you talk about?"

"Me, usually. He was always concerned about the people around him. He rarely spoke about himself. I didn't realize until now how little I knew about him."

"What about his relationship with Stephen Robb?

"They were friends."

"You didn't know they were lovers?"

"No. But like I said, he didn't talk about himself."

"What do you know about Page Salinger?"

"Nothing. I've never met her."

"What about this letter?" Mahler took a piece of paper from his pocket and handed it to me. "It's a photocopy of the letter he gave you the night he was killed. It's from Barkley to Howard Miller, who's a lawyer here in town, setting up a meeting."

I read it and handed it back to Mahler. "I don't know. He didn't talk about it. He just gave it to me."

"Did you read it Thursday night?"

"No."

"Were you involved in any kind of association with Barkley that involved his lawyer?"

"No. I never heard of Howard Miller."

"Miller's a criminal attorney. Can you think of any reason Barkley may have had for consulting with him?"

"Not really. Why don't you ask Miller?"

"I will, but I wanted to hear what you had to say. Doesn't all this seem odd to you? He wanted to talk to you about this meeting, and you don't know anything about it?"

"A little odd, but Paul was like that. The first time he met anyone, he treated them as if he had known them for a long time."

"So that's how he treated you?"

"I had the feeling that he saw me as someone older, who had lived outside this town and had experience of the world."

"So he confided in you?"

"No, confided is the wrong word. In his café and catering businesses, he ran into people from show business, and he seemed to think that was an experience we shared in common."

"Our forensics people say that something else may have been in the envelope. You recall anything else being there?"

"Not that I remember," I said, not looking at Mahler. "If you've already arrested Stephen, why are you asking all these questions?"

Mahler grinned. "Oh, we're looking at several lines of investigation," he said. "There may have been more than one person involved. We like to make all the pieces of the puzzle fit together. Don't you like the pieces to fit together before you start a book?"

I held the bottle toward Mahler, and when he nodded, poured him more water.

"In my experience they don't usually fit together," I said. "There're always loose ends. Life's messy."

"Some mysteries that can't be solved?" Mahler asked. "Does that sell more books? Let the readers figure it out?"

"No, it's more like there are few simple explanations for why a person does something," I said. "But then I've never written about a murder. Maybe it's different."

"It's pretty much the same," Mahler said. "We're both dealing with small pieces of information, which in themselves don't mean anything. But they can come together to make a picture."

"What do you know about Paul Barkley and drugs?" Mahler asked.

I finished my glass.

"Nothing," I said. "I never saw him with anything like that. He seemed like a pretty clean-cut guy."

"We're getting some information from our drug investigation unit."

"Well, I can't think of anything helpful to say. I never saw any street sellers or junkies hanging around his place, if that's what you mean."

"How about his friends?"

"They're a pretty clean bunch. But I'm probably the wrong person to ask. I'm still new in town."

"We're talking to the others. But I'm interested in you. Didn't you have a drug problem a few years ago? I seem to remember reading something."

"In the rehabilitation community, it was called an amphetamine dependence. But that's in the past. For the last three years, I've been declared drug-free by the American Booksellers Association. It's safe to read Charlie Teller again."

Mahler smiled. "Glad you haven't lost your sense of humor."

"Part of the twelve-step program. Step ten: learn to laugh at yourself as much as those laughing at you."

"See that's just it," Mahler said. "You're a smart guy, Boswell. I think you know something you're not telling me. You're not just sitting up here in this little room, writing the fascinating life of Rajiv Patel and poured-in-place concrete. You've got something else going on."

"What makes you think that?"

"You must have learned something from writing all those biographies," he said.

"And yet it never made me smarter," I said.

"I never said anything about being smarter," Mahler said, with his wise-guy grin. "There's more to learn than that." He closed his jacket and stood to leave.

"I don't think I ever uncovered much," I said, leading him to the door. "It was pretty obvious stuff,"

He stopped in the doorway. "You give yourself too little credit, Teller," he said. "You can't help wanting to find out what you don't know. There's always one more question for you. For instance, I heard that earlier this afternoon you visited Stephen Robb in jail."

"Are you keeping track of me, detective?"

"Pieces of the puzzle," he said, as he went down the stairs. "Just trying to fit them together."

CHAPTER **9**

I AWOKE EARLY the next morning and ate breakfast in front of my computer. I plugged in Barkley's memory stick and opened the file. It was a spreadsheet of numbers. On the left side, over the first column, the heading was "Location." Down the column were single words: Fieldcrest, Armory, and Greene. The next column contained dates—months and years—all in the last five years. After that was a column labeled "Condition." The rest of the columns were titled with expressions that looked like filenames: sysdat, spectot, and util-reg.

I stared at the screen. Barkley had read all my books. Several times we talked at length about Virginia Hardy and Tina Terrill. What had he wanted to tell me about this spreadsheet, and why had he chosen to give it to me?

At nine I looked up the phone number for Barkley's lawyer, Howard Miller, and called. I got his service and left a message.

I called Molly to tell her about my conversation with Mahler. When she answered, she said she didn't have time to talk. She was on her way to Barkley's house to meet his parents, who were driving up from San Francisco to choose burial clothes for their son. She suggested we meet there in half an hour.

Barkley's home was a condominium in the Bennett Valley section of Santa Rosa—one of a cluster of two-story homes surrounded by pine trees. I spotted Molly's car and saw her standing by the condo's front door. Her face was drawn and tired-looking.

"The cops gave us permission to do this," she said as we went inside. "The crime scene techs already finished here."

We walked into a living room, and could see beyond to a kitchen and dining room; upstairs were two bedrooms. The rooms were uncluttered. The furniture looked European, made with polished hardwoods in simple lines. A few black-and-white photographs of Barkley and his family and friends were mounted on the walls.

Molly made tea, and we talked at the kitchen bar. I told her about my visit with Stephen. She opened her hands in a gesture of helplessness when I described his distress. "I hope he can hang in there," she said. "It's going to be tough to get a release on a homicide charge."

"Do they have evidence against him?" I asked.

Molly shrugged. "I have a friend, Kim McFarlane, who works for Eddie Mahler," she said. "She's willing to tell me a few things, because I helped her in a custody hearing six months ago. She said they confirmed the twenty-two was the murder weapon. Three rounds are gone. It's a Taurus PT22, semi-automatic. Nearly brand new. It's a really small gun, about five inches. A concealment weapon, what a woman might carry in her purse."

At this last remark, I raised my eyebrows.

"I'm just saying it's that kind of gun," Molly said. "Anyway the crime scene guys found it in some tall grass at the back of the parking lot. Stephen's prints are on it, and it's registered to him, but Stephen didn't have any powder residue on him or his clothes when he was arrested."

"What's that mean?"

"Not much. He could have cleaned it off and thrown away the clothes. They're interviewing other people who were at the café to see if anyone saw Stephen with the gun."

"Did you?"

"No, but someone else may have. Mahler's team has figured out that the pickup you saw wasn't Stephen's. But they also don't know if it was connected to the murder. They're trying to track it down, but there's not much to go on. Kim said there was also some other physical evidence at the scene that they think they can tie to Stephen."

"Like what?"

"She wouldn't say. I think she doesn't want me to get out ahead of them on anything that might get her in trouble."

"It still doesn't explain why Stephen would do it. He told me the argument Thursday night was not a big deal."

"Kim said Mahler's guys found some hints of a disagreement between Paul and Stephen over partial ownership of the catering service. Stephen thought Paul was reneging on a promise."

"From what you know, do you think Stephen was involved?"

"It's hard to know. It doesn't look like it was a robbery. Paul had a lot of money on him. The other thing is, he took three rounds. There's a cop wisdom: one bullet's a robbery, more's a statement."

"Anyway, it's early in the investigation," she said. "I've been doing this long enough to know people will surprise you. Given the right circumstances, any of us is capable of killing someone. It just takes stepping over the line for an instant."

"It seems unreal though, doesn't it?" I said. "Mahler told me last night they're getting information about Paul from the drug investigation unit."

Molly smiled. "Eddie talked to you again?"

"At my place. He was waiting for me when I got back last night about midnight. He seems to think I know something."

"Eddie's an interesting guy. Watch what you say to him."

"It's hard for me to imagine Paul having anything to do with drugs."

Molly finished her tea and took a deep breath. "Kim said they discovered cocaine traces in Paul's office safe and some interesting files on his hard drive. That's all she'd say. Anyway, why are you so interested in all of this?"

I hesitated. "I just thought I'd do some checking around on my own," I said. "I know how to do research. I knew Paul and I know Stephen, and I was there the night Paul was killed. I thought maybe I owed it to Paul for helping me when I first got here. Besides, maybe I'll even feel useful again." This was the first time I had said it out loud, and I was surprised at my own words.

Molly smiled. "He got to you, didn't he?" she said. "For me, the thing about Paul was he was always talking about a new venture, a new idea. It was never just a good idea. Each one was going to be the best thing that had ever happened. He'd say he'd just mentioned it to his friend, Jerry Bernstein, the film producer, or Joyce Cross, the actress. And they loved it. Two weeks later, of course, he'd have forgotten it, and there'd be another new best idea. I think it's how he kept himself going. It was like fuel to him. The funny thing is, I always believed him. He'd have me believing that *this* one was *the* one."

We heard a car pull up outside. From the kitchen window, we saw an elderly couple emerge. Molly went to meet them at the door. The couple walked toward the house, the man gently supporting the woman's arm. Seeing Molly in the doorway, they paused.

The man pointed to the hydrangea bush by the entranceway. "These houses all look alike, but I could always tell which one was his by that hydrangea."

Molly hugged each of them in turn and led them into the house. Eileen and Martin Barkley were in their late seventies. They were dressed formally—she in a black silk dress and he in a suit and tie. There was air about them of protected gentility, which was rare in California, as if they had been imported untouched from the East Coast.

Molly introduced me. "This is a friend of your son's, Charlie Teller," she said loudly. "Charlie's a writer. He wrote that book on Tina Terrill. You remember, the skater?"

Eileen peered at me. "You're a skater? I didn't know Paul skated. We lived in the city when he was growing up."

"No, no," Martin corrected her. "He's a writer. He wrote about a skater."

He shook my hand. "Paul spoke of you," he said.

I smiled and tried to imagine what Barkley would have said about me. Before I could reply, they both turned and headed for the safety of two wing chairs in the living room.

Molly made more tea, and the four of us sat together in the living room. At first there was an awkward silence.

"I remember when he bought this house," Martin finally said without looking at any of us. "I thought he paid too much for it. Now look at what it's worth."

"He rented an apartment before this," Eileen said. "I never cared for it. Too noisy."

"He asked me if I thought he should buy it," Martin said. "Of course I don't know the market up here."

"He had a roommate for a while," Eileen said. "A young man named Andrew who worked at the restaurant."

The two of them talked like this for a while, as if alone in separate rooms. Then Molly asked if they had made arrangements for the service. Martin explained that they had decided to hold it in Santa Rosa, where Paul's friends were. It was scheduled for Tuesday.

Molly suggested she and Eileen go to Paul's room to find a suit.

I turned to Martin and asked how his son started in the restaurant business.

"It was all he was ever interested in," Martin said. "While he was in high school, he worked in several restaurants. He loved it. He majored in business administration at UCSF. When he got out, he started managing. First Café Ritz on Market. Then Del'Oro's in the Marina."

Martin stood and walked around the room. He stopped and studied a candle holder and then peered at a photograph of Page and Paul on the beach.

"Paul worked hard," he continued. "It was a time, you know, when many young men of his generation . . . what would you say . . . lacked direction. But Paul worked hard. And he changed those restaurants, both of them."

"How so?"

"It was everything. The way the room looked. The lighting, the tables. The way the waiters spoke to you. The food, of course. He made it a place where people wanted to be."

He resumed his tour of the room. "Pretty soon they were discovered," he said. "Politicians, film stars, they all started hanging out there. That became Paul's thing."

"What do you mean?"

"Oh, I think he liked being in the presence of those people. The reflected glow, I suppose."

He returned to his wing chair and sat down. "I worried sometimes. Thought he took it too seriously. It was a distraction from the business." He stared straight ahead for a moment in silence.

"Why did he move out of the city and come up here?" I asked.

Martin shrugged. "He wanted his own place, and it was cheaper up here. He liked being in a smaller pond, so to speak. He built Galileo's from the ground up, and it became the place to be in this town."

"So the restaurant came before the catering and the fitness club?"

"The other businesses were an afterthought. His customers, the wealthy ones, asked him to put on parties at their houses. Pretty soon it was a business. Then he hired John as a personal trainer for a few customers, and that started the fitness club."

"They all seemed to be succeeding. Every time I saw him he was busy." As I said this, I remembered what Stephen had said about money troubles.

"Paul was good with people," Martin said. "That was his gift. He knew how to take care of people, particularly those who were used to being cared for. He knew what they wanted. He told me once he understood the rich and famous and why they lived the way they did."

Martin looked tired. "The past year he was different," he said. "He wasn't as focused. And then there was Page. I never understood her."

Behind us we could hear Molly and Eileen coming down the stairs. Molly was holding a dark suit on a hanger, and the empty suit seemed to be descending in front of the two women.

Martin watched them. "Anyway," he said, "I guess it doesn't matter now."

CHAPTER 10

ON SUNDAY MORNING I packed a lunch for the day's canoe ride with Jill and Lucy. In a knapsack I put a loaf of ciabatta, a block of goat cheese, olives and apples, a bottle of juice, and a bottle of pinot noir.

I drove first to the jail to accompany Carl on his visit to Stephen. In the parking lot Carl stood leaning against his car, with his hands stuffed in his pockets. He was tall and thin and had an odd way of standing with his back curved forward and his shoulders hunched. His anxiety about the visit had made him overdress. He wore a white shirt, chinos, and a dark sports jacket. When he saw me, he gave a short wave.

A burly sheriff escorted us into the visitors' room, and we found Stephen already seated at a window. I stood in the corridor to give the pair some privacy. After a few minutes, Carl motioned for me to join them. Stephen looked less fearful than he had two days before. His face was freshly shaved, and the dark shadows under his eyes were gone.

"Can you tell me what was going on between you and Paul Thursday night?" I asked Stephen.

"It was about Seasons, the catering business," he said. "About a year ago, Paul asked me to take it over. It was booming. We had more business than we could handle."

"Some weekends we had separate bookings for Saturday and Sunday," Carl said.

"The problem was Paul couldn't let go," Stephen said. "A lot of the business came from his contacts among his wealthy friends. So even though I was supposedly in charge, he kept trying to make decisions."

"So that's what the phone call was about on the patio?"

"The call was from a woman in Healdsburg who had a question about her party next Saturday. I didn't even know we had the booking. It's not the first time it happened. I told him if he wanted to run the business, he should run the business."

"That's all it was?"

"More or less."

"Molly said the police think there was some dispute between you and Paul over partial ownership of Seasons."

Stephen looked at Carl. "It was one of those on again, off again things. There was nothing on paper. That's not what we were fighting about."

"Molly said the police found some cocaine traces in Paul's safe," I said. "You know anything about that?"

Neither of them said anything.

"Look," I said, "You don't have to tell me, but you need to tell Molly if you know anything."

"I saw a bag once in Paul's' briefcase when he left it open," Stephen said.

"There was a weird guy who used to hang around the bar," Carl said.

"Yeah," Stephen said. "Greasy hair. Had a tattoo of the Zig-Zag guy on his neck. Ordered rum and cokes and talked with Paul in his office. Never paid."

"What'd Paul say about him?" I asked.

"Nothing," Stephen said. "He never mentioned him, and I stayed away from the subject. I figured the less I knew, the better. You can see how successful that's been." He raised his hands in a gesture of resignation.

"Do the words Fieldcrest, Armory, or Greene mean anything to you?" I asked both of them.

They shook their heads. "Why?" Stephen asked. "What are they?"

"I don't know. Maybe nothing. Do you know why Paul wanted to talk to me Thursday night?"

"He didn't say anything to me," Carl said.

"Maybe he wanted you to write something for him," Stephen suggested. "He was always talking to one of his friends in the film business about something in his life that he thought would make a good movie."

"It was something else," I said. "He wanted me to meet him at a lawyer's office."

"I don't know anything about that," Stephen said.

I stood to leave. Carl said he wanted to stay longer. I waved through the glass to Stephen and asked for a guard to escort me out.

*   *   *

I drove north on the freeway to Jill's house in Windsor. It was a fast-growing town, with new housing developments on either side of the freeway. Jill had bought a two-story house in a tract where the streets were named after famous California authors. She lived on Chandler Way, a gently curving street of identical houses that somehow managed to transplant the master of LA noir to a sunny suburban landscape. Each time I visited, I tried to imagine how Chandler might have used one of his famous similes to take his revenge on the scene. This morning I thought: The street was like a ribbon, wrapped around the package of houses that hid all the misery within.

Lucy was waiting for me on the porch and ran to the street to give me a hug through the car window.

"Hey daddy," she said. "Is there going to be whitewater where we're going?"

"Sure," I said. "There's been a lot of rain in the mountains that feed this river."

For all the problems Jill and I had between us, I was always surprised that we had managed to raise such a cheerful teenager. She opened her knapsack and showed me a waterproof case she had bought for her camera. As we looked at the case, I heard Jill walk up behind us and felt her hand on my back.

"Hi Charlie," she said. We exchanged a quick kiss. For me, the touch and the kiss were sad emblems of our current relationship, in which it was safe to exchange small gestures.

Lucy climbed in the front, and Jill sat in the back. By now the sun had burned off the morning fog, and the day was warming. We drove a few minutes north on the freeway.

At the river, the canoe rental company fitted us with life preservers and helped launch us on the water. The river had a strong current, and I was soon busy trying to keep us pointed downstream. On either side, canoeists unfortunate enough to get turned sideways were quickly dumped into the cold water or sent into the riverside brush.

After an hour, we found a sandy beach, spread a blanket, and ate lunch. Lucy chattered about her school assignments and her friends. When a canoe with young boys overturned on the river near us, she ran to help them retrieve their floating packs.

"She likes it here much better than LA," Jill said. "She can ride her bike to school. One of her friends has horses. She's had three sleepovers this month."

"How about you?" I asked. "How's the teaching?" Jill was a professional violist, and had come north to teach at Sonoma State.

"Good. So far, I've just got one class, but I put in a proposal for a Mozart class like the one I taught at Fullerton. The private lessons are starting to pick up. And I've been accepted, provisionally, as a member of a local string quartet."

We watched Lucy at the river's edge, lifting an ice chest for the boys in the river.

"I saw the story in the paper about Paul Barkley," Jill said. "Do you know the man who's been arrested?"

"Stephen Robb. I visited him this morning in jail."

Jill looked surprised. "Really?" she said. "You never mentioned him. How do you know him?"

"He was the manager of Galileo's. I saw him there when I had dinner."

"You think he did it?"

"He says he didn't, and I guess I believe him."

Jill broke off more bread and cut a piece of cheese. "So what's your involvement?" she asked.

"I'm going to ask a few questions, poke around a little," I said.

"Why not let the police deal with it?" she asked.

"I think I can help," I said. "Paul was very generous to me. I feel like I owe this to him. This is something I can do."

Jill shook her head and looked away, but I recognized her disapproval. This was the essential part of our relationship the last five years. Her skepticism and the probing of motives that had once been directed toward college administrators and members of her string quartet were now aimed at me.

"Do you think I shouldn't help these people?" I asked.

"I can't tell you, Charlie," she said. "I don't know them."

"But you have an opinion. Why don't you tell me?"

"It's up to you. It's just that I came here to leave the stuff in LA behind, and I agreed you could move up here for Lucy's sake on the condition you keep a low profile. I don't want to go back to what it was like."

"I'll do my best."

"You don't have to look all injured either. You made some bad decisions. You brought it on yourself."

"I know. I never said I didn't."

If they're together long enough, every couple has one conversation over and over. This was ours.

Lucy ran towards us. She could sense the tension. "Did she tell you about 'Dave'?" she asked, using a deep voice as she said the name.

Jill's face blushed. "No," she said. "I hadn't told him." She turned to me. "I've been seeing a guy named David Reynolds."

"Dave," Lucy said again in the mock deep voice.

"We've gone out a few times. He's a sweet guy."

"He's a farmer," Lucy said.

"A vineyard manager at Myers Creek Winery. We met when my string quartet played at the winery."

Lucy found the olives and bit into one. "He drives a Dodge Ram," she said. "He's hulking."

"He's not hulking," Jill said. She was embarrassed and wouldn't meet my eyes.

Seeing another canoe caught in the currents, Lucy ran back to the river to help its occupants, leaving Jill and me alone again. The two of us sat, without speaking, watching our daughter.

Like most men, I didn't know much about the human heart, especially my own. Which meant that, as I sat beside the woman to whom I had been married for six years and divorced for another ten, I didn't know if I was mourning the life we once had, if I was just wishing again for a shared intimacy with anyone, or if I was, in fact, still in love with her. What I wanted was for Jill to lean across the space between us, past all the terrible things we had said and done, and put one hand on the side of my face the way she had the first time and kiss me, and I, tasting her kiss, would kiss her back and feel that familiar ache of joy.

CHAPTER **11**

Nick White

FOR SIX WEEKS in the fall of 1979, I rode through Europe in a motor coach with Nick White and what was left of the legendary rock band Circle of White. It was the Blessed Hope Tour, later to be remembered as the last tour to feature lead singer Sylvie Beckett. The schedule included concert dates in twelve cities from northern Germany to Madrid, Spain. We spent hours in the coach, lurching from one city to the next. The founding members—Sylvie, Jeremy Wilson, and Peter O'Callaghan—sat in the rear, passing a joint between them. The nameless new kids, recently recruited from Christian rock bands, sat up front and took snapshots out the window.

In the middle sat Nick White. Shorn of his long hair and clean shaven for the first time in ten years, he resembled a pre-formed version of himself. Rock star as embryo.

Just a few years before, Circle of White had been one of the most popular rock bands of all time. Five double platinum albums, the best-selling album in history (Sweet Love), three Grammys, and an Oscar-nominated song ("Ever in Your Heart").

They were *the* band of the 1970s. Their clothes set fashion trends, they were in and out of marriages with film stars, and for years they toured worldwide, performing in sports stadiums. Always at the forefront, prancing at the stage's edge, just out of reach of the girls in the first row, was the bad boy of London—Nick White.

But in 1977, Nick White's renown was overshadowed by a single late-night incident in Chicago's Oak Park Hotel. Alone in his room, roiling with Quaaludes, cocaine, and Black Label, Nick had a vision.

In the version of the story in his autobiography, Nick said his hotel room filled with light—and something else, a presence. At first he thought it was the electrical glow of his own overloaded nerve endings. But as he gazed at the light's pulsing heart and watched the aura brighten and fade, he read a message in the rhythm. It said that it was possible to return to the origin of the cycle, to reclaim innocence. After that Nick White began a new life.

The following day, Nick met with his fellow band members and told them the story. He was going to take time off from touring to study the gospel. He planned to write new songs—not pop love songs but songs worthy of his vision. In the future, accompanying the band on tour would be his new friend, the Reverend Albert Heywood, a young minister Nick had found the night before in the Harvest Fellowship Baptist Church, a few blocks from the hotel. Nick said he would also seek the forgiveness of his former wife Leslie Anne. And he was going to cut his hair.

With the label and his management unable to dissuade him, Nick canceled the rest of the band's North American tour and went home to England. Two members of the band quit immediately. The others stayed on, and the band re-formed, with the same name but now playing a mix of old hits, gospel songs, and "Christian rock."

It was a global media event. Headlines read "Pop Singer Meets Christ" and "Son of God Calls on British Rocker." The record label sued. Fans deserted. A fan club in California sponsored a return of records to stores.

Nick was undeterred. Over the next two years, he continued to talk about being saved. He decided to tell his side of the story, and he needed some help. He called and invited me to visit him before the band's next tour.

I had just finished my second book, an autobiography of the fifties-era western film star, Jack Evans, and was looking for a new project.

I flew to London and met Nick in a Chelsea recording studio. If some entertainers are smaller and quieter in person than their public personas, Nick White face to face was larger and louder than he appeared on stage. "Charlie Teller," he boomed as he greeted me with an enthusiastic bear hug. "How're they hanging, mate?"

We were in an office next to the studio's control room. Nick wore a leather bomber jacket, jeans, and wire-rim sunglasses. In a corner of the office sat the minister Heywood, a thin, awkward man dressed in a suit too large for him.

"I need your expertise to tell my story," Nick said. "Not just the lowdown dirty version. No offense, mate, but I know that's the stock-in-trade."

He cleared a chair for me and walked back and forth the length of the small room while he spoke.

"What do you want?" I asked.

"Sanctification," he said, his eyes shining.

"Sanctification?"

"Separation from evil and dedication to the divinity of Christ. Did you hear my song on the album before this one—'I am Sanctified'?"

Nick was famous for sly jokes, so I waited to see if this was a put-on. "You want your autobiography to separate you from evil?" I asked.

"I'm going to put the sins of the past in this book and let them go. That's the heart of the matter. We only torture ourselves with the past, Charlie. This book's going to redeem me—I can feel it. And I need your talents to write it."

I stared at the two of them. Nick appeared to be glowing, charged by an invisible electric current. Heywood had a quiet otherworldliness, as if something had granted him the power to deny reality—to believe that, even as he sat there in the Chelsea recording studio, he was still a provisional minister in a failing Chicago church, not the companion to one of the greatest English rock stars of our generation.

"This'll be a new step for you, Charlie," Nick said. "This book's not just going to tell the story of my life—it's going to heal my soul. And you'll be the vessel for that."

Heywood clasped his hands on his lap. "Mr. Teller," he asked, "have you accepted Jesus Christ as your Lord and Savior?"

Nick laughed a big booming laugh. "Albert," he said. "I've read Mr. Teller's books. I can tell you he's not been blessed with the waters of salvation. But he's not without hope. No one in this world is without hope."

For a moment, I didn't say anything.

"Not what you were expecting?" Nick asked more quietly. He sat on the desktop and pushed the sunglasses on top of his head. His bright green eyes watched me.

"Not exactly," I said.

"Not exactly what I was expecting either. I know what you're thinking, but I'm not going to ask you to write a load of bollocks about being born again. We're going to write my story, and it's a good one."

"Why do you need me? You know the history and the stories."

"Discipline, mate. I need someone to hold my hand, keep me on the straight and narrow. Ask Albert here, I'm a man of appetites. I've got to be held to task."

"Why me, of all writers?"

"Worried this one's going to wreck your reputation, are you? Listen, believe it or not, I'm not just a daft guitar player from the Midlands. I read your autobiography of Virginia Hardy. It's a beautiful book. I need your skills. I want to describe something special. Any one of those *Rolling Stone* monkeys can write the rock and roll. I need someone to do the more serious work."

"It doesn't always work out when I try to help someone. Sometimes it's not a match."

"Like a marriage, I expect. But we won't know if we don't give it a go. If nothing else, it'll be a bit of fun."

To my credit, I knew even then that writing Nick's life story would not be just a bit of fun. It would be difficult without the articulateness of Virginia Hardy and the patience of Jack Evans. I'd be working with an impulsive hedonist, who may have addled his brain with drugs and who was used to the highs of performance. On the other hand, I was being invited to help write the autobiography of a rock legend. Who would say no to that?

In the end, I agreed to try to work with Nick, to conduct a few interviews and see how it went. I said I'd ask my agent to draw up a business arrangement.

Nick smiled broadly and pumped my hand. "Brilliant," he said. "Good man."

He looked at Heywood. "A few years back, I might of offered you a pint. But now I'm going to ask Albert for a blessing."

With that, the born-again rock star, the small-time minister, and the ghostwriter knelt on the floor of the recording studio office and asked Jesus Christ to bless the writing of an autobiography.

. . .

Our routine on the Blessed Hope Tour was for Nick and me to talk in his hotel room in the early morning hours after the concerts, while Nick unwound from the performance.

He had been born in Leicester, in the country's industrial Midlands. It was a nineteenth-century mill town, with densely packed, brick row houses, and when Nick was born in the late 1940s, the country was stuck in the post World War II depression. The family lived on Edgehill Road, in a cramped two-up, two-down with the "facilities" in the back garden. Nick's father, an unemployed construction laborer, left home when Nick was an infant. His mother, Penny, sang for drinks in a local pub. He lived for much of his childhood two doors down with his Aunt Brenda. Determined he should learn one thing more than his parents, his aunt taught the young boy to play the upright piano in her front room. By the time he was ten, he was able to join his mother at the pub and accompany her on popular songs of the day—"You'll Never Know" and "Goodnight Sweetheart."

After that, it wasn't long before he began to write his own songs to play at the pub. He had tunes in his head, and he knew the kind of songs people liked to sing. His mother announced the title, the two of them sang, and the boy stood on the piano bench to take his bows.

At fifteen, Nick formed a band with two boys on his street. They called themselves The Outlaws and played talent shows with a borrowed set of drums. On Saturdays they listened to a radio program of the new American rock and roll: songs of anguished teenage love and fast cars. For the young boy living in the narrow world of postwar England, they awakened a unique sensibility.

Nick's songs took that American teenager's voice and turned it into a deeper and darker yearning for love. In his lyrics and melodies, the young boy found a new way to tell the world about everything he longed for in that cramped life on Edgehill Road.

At nineteen, out of school, Nick and one of his boyhood friends, Jeremy Wilson, moved to London. One night in a club, Nick met a singer named Sylvie Beckett from a wealthy Kensington family. In awe of her sophistication and style, Nick wrote a song overnight and presented it to her the next day. It was called "This Dance," and told the story of a boy too shy to ask a girl to dance. Sylvie loved the song and took it to her friend, the legendary Johnny Summers, whose band, Johnny and the Dreamers, was the leading English pop band of the time. Summers recorded the song with Sylvie doing the vocal.

The song was the beginning of the passionate but off-balance relationship that Nick and Sylvie would have for the next ten years, a relationship of two restless musical talents never in love with each other at the same time.

Summers invited Nick and Jeremy to join his band, and they played concerts first in London and later in Europe. The group was a revolving door of top talent. It was here that Nick met several musicians who would one day join his band.

When "This Dance" hit the charts, Summers asked Nick for more songs. By then, he had a trunkful, dating back to tunes written for his mother's pub singing. Together, they assembled the songs that would become the Dreamers hit album *Northern Lights*.

The music had a fresh sound. The lyrics were filled with a wonderful British colloquialism new to American audiences. The melodies were catchy and fun to sing. In the ballads was the authentic voice of the young kid from Leicester, dreaming of love.

Just like that, Nick White was a star. For six months he toured with the Dreamers. When the band broke up, Nick formed a new group. He hired the best musicians from the Dreamers, his old friend from Leicester, Jeremy Wilson, and his lead singer Sylvie Beckett. He named his band Circle of White.

. . .

In 1967, the band's first album was released. It contained all new material, and three songs—"Faded," "Lost in Your Love," and "Betrayal"—ended in Billboard's top ten. On the album cover, the band members were dressed in Renaissance clothes, and their photograph was enclosed in a psychedelic design. For the next six months, profiles of Nick and the other musicians filled newspapers and magazines. On a yearlong worldwide concert tour, called "Circle the Globe," the band sold out venues on four continents and established a model for touring.

The band was famous for its excesses. Here and there band members fell by the wayside. Experimenting with opium, the keyboard player suffered a nervous breakdown and was forced to leave the tour.

Before leaving London, Nick had married his childhood girlfriend, Leslie Anne, and at the start, she toured with the band. But the travel and long hours were too difficult for her, and once she learned of her pregnancy, she returned home. Alone on the road, Nick was surrounded by young women who followed the band from city to city. He found them in his hotel room in the early morning, sitting on the floor with rolled joints and trays of room service food.

In 1969, Nick took time off from performing to be with his family. He worked in a renovated shed behind their London flat and wrote the band's second album, called *Sweet Love*, which contained a dozen of the best songs Nick would write and set an all-time sales record.

The band's third album, *Return*, was dark and moody, and was released to mediocre reviews. When the album tour ended, Sylvie quit and announced her intention to begin a solo career. Nick hired a replacement singer, an American named Cheryl Owens. When the tabloids ran photos of Nick kissing Owens at a late night dinner, Leslie Anne filed for divorce and custody of their daughter.

In 1976, most of the original band members returned to Circle of White. The group released a Greatest Hits album and set out on a yearlong tour.

The euphoria of the reunion lasted six months before the old tensions returned. The virtuoso guitarist Donovan Breslan was bored playing the old songs. On the European portion of the tour, O'Callaghan was too strung out on heroin to perform. Sylvie demanded the middle third of each concert be reserved for songs from her solo album. Nick tried to balance it all, finding his own middle ground between the pre-concert coke rush and the early-morning Quaalude sedative.

Then in the Oak Park Hotel, he experienced the visitation, and everything changed.

When I arrived in 1979, Circle of White had just released a new album, *Blessed Hope,* and the European tour was intended to showcase it. The concerts themselves were an odd mix of the band's classic hits and new songs with a Christian message.

Jeremy Wilson and Sylvie Beckett were the casualties of the tour. Wilson sat alone in the coach and at meals, reading science fiction. Sylvie, once a rock diva, held a tambourine on stage and sang backup with two "Christian rock sisters."

. . .

Following the tour, I worked for two months in London, writing from the tape transcripts and continuing to interview Nick and his friends. Nick and I first wrote the story of his life as a rock star. We covered the escapades—a bong catching fire in the dressing room before a concert in Melbourne and the three girls photographed in his bed in Berlin.

After that, we tackled the story of his new life as a Christian. The struggle was to find an authentic voice. What he believed in, when we got past all the doctrinal clichés, was something neither complicated nor strange—it was goodness. But while the English language has a rich vocabulary for describing transgressions and the weaknesses of the flesh, it is difficult to describe goodness without inviting skepticism. Nick had the extra burden that he had spent years in the public eye as the prince of facetiousness. His witticisms and wordplays had turned his voice into the sound of comic insincerity.

To write his book, Nick and I worked together five mornings a week in his flat. He read the tape transcripts and explained them while I sat at an electric typewriter and typed.

One morning he suddenly stopped and held the pages in front of me. "You don't believe this, do you?" he shouted. He was dressed in a faded tee shirt and sweat pants and was carrying a soup bowl filled with coffee. Waving his arm, he splashed coffee down the front of his pants.

I looked back at him.

"We're buggered, you know that?" he said.

"Imagine one day you wake up, and nothing makes sense," he said. "This writing job is not everything you thought it would be. The people in your life are strangers. You've got nothing. I mean, sure, you have a house, money in the bank, a few cars. But really, you've got fuck-all. What do you do?"

He laughed and put down his coffee. "Hang on a tick," he said. "Take off your clothes, mate."

"What do you mean?" I asked.

"Just do it. I want to show you something."

I removed my shirt and trousers.

"Bloody hell," he said. "Do you think I'm going queer on you? Take 'em all off."

I fully undressed and stood naked before him. He headed downstairs and led me through the kitchen to the back door. There he put his hand on my shoulder and said, "I want to show you something." Then he pushed me outside and locked the door.

I stood in a small garden enclosed on three sides by a brick wall. The morning was foggy and cold. I rubbed my bare arms and shifted my weight on the flagstones.

In a minute Nick opened an upstairs window.

"You're all alone," he yelled. "You've got nothing. What are you going to do?"

I looked up at the windows of the flats on either side of Nick's house.

"What about your neighbors?" I said.

"What about them? We're all naked, Charlie."

"So why am I here?"

"I want you to write this so people feel it in their fucking marrow—the way I felt it. What do you feel?"

"Cold."

"Sorry about that, mate. What else?"

"A little foolish."

"Right as rain. I'm the world's fool. Everybody laughs at me. But what do you want?"

"Respect for my work."

"It's fleeting. What else?"

"To create something that moves people."

"Great feeling. What else? What do you want?"

I tried to balance on one foot to avoid the cold flagstones. I cupped my hands in front of my mouth and breathed into them. "I don't know," I said. "I don't know what I want."

I looked up at the window, but Nick was gone.

"I don't know what I want," I called louder. My voice echoed against the building.

A moment later Nick opened the back door and stepped into the garden. "Love, Charlie," he said. "Love was the right answer. First Corinthians, verse thirteen, line thirteen: 'And now faith, hope, and love abide, these three. And the greatest of these is love.'"

He handed me a raincoat. "We're a pathetic species, mate, who doesn't know ourselves," he said. "But standing out here, your jewels for all the world to see, that's what it's like for a bloke like me to take Jesus Christ as my savior."

. . .

By the time Nick hired me, I had earned a modest reputation in the literary world, based on my work on the Hardy and Evans books. I had an agent, who fielded book offers and found opportunities for me to write articles. Publishers began to solicit my endorsement of other writers' books. For a while, I was a bright light in a small universe.

But there was something missing too. Each afternoon while I worked on Nick's book, I returned to my two-room flat in Bloomsbury, where I sat at a desk writing and rewriting chapters. The winter turned into one of the wettest in London history, and no matter how many lights I turned on, the apartment was as dark as a cave. In that winter's gloom, I suffered a kind of break.

It began with my arranging for a box of my unfinished fiction to be shipped from LA. Commercially, nothing much had come from my stories. From time to time, I published one in a literary review, but my success as ghostwriter gave me no advantage in publishing fiction. Sitting in that dark room, re-reading the stories, I felt their failure. Like many others, I had fallen into my work without ever choosing it. I had written Virginia's autobiography to see if I could. That book led to the Evans book, which in turn made possible my work on Nick's autobiography. I was borne along on the stream of my career.

As a young man, I had believed that writing would change my life, make me larger. Maybe also, if Nick was right, it was love that I was after. Deep in our hearts, if we're honest, lie the most pathetic of dreams. But now, as my stories receded further from what I imagined in my mind, I doubted my own ambition.

I was dating Nick's publicist, a beautiful young woman named Annie Powell, who had black hair and freckles across her nose. She called me Charles, in a way that I first took to be a parody of formality and later discovered was just a sign of her upbringing in a conventional middle-class English family. At Christmas, when I visited her parents in Kent, the four of us sat around the table after dinner, and in a stiff little drama, one by one exploded our Christmas crackers and sat facing each other in paper party hats.

One night I told her I didn't know who I was, that I felt lost. I talked nonstop for ten minutes. She listened without a word, and when I finished, she frowned and said, "I think you're making too much of this, Charles. You've already written two books. Nick likes your work. Isn't that enough? I mean, *really*."

Annie was inclined to say "I mean, *really*" whenever we had a serious conversation; it was her way of ending a train of thought emphatically when she had run out of ideas.

I was her American experiment. She was trying me out—like a new outfit that she had not made up her mind about. As she wavered in her opinion, it was clear I needed to supply the passion for both of us. We made love in my chilly room, and she dressed with her back to me. Near the end of the year, on her birthday, I gave her a card with a line from Yeats ("a meteor of the burning heart"). She stared at the card for a minute longer than it would take anyone to read it and looked up at me. Her face, with its little girl freckles, blushed red. Searching for a way out of the moment, I thought of what Nick had told me in the garden behind his flat. And so in that awkward minute, I said I loved her. When we hugged, I felt one of her hands patting my back.

• • •

Nick White's autobiography, *White Nights,* was my first best-seller. It sold a hundred thousand copies in the first six months, and was on the best seller list for a year.

On the cover was a photograph of Nick caught in the glow of stage lights, his guitar at his waist and his hair flying behind him. The first chapter told the story of a Paris concert, when Circle of White had been at its peak, and the band and the concert crowd were joined in a euphoric union that many afterward called the best rock concert of all time.

An excerpt appeared in *Rolling Stone*. The cover headline read: "Nick's Back!" The *Newsweek* music critic wrote, "This is what rock music's all about."

For a while, I was famous. According to a handful of magazine profiles, I was part of a new generation of biographers who were bringing seriousness and craft to the profession. Critics began to identify something called the Teller style.

For Nick, unfortunately, despite the sales and critical attention, his autobiography was a failure. The book did not put his sins behind him but brought them roaring back. In interviews, the stories of the Circle of White's touring were the first thing most interviewers wanted Nick to retell.

His autobiography also failed to heal Nick's relationship with his former wife, Leslie Anne, who mocked his religious conversion and publicly declined Nick's request to remarry. She told a British tabloid, "Nick can't ask you to pass the butter without talking about Jesus."

The book did not succeed either in converting readers to Nick's faith. Even the reviews that praised the book advised readers to skip the later chapters. The book stranded him between two worlds. His renunciation of his past misdeeds and his commitment to the new Christ-oriented songs separated him from his family and friends in the music business. At the same time, the recounting of his wild youth made his new Christian acquaintances wary.

On the book tour, the failure for Nick was evident in city after city. When he and I appeared on talk shows, Nick began with a story from his early days. Then I described our collaboration. After that, Nick had a few minutes to explain the meaning of his spiritual transformation. The interviews usually ended with Nick singing.

Many interviewers sat awkwardly silent while Nick retold the Oak Park Hotel story; others interrupted him and asked him to sing. Over and over, it was as if he were alone and naked, as I had been in his London garden, trying to tell the story no one wanted to hear.

As the weeks went by, Nick became more dispirited and seemed to grow smaller and quieter. Near the end, we were invited to the studio of a small Midwestern radio station. When it came time for Nick to sing, he strummed a few chords, stared at his fingers, and put down the guitar. Panicked looks filled the faces of the disc jockey and station engineer. "When I first started," he said softly, "I sang songs with my mother. They were older songs." He cleared his throat and sang *a cappella* the Irving Berlin classic "What'll I Do."

What'll I do
When you are far away
And I am blue,
What'll I do?

The next day he flew home to England. He left a message of apology on my hotel phone. "Sorry, mate," he said. "We gave it a go."

In the years after that, Nick never released another album or toured with his band. He became a kind of elder statesman of rock and roll. He wrote songs for other singers in a desultory way, and received an Oscar nomination for a song sung by a turtle in an animated film.

Ten years after his autobiography's publication, I met Nick once alone for lunch in a New York restaurant. It was a bright day, and we were shown to a table beside a tall window, where the sunlight flooding the space made Nick look pale and fragile. He was nearly fifty then. His hair was long again, and it hung in slack strands and joined with a dense, grey beard so that his eyes seemed to be looking out from behind a mantle.

He glanced at the menu and ordered food that he never touched. At first, he talked about the flowers in the garden behind his country house in Surrey. His voice still had its Midlands accent but was soft now and barely audible. He knew the plants by name and took a few minutes with each of them: ageratum, coreopsis, echinacea, rudbeckia. The yarrow, he said, had rose-red flowers on two-foot stems. *Achillea millefolium*, the plant Achilles used to heal wounds.

But he had come to tell me something, and eventually he came to it. He had lost his faith a while before. He wondered if I had known. "It took two years," he said. "I'm not sure what did it. I think I heard myself talking once, and I sounded like one of those skivers, selling you something you don't want. I found out people don't want faith. What they want are things—things they don't have mostly. Anyway, one morning I woke up, and it was gone. Like someone in the next room, rattling around, had moved on."

I probably told him then that, whatever the outcome, his conversion had made people see him in a new way, as a genuine person with real conflicts, but he had not come to listen to me.

He put a finger in his water glass and pushed at an ice cube. "After that, everything was, what would you call it? . . . not relevant," he said. "I couldn't go back to the music. I'd seen through it by then. Not that I can ever escape it. You hear the bloody things everywhere, don't you? In the frozen foods aisle of a supermarket. Airport waiting rooms. Some git in front of a microphone, going on about love in three verses and a bridge. Have you learned anything about love in your life, Charlie? Or, are you still trying to figure it out? Unlike you, my sad American friend, I have twelve million pounds a year in royalties. My accountant reckons it's not a bad trade."

I must have said something here about his memoir continuing to be popular years after its publication.

He looked levelly at me. "They were just stories," he said. "I would have expected you to know that, Charlie."

When I didn't say anything, he said, "Oh, I don't blame you. You were the right man for the job. The bloody historian, weren't you. Tell me what happened, you said. Charlie Teller. Tell me this. Tell me that. Only it turns out, even the stories weren't really mine; they belonged to those faces in the stadiums. They were their stories, their concerts, their songs. They didn't need me. Forget that crazy bugger over there. Lost his mind, poor chap. Too much of the drink, too many pills." His long, thin fingers came to his hair and pulled it back like curtain ends.

"They were just stories, Charlie," he said. "I thought you knew what your books are, being as how it's your business." He said these last words with a recreation of his younger self's sly smile, so that I was not certain how deeply they were meant to wound.

I said something about the objectifying nature of autobiography, and he watched me as he had years before in his kitchen, as if he were being schooled. Then he looked out the tall restaurant window. "The joke was on me in the end, wasn't it?" he said. "I wasn't reborn; I just lived on after I died."

Neither of us said anything. Around us, the room was filled with the busy clatter of the luncheon service and the mingled conversations of half a dozen tables. But I was suddenly aware of the silence between us. I left to find a restroom, and when I returned to the table, two hundred-dollar bills were tucked beside my plate, and the chair where Nick had been sitting was empty.

CHAPTER **12**

ON MONDAY, I sat down to write a progress report for DeVries. I began by reading through the two binders I had already compiled on Patel's life.

The binders were part of my system for writing an autobiography. At the start of each book project, I conducted interviews and had them transcribed and stored in the first binder. As I continued to conduct more interviews, I read and re-read the transcripts, marking passages with a highlighter and writing notes to myself in the margin to flag useful information and areas where I needed more. After a few weeks, I cut and pasted excerpts from the transcripts and compiled them in a second binder, with tabbed dividers for different time periods.

Now, as I read through the second binder's contents, I opened a new file on my computer and made a list of the information I had so far—a crude table of contents for the book. Each item consisted of two or three sentences, describing a period or event in Patel's life. This step was always a moment of truth for a book. The list showed in stark terms how much useable information I had collected and what more was needed. It was an effective way of identifying problems—repetition of stories or areas where there was a lack of information.

By mid-afternoon I had written a five-page list of possible chapters. I projected the book would have about 35 chapters, and I had bits and pieces for about 15. But there were serious problems: long periods of Patel's life for which I had almost no information. I summarized this in a memo that described the positive progress made to date and what was still needed.

At four, having written a first draft of the progress report, I quit for the day and went for a walk. I took a familiar path that climbed the hillside behind the estate to the ridgetop. As I walked, a stream of thoughts crowded my mind. Molly's account of the police drug investigation and Stephen's story of seeing the bag of dope in Barkley's briefcase seemed unreal. The Paul Barkley I knew was concerned about the fat content of his restaurant recipes and how to schedule more cardio classes in his club. He wasn't selling drugs.

When I returned, I was sweating. I opened a bottle of beer, and while I drank it, I found a red pepper, an onion, and leftover chicken in the refrigerator and chopped them into small pieces. In a large pot, I cooked a cup of white rice, and stir-fried the vegetables and chicken. I opened a bottle of pinot blanc and had two glasses with dinner.

As I was finishing, Molly called to say she had appeared with Stephen at his arraignment. "The district attorney's putting together a case," she said. "The physical evidence at the crime scene turns out to be a footprint in the mud in the parking lot near Paul's car. If Mahler can match it to Stephen, that'll be pretty damning. Also apparently Paul and Stephen got into a shoving match at a catering event a few weeks ago."

"What'd Stephen say?" I asked.

"It was a spur-of-the-moment thing. It got out of control. They later apologized. None of these things means much in itself, but they add up to motive."

"You think Stephen's telling you everything he knows?"

"If he did, he'd be the first client who did. The other problem is that Kim tells me the police are tearing apart Paul's business records, and all kinds of things are falling out."

"Like what?"

"Who knows? Paul was a friend, but we never talked much about his businesses. About a year ago, I helped him with some permits, but mainly I steered him to another lawyer."

"Howard Miller?"

"No. Howie's a criminal attorney. But the point is Paul had a bunch of enterprises going on at once, and he kept things pretty close to his chest. I had glimpses inside here and there, but I don't know the whole picture. I don't think anyone did."

"So you're saying you don't know what the police might uncover."

"More or less. Paul was a sweet guy. But there was something dark, too."

"What do you mean dark?"

"It wasn't what you saw, it was what you didn't see. Paul was a guy who could get things done. He found you that job with Patel. He was always doing something like that. But sometimes you wondered *how* he could do all those things."

"He knew a lot of people."

"I think it was more than that," Molly said. "But it's been a long day. I've got to get some sleep. I'll see you tomorrow."

After the call, I washed the dinner dishes. Then I found my copy of *Return of the Native*, read for an hour, and went to bed.

* * *

The memorial service for Paul was held at eleven o'clock the following day at Santa Rosa Memorial Park, a grassy hillside cemetery on the east side of town. I arrived early to help Molly with Barkley's parents. We met in the parking lot and escorted the pair to the gravesite, which was a narrow plateau on a treeless slope, where a white canvas canopy had been erected. Folding chairs had been set up in a ring around the grave, and the four of us sat in the front, facing back down the hill to watch the other guests arrive.

Barkley's friends and employees came—John and Carl were there early, along with Nico, who wore a vintage dress and lace arm warmers. John shook my hand. His eyes were red-rimmed. Nico sat beside me, looped her arm in mine, rested her head on my shoulder, and cried.

Rajiv Patel arrived in a tailored pinstripe, with Shawn three paces behind, in his aviator sunglasses, looking like a Secret Service agent. Among the 50 or so other guests, I recognized prominent local business people and a cross section of the celebrities who had fled Los Angeles and found rural retreats in the county. Eddie Mahler, in a somber dark suit, stood apart from everyone else. Then, among the last guests, I saw a familiar face. I turned to Nico and asked if she knew him. "Your generation," she said. "Kenny McDonald."

I stared at the approaching figure. A large, overweight man, slowly climbed the hillside, his feet splayed outward to balance his broad frame. He wore an expansive, light-blue, double-breasted suit, open in the front and flapping as he walked. His hair was thinning and combed straight back in a shoulder-length ponytail. If he was Kenny McDonald, he was the ghost of Kenny McDonald.

I had seen him in person more than forty years earlier at the Hollywood Bowl. His band, The Jays, had taken the rock scene by storm, with six top songs in two years, platinum albums, sold-out concerts, mobs of fans. The lead singer, Kenny McDonald, was a thin, clean-cut twenty-year-old with boyish features and a golden voice that sang the lead melodies above the harmonies of his three childhood friends. Innocent, fun songs from a time before the Vietnam War, all about falling in love and driving fast cars.

He had disappeared from public view fifteen years before. There had been speculation that he joined a cult or that he died. But here he was, a rock and roll legend, finding a seat in the gallery of chairs facing me across from Barkley's coffin. I had trouble taking my eyes off him. His size was prodigious—more than 300 pounds, I guessed—but his face had barely aged. The same boyish look, now on an oversized body.

The minister took his place at the head of the casket and began to speak. Barkley's mother held a handkerchief to her face and softly cried. Nico broke down again and squeezed my hand. It was beginning to sink into everyone that Paul was gone.

I looked across the casket, over the heads of the other mourners, down the slope we had climbed. Two figures were walking toward the gathering. I recognized Page Salinger with a young man at her side. She wore a brightly colored silk jacket over a short black dress. When she came closer, I saw the jacket was covered with a reproduction of one of Toulouse-Lautrec's famous Moulin Rouge paintings, the gay figures of Parisian nightlife dancing across her torso as she moved. The man beside her looked like a bodybuilder. He had a square head with a stiff crewcut, and a developed upper torso that barely fit into his dark suit. They sat in the last row of seats outside the canopy's shade.

The minister finished with a prayer, and a woman from the mortuary walked among the mourners with a wicker basket filled with white rose buds. Each of us took one and laid it on the casket as we filed past. Kenny leaned toward the casket to place his flower in an empty spot. He was sweating heavily. Page tossed hers so that it hit the rim of the casket and fell into the grave.

When each of us had taken a turn, the casket was lowered into the ground, and the minister announced we were all invited to a reception at Crane Ridge Winery.

* * *

The winery was a 20-minute drive west, along the valley that follows the Russian River to the coast. The winery was a flat stone building perched on a hillside and surrounded by vineyards. The building housed a tasting room, and on the backside, an open patio where the reception was held.

Some of the guests—among them, Eddie Mahler, Rajiv Patel, and Kenny McDonald—did not attend the reception, and the gathering was down to about 30. One side of the patio was lined with tables of food platters and bottles of wine. The winery's owner helped Barkley's parents choose their food and find seats at the round tables on the deck.

Relieved of her escort duties, Molly joined me at a table with Nico and John. "Howard Miller called," she said. "He got your call, and he wants to talk, but he wants me there, too. I'll call you with details."

Nico looked at me. "Does this mean you're actually doing what I said, trying to figure out who killed Paul?" she asked.

"I guess I'm going to try," I said.

"Can I come, too?" Nico asked.

Molly looked at me and hesitated. Of the four of us, Nico looked the most visibly affected by Paul's death. Her face was still red and puffy from crying.

"Sure," Molly said. "Charlie'll let you know."

For a moment we sat watching the scene around us.

A large man in a wrinkled suit approached our table. "How're you folks?" he said. Raising one hand, he aimed a camera at us and took several photographs. There was something familiar about him, and when he saw me, he said, "Hey Charlie. Long way from home," He pointed the camera at me and took a couple more photos.

His name was Bud Platt. He was an aggressive news photographer whom I had known years before in Southern California. When the story about Susan Sparrow broke, he had staked out my house for a week.

"What do you want?" I said.

"It's a reception," he said. "Lot of newsmakers here. Now I know you're around, I'll keep a look-out." He moved on to the next table.

Watching him go, I looked across the patio to where Page was seated with the bodybuilder. "Who's the guy with Page?" I asked Nico.

"Ray Brenner," she said. "Used to train at the club. Basic Cro-Magnon. Brain the size of a pigeon's."

"Ray was a semi-professional bodybuilder," John added. "Busted for steroids a couple years ago. I think he works construction."

"Are he and Page friends or what?" I asked

Nico shrugged. "Who knows? Does Page have friends?" she said.

"Would you introduce me to her?" I asked.

"Jeez, Charlie, are you kidding me?"

"No. I want to ask her something."

Nico rolled her eyes and said, "Is this what it's going to be like?" She stood and led me across the patio. Page and Brenner were silently eating the last of their meal. Brenner looked up, his large square face a mask of impassivity. Nico waited a moment for Page's attention, but Page continued to focus on the slice of cake that she was eating.

"Page, this is Charlie Teller, a friend of Paul's," Nico finally said.

"What can I do for you?" Page said without looking up.

"I'd like to talk to you about Paul," I said. "I have a few questions."

She speared a piece of cake and held it in the air and looked at me. She wore thin sunglasses so I couldn't see her eyes. "We have to do it now? I feel like shit, you know?"

"Sure. Maybe we could get together another time. I was wondering if you could explain a few things Paul said the night he passed away."

She ate the cake. "He didn't pass away," she said. "Somebody fucking shot him."

Brenner watched us, enjoying the show. He seemed to grow inside his suit.

Nico and I stood behind the empty chairs at the table. "Before he was shot, he wanted to talk to me about something," I said. "But I don't know what it was."

"So what," Page said. "Paul's dead. Whatever it was, you can forget about it." She returned to stabbing her food.

It was an odd combination—the stylish sexuality of the clothes and the manner of a street punk. I tried to imagine her with Paul Barkley, who had been affable, gracious, and well-mannered.

"It may turn out to be unimportant, but right now . . ."

"Oh I get it. You're that fucking writer guy who did that book with what's-her-name—Susan Sparrow. Then screwed it up. Paul told me about you. Christ, what the hell do you want?"

"I wanted to ask . . ."

"This isn't Hollywood. We aren't the bimbos and losers you're used to. You might be out of your league."

I waited a moment to see if she had anything else to say. She took a drink of her wine.

"I realize this is bad timing," I said in a measured voice. "I don't mean to intrude. Maybe we could get together another time and talk for a few minutes."

"Do you have even a clue? I don't want to talk. *Ever.* Do you get that? Stay the fuck away from me."

As we walked back to our table, Nico said, "So was that everything you hoped it would be?"

"You bet," I said. "I think we broke the fucking ice."

CHAPTER 13

IT WAS LATE afternoon when I returned home. On my doorstep I found a small box of file folders from DeVries. As promised, he had prepared background materials. On top was a cover memo, listing my questions, which were keyed alphabetically to the folders.

The materials included histories of several of Patel's companies, a recent internal audit, two speeches, a genealogical history of the Patel family, photocopies of personal correspondence, a deposition in a lawsuit between Patel and a neighboring winery, and a partially completed draft memoir written by a local writer named Anita Kleinman.

I read each of the documents carefully and made notes. After an hour I was startled from my concentration by a phone call from Molly. She said she was having trouble reaching Miller to set up our meeting and would call me back if she got through. I returned to my reading.

Surprisingly DeVries had provided genuine answers to several questions. Keyed to my question on Patel's grandparents, the genealogical history included their names as well as a short account of their lives. In response to my queries about Patel's wife, Safia, who had died of cancer in the early 1990s, there was a long section in the Kleinman memoir with interesting anecdotes.

After two hours of reading, I found a text message on my cell. It said 9 pm and gave an address on the west side. I called Molly to confirm that it was the meeting with Howard Miller, but she didn't pick up. I called Nico and left a message with the time and address.

*　*　*

To reach the meeting address, I drove along a flat, straight highway that led out of Santa Rosa to the west. Past the last strip mall, the highway met a rural landscape of open fields. On either side, the highway was intersected by narrow gravel lanes that disappeared into the countryside. The address was on one of those lanes. The road was unlit, and a canopy of pine trees blocked the moonlight. I drove slowly down the dark path, searching the mailboxes for the house number.

After about a mile, I saw a car in a driveway with its headlights on, and ahead of me in the road, another car parked sideways and blocking my way. A young man appeared in my headlights and raised his hand. He wore a numbered athletic jersey and flat-billed baseball cap jammed sideways on his head. He was holding something that looked like a pole. "Excuse me, sir," he yelled, running toward my car. "Can you give us a hand? We had an accident."

I peered ahead at his car, an ancient, rusted Oldsmobile, and opened my door to meet him. "Sorry, man," he said. "But we hit a fucking dog." His face glowed in my headlights.

In an instant, I noticed his eyes shift slightly away from my face, to see behind me, and something crashed onto the back of my head, and I fell face down on the gravel road.

"Hey, bright boy," a voice yelled. "What's wrong? You fall down?"

I jumped up, but felt a sharp pain from the point where I had been hit. Behind me was another young man in a hooded sweatshirt. He was holding a pole, too. It was a long wooden grape stake.

"Daryl," the first man said. "I think you hit a double." He came toward me, holding his stake in both hands.

I backed against my car to keep both Daryl and the first man in view. The first man swung his stake. I raised my arm, and the stake cracked across my forearm. "Shit," he said.

"What do you want?" I said. "Money?"

"No, not money," said Daryl. He turned the stake in his hands and pointed one end toward me. "We don't want money, do we, Mitch?"

"No, bright boy," Mitch said. "We want to be major league baseball players."

From the direction of the Oldsmobile, I heard footsteps, and a third man carrying a stake appeared in the light.

With my attention turned, Daryl swung his stake again and hit my left arm just above the elbow. The blow sent a shooting pain through my arm.

"What'd you say, bright boy?" Mitch said. "Was that a single?"

The third man stepped toward me. He was younger than the other two. A thin, nervous-looking teenager. He wore a denim jacket and baggy pants.

"Christopher's in the batter's box," Daryl called.

Christopher swung his stake wide and missed. As it passed, I reached out to grab the stake, and for a moment caught it before he jerked it back. But the effort pulled me away from my car, allowing Daryl to step behind me. I was surrounded.

The men faced me, rocking on their feet. Daryl twirled his stake in his hands.

"Oh, Christopher. Strike one," Mitch said. He slashed his own stake at my legs and hit me low across my shins.

"Bright boy, you'll be famous, too." Daryl said. "A famous baseball."

"What do you want?" I asked again. My voice sounded thin and far away. I could feel the skin cut on my legs and the blood running down one side.

Christopher came toward me, holding his stake over his shoulder like a bat. This time, when he swung, I blocked the blow with my left arm and caught the stake with my right hand. I wrenched it away from him and thrust it back at him, catching him in the stomach and doubling him over.

As I straightened, Mitch hit me on the right side with a blow that skipped off my shoulder and hit my face. I reached to hold my face, and Daryl drove his stake end-first into my ribs, and I fell to the ground.

I sat crouched on my hands and knees. The ground swam toward me.

"I think we have a home run, hey bright boy," Daryl said.

"Over the fence, out of the park," Mitch said.

Christopher came close, grabbed back his stake, and hammered it across my back. I folded myself away from the blows.

"Come on, man, you want to fight?" Daryl said.

"Get up and fight, bright boy," Mitch said. He prodded me with his stake.

I felt the men come closer, tightening the circle. I wrapped my arms around my head and tucked my legs to my chest. "You stay on the ground, we have to play golf," Daryl said. He swung his stake and hit the top of my head where it was exposed.

Suddenly I heard a sound from outside our circle. It was the Oldsmobile's engine starting. The engine raced with a loud roar that filled the air.

"What the fuck," Mitch yelled, turning to the car.

Christopher dropped his stake and ran, and I felt Daryl go past me.

Turning my head, I saw the Oldsmobile, with no one inside it, lurch into gear and fly over the shallow ditch that bordered the road, smash through a wooden fence, and bounce across the field, the red taillights quickly receding in the dark. The three men raced after it, tearing through the brush and yelling at one another.

I balanced on my knees, watching them. Then I felt two hands come under my arms from behind and lift me to my feet. When I turned, I saw Vincent's face. "Vincent?" I said.

"Come on, Teller," he said. "Let's get out of here."

I leaned against him to regain myself. "What happened?" I asked.

"I tore out the throttle housing," he said, looking out toward the field. "They really ought to build those things better."

"But what's on the other side of that field? Won't it hit something?" Across the field, we could see the lights of the car, still moving, at the far end.

"I think there's a concrete block wall."

"You *think*?"

Just then, from out of the darkness, came a loud crash.

"OK," Vincent said. "I'm sure."

CHAPTER 14

I DREAMED I was flying. I was coasting through a sea of clouds. The ground below was a miniature game board of dark cities, arterial highways, and patchwork fields. The air flowed gently around me, and a warm atmospheric current, sweeping through the sky, held me aloft. I marveled at the lightness of my own limbs. They looked as if canvas fabric had been stretched across them, like the fuselages of early airplanes. Is this what it's like to die? I wondered. I looked down and watched a small car traveling along an interstate. It seemed to move more slowly than my former earthbound sense of vehicle speed. Or, was that just the perspective? I could never remember the principles of physics, which were so simple and complicated at the same time. Then, in my dream, I thought: In the afterlife, would I be asking questions? Wouldn't there just be answers? In that case, how was I, who had spent my whole life conducting interviews, asking a million stupid questions, qualified for *this* eternity? I looked at my arms. Were they as light as a minute ago? Physics again. It was difficult to know before you died what was important to learn.

I awoke suddenly and found myself lying in a strange bed covered with a down sleeping bag. I could smell incense and hear the Enya CD with children chanting in an imaginary language. A few feet away, Nico sat in a rocking chair, reading a *Cosmo* with the cover headline, "14 New Positions for Valentine's Day." She was wearing a flannel nightgown and a hooded sweatshirt. When she saw my eyes open, she put down the magazine and smiled. "Hey, Charlie," she said.

I tried to sit up and got halfway on my elbows before it felt like a knife being stuck in my abdomen. "Take it easy," Nico said.

She drew back the covers and supported my right shoulder while I pulled myself upright.

"What time is it?" I asked.

"About six," she said.

I remembered parts of the night before—sitting in the front seat of my car while Vincent drove, the radio playing a left-wing talk show from Berkeley, being licked in the face by Verlaine, and falling into the soft bed.

I was wearing flannel pajamas. Pulling up the front, I found an ice pack, and under it, a large, dark bruise on my abdomen, where Daryl had driven the end of his wood stake. I replaced the ice pack, let the pajamas fall, and sat back. "So what do I look like?" I asked Nico.

"Not bad if you like purple," she said with a smile.

She reached a small bottle toward me. "Open your mouth," she said. She dropped half a dozen tiny pills into my mouth.

"What is it?"

"Arnica. It's a homeopathic medicine to heal the bruising. Hold them under your tongue."

I obeyed her and felt the pills dissolve.

"You've got bruises on both arms," Nico said. "A goose egg on the back of your head, a bruise on your forehead, and that big bruise that you saw on your stomach. Vincent thinks a couple of the ribs might be cracked."

"Other than that, they barely touched me."

"If we keep ice on the bruises, they'll feel better in a day or two. Want something to eat?"

I asked for coffee, and when she went to get it, I heard footsteps in the hallway and saw Vincent at the door. He was holding his own coffee mug and seemed shy about entering.

"Hey," he said.

"Morning," I said. Two guys communicating.

"What was that about last night?"

"Some kids."

"Come on. Someone sent me a text message to go out there."

Vincent shrugged.

"How was it you were there?" I asked.

Nico came in with my coffee. "He heard your message for me on our answering machine. I wasn't home, but Vincent thought it sounded funny."

"What do you mean?"

"The address didn't sound right for your meeting," Vincent said.

"But why'd you come?"

Vincent stared at me without speaking.

Nico said, "He knows I like you and would be upset if you called and he didn't do anything."

I watched the two of them. It was as if I were working with a translator.

"Before you picked me up, Vincent," I said. "I thought those kids were your friends."

Vincent gave me his Special Forces glare.

"Why would you think that?" Nico asked.

"Because," Vincent said. "last Friday night Teller tried to extort some information from me, and we . . . reached an impasse."

"Oh, man, Charlie," Nico said.

"I asked him a few questions."

Vincent snorted. "It was more than that," he said.

"And then your husband offered to throw me off the deck."

"What is it with you guys? It's like, 'women learn to be women, men learn to be men.'"

"Who said that?" I asked.

"One of Ani's songs," Nico said.

"Annie who?"

"Ani DiFranco. How old are you anyway?"

Vincent looked at us impatiently. "I spoke with you directly," he said. "I didn't send kids."

"So who would?" I asked.

Vincent didn't say anything.

"Who else have you been talking to, Charlie?" Nico asked.

"Just Stephen and Carl." I looked at Vincent. "Why were you in such a hurry to leave last night?" I asked.

"You wanted to lie on the ground a while longer?"

"Something else was going on, wasn't it?"

He didn't answer.

Nico was watching him now.

"Was someone else there?"

Nico reached over and put her hand on his arm.

Finally Vincent said, "Brenner."

"Ray Brenner? The guy with Page at the funeral?"

Vincent nodded. "When I arrived, I left my truck near the highway. I went on foot through the field and came onto the road in front of the Olds. There was another car parked out there. It was Brenner."

"What was he doing?"

"Sitting in his car."

"But why would he go after me?" I asked.

"*He* wouldn't," Vincent said.

"Ray Brenner doesn't put on his pants in the morning until someone tells him to," Nico said.

"So it was Page?" I said.

Vincent didn't answer.

"Must have made a bad first impression, Charlie," Nico said.

"Should I report this to the cops?"

"What for?" Vincent said. "You've got no evidence Brenner or Page was involved. You'll spend a year talking to your lawyer, and the kids'll do six months."

I looked at Nico. "You're the one who wanted me to get involved with this thing," I said. "What happened last night looks like someone doesn't want me poking around. And that makes me all the more interested."

Vincent shook his head. "What happened last night is about you asking the wrong questions of the wrong people," he said.

"So what are the right questions, and who are the right people?"

Vincent didn't answer.

"This is just like Friday night. If you didn't know anything, you wouldn't be doing your laconic Zen thing."

Nico frowned, and I regretted my sarcasm.

"OK," I said. "Molly told me the cops found cocaine traces in Paul's office. Is that what this is about?"

Nico sat up straight and raked her fingers through her short hair. "Paul was involved in a bunch of businesses," she said. "When I first met him, he had a limo business. People came to him for stuff. He ran their parties, hired their fitness trainers, helped them meet each other."

"He was a drug dealer," Vincent said without looking up.

"You know that for a fact?" I asked.

"Sure. He ran it through his catering service. It was a select clientele. Small quantities."

"This is what you were referring to Friday night—why you didn't like him?"

"He was a hypocrite. He had a clean-cut image, but he sold coke."

"And that's different from your enterprise in the garage?"

Vincent gave me the stare again. "I grow marijuana for my own use."

"OK. But what does this have to do with someone shooting Paul?"

"I don't know, but it's a good place to start. You go where Barkley was going, and you'll meet some hard people."

"You know any of these people?" I asked.

"A few," Vincent said. "I know Barkley's supplier was Kenny McDonald."

"The singer who was at Paul's funeral?"

"He hasn't been a singer for twenty years. He's a dealer."

"How do you know?"

"I know Kenny," Vincent said.

"Could I talk to him?"

Vincent shook his head.

"Kenny's pretty reclusive," Nico said. "He lives by himself, way out in the countryside."

"So introduce me. I'll say I'm doing an interview for a magazine."

"And then what?"

"I'll say I was buying coke from Paul, and now he's gone, I'm looking for someone else and see what Kenny says."

"What do you expect he's going to tell you?" Vincent asked.

"I don't know. You have a better idea?"

Vincent shook his head.

"So will you introduce me?" I asked.

"Why would I do that?" Vincent said.

"Because if something happens to me, it'll make you look bad here at home."

Nico rolled her eyes.

"All right," Vincent said after a long pause. "I take you up to Kenny's for an introduction. But that's all. You do your phony interview and drug buy when I'm not there."

CHAPTER 15

Paul Barkley

DURING THAT DISGRACED period of my career, when I couldn't get a contract for an autobiography, I thought of writing a detective series. I even made a pitch to a New York editor, who had gone to school with Jill and who agreed to listen to me out of allegiance to their history. In her early thirties, this editor had recently signed several hot literary stars. She was brimming with optimism—on her own path, she was scaling one of those upward slopes. There was an air of expectation in her office that day. We sat on either sides of a gleaming desk, cleared of everything but a pencil and a new legal pad, as if that was all that was needed for greatness to succeed.

I told her my plan was to take distinctive American literary characters and imagine them as detectives. The idea was to retain their original physical presence, voice, and setting, but introduce a crime to be solved, and exploit the incongruity. I proposed Holden Caulfield, Isabel Archer, Jake Barnes, Rabbit Angstrom, and Moses Herzog.

Of course, I intended the idea to be new and edgy. But once I started, there was little to disguise my inability to imagine an original detective. A lifetime of speaking in someone else's voice bred certain habits. I talked on and on, in an unstoppable stream, unable to quit even as I watched the cheerfulness drain from the editor's eyes to be replaced by mortification. Later I learned she phoned Jill after I left, worried about my mental health. Did I have a compulsion to humiliate myself? Apparently it was common among men of a certain age and circumstance.

Investigating a murder and ghostwriting an autobiography have a natural intersection in their reconstruction of a life. In a murder investigation, you start with the clues left behind by the deceased's passage on earth. In an autobiography, you and your client stand over the corpse of a personal history, prodding it with your toes to hear the story it has to tell.

In both cases, the occupation lies in climbing into the skin of the prone figure and breathing life back into its limp frame. My profession is known as ghostwriting, not only because I labor unseen behind the authors of my books, but because I'm paid to haunt their past.

After Paul Barkley's murder, I replayed what I knew of him. On two occasions in those months of our acquaintance, he and I talked alone. It was late at night at the café, after the others had drifted home. All the lights were switched off except the ones behind the bar, and we sat together while he mixed cocktails. He made gimlets, half gin and half Rose's lime juice, because he read about them in a Raymond Chandler novel.

On the first of these occasions, he said, "Did you see Madeleine Fitzgerald here tonight? She sat over there with a guy who never took off his sunglasses. I always liked her in that cable series where she played the wife of a mafia don." He held up his glass, examined his drink in the dim light, and drank some more.

"You know, Charlie," he said, "when I first met people who live in the spotlight, I was surprised at how ordinary they are. You meet them up close, and they talk about the same things as you or I. I don't know why that surprised me. Maybe I thought their conversations would be like film dialogue."

"That ordinariness always made them seem less remote," he said. "It's as if any of us could achieve what they did. It must be that American thing of believing we can become whatever we want."

As with other men of my experience, gin made Barkley take the long view. He looked at the café's dining area. "In my business, you work hard and make a thousand decisions," he said. "But you know what it all turns on? One thing."

"It's the same way with those people," he said. "One part in one film and they're big. If you ask me what I believe in, that's it. That one thing."

Barkley's eyes shone in the dim light. His voice was calm and sure of itself, as if he were settling into something he had always meant to tell someone.

At that moment he might have launched into a late-night, alcohol-sodden revelation. He might have talked of his childhood or his love for Page. But it was as if he assumed the two of us were beyond talking about the simple business of ourselves.

I think now of Molly's concession that she believed Paul every time he told her a new venture was *the* one that was going to succeed. Barkley persuaded me, too, and made me a confidant in his scheme. I don't remember exactly what he talked about that night, but Barkley's subject was always the same—success, not of an ordinary kind, but something capable of sweeping away everything that had come before.

He was besotted with the possibilities of his own large hope. He was at once the star and the fan of his dreams, the wonder and the celebration of the wonder. The more he talked, the more he drew me in, and somewhere in my not protesting his generous assertion that we were already friends, I became his friend.

With only this behind us, when Barkley came to me the night he was killed, I was ready to help him. "I'll talk to you later," he said. After that, the words hung in the air.

Had he wanted to ask my advice, or show me what he had done? Over and over I replayed the scene. I saw his face close to mine. It swayed back and forth, and he continued to dance even as he spoke. He had a goofy, carefree smile. Whatever his fears or worries that night, they were held in check for a brief interlude by the fresh new air of the spring evening and the wonderful freedom of moving his body in time to the music.

"This is the beginning, pal," he shouted above the sound system as he handed me the envelope. That envelope and the memory stick inside became a symbol of his legacy, not the gift of writing Patel's biography but the puzzle of his own.

Years before, the elderly English actor, who wanted to hire me to write his autobiography, had showed me the story of his life drawn as a single line across a page. With Paul Barkley, what I was after was the line that led him at the end of his life to be shot late at night in a parking lot—and the line that brought me to be there with him.

Part II

CHAPTER 16

VINCENT PHONED KENNY and arranged our meeting for the afternoon.

"Did he agree to an interview?" I asked.

"That's for you to ask him," Vincent said. "All I did was tell him who you are."

"What'd he say?"

"Said he never heard of you. He asked if you were some asshole writer, and I said something like that."

"Thanks, Vincent. I knew I could count on you not to oversell me."

I used the time before we left to clean myself up from the night before. Standing before a full-length mirror outside the shower, I examined my injuries. The worst was the bruise on my abdomen. It hurt to bend at the waist and take a deep breath, confirming Vincent's speculation that I had broken ribs. The swelling on the back of my head had turned into a tender, sore golfball-sized bump. Once I was fully dressed, the only visible damage was the forehead bruise.

I called Molly and told her what had happened the night before.

"You need to report it," she said.

"I didn't get a very good look at the kids," I said.

"Doesn't matter. If you don't report it now, it'll be difficult later."

I promised to call, but I could tell she didn't believe me. She said our meeting with Howard Miller was scheduled for the following morning at his office in Santa Rosa.

* * *

Vincent and I drove together in my car back to the country road where Vincent had left his truck. We looked across the open field, but the only signs of the Oldsmobile's wild ride were the crushed fence and the tire trails across the dry grass.

Vincent followed me to my house so I could change my blood-stained clothes, and then we took Vincent's truck to Kenny McDonald's house. On the way, Vincent said, "When Kenny's talking, keep eye contact with him. He tends to be suspicious of strangers and a little high strung."

"What do you mean 'high strung'?"

"You'll see."

Kenny's house was on Chalk Hill Road, a secluded rural road across the Alexander Valley. As we drove north, vineyards covered the western plains, the grape plants arrayed in trellised rows and bathed in sunlight against a blue sky. Where the road sliced through earthen embankments, it exposed small road cuts of white clay that gave the highway its name. The eastern side was rugged, with rocky hillsides rising steeply from the valley floor amid dark groves of madrone and oak. The madrones were old, their red bark blistered and peeling. The oak trunks were black from the recent rains, and their limbs wheeled in crooked and strangled flights. Many of the stands appeared dead, the wood veiled in pale-green lace lichen that enshrouded whole branches and draped down like desiccated fruit.

Here and there, narrow private roads rose up the eastern hillside and were swallowed by the tree cover. Vincent pulled into one of these roads and drove a hundred yards to a metal gate. He got out and worked the gate levers and pushed it open. We crossed a dry creekbed and followed a steep dirt track up the hillside. On either side was eight-foot-high fencing, capped with barbed wire. At the summit, the road met an open plain covered in dry grass and manzanita. Here the dirt track turned into a gravel drive that straightlined across the plain. At the far end, just before the plain dropped off into another valley beyond, lay a large one-story structure.

The house was a long, flat arrangement of aluminum beams and glass panels, and looked like something alien that had dropped out of the sky.

A Corvette and a couple of pickup trucks were parked in front. As we walked toward the front door, a small man wearing a straw hat and carrying power hedge trimmers passed us without looking up and headed toward the back of the house.

Vincent rang the bell. On the porch a giant wind chime clanged gently in the wind. Somewhere behind the house the hedge trimmer began to whine.

A thin Asian girl opened the door and bowed. Vincent said something in an East Asian language. The girl bowed again and motioned for us to follow her down a hallway. Her sandals slapped on the tile floor she walked.

"Her name's Kim-Ly," Vincent told me. "She lives here and takes care of Kenny."

Built into the walls on either side of the hallway were small audio speakers that were playing Sam Cooke singing "You Send Me."

The hallway led to a living room with a sunken floor and a u-shaped white leather sofa. Here ceiling speakers played Marvin Gaye's "Let's Get It On."

I followed Kim-Ly and Vincent to a sliding door that opened to a redwood deck behind the house. The deck surrounded a long, rectangular swimming pool. Along the far side of the pool were shrubs, a low rock wall, and beyond that, a view of the valley.

Cast-iron patio tables with bright red and white umbrellas were positioned around the pool. At one of these, alone in the shade, sat Kenny McDonald. He looked even larger and heavier than he had at the funeral. He wore an unbuttoned Hawaiian shirt, swim trunks, and a baseball cap with a Japanese character stamped on the front. He sat slumped in a cast iron chair. His belly fell over the top of his trunks. In front of him on the table was a silver handgun with a diamond-patterned handgrip.

Kim-Ly went back into the house. As Vincent and I walked toward Kenny, I saw his eyes were closed and thought he might be sleeping. Then I noticed the earbuds in his ears and saw his head bobbing up and down. His lips moved, and his hands beat on the edge of the table.

When we reached his table, Kenny's hands stopped drumming, and his eyes opened. He looked at Vincent and then at me without saying anything.

"Hey man," Vincent said. "I brought someone who wants to meet you." He spoke slowly as if talking to a person unfamiliar with the language.

"This is Charlie Teller," Vincent said. "He's a writer. He wrote that book a few years ago with Nick White, called White Nights."

As Vincent spoke, I suddenly remembered a passage in Nick's book where he had written disparagingly of Kenny's band, The Jays. They were dragged down, Nick said, by the excesses of their lead singer, Kenny McDonald. My stomach lurched. Kenny looked me. His eyes were blue but with a dead light in them. I thought of Vincent's admonition that I maintain eye contact, but it was an effort to look at his face. He still had not said a word.

"I wanted to talk to you about a profile for *Rolling Stone*," I said. "Part of a series. Bands from the sixties and seventies."

"They've got a guy watching me," Kenny said, staring at me. "Did you know that?"

Was I supposed to answer this question? I wanted to look at Vincent for guidance, but I kept my eyes on Kenny.

"I've seen him a few times," Kenny said. He yanked the earbuds down around his neck. "Just a kid. They're paying a kid to do this."

"The interview wouldn't be today," I said. "I would come back another time." My voice sounded far away, as if I were on a different stage from Kenny. Vincent and I were still standing in front of the table. The sick feeling in my stomach intensified.

"They hand-pick those guys, did you know that?" Kenny said.

I searched for a response. But before I could speak, there was a sound in the manzanita on the other side of the pool. Kenny picked up the gun and fired three rounds in the direction of the sound. The gun's explosion echoed off the rock walls. The bullets ripped through the brush, splintering the red branches and blasting puffs of leaves into the air. Shell casings clattered onto the tabletop.

Vincent and I stood still. There was no sound from the bushes. I wondered where the gardener had gone. Kenny stared at his target, then threw the gun on the table.

"I don't write music anymore," he said. "The good songs are written."

It was a moment before I realized he was speaking to me. "I was thinking of a retrospective piece," I said. "Looking back. Your memories."

Vincent pulled out one of the cast iron chairs and sat down, and I did the same.

"Which songs?"

For a terrible moment my mind went blank. Then I said, "The first two albums. *The Jays* and *Trade Winds*."

"Good songs." He looked at Vincent. "Even though we didn't make any goddam money off them."

"We could talk about that."

"Later stuff's good, too. The *Stone Cloud* double-pocket album."

Stone Cloud was a dark, almost unintelligible album made in the studio, after the band had stopped touring, and the keyboard player Tom Kennedy left the band.

"We could talk about that, too," I said. "You guys pioneered some . . ."

"I call Henry Palmer at *Rolling Stone*, he's going to know about this article of yours?" Kenny asked, looking at me.

"Henry left the magazine two years ago. And I haven't spoken to anyone there. I wanted to talk to you first and then make a pitch to them. You want to check me out, you can talk to Susan Knowles. She's the features editor."

I looked over at Vincent. He was leaning back in his chair, but his eyes were fixed on Kenny.

"You gonna tape what I say?" Kenny asked.

"I usually do," I said.

"I don't like tapes."

"I'll do notes."

"I want to read what you write before it goes in the magazine."

"The magazine doesn't allow that."

Vincent shifted in his seat.

"I don't want you writing a bunch of crap about me," Kenny said. "There's been a lot of that."

"It's going to be about you and your music, how you and Tom Kennedy wrote it."

Kenny seemed to have lost interest. He was pushing the dial on his iPod.

"Could we schedule a time?" I asked.

Satisfied with his player, Kenny readjusted his earbuds. "Friday, one," he said. He looked at Vincent. "You see that guy watching me, you give him a message."

"Sure," Vincent said.

"You tell him I'm not bound by international treaties. So he better watch his back."

"I'll tell him," said Vincent.

Vincent and I pushed ourselves away from the table and stood to leave. Kenny closed his eyes again and bobbed his head in time with the music.

When Vincent and I were halfway across the deck, Kenny's voice called after us. "Hey Teller," he said, "Your friend Nick White doesn't know shit about me."

CHAPTER 17

ON THURSDAY MORNING I met Molly in front of Howard Miller's office in downtown Santa Rosa. The law firm of Pilgrim, Miller and Sandstrom was located in a restored two-story Victorian. Dressed in a navy blue suit, Molly was sitting at the base of the front steps, reading a file on her lap. She inspected me as I approached.

"You don't look too bad," she said. "From what Nico said, I was expecting worse."

"You want me to lift up my shirt and show you my wounds?" I asked.

She smiled and stood up. "Maybe later, tough guy," she said. "Nico can't make it. She has a massage this morning and didn't want to pass up the money."

Molly studied my face. "Look," she said. "I'm really sorry about not getting back to you. Howie wasn't returning my calls."

I shrugged. "It's not your fault. Vincent said I was asking the wrong person the wrong questions."

"Occupational hazard."

"Or stupidity."

"Speaking of which," Molly said, "Eddie just received a tip that Stephen was seen two weeks ago at a firing range outside Petaluma. Some helpful citizen saw Stephen's photo in the paper and called it in. The firing range records bear it out. Stephen test-fired a Taurus PT22, same registration as the murder weapon. Stayed for half an hour. Brought his own rounds."

"Stephen didn't tell you?" I asked.

Molly shook her head. "It's innocent in itself. But it dispels his whole contention that he shoved the gun in a drawer and forgot about it."

"Mahler know any more about what Paul was doing with the coke?"

"Not exactly. But apparently when Paul was killed, somebody in the district attorney's office made a cross-match to Paul's name in an ongoing state-local drug investigation. Paul was on a watch list."

"A watch list?"

"They were keeping an eye on him."

"So it's true? He was dealing?"

Molly shook her head. "I don't know. Kim couldn't tell me more than that. But I wonder if Paul got in over his head. He always thought he could do anything—juggling three businesses, hyping new ideas. Maybe he got mixed up in something he couldn't handle."

I looked at the Victorian. "So who's this guy?" I asked.

Molly led me up the steps. "Criminal attorney, at the top of the food chain."

The office reception had three chairs and a low table that held a small tray with smooth stones arranged in a circle of sand. Molly gave our names to a young receptionist, and after a few minutes Miller emerged from the nearest doorway. He smiled and winked at the receptionist and led us into his office.

Miller was a tall, athletic-looking man in a starched white shirt, charcoal trousers, and an Italian silk tie that probably cost more than my car. His thick, black hair was combed straight back and looked as wet as if he had just stepped out of a shower. He had the bluff manner of someone used to winning.

"Hey kiddo," he said, wrapping his arms around Molly in a bear hug. "You doing that 6K next Sunday in Napa?"

"As long as Larry and I get through our depositions this week," she said.

Molly introduced us, and after Miller shook my hand, he pointed his finger at me and said, "I've always wanted to talk to you."

The Leslie Hartford lawsuit, I thought to myself. Hartford was a concert pianist and the subject of my last unpublished book. He sued me for contract violations, and the case got a lot of press. Whenever I sat next to lawyers on planes, they brought it up.

"It's that goddam Hartford thing from a few years ago. When Molly told me you were living up here, I thought about it right away. I suppose you hear that a lot from lawyers."

"No," I said. "What is it?" Usually they said that if they had been representing me, they would have buried Hartford.

"It's just that his case was pretty weak." Miller turned and smiled at Molly. "You know me, Molly, I'd have buried the guy."

Molly flashed me a sympathetic look, and we sat in chairs facing Miller's desk.

"Hey, like I said over the phone, I'm sorry as heck about what happened to Paul," Miller said, looking at Molly. "What a shock, huh?"

He turned to me, "Small town like this, we don't see a lot of this sort of thing, although it's coming everywhere isn't it?"

"We were wondering what you could tell us about the letter Paul wrote to you," Molly said, trying to get him on track.

"Not much. It's like I told Mahler. Eddie was all over me, like I wasn't telling him something. You know Eddie."

"Yeah, I know Eddie," Molly said.

"The thing is, I hardly talked to Paul. I met him a few times at parties where he was catering."

"But the letter implied you had some sort of an agreement with him?" I asked.

"If you want to call it that," Miller said. "The last time I saw him was at Preston Winery, when they did a reception for their new tasting room. Paul catered it. Some amazing Thai stuff. Anyway we talked, and he said he needed to hire me."

"For what?" Molly asked.

"He didn't say. He just said he'd need me to represent him. Some shit was coming down, and he wanted me in his corner."

"Did he say what this 'shit' was?" I asked.

"Not really. Look maybe it's not true, but word is Paul may have been involved in some drug stuff. Anyway that's what I thought it was. I do some drug-related defense work, and I assumed that's why he picked me."

"But Paul didn't say that?" Molly said.

"No, he didn't go into any details. He asked me what my retainer was, and I said it was ten grand, and a couple of days later he messengered over a cashier's check for the whole 10K." Miller opened a manila file and passed a copy of the check across his desk to Molly.

"The check came by itself, without a cover letter?" Molly asked.

"Yeah. Not even a post-it. I made some notes myself of our conversation up at Preston. That's what this page is. Otherwise, nada."

"Did Paul say anything else that night?" I asked.

"He said if anything happened, I should talk to you."

"Me? He actually used my name?"

"Yeah, he said talk to Charlie Teller. He'll know what happened. I was about to call you when Molly phoned. But I take it you don't know what that meant."

"Not a clue."

"Well, I don't see there's much I can do at this point. I'll return the money to the estate, of course. I never really did anything."

"I'm curious," I said. "The letter that Paul gave me the night he was killed was to set up a meeting with you. Why wouldn't he just call?"

Miller frowned. "I don't know. He may have also called. Let me check. We keep an incoming log." He punched a few keys on his keyboard and looked at the screen.

"No. Nothing here. If he called and left his name, it would be here. My admin's pretty good about that. Sometimes people send a letter if they want a paper trail."

"Paper trail?"

"Yeah. Proof of a course of action or intent."

"What else did Eddie ask you about?" Molly asked.

Miller smiled. "Nice try, Molly. You know I can't tell you that."

"Doesn't hurt to try."

"I can tell you he thought Paul might have given me something."

"Like what?"

"Something that was separated from the letter."

"But he didn't say what it was?"

"I don't think he knew." Miller stood up behind his desk. "Listen I have to be in court in thirty minutes."

Molly and I stood to leave and shook Miller's hand.

"You know," Miller said at the door. "Paul said one weird thing that night at Preston. He said, 'I need someone representing me who doesn't get scared.'"

"Scared of what?" Molly asked.

"He didn't say."

*   *   *

After the meeting with Miller, Molly and I went our separate ways, and I drove home with a sense of dread. The next day I had a meeting with Patel and DeVries, and I had promised to give them a progress report. It had not been a great work week. DeVries had given me what I had requested, and all I had to show them was the chapter list and memo that I had written on Monday. I needed a place to start the biography.

When I reached my apartment, I took out the contents of DeVries' package and put them in neat piles on the floor. Then I slowly read each file. About three o'clock, when I was feeling discouraged, I saw something. In my own interview transcripts, Patel said his first major construction project was the Pine Grove Shopping Center in Bakersfield. All he said was that the project was a big step for his young company. In Anita Kleinman's memoir, Patel's wife said that Pine Grove nearly bankrupted them.

Patel's speech to the business roundtable had a section on state permitting reform. One of his examples was a crucial permitting delay in the Pine Grove construction, when the building plans were found to have too few parking spaces for the projected retail space. When the building permits were denied, the project could not have proceeded without an innovation by Patel and a junior engineer named James Bartlett. Together the two men pioneered a construction design that legally allowed an extra ten parking spaces on every level of the structure. The brochure on Bartlett Precast Construction, a Patel subsidiary, described how the two young men invented the design one night on Bartlett's kitchen table.

I sat at my computer and started typing. After an hour I had a pretty good first chapter. It told the story of a young Rajiv Patel, long before he had made his billions, embarking on a high-risk construction project. The chapter captured the essence of Patel—his engineering insight and his calmness under pressure.

The story also had the potential to introduce the central image for the whole book: the spirit of American building, the power of the individual to imagine something big and bring it into existence.

I printed out a copy and went through it slowly with a red pencil, editing to sharpen the drama. By seven o'clock I finished. I made copies of the chapter and the outline and put them in a folder for the next day's meeting.

CHAPTER 18

AFTER DINNER I felt restless. I paced around my apartment and stared outside at the vineyard, looking for something. The sun had already set behind the mountains, and the sky had been drained of color. The trellises of sauvignon blanc flowed down the hill in even rows toward the valley floor. Whatever I was looking for, it wasn't outside. As far as I could tell, the grapes were minding their own business.

After a while I looked up Page Salinger in the phone book and found an address on the east side of Santa Rosa. On the spur of the moment, I went down to my car and drove into town.

It was dark by the time I reached Santa Rosa. A strong, warm wind was blowing, whipping tree limbs back and forth, and scattering debris across the road.

The address was an apartment complex bordering a large public golf course. I parked across the street and sat staring at the windows of Page's apartment. Lights were on inside, but I couldn't see anything. After a few minutes I felt stupid sitting there. As I was about to drive away, I suddenly saw her in the front window talking on her cell phone.

I walked across the street and rang the apartment bell. Page opened the door. "What do you want?" she said. She was still holding the phone.

Without thinking, I pushed my hand through the gap in the doorway and shoved her hard. She fell backward into the apartment, sprawling on the floor, with the cell phone shattering across the uncarpeted tile. For an instant I stood still, looking at her, surprised at my own anger and strength. Then I went into the apartment and closed the door.

She got to her feet and swept her hair away from her face. She wore a pair of tight jeans and a baggy sweater. "What are you doing?" she yelled, coming toward me, her eyes filled with anger.

I shoved her again, and this time she fell against a chair that overturned behind her.

"What'd you tell those kids to do?" I said, suddenly flushed with the anger and frustration of the last two days.

Page untangled herself from the chair and stood, more slowly, but before she was fully upright, I pushed her again and she fell back onto the floor. This time she stayed still. "I'm going to call the cops," she said.

"Good," I said. "We can ask them about Daryl and Mitch." I found myself standing over her, shaking. I stepped away and took a breath.

She sat on the floor, with her back toward me. "You jerk," she said. "You really don't know what's happening, do you?"

"I know you hired some guys to beat me up."

"You think that's what this is about?"

"It's enough."

For a moment neither of us spoke. Then she said, "Why're you involved anyway? What do you think you were to Paul? Some guy he helped find a job."

"Paul did me a favor when he didn't have to."

"So what?"

"What were *you* to Paul?"

She ignored me.

"The hot girlfriend? Not as easy to play that part these days, is it?"

Without speaking, she looked up at me. The anger was replaced by a look of weariness.

"And now you're going to have to run your act all over again, with some other poor guy," I said.

She looked away again and said, "We were engaged."

"What was the plan? He was going to supply drugs to his rich friends, and you were going to keep house?"

She looked stung. "Is that what you think?" she said. She stood and faced me.

"I know Paul sold drugs. And that's what probably got him in trouble. And you use people to get whatever you want. You deserved each other."

"Who are you to say anything about me?"

She ran her left hand through her hair again. She stepped toward me. "Speaking of using people, what do you do?" she asked. "You hang around people while they tell their stories. What's that make you?"

She was close to me now, her face even with mine. I took a few steps back.

Page smiled. "What's wrong?" she asked. "Women make you uncomfortable when you're not beating them up?"

"You're pathetic," I said, but felt myself off balance.

She came closer until her face was a few inches away, her eyes watching me. "Afraid?" she asked. Her hair fell in tangles on either side of her face. I could smell her perfume and feel her breath.

She laid her right hand on my chest, held it there, and then ran it slowly down to my abdomen. The whole time her brown eyes looked straight at me.

I put my hands on her shoulders to push her back and felt her straining toward me.

She smiled again. Her head came toward me, and for a moment I thought she was going to kiss me. But she leaned past me so that her hair fell into my face, and she put her lips against my ear. "Make up your mind," she whispered.

I felt suffocated.

For a moment neither of us moved. We stood together, waiting.

Outside there was the sound of a car door closing.

Page pushed herself away from me. She lifted her chin and shook out her hair. The doorbell rang.

She walked slowly to the small oak desk outside the kitchen, picked up a laptop, and put it inside the desk drawer.

Outside a voice said, "Santa Rosa Police."

Page walked past me without looking up. When she opened the door, Eddie Mahler stood in the doorway, in his usual golf jacket and jeans, his wiseguy smile already turned on.

"Ms. Salinger," he said, and then looking past her at me, "And Boswell."

Mahler entered the apartment and came toward me. "Your presence here tonight biographical or personal?" he asked.

"I came to offer my condolences."

"Really? Last time I asked, you said you weren't acquainted with Ms. Salinger."

"We just met."

Mahler looked beside me at the overturned chair and broken cell phone parts. "And having fun already," he said.

Studying my face, he saw the bruise. "What happened, Teller?" he asked. "Walk into something?"

"Something," I said.

Page joined us, and we stood together in a circle. "What do you want, detective?" she asked impatiently. "I thought we covered everything."

"Just a few follow-up questions. People don't always tell me everything the first time. You have that experience, Teller?"

"All the time," I said.

Page sat in a stuffed chair, and Mahler and I sat side by side on a sofa facing her.

"Do you mind if we speak in front of Mr. Teller?" Mahler asked.

Page looked bored. "Why should I?" she said.

Mahler pulled a pen and a small notebook from his pocket and flipped through the notebook. "Last week you said Barkley wanted to postpone your wedding, that he expected to be away for a while."

"Yes."

"And he didn't say when or where he was going?"

"No."

"And for something as important as your wedding, you didn't ask him?"

"I trusted him to tell me what I needed to know."

"The interesting thing is, Barkley doesn't seem to have told anyone else about this trip. Including his business partner and his other friends and associates."

Page folded her arms. "What do you want me to say?" she said. "I don't know Paul's friends."

"So you don't know Stephen Robb or why he would want to kill Barkley?"

"I just said I didn't."

"You didn't witness any arguments between the two of them?"

"No. Paul and Stephen talked sometimes when Paul took me to Galileo's, but it was just business stuff. I didn't listen."

Mahler looked at me. "We've also learned," he said, "that what Barkley was referring to when he talked about postponing your wedding might not have been a trip but something else. Apparently he was expecting to be arrested."

"He didn't mention it to me," Page said. "Besides, if he thought he was going to be arrested, wouldn't *you* know about it?"

Mahler ignored her and wrote something in his notebook. "Did Barkley talk to you about any money problems?"

"We never talked about that stuff. When he wasn't working, he didn't talk about business."

"You see any evidence he was short of money?"

"He didn't spend his money on me. I take care of myself."

"What do you know about his selling coke?"

Page looked back at Mahler. "Paul didn't do that. It's the kind of thing people make up after someone's been killed so it looks like it was *their* fault."

"We found traces of coke in his briefcase and his office."

Page shook her head. "I don't know anything about it," she said.

Mahler turned a page of his notebook. "Did Barkley leave a laptop computer with you?" he asked without looking up. "According to his associates, Barkley kept one with him all the time. But after his death, it wasn't in his office, apartment, or car."

"Haven't seen it," Page said.

"Our forensics indicates someone downloaded files from his office computer to an external device the day he was killed. We were wondering if he might have left it here."

"He didn't live here."

"We can get a search warrant. We find it here or in your car, you could be charged with obstruction."

"I told you, I haven't seen it."

Mahler turned toward me, "How about you, hot shot?" he said. "You seen a laptop lately?"

I faced Mahler beside me on the sofa, but could feel Page watching. "Just my own," I said. "You're welcome to look at it, but since it has confidential files from Rajiv Patel, you'll need to get his release."

Mahler looked at me steadily for a moment. "Maybe we'll do that," he said.

He rose, put the pen and notebook back in his pocket, and walked to the door. In the open doorway he turned back. "Don't forget to take notes, Teller," he said.

For a moment after Mahler left, Page sat staring at me. Then she said, "You think I owe you something now?"

"Why would I think that?" I asked, standing to leave.

"In a situation like this, somebody usually does," she said.

CHAPTER 19

EARLY THE NEXT morning Nico called to invite me to have lunch with Vincent and her at the downtown Denny's in preparation for my meeting that afternoon with Kenny.

At nine I walked from my tower down to the estate house for my Friday meeting with Patel. When I arrived, Patel and DeVries were waiting for me. I could see them notice my bruised forehead.

"Quite a bump you've got there," DeVries said.

"Would you like me to call Dr. Carlton?" Patel asked. "He's just across the courtyard in his clinic."

"It's okay," I said. "I hit a tree limb when I was jogging."

As usual, Patel sat in a recliner, DeVries was positioned at a table beside him, and I faced them in an uncomfortable high-backed chair. I handed each of them a copy of the book outline and the sample chapter. "This should give you a sense of how the book is taking shape," I said.

DeVries handed me a file folder. "While we're reading," he said. "Perhaps you'd like to see the photographs we've collected for the book."

"Shawn, my friend," Patel said, "Please bring us some coffee." For the first time I saw Shawn in a chair behind the entranceway. He was balancing a tennis ball on the back of one hand, withdrawing his hand, and then catching the ball in mid-air. Without a word, he stood and left the room.

DeVries read the pages quickly. He sat stiffly in his chair, looking down through a pair of narrow reading glasses. When he finished, he remained still, waiting for Patel.

Shawn returned with three cups of black Turkish coffee on a tray. Sitting back in his chair, he resumed his game with the tennis ball.

I looked through the photographs. Most were pictures of Patel shaking hands with famous people—former American presidents in golf clothes, movie stars, and comics.

Patel read slowly, sipping his coffee. Once he said, "Yes, yes." Later he handed a page to DeVries and said, "This word 'reticulating' is not correct."

When he finished, Patel said, "Well done."

"Thank you," I said. "Is it accurate?"

Patel smiled.

"I thought I might speak with James Bartlett. Perhaps he could fill in some of the details on the project."

"That would be difficult," Patel said.

"Jim Bartlett's retired," DeVries said.

"If you'll give me his number, I could phone him to confirm the timing."

"We don't want to run up the charges on this project," DeVries said.

"In your outline," Patel said, "you devote Chapter 12 to an account of my late wife Safia. Where will you find this information? My dear wife is deceased."

"I thought you might tell me."

"Her memory is painful," Patel said.

"Liver cancer," DeVries explained.

"I could use Anita Kleinman's memoir," I said.

"My goodness, Anita Kleinman," Patel said.

"Her account was unreliable," DeVries said. "It's the reason she was fired. I only showed it to you as a point of reference."

"But we have to say something about your wife," I said.

"The focus of this book should be on Rajiv's accomplishments in the business arena," DeVries said. "There will be photographs of Mrs. Patel."

"A formal portrait was taken before she became ill," Patel said.

"If I may say," DeVries said. "While I agree with Rajiv that you've written an acceptable first chapter, I'm surprised you've not made more progress."

"It's difficult to see the progress at the start because I'm collecting information," I said.

"But you've been with us for more than two months, and you've had unprecedented access to Rajiv and our files. Frankly I expected you to be farther along. Perhaps at our next meeting you could provide us with several more chapters—let's say four—and a schedule"

"A schedule?"

Patel, who had been looking distracted, now spoke up. "You'll forgive us," he said, "In building construction, we face deadlines and fines if we don't meet the deadlines. Whit is accustomed to browbeating my site managers."

"The publisher has given us a deadline," DeVries said.

"I didn't realize you'd already contacted a publisher," I said.

"Landner and Giles in New York," DeVries said. "They expect a draft by July. It'll be on their spring list."

"Perhaps, Whit," Patel said, smiling, "Charlie's bored. He's used to more drama."

"We've given him interesting accounts."

"Maybe you'd like me to hit a baseball like Mister Kenneth Styles?" Patel asked, rising out of his recliner and posing as a batter in front of me.

I smiled and shook my head. "Not necessary," I said.

"Or skate like the young girl with the short hair. What was her name?" He bent at the waist and swung his arms in rhythm. Shawn stopped catching the tennis ball to watch him.

"Tina Terrill."

"Yes, the sad Tina Terrill," Patel said. "I've been in many races but never fell. A better story, I guess, if I'd fallen."

"We've already provided a great many anecdotes of interest to the business community," DeVries said.

"But dull to everyone else," Patel said. "Charlie's used to drug rehab and sexual escapades. What are a few buildings to a writer? Maybe we should ask our friend, Mr. Lawrence, for some stories? What do you say, Shawn?"

Shawn looked self-conscious as the attention of the room turned to him.

"Shawn's lived an interesting life, haven't you?" Patel said. "You attended college in the East somewhere, wasn't it?"

"Yeah," Shawn said. "Duke."

"Ah, yes, Doook," Patel said, imitating Shawn's accent. "Played football there, too. What position was it?"

"Tight end."

"Tight end. Shawn has many talents. A few weeks ago, he had to intervene when a former employee tried to assault me, didn't you?"

"Yeah, sure."

"He hit the gentleman in the nose. Broke it, I believe. Quite a lot of blood. More than you would think. We've only just cleaned it all up."

Shawn sat still in his chair, with an impassive look on his face.

"What do you think, Whit? Shall we include a few of Shawn's stories in the book? Spice things up? Get Charlie's engine revving?"

"Your autobiography is a story of great success, Rajiv," DeVries said. "One of the greatest in our country."

"But not glamorous and sexy. Charlie here wants glamorous and sexy."

"No," I said. "I think I understand what you want."

"Perhaps, Whit, we could invite Charlie to our party in a week's time?" DeVries frowned.

"There you'll see that I'm glamorous and sexy," Patel said. "We've invited film stars and entertainers who make their homes in this valley."

"Rajiv hosts parties every year to coincide with milestones in the winery season," explained DeVries. "Our grand ball is at harvest, but we also have parties throughout the growing season. This party is the first of the season—at bud break."

"It'll be a small gathering," Patel said. "Two hundred guests. There'll be dinner and dancing. Sometimes the guests sing a song or tell a funny story. We'd be honored if you'd join us. You may bring a female companion if you wish."

"An acquaintance of yours will be in attendance," DeVries said, consulting a list on his desk. "Jill Bennett. Wasn't she your former wife? She's coming with David Reynolds, one of our vineyard managers." He smiled.

"Small world," I said, smiling back.

* * *

I drove to Denny's. The restaurant was noisy and crowded. Nico and Vincent sat in a booth near the back. Nico's hair was combed straight up, stiff with mousse, the tips dyed the color of traffic cones. She wore a bolero top and a set of lacy wrist cuffs. Vincent acknowledged me with a slight nod.

"I'm getting the Twin Stacks," Nico announced. "Waffles and pancakes."

"How about a side of donuts?" I suggested.

"Where do you see that?" Nico asked, looking back at the menu.

After the waitress had taken our order, I told them about my meeting with Howard Miller.

"The part about Barkley expecting to be arrested doesn't make sense," Vincent said. "With drug busts, the cops don't signal their intentions."

"Maybe Paul saw something inside the drug operation itself that tipped him off," I said.

"I don't understand what Miller said about being scared," Nico said. "What was Paul afraid of?"

"Maybe he thought he'd have to testify against his suppliers," Vincent said.

"Like Kenny," I said.

"Or someone higher up in the organization."

"You mean there's someone scarier than Kenny?"

Vincent shrugged. "Kenny buys from somebody," he said.

The waitress returned with our food, and for a few minutes, the three of us were preoccupied with our meals.

"Paul might've been frightened about the publicity," Nico said between mouthfuls of pancakes. "He was always worried about how things would affect his businesses."

"The strange thing is," I said, "Mahler himself didn't seem to know Paul was going to be arrested."

"Where'd you see Mahler?" Vincent asked.

"At Page's apartment," I said. "He came to ask her some questions."

"And why were you there?" Nico asked.

"Just trying to clarify her role in that business with Daryl and Mitch Tuesday night."

"Did you get it clarified?" Nico asked.

"More or less. By the way, Page insisted Paul wasn't a dealer."

"She's kidding herself," Nico said. "But don't you think it's strange that Paul never said anything to us about the possibility of being arrested?"

"You told me he had separate worlds."

"Yeah, but he didn't say anything to John or Stephen, who run his businesses. Those businesses were his whole life. I can't believe that if he knew he was about to be arrested and unable to manage things, he wouldn't talk to them."

"He told Miller that Charlie would know," Vincent said, looking at me.

"But you don't, right?" Nico said.

I shook my head.

Vincent and I finished and waited while Nico ate her way through the Twin Stacks. I looked at Vincent. He was staring ahead—like a monk measuring eternity in the Nepalese foothills or, in Vincent's case, a former Special Forces soldier reviewing the nineteen sequential steps required to wire a Denny's with explosives.

"All right," I said. "I have to know. How'd you two meet?"

"Why's that important?" Vincent growled.

"It's probably not. But I've been trying to picture it."

Nico smiled. "What've you been picturing?" she asked.

"Vincent sneaking up behind you and shooting you in the back with a tranquilizer gun."

Nico laughed and put her arms around Vincent. "Oh, it was nothing like that. It was very romantic. We met at the Club Flak, when the Maniacs were in town."

"Nothing says romance like the Maniacs," I said.

"Vincent gave me a flower."

"A flower? What kind of flower?"

"A bud rose. Because our love was new."

I looked at Vincent. I tried to imagine him holding a bud rose. Then I tried to imagine him saying the words "bud rose." He was staring ahead again, probably remembering where he left off in the explosives wiring sequence.

Nico ran her fingers through Vincent's hair where it was tucked around his left ear. "'Love is like falling, and falling is like this,'" she said, smiling.

"Ani DiFranco?" I asked.

"Yeah. You know how cool people look in movies when there's a sound-track behind them. I always wished we had soundtracks in real life. Mine would be an Ani song. Every time you saw me, there'd be one of her songs."

The waitress refilled our coffees.

When the waitress had gone, Vincent looked at me. "Are you two finished?" he asked. "Can we talk about what you're going to say to Kenny?"

"I'm going to start off talking about the article I'm writing. Far as he's concerned, that's why I'm there."

"Then what?"

"When the time's right, I'll just ask if he was dealing with Paul?"

"That's exactly what you don't want to do," Vincent said. "You don't want to ask him anything that forces him to give you information. Act like you already know, and you want to make a buy. That way, you don't box him in a corner. If he doesn't want to do it, he doesn't have to."

"What if he asks how I know about it?"

"Paul told you. If you'd been one of Paul's buyers, that could've happened. The main thing is, don't screw around with small talk. Keep your body still and look back at him."

"He's not an easy guy to look at," I said.

"He thinks you're fucking with him, he's liable to do something," Vincent said.

"Center yourself on your throat chakra," Nico said, putting one palm over the front of her neck. "It'll help you know what to say."

Standing, I paid for my lunch and invited them for dinner at my apartment to tell them what happened. "Good luck, Charlie," Nico called when I was halfway across the restaurant. She had returned to rearranging the hair over Vincent's left ear, and he was staring straight ahead.

CHAPTER **2 0**

Ken Styles

IN HIS MAJOR league career, Ken Styles had a singular gift for hitting towering home runs. Wherever he played, he hit baseballs to the farthest reaches: off the dome in Houston and onto Waveland Avenue in Chicago. A St. Louis sportscaster coined the term "Styles Miles." When he batted, even the dullest, mid-season game seemed to pause to see what would happen.

Styles loved the frozen frames of time at the plate: the moment just before the pitcher's release, the moment of the ball in flight toward him, the moment of his swing, and the moment of the ball climbing in the air. What he wanted most was to be inside one of those moments all the time.

In his first year, Styles was named rookie of the year. A year later, he won the batting title, was voted Most Valuable Player, and his team, the Atlanta Braves, won the World Series. In his third season, he joined the team's partying contingent and began drinking. His ball playing became erratic. Three years later, he broke three fingers in his left hand in a collision at the plate and was out for two months. In the off season, he was arrested for a DUI. The commissioner forced him to enter a drug rehabilitation program. Three years after that, coming home from a late-night party, drunk and high on cocaine, he ran a red light and hit another car. The other driver was seriously injured. Convicted of a felony DUI and drug possession, Styles was sentenced to the California State Prison at Corcoran for five years.

I met Styles three years after his release. He was living in Southern California, where he had opened a string of KT Steakhouses. Styles' brother-in-law and manager, Claudell Taylor, called me and said Styles wanted to talk about a book. I said I didn't know much about sports and suggested he contact a sportswriter friend of mine who wrote for the *Times*.

There was silence on the other end. "Ken wants to talk to you," Taylor repeated.

We met in a KT Steakhouse in Anaheim, a one-story building with smoked glass windows and a view of the Santa Ana Freeway a block away. The restaurant sign had a neon caricature of Styles' smiling face with a baseball bat and ball beneath it. The caricature was repeated above the lounge bar and on the front of the menus and the napkins. I waited with Taylor in a booth of the nearly empty restaurant.

After a few minutes Styles arrived. He was a tall, powerfully built black man dressed in a cashmere sweater and dark trousers, who loped across the room in a defiant style. He slapped a national sports weekly on the table, with a cover photo of Styles and the title "Wasted" across the top.

"You read that?" he asked.

"No," I said. "I don't follow sports. As I told Mr. Taylor, I'm not a sportswriter."

Ignoring me, Styles continued to look at the cover photo, which had been taken shortly after his arrest for the auto accident. His face was blurred, his hair disheveled. He looked like a bum.

"They interviewed people who used to work for me," he said. "People *I* paid a lot of money."

He pulled himself into the booth. The leather seat and table seemed too small for him. His eyes focused on me. "You look at me, what do you see?" he asked.

I hesitated. "An athlete," I said.

"I look old to you?"

From news accounts, I knew he was just thirty-four. But, in baseball parlance, he was an "old thirty-four." His lined face and heavy body made him look ten years older. "No," I said.

He held a menu toward me. "You think I look like this cartoon? You think I smile like this? Shit, I don't smile like that."

At that moment, it was hard to imagine Styles ever smiling.

"Man developing these restaurants, he says, Ken, this is the way people want you to look. Bullshit."

While Styles stared at the menu, I said, "When I write books, I try to choose subjects that I'm familiar with. That way, I can bring something to the writing. I knew Virginia's Hardy's books and Nick White's music before I started writing their stories. I'm sorry, but I don't know baseball very well. I don't think I could do a good job of writing your biography."

"This isn't about baseball," he said. "This's about me, and I'll tell you everything you need to know. You just have to listen."

"But I need to understand your work in order to describe your life."

His face tightened. "Look here," he said. "You know what happened to me? You think I don't have a story to tell?"

"I'm sure you do."

"There're fifty writers who'd give their left nut to write my story."

"So why do you want me?"

"My wife, Ricki, tells me you're the best. Man, I deserve the best."

"If I did it, we'd have to talk about everything—your drinking, divorces, the accident, prison."

"What I want."

"I'll need some time to think about it."

"Sure. Take a minute."

We stared at each other.

"All right," I said. "I'll do it. Soon as I finish the final changes on Nick's book."

Styles held out his huge right hand to shake. "What do you want to eat?" he asked.

"Just coffee," I said. It was ten o'clock in the morning.

"Have a steak," he said. He called across the room. "Bring us a T-bone." He left the table to find a waiter.

I looked at Taylor, who shrugged and spoke for the first time. "Looks like it's all happening for you now, brother," he said. "And the good news is, you get to keep your left nut."

. . .

I stayed with Styles and his family in his home in Palos Verdes while I wrote his book. Styles was living with his third wife, a local television personality named Ricki Taylor, and her two children from an earlier marriage.

My living quarters were in a self-contained apartment next to the workout room, and our routine was to meet there at six each morning and talk while Styles worked through his regimen.

Styles had grown up in a middle-class household in Oakland, California. His older brother excelled at sports. Shy and unsure, Ken had to be coaxed to join Little League. He hated anything that drew attention to him, and dreaded standing at the plate. When he swung and missed, he heard kids laughing behind the batting cage.

He stopped swinging. He stood at the plate and leaned the bat against his shoulder. His at-bats became a test of wills between the seven-year-old Styles and the umpires, who would urge the young boy to swing and then give up and award him a base-on-balls.

At the plate, Styles watched the baseball coming toward him. He noticed how fast it was thrown, how it left the pitcher's hand, and the arc it traveled toward the plate. He saw the ball move left and right and up and down. He began to know the pitchers' grips, windups, and delivery.

After several weeks, he could tell where pitches were going to be at the plate. He played a game of guessing where the ball was going to end up. Then one day he swung.

And missed.

It took him another two weeks to judge his bat speed and where to swing.

Near the end of the season, he batted against a boy he had watched all summer. Styles watched three pitches arrive at nearly the same spot, and on the fourth one, he leaned back slightly on his heels, turned his right shoulder away from the plate, and swung. He hit the ball over the short-stop's head into left field. It was a routine single, but Styles never forgot the feeling of the bat connecting with the ball.

"You feel it in your hands through the wood," he said. "If it's a clean hit off the barrel, you feel this jolt in your hands, and you know the ball's going somewhere. There ain't nothing in life like that feeling."

In high school, Styles' baseball coach was a former minor leaguer named Bobby Morgan, who awakened the shy teenager's mind to the game within the game. Styles learned to watch how the infielders shifted their positions for different batters and with runners on base. He learned to visualize the pitcher's strategy for each count.

More than anything, Morgan taught Styles the smallness of the game. "You play 25 games a season, bat four times per game, and you get one hit a game, you're batting .250," Morgan told him. "You get one more hit every other game, you're batting .370. You get that second hit by swinging a tenth of second earlier on a pitch, or you hit a line drive six inches higher than the second baseman's glove. It's all small."

As a senior, Styles received offers from four major league teams. Over his mother's insistence that he attend college, Styles signed with the Atlanta Braves and spent half a season on the Richmond Braves, Atlanta's AAA team. He was called up to the majors in the spring of 1970. By May he was in the regular lineup and batting over .300. With his middle name Thomas, he became known as "KT".

In his third season, Styles was embraced by a trio of top stars who went bar-hopping every night. Returning to the clubhouse the following day still drunk and hung-over, Styles and his new friends drank coffee and took amphetamines to recover their senses. For the first time Styles felt his body's heaviness. He had trouble seeing the ball and swung at bad pitches.

Then someone gave him cocaine, and he fell in love. It embraced him with such gentleness he was hardly aware he had surrendered to it.

At the end of his fifth season Styles signed with the Dodgers. The following year, he was arrested outside a bar in Hollywood for driving under the influence and spent a night in jail. The commissioner conducted an investigation and required Styles to enter drug rehab. He missed the first half of his seventh season and relinquished his salary.

. . .

When Styles finished his daily workout and grew tired of talking to me, he wandered around his house, rough-housing with Taylor's children and pulling leftovers from the refrigerator. All the while he carried a base-ball bat in his left hand. Lying around the house were a half dozen of them, all identical—white ash, 34 inches long, the Ken Styles brand burned into the 2-1/2-inch barrel. He picked them up unconsciously, as if they were a part of his arm.

"I know more about hitting a baseball than anything in life," he said, swinging the bat idly. "I can tell you what happens if I move my plant foot back two inches, where I'm going to hit that ball. When I was playing, I knew all the pitchers and the kind of stuff they had. Man, half of them, I knew what they were thinking before they thought it."

"First few years, there was something else. My body knew where the ball was going to be at the plate. I'm talking about my *body*. I didn't have to think. It wasn't practice or studying film. It was just there, like a connection between me and the ball. That's something only the great players have, and I had it. It was fragile—only I didn't know that. It wasn't nothing else but magic."

"Then the drinking and the dope . . . and one day it wasn't there. Even with detox and getting sober, I couldn't find it. Magic was gone." He lifted the bat and let it rest on his shoulder.

. . .

Styles' eighth season was a comeback year for him, and the Dodgers lost a tough championship series to the Braves. But his next season was a nightmare. His second wife, Melissa Richards, filed for divorce and charged Styles with physical abuse. He got off to a slow start, below .200 for the first time in his career. Fans heckled him. In July, he was suspended for shoving an umpire. A tabloid published photos of Styles in a New York restaurant with a drug dealer. The Dodgers finished in fourth place, and Styles asked to be traded.

Two weeks before Christmas, Styles attended a party with friends in West Hollywood. A police investigation later determined Styles had drunk three Tequila and tonics and snorted half an eight-ball of cocaine. He left the party just after midnight and drove home in his Mustang. At the inter-section of Melrose and Fairfax, Styles went through a red light and hit a Corolla on the rear passenger side. Police estimated the Mustang's speed at the time of impact at 75 miles per hour. The Corolla was nearly torn in two, and the young female driver was critically injured.

· · ·

After six months in England, I used my advance from the Nick White book to buy a house in Pacific Palisades, where I stayed on the weekends while I worked on the Styles book.

Partway through my interviews with Styles, Nick White's biography was released, and I accompanied him on a four-week tour of the United States. This was at a time of Nick's full embrace of the book, before his dis-illusion with it and me. The tour started in Los Angeles at MacArthur's Books in Brentwood.

During the signing, a young woman left the line leading to Nick and approached me. She had a shy smile and large brown eyes. Her hair was pulled back in a ponytail, with a spray of uneven bangs and a pair of glasses balanced on top of her head. She held her book with both hands against her chest. "I've read your books," she said. "This one and the ones on Virginia Hardy and Jack Evans. I mean, not *your* books, I guess, but the books you helped write. And I just wanted to say that I like the way you let the life stories unfold. I assume that's your choice, or partly your choice."

I smiled and said, "The sequence's usually a negotiated choice."

She opened her arms and held the book toward me. "Would you sign it please?" she asked.

No one had ever asked me to sign a subject's book. When I asked her name, she said Jill, and she took a breath for the first time since she approached the table.

While I was signing, she bent toward me and said, "I'm a musician, and where you describe how a musician listens to music is really true. It's the first time I've ever read it anywhere."

Hearing this, Nick leaned in front of me and said, "Young lady, I'll have you know that particular passage was mine. The only contribution this bloke made was to translate words like 'chips' into American. Otherwise he was bloody useless."

Jill laughed. Nick asked her what instrument she played.

"Viola," she said. "But not in a rock band."

"Not much call for it, is there?" Nick agreed. "But a beautiful instrument nonetheless. Brandenburg Concerto No. 6 has some nice viola bits. I heard it played once in Scunthorpe or some place."

"Wow," Jill said. "Not many people know about the viola in the Brandenburg."

"Course they don't," Nick said. "But I do, because I'm a musician, whereas Charlie here, when we started, didn't know a G clef from his bum."

I handed the book back to Jill, and she folded it in her arms again. "The other thing I wanted to tell you," she said, "was I loved that place in Nick's book where you quoted Yeats on the 'out-worn heart, in a time out-worn.' I mean it was corny, but it was perfect." Her face blushed, and she walked away.

Nick and I watched her walk to the door, where she paused to open the front of her copy and look at my signature. "I think, Charlie," he said, "That woman is your groupie. Utterly delightful in an American way. Freshly scrubbed."

Nick returned to signing books. Then he looked back at me and said, "What's important, mate, is that she's the only woman in this galaxy who's ever actually fallen for your Yeats. You ought to chat her up before she leaves, or you'll die a broken and lonely old geezer."

On our first date, Jill told me that for years she had patched together several jobs as a musician. She was an untenured professor at Cal State Fullerton, she performed at wedding receptions with something called the Toyon String Quartet, and she gave private lessons. She said she had begun playing the viola at age eight, when it was recommended by a music teacher. "Violas are usually given to children who want to be in the background, supportive players, not soloists," she said.

"Was that true for you," I asked.

She shrugged. "I don't know if I was given the instrument because I was shy," she said, "or if I became a background person because I played the viola."

"Well, we have something in common. We ghostwriters are definitely background people."

"Maybe that's why I wanted to talk to you at the signing." She blushed again as she had at the signing.

On our second date, after a movie, we went back to her apartment. She opened a bottle of wine, and I asked to see her viola. She played a few measures of the Dvorak Quintet. Then she handed the instrument to me and showed me how to hold it and draw the bow across the strings. "Most people," she said, "who have never played a string instrument are surprised the first time they hear a violin or viola so close to their ears." She put her fingers around my bow hand and drew the bow across the strings. The sound filled my head.

"That's the tradeoff of playing the viola," she said. "The fingering is excruciating, and you spend your life sawing away in the service of violins. Violas are designed for playing the inner harmonies, not the juicy melodies."

Conscious of her hand on mine, she drew the bow across the strings again. "But despite all that," she said, "you produce that sound. The larger size and lower pitch make the timbre deeper and darker than a violin's. Because the strings are thicker, people also say a viola 'speaks more slowly.' I like to think it's the sound of feelings deep within us."

"It's about voice, isn't it?" I said. "Finding the viola's voice and understanding how to use it to express something. When I help my clients write their books, I have to find what's distinctive about their voice and then use it to tell their story. It's about listening and then imitating that sound."

"And staying out of the way of what's being said," Jill said. She smiled at me and gently lifted the viola from my shoulder.

On our third date I made dinner at my house, and after dinner, we sat on the deck, looking out on Santa Ynez Canyon. "Let me ask you a question," she said. "Each of your autobiographies begins with a chapter about something in the subject's life that defines them. Did I get that right?"

"More or less," I said.

"So if you were helping me write my autobiography, what would the first chapter be about?"

"Your fingers."

Jill laughed and held up her hands to look at them.

"Haven't you ever noticed, people's fingers are very different," I said. "They're our most distinctive part. They express who we are. The windows to our soul."

"I thought the eyes were the windows to the soul."

"No. It's the fingers. For instance, yours are unusually long and thin. Especially the last segments—the distal phalanges."

"The distal phalanges?"

"Sorry. The fingertips. I had to learn the names of bones when I was writing about Ken Styles' broken hand."

"Well, in my case, I need long distal phalanges to reach the C string".

"That's right. You're a professional string musician, so you express yourself through your fingering. It's a defining characteristic."

"But what's that say about my soul?"

"It's how you move your fingers. You have unusual grace."

Jill laughed. "Other men look at breasts, and you've been watching my fingers?"

"I couldn't help it. It's the first thing I noticed about you."

Jill smiled hesitantly, still unsure if she were being put on. She moved her fingers through the air in front of me. "So that's what you'd write about?"

"No," I said. "I'd have to know more about them. Like how they feel."

"How they feel? You mean like this?" She laid her left hand on the side of my face.

"See," I said, "that tells me a lot. Your fingers are cool. They're soft. And I was right about those fingertips."

Jill laughed again and ran her fingers across my cheek.

"But it's *your* autobiography," I said. "I always ask my clients what they want in the first chapter."

"I think I'd want something more dramatic," she said. "Something that the rest of the story could build on. Like this." With her left hand still on my face, she drew my head toward her and kissed me slowly on the lips.

She sat back and smiled. "Isn't that a good beginning?" she said.

·   ·   ·

The other driver was a twenty-eight-year-old nurse from Glendale. She suffered a broken arm, three broken ribs, a fractured pelvis, a ruptured spleen, and head injuries that left her with short-term memory loss.

The legal proceedings following the accident were a media showcase. A newly elected district attorney announced that if the victim died, he would charge Styles with second-degree murder. When it was clear that the victim would survive, the charge was reduced to felony driving under the influence and causing great bodily harm, with additional charges for possession of a controlled substance. In a plea agreement, Styles pled guilty and accepted the maximum sentence of five years. The judge ordered Styles to report to Corcoran State Prison. A photograph of Styles arriving at Corcoran in shackles and an orange jumpsuit appeared on every sports page in America.

He was released after three and a half of the five years and went to live with his sister, Tanya, in Long Beach. Tanya required that her brother accompany her to services every Sunday evening at the First Baptist Church.

A film crew from a local Los Angeles television station filmed Styles in the church, and the clip ran on the local news. Ricki Taylor, who was hosting her own morning show on the station, happened to see the news story and went to meet Styles.

As Styles later described it, his first meeting with Taylor did not go well. "I thought she's going to ask me to be on her show or something," Styles said. "But right away she tells me the black community is watching me. Just like that, she's in my face."

The turning point came during another of Taylor's visits with Styles. "She said, 'Ken, no one's going to pitch to you for the rest of your life.' It was the worst thing anyone ever said. I just stood up and walked out."

Taylor took him to AA meetings and prodded him until he stood up and told his own story, and later she took him to a boys and girls club in Hawthorne, where he spoke to a room of children. When he told them he'd been a baseball player, one of them called out, "How come we never seen you?" Another answered, "He played a long time ago." Another said, "He fucked up. They bring somebody here, it's cause they fucked up."

Much of what Styles told the children that day would be part of a speech he would give for the next fifteen years. He told them about feeling a clean hit through the wood of the bat. He told them sports were not just about strength and power but about vision, being able to see what was going on in the field. He told them about the smallness of baseball—hitting a ball just six inches higher than the second baseman's glove. He said sometimes in life, if you did a small thing, it might be important to another person.

He appeared on Taylor's TV show. The show caught the attention of a group of local black investors, who approached Styles with the idea for a chain of restaurants.

Styles' book, *Full Count,* was published at the start of spring training in 1986. The cover photograph showed Styles hitting the winning home run in Game Four of the 1971 World Series. To coincide with the book's release, *Sports Illustrated* ran a cover story and a long interview with Styles. In the months following the tour, he received offers to join several sports shows and in the end chose to host a weekly LA radio talk show.

If Ricki Taylor was right about many things in Styles' life, she was wrong about one thing. He did have someone pitch to him again. It was in the mid-1990s, ten years after his book was published. The occasion was an old-timers exhibition, prior to a regular season game at Atlanta-Fulton County Stadium, where Styles had played the best years of his career.

That day Styles looked older than forty-six. His loose jersey could not hide his heaviness, and when he jogged onto the field, he was winded. Fans who had seen the TV movie based on *Full Count*, which starred the young black actor, John Allen, were surprised to see the graying man on the field. Recent press stories hinted his marriage with Taylor was ending, and his talk show contract had not been renewed.

But that day at the ballpark was not about Styles' troubles but about his return to baseball. In the shortened exhibition game, he batted just once. He faced a long-retired pitcher, whose fastballs now floated across the plate. Styles fouled off a couple and looked at pitches outside the strike zone, until the count reached three and two. He fouled off three more pitches into the seats behind first base. On the ninth pitch, a pitch down and in, he pulled out his hips, raised his shoulders, and turned his body into a swing, launching the ball in a long, high, slow arc that carried it above the field in fair territory and into the upper deck of the right field stands. The fans jumped in their seats and cheered, and at the plate, Styles stood for a few seconds without moving, the bat in one hand, the impact of the ball ringing in his fingers, and his head turned to right field, as if he were still watching the flight of the ball through the air.

CHAPTER **2 1**

LEAVING THE RESTAURANT, I drove north to see Kenny. I exited the freeway and headed east to Chalk Hill Road. Without much trouble, I found the turning for Kenny's private road, opened the latched gate, and drove up the steep hillside.

Kim-Ly greeted me at the door, and I followed her down the hallway. There was music playing again from the hallway speakers. It was Elvis Presley's "Love Me." This time, instead of going outside to the deck, Kim-Ly led me past the living room and down a windowless corridor. We passed open doorways of an office, an exercise room, and several bedrooms. Speakers were mounted in this corridor, too, and they were playing the Four Tops' "It's the Same Old Song."

Near the end of the corridor, Kim-Ly stopped beside an open door, bowed slightly, and walked away. From inside the room came the sound of one of the Jays' biggest hits of the 1970s, "Get to You." The room was a home theater. At the front was a large screen television, and facing it, were a dozen cushioned chairs. In the back was a bar. The room was dark and stuffy and cloudy with marijuana smoke.

Across the room Kenny stood, bent over an instrument console. He wore an enormous yellow polo shirt and khaki shorts. His long hair was loose and falling over his shoulders.

The Jays' song was blasting from speakers in all four walls, so loud that it vibrated the floor. Wearing a headset, Kenny was adjusting the sound mix and dancing to the music. I waited to approach him. After a few minutes he looked up at me. "Listen to this, man," he said.

He pushed a button and started the song over. "The first thing you hear is the organ," he said. "It's a slow, scary sound, like something rising out of the swamp."

The room filled with an organ playing deep bass notes. "Tommy would be on the left side of the stage playing it, weird ass smile on his face. Here come the congas, setting up the beat. Boom, boppa, boom. It's coming toward you, and you can't stop it."

Kenny watched me. "You hear this? That's T.J. on the bass. See how he's changing the tempo, picking up the speed. Then the sax. On the road, man, we had this big black fucker on sax, hardly spoke to us. Right there. That's lead guitar, Mike in those days. Seven notes over and over. Beautiful liquid sound. Faster and faster. The whole thing's rolling now, like a train."

Quick guitar chords rang out of the speakers. Kenny laughed. "At this point, the kids in the front row, the ones in the stage lights, are rolling their heads with their eyes closed. Then listen. Right there. That's me. I made that sound. It's like an animal call, some shit like that. Then somebody else, T.J., does it too. In the studio we dubbed in jungle birds. It goes faster and faster. And you think it's going to run over you. Then all of a sudden, at eighteen measures, *wham.*"

Suddenly the room fell quiet. "The whole sound stops dead. It's completely silent for two bars. In concerts sometimes the kids in the back would be still screaming here. It would take them a few seconds to realize we stopped. Then, when it's still, Mike starts with the guitar again. Hear it? But this time, all by himself. Those same seven notes. That's when I start to sing."

Kenny held his right fist near his mouth and mouthed the words. From the speakers came the sound of his voice whispering. "I'm coming to get you now. I'm coming to get you now."

Kenny pushed a button and the music stopped. He looked at me. His hair fell into his face and his eyes were clouded. He looked unsteady. "Nobody did concerts like us," he said. "Kids came out of those concerts, and their heads were changed. We killed them."

"I went to a lot of your concerts," I said. "Hollywood Bowl in sixty-eight. Fillmore East in seventy."

He didn't seem to hear me. He dropped into one of the theater chairs. They were mounted on swivels, and he turned to face me. I sat a few seats away in the same row. He picked up a joint from an ashtray. He put it to his lips and inhaled, and as the smoke from the still burning joint curled in front of his face, he sniffed it through his nose.

"We were a bar band," he said, blowing the smoke toward me. "We should have played there, where kids could dance. Last five years, it was nuts. Stadiums. Thirty, sixty thousand seats."

He put down the joint and reached behind to the console, picked up a glass, and drank from it. "It stopped being fun. First Tommy left. Then Mike. Couple years, it was nothing but lawyers."

I took out my notebook.

"Only one I miss is Tommy. We were in high school together in Torrance, you know that? That's when we started writing songs."

Kenny pushed the hair from his face. "Tommy was a real musician," he said. "Mike and I—we were in it for the scene. But Tommy was a genius. He loved all kinds of music. Classical, blues, show tunes. He knew Cole Porter lyrics by heart. 'If she says your behavior is heinous, kick her right in the Coriolanus.' All that shit."

Kenny drank from his glass. "Tommy'd sit at his piano and work out the melodies. Playing the same phrases over and over. First in his room at his parents' house and later in a house we shared in Malibu. He'd play the song for me a few times, and I'd go away and come back with a lyric. He didn't like something, he'd tell me. He knew the song he wanted."

Kenny looked at me. "You want to hear a story?" he asked. "In 1973, there was this dealer who hung around us named Jelly Green. Big dopey guy. He gave Tommy some acid. Tommy'd done acid before, but this time it was different. Bad shit."

"First couple months he couldn't talk. I mean he said things, but they didn't make sense. And he couldn't play piano. He just looked at the keys. It freaked out everybody, man. Tommy went to hospitals and rehabs. But they couldn't do anything with him. So he came back to us. He was like a lost kid. He hung around the bus and sat on the side of the stage when we played. If he talked, it was like two sentences a day."

"After about a year, one night in Detroit, in the middle of a set, he comes on stage. We just finished 'Crystal.' Tommy goes to the electric piano, and our replacement guy gives him the bench. Tommy starts playing some Chopin shit. It's beautiful. But I mean no one—none of us or the kids in the hall—knew what the hell was going on."

"He finishes, goes back stage. Never does it again. After a few days he flies home. Lives with his mother, watches TV all day. Few years ago his mother died, and the family put Tommy in a nursing home."

Kenny drank from his glass again and looked at me. "You like that story? That the kind of thing you want in the article? It's not real funny, is it?"

"No," I said. "I didn't know what happened to Tommy."

He didn't seem to hear me. "What'd you want in this article?" he asked. "You want the parties and the girls, that shit?"

"The music. I want to write about your songs."

"Yeah, the music. It was important in those days, wasn't it?"

"When *Trade Winds* came out, my friends and I listened to it over and over."

"Our songs meant something. They all did then. It's not like that now. It's all a lot of shit."

"That's why I think an article would be good. Remind people about the way your music was."

Kenny stared at me. "You gonna write about the way I look?" he asked.

"I don't have to," I said.

Kenny stood up, lumbered back to the bar, and poured tequila into his glass. "I thought that's what your books did," he said with his back turned. "Reveal what people are hiding."

"This is an article. It's different."

Kenny turned around and came back toward me. In one hand he held the glass, and in the other, the silver handgun. He fell into his chair and threw the gun on the chair between us. "What're you doing around here, Teller?" he asked. "I never saw you until last week."

"I came to be near my ex-wife and daughter. I didn't know anyone until I met Paul Barkley."

"Paul Barkley?" Kenny said.

"Paul helped me get a job with Rajiv Patel. I'm writing Mr. Patel's memoir."

"I thought you're writing an article about me?"

"Actually I'm doing both. Anyway Paul helped me get the job with Patel. I guess you knew him, too. I saw you at his funeral."

"Who're we talking about?" Kenny asked. He drank the rest of the tequila.

"Paul Barkley," I said.

"You *guess* I knew him?"

"Paul said you worked together."

"Worked together? That's what he said?" Kenny asked, leaning forward, interested.

"Yes."

"He used those words?"

"Yes."

"You're sure?"

"Yes."

"He said 'worked together'? Just like that? It wasn't something else?"

"No," I said. I looked at Kenny the way Vincent had told me to. Kenny's eyes stared at me. "Paul got me some coke a couple times," I said.

"Coke?" Kenny asked.

"Yeah," I said, still looking at him. "Paul said if anything happened, and I wanted more, I should talk to you."

Kenny put the glass on the console behind him. "Who the fuck are you, man?" he said.

"I told you. I'm a writer."

"Yeah and something else, too, or we wouldn't be talking about cocaine and this Paul Barkley shit. You work with that kid who's watching me?"

"No, I don't know anything about that."

"You act like him, man. Like you're watching me."

"I just want to do the article, is all."

"But not everything belongs in the article, does it?"

"No."

"I mean it'd be important for someone like you to know that, wouldn't it?"

"Yes, I know that."

"I knew you would," Kenny said. "Come back Tuesday. I'm tired of this shit." He picked up the joint again and squeezed it between his lips. Then he closed his eyes and held his breath.

CHAPTER 22

ON MY WAY home from Kenny's house, I stopped at a market and bought groceries for dinner. At my apartment, I cooked a pot of vegetarian chili and made a salad. About seven Nico and Vincent arrived.

I opened a bottle of cabernet sauvignon, and we sat on the balcony. The sky had begun to darken. On the eastern horizon a pale moon was just visible.

I gave them a brief account of what Kenny said. "He was definitely freaked when Paul's name came up," I said. "I don't think there's any doubt that Paul was dealing for him."

"I told you that," Vincent said.

"Yeah, but we didn't have it from Kenny."

"So in the end Kenny didn't actually agree to sell you coke?" Nico asked.

"No, he was too uptight," I said. "I'm going to see him again on Tuesday."

"What for?" Nico asked.

"I don't know. Maybe he'll talk about Paul some more. People say things even when they're trying not to."

"I'm curious about when Kenny asked you the exact words Barkley used," Vincent said.

"It was like he fixated on the phrase 'work together.' He didn't like that."

"But maybe it was something else. Maybe it was the difference between 'worked' and 'working.'"

Nico and I looked at Vincent.

"Maybe," Vincent said, "something happened, and they were no longer working together. Maybe it was the past tense."

"So you think Paul stopped selling?" Nico asked.

Vincent shrugged. "Who knows?"

"If it's true," I said. "It would give Kenny a motive for killing Paul. He'd be losing a big customer."

"I don't see Kenny having the concentration for something like this," Vincent said. "Spur of the moment, maybe, but not anything requiring planning."

"Besides," Nico said. "Whoever did this, set up Stephen and knew something about the café."

By the time we finished the wine, the evening had turned cool, and I suggested we go inside. We sat around my small kitchen table. I filled three bowls with chili and put fresh tomato slices and grated cheese on top. Nico brought three bottles of cold beer from the refrigerator.

"So if Paul stopped dealing, why would he contact Howard Miller to represent him?" I asked.

"Maybe he suspected the police already had evidence," Vincent said.

"OK," I said. "Why did he choose to tell me? He knew the rest of you better. Molly would be more helpful."

"I know why he chose you," Nico said. "I used to give Paul massages twice a week, and he liked to talk on the table. A few weeks ago, I said how cool it was you were living here. And he started talking about you."

"He said all your books are about the same thing," Nico said. "The subject of the autobiography is renowned for something—their films or music. But that's not who they really are. So they struggle to find the core of their identity in the face of public adulation for what they've done."

"But what's this have to do with Paul wanting to talk to me?" I asked.

"Paul thought you had insights into the conflict between the public and private person. He thought you'd understand him."

"He told you that?"

"Yeah, he said you were underrated. He said your autobiographies had thematic unity. Paul was deeper than a lot of people thought he was. He had this spiritual side that he didn't show much. I think he was trying to resolve something in his own life."

"Like what?"

"I don't know. But it doesn't surprise me he stopped dealing. That makes sense with the things he was telling me. It was like he was coming to a crossroads."

"But he didn't say what it was?"

"No. That was too personal, or maybe he just wasn't ready to talk about it. But he was about to get married, so maybe it had something to do with that."

I cleared the table and made coffee. When I returned to the table, Vincent, who had been quiet for several minutes, said, "I want to come back to something you told us earlier. The letter that Paul gave you was just to set up the meeting with Miller, right?"

"Yeah," I said.

"But Miller said the cops think something else was in the envelope. Was there?"

"You looked inside the envelope that night," Nico said. "I remember."

I didn't say anything. They both looked at me.

"I've dragged people into my trouble before," I said. "I'm trying not to do that anymore."

"Hey, that's sweet, Charlie," Nico said. "But we don't know what you're talking about."

I went to my computer and brought the memory stick back to the table. "That was with the letter the night Paul was killed," I said. "When I gave the letter to the police, it must have fallen out of the envelope. By the time I found it in my pocket, I thought it might look suspicious to give it to them."

"As opposed to now, it doesn't look suspicious that you still have it?" Vincent said.

"No, but since Paul was going to give it to me, I wanted to see what it is."

"It's obstruction of justice," Vincent said. "It's a felony."

"I know it was stupid."

"Did you look at what's on it?" Nico asked.

"Yeah. But it doesn't make sense. It's a spreadsheet."

"I want to see it," Nico said.

I looked at Vincent. "You guys can walk out of here right now," I said.

Vincent stared at the memory stick on the table. Then he picked it up, walked to the computer, and put it back in the port. Nico and I followed him and stood behind his chair. He opened the Robles file and scrolled through the pages. He clicked on "Properties" and opened a tab called "Statistics." It showed the file had been created by someone named Andrew Sutter about a year ago.

"That mean anything?" Vincent asked.

"No," I said.

Vincent went back to the main view and stared at the columns. "They're quantities of something," he said.

"Drug sales?" Nico asked.

"I don't think so," Vincent said. "Some of the columns have an 'm' for meters. They're distances."

Vincent leaned back in his chair. "I have to spend more time with it."

"You're joining the felony?" I asked.

"No, that's your problem," Vincent said. "I don't plan on getting caught."

CHAPTER **23**

THE FOLLOWING MORNING I arranged to meet John Coffey at the fitness center to find out what his forensic accountant had learned about the business accounts. When I arrived, Coffey handed me a file folder. "It looks like Paul was transferring large sums from the fitness center to the catering business for about two years," he said.

"Isn't it normal for the owner of several businesses to shift money around as he needs it? Wasn't the catering business a startup that would need capital?"

"Seasons was long past being a startup."

"Stephen said it was booming."

"Yeah and the thing is, the money from the fitness center wasn't even staying in Seasons."

"What'd you mean?"

"The money was deposited, then withdrawn in cash. Fifteen grand a month. Some months twenty. Enough so that most months the fitness center didn't show a profit."

"Does the money show up in other accounts?"

"No. We even checked Paul's personal accounts. It just disappears."

I looked at Coffey's face. The weight of what he had told me was caught in the dark lines around his eyes. I had spent enough time around athletes to know that devoting your life to amateur sports, as Coffey had done, would mean believing in a measure of fair play and honesty. In the past week, he had learned that his business associate and friend had engaged in a secret business.

"Molly told me the police found traces of coke in Paul's office," he said. "I think I knew about it, but I didn't want it to be true."

"What'd you see?"

"The last nine months, Paul was less engaged. Our routine had always been to have a management meeting every Tuesday morning. In the beginning, Paul wanted to know everything—class curricula, attendance levels, brands of squash balls. He was on top of it all."

"Didn't that drive you crazy?"

"No, that's just it. When Paul was involved, he made it fun. That's what he said when he hired me. 'Come on, it'll be fun.'"

"So you liked working for him?"

Coffey leaned forward toward me. "Man, I *loved* working for the guy," he said.

"And *was* it fun?"

"For a while, sure. Couple years ago he was running on all cylinders. Filled with ideas. Classes for seniors and postpartum moms. After-school classes for teenagers to get them interested in body awareness."

"What changed?"

"He just backed off. Cancelled meetings. First one, then it got to be a regular thing."

"Maybe he wanted you to take responsibility?"

Coffey shook his head. "No, that wasn't Paul. He was a real hands-on guy. I thought maybe he was pre-occupied with the restaurant, but Stephen said Paul was letting things slip there, too. It was like he was putting everything into Seasons, the smallest of his businesses."

"What do you think happened?"

"Over the years, the fitness club has arranged to get endorsements from local professional athletes," he said. "Whenever we did one, Paul was like a kid. Those guys were larger than life to him. Most of us figure, deep down, the lives of pro athletes probably have as good a chance as our own of being screwed up. But to Paul, they were heroes. It was like he always wanted to see the good in people. All I can figure is, he trusted someone, believed in something he shouldn't have."

Coffey checked his watch and stood up. "I've got to teach a class," he said. At the door, he paused and said, "I hope this helps. It's funny, but sometimes now, with the things that are coming to surface, I think about all the time Paul and I spent together and how he never talked about what was going on out of sight. I wonder if he tried and I didn't listen, or if he wanted to spare me. As much as I want to know who killed him and why, I think what I really want is to know why he didn't talk to me."

* * *

As I headed to my car in the fitness center parking lot, I saw a small crowd watching a man and woman arguing. The woman's car was backed partway out of her space, and the man was blocking her with his pickup truck. They were yelling back and forth from their drivers' windows. I started to walk past when I noticed that it was Page Salinger and Ray Brenner.

"You want me to run into you?" Page yelled. She had backed her red Camaro to within a few inches of Brenner's pickup, a Ford F-150, whose over-sized wheels raised it three feet off the ground.

"Go ahead," Brenner answered. "I'm not moving." He revved his engine.

I went over to Page's car. "Excuse me," I said. "You two think you can take this somewhere else so that the rest of us can get our cars out?"

She wore sunglasses and an open-fronted wind breaker over a dark leotard. Her hair was pulled back in a ponytail, and her face was flushed from yelling. She looked at me and seemed to catch herself from speaking. Then she sank back in her seat and said, "I just want to go home."

I walked over to Brenner. "You want to let her out?" I said. "You know where she lives if you want to talk to her."

"This doesn't concern you, chief," he said.

I reached into my jacket and took out my cell phone. I tapped in 911. When the dispatcher answered, I said I wanted to report a fight in progress and gave her the address. When she asked my name, I said Ray Brenner. I walked to the front of Brenner's truck and read the license number. As I did this, Brenner stopped gunning his engine and watched me.

The dispatcher asked me the nature of the incident. I said I was in a big truck and was about to beat the crap out of a young woman. In a level voice, the dispatcher said, "Sir, the police will be there in two minutes."

I held the phone toward Brenner. "Anything you want to add?" I asked.

Brenner opened his door and started to get down. Then he got back in and slammed the door. "You're in trouble, man," he said. Then he called to Page, "This isn't over."

He revved his engine again to clear the spectators away from his truck and then he roared out of the parking lot.

I walked back to Page's car. She lifted her sunglasses onto her forehead and peered at me. "Thank you," she said. She backed her car out and drove away from the parking lot.

The small crowd dispersed. A few blocks away I could hear a police siren. I found my car, and as I reached the exit of the lot, a patrol car entered. I waved to the officer and drove away.

CHAPTER 2 4

ON SATURDAY AFTERNOON I sat at my desk and wrote two more chapters for the Patel book. The chapters covered the success of Torana Construction during the 1980s building boom. With its completion of the Pine Grove Shopping Center, the company quickly won contracts for a series of huge, high-profile projects—a housing tract outside Sacramento, a mall in Orange County, and an industrial park in San Diego.

Patel introduced building innovations: a new process for pouring foundations and new framing templates that could be delivered pre-made to construction sites. For Patel and DeVries, the volume and speed of the construction were at the heart of the autobiography. In their version of events, these business practices represented Patel's contribution to the industry. It was the story of an Indian immigrant who had not only mastered the procedures of American industry, but had advanced the state-of-the-art.

With the two chapters complete, I reviewed the shape of the book as a whole. Already the business information was overwhelming the personal story. Despite the request by Patel that I reduce the story of his wife, Safia, I went back to materials on her in my file.

The portrait of Safia in the Anita Kleinman biography was spare. She had been born of Gujarati Hindu parents in Chicago, married Patel when she was in her early thirties, gave birth to two children, and died of cancer at age 58.

Nevertheless Ms. Kleinman had spoken with Safia on three occasions, and the passages in her book contained a few intriguing details. Safia is described as making a fist while describing her husband and as saying that the devil is in their house.

In the phone book I found a listing for Anita Kleinman and called the number. The address was in Oakmont Village, a gated community for "mature residents" across the valley from my tower. A woman answered the phone. "Anita here," the voice said brightly.

I introduced myself and was about to explain the reason for my call, when I was interrupted. "Are you *the* Charles Teller?" she asked. "The great biographer."

"Yes, I write biographies."

"Oh, my. This is unexpected."

"I'd like to ask you . . ."

"As you're aware, Mr. Teller, from the letters that I've sent you, you are my *muse.*"

"I didn't realize . . ."

"My own writing is on a lesser order, but I think myself a colleague, a historian of people's lives, a female Charles Teller."

"That's very generous . . ."

"My own books are self-published and sell on a smaller scale, Mr. Teller, but several have had a wide circulation. You may be familiar with my book on Henry Talbot, the apple grower and car dealer who transformed this valley. *Henry Talbot: Man of Vision.*"

"Mrs. Kleinman, I would . . ."

"Please call me Anita."

"Anita, I'd like to ask you a few questions about your biography of Rajiv Patel."

"An unfortunate experience. My only unfinished work. I'm afraid Mr. Patel and I did not see eye to eye. But I would not yield my professional integrity. I know you've had to wrestle with that yourself. So there we are in the same boat, you and I, or you and me."

"Yes, of course. If I could come by sometime next week and talk to you about your experiences with Mr. Patel, that would be very helpful."

"It would be my pleasure to give back to the man who has given so much to me."

We made arrangements for me to visit her for tea on Monday afternoon.

That evening Molly called and invited me to come along the following morning when she talked to Stephen at the jail. I also got a call from Nico, who said Vincent had made some progress in decoding the spreadsheet but that he was going to have to wait until Monday, when businesses were open, to confirm it.

Later, Jill called and said she and Lucy wanted me to come to their house for dinner Sunday evening. After I agreed, she said, "My friend Dave will be there, too." I couldn't think of anything to say. After a long silence, I said, "Well, that's . . . good."

*　*　*

At ten the following morning I met Molly in the jail parking lot. She looked tired and serious and said nothing as a guard escorted us to the visitor's section, where Stephen was waiting. Molly started by telling Stephen about the police case against him. Her voice was measured, and I could tell she was trying to control her anger. "It's all circumstantial. There's no physical evidence putting you in the parking lot or connecting you to the killing. But they have the two arguments between you and Paul and your lying in initial testimony about Paul's coke dealing."

"None of that means anything." Stephen said.

"Actually it does," Molly said, her anger erupting. "It gives you motive. Believe me, I've seen people convicted on stories like this."

"It's all out of thin air."

"No, it's not. Just like your shooting at the target range isn't out of thin air."

"Is that what you're mad about? The target range?"

"Of course. When you first talked about the gun, it was like you didn't remember you owned it. Then we find out you were shooting it a week before the murder."

"I told you I forgot."

"You can't forget, Stephen," Molly yelled. "Kim says Mahler's looking at the drug sales. They think you and Paul were fighting over control of them."

Stephen closed his eyes and shook his head.

To interrupt their exchange, I told Molly and Stephen about my meeting with Kenny and about Vincent's speculation that Paul may have stopped working for Kenny.

When I finished, Molly looked at Stephen and said, "Do you know anything about him stopping?"

Stephen sighed. "Look," he said. "I keep telling everybody I don't know about this stuff. I didn't tell the police about the drug business because I thought it was irrelevant."

"Tell me everything. Let me worry about what's irrelevant."

"All right," Stephen said. "A lot of the people who ate at Galileo's and who hired Seasons were part of a certain crowd who lives in this county. They're rich, and many are in show business. Paul wanted more than anything to be part of that crowd. It was like an obsession."

"So he thought that selling coke would give him an entrée?" I asked.

"More or less. To Paul, the drugs were just a means to an end. The joke was he was a full-service caterer. I don't know if he stopped dealing. We never spoke about it. All I know is around the end of January Paul backed away. He cooked but left everything else to Carl and me."

"What about the night he was killed? Didn't you say he got a call about a catering job?"

"Customers still called him. For a lot of them, Paul was the point of contact."

Stephen sat back in his chair. "Paul was a middle-class guy who ran a restaurant. But he tried to dress and act like someone else. It was like he was trying to be as young and rich and hip as the people who hired him. He thought he could do it, but he couldn't. To them, he was always the caterer or the drug dealer."

"What do you know about Paul transferring money through the Seasons accounts?" I asked.

"I saw it in the books. Paul told me to mind my own business, but it was obvious it was cash to buy the coke."

"There's something else," Stephen said. "Until January Paul was adding names to the guest lists for the catered parties."

"What do you mean?" Molly asked.

"Our parties were invitation only. The clients gave us the guest lists, and we hired security guards to check people at the door. But before the parties, Paul added names, and he wouldn't let us see the final list. He just told us the total number. He said the guests wanted confidentiality. But I knew something else was going on."

"Like what?"

"They were his buyers."

"What happened after January, when Paul stopped going to the parties?" I asked.

"No more added names," Stephen said. "We used the lists that the clients gave us."

Molly looked at Stephen for a moment. "If we can find Paul's lists," she said, "they might tell the cops something about Paul's dealing and who wanted him killed. It could help your case."

"Were the lists were on his office computer or his laptop?" I asked.

"Office. He printed them out from there."

"We could ask Eddie Mahler to check," Molly said.

As Molly and I walked to the parking lot, she said, "By the way, Kim told me the cops have opened an investigation on you."

"Yeah, I know. Mahler talked to me."

"I think this goes beyond Eddie. You showed up on surveillance."

"You're kidding."

"Just be careful, Charlie," she said. "This is still a small town. They want to solve this thing."

CHAPTER 2 5

Skye Lurie

I MET SKYE Lurie on a Nantucket beach in late January. It was a damp, gray afternoon, already turning dark at three. A cold wind scudded across the dunes, carrying flakes of snow that had fallen the night before. As I approached Skye's cottage, I saw her sitting on top of a bluff behind the house. She wore no coat but held the edges of a wool cardigan close together at her chest. When I neared, she looked up at me. Her face, which I had seen many times on TV and in newspapers as she emerged from a drug treatment center, looked swollen and white. Her appearance seemed to have been thrown together by an angry child—smeared liner rimmed her eyes, and patches of scalp showed through hair that had been hacked close to her head. She took a drag from a hand-rolled cigarette and squinted at me. "Here for a swim?" she asked.

I cleared snow from a spot near her and squatted. "Just a tan," I said.

"Came to the right fucking place," she said.

Skye was the daughter of two famous parents—Tom Lurie, the liberal Connecticut congressman, and Addie Huston, the leading singer-song-writer from the sixties and seventies. When I met her in 1987, Skye had a national prominence of her own. For seven years, she had been the country's most visible celebrity teen drug offender.

A month before our meeting, my agent told me Skye had written a journal that showed promise as a memoir. The writing needed work, but it contained graphic stories of her struggles to get clean and genuine insights into her emotional distress. Tom Lurie asked my agent if I'd consider working with Skye to improve the journal for publication. I called Skye and arranged to meet and read the journal draft before deciding if I could help her.

"Mind if we go inside to talk?" I asked. "It's pretty cold up here."

"In a minute," she said. "A guy in the house down there named Seth wants to steal some money from me, but he won't do it while I'm there. So I'm giving him some time."

"Who is he?"

"Drug dealer I knew in rehab."

When she finished the cigarette, she crushed it into the snow, and we walked down to the cottage. The living room had a careless, squalid quality. The floor was strewn with clothes, and the air smelled of rotten food. A TV blared a football game. On the coffee table was a spilt pile of green capsules, empty beer bottles, and a buck knife.

Seth lay on a sofa. His large dirty work boots were defiantly planted on the sofa cushion, all his energy focused on smoking a cigarette, as if it were a job.

Skye led me to the kitchen. She cleared dishes from the table and took two bottles of Corona from the refrigerator. "I read your book on Nick White," she said, handing me a beer. "Some of it was stupid, but I liked the part when the band was getting started."

"I didn't write it all," I said. "My job was to help Nick write it."

Skye ignored me and pushed a ring binder across the table. "This is my journal," she said. "In the last rehab, it was a condition for release."

The binder held lined pages with a small, tight cursive scrawl. "My dad thinks you could make it sound better, and people might want to read it," Skye said.

"What do you think?"

"Know who was on the cover of *People* more than anyone else for the past four years? It's like there's this fascination with why I'm so fucked up."

"Is this book going to tell them?"

She tipped the bottle back and drank. Some of the beer ran down her chin, and she wiped at it with her hand. "I don't know. I don't give a shit," she said.

I stared at her. He face was round like her father's, and her brown eyes looked like her famous mother's on a dozen record albums. But despite the boarding schools, tutors, and treatment centers, her tough, beaten air seemed a world removed from her wealthy, privileged parents.

That night in my hotel room I read the journal. It was a wild, undisciplined account of her feelings and memories, as well as exercises assigned by the center's counselors. There were childish poems and boring dream interpretations. But it also included behind-the-scenes tales of her family's strife, hair-raising accounts of drug adventures, and thoughtful reflections on growing up in the shadow of famous parents.

The following morning I returned to Skye's cottage. I agreed to work with her and arranged for my agent to work out the terms of a contract with Tom Lurie's advisor, Sawyer Stevenson.

We wrote the book over the following six months in the Nantucket cottage. I slept in the guest room, and we set up a desk for writing in the living room.

Skye's story began at age six, with a memory of her parents fighting. Addie had seen Tom whispering to a woman at a fundraiser and drove home without him. Skye awoke to find her mother in their bedroom cutting Lurie's trousers in half with a pair of scissors and carefully hanging them back in his closet.

When Skye was eight, her parents divorced. Huston declined custody of her daughter. Her album "Finding My Way" went double platinum, and she was booked on an eight-month tour. Congressman Lurie had been named to the Finance Subcommittee, which was holding hearings on the President's new budget.

Skye lived in the family estate in Connecticut with her older brother Bobby and a nanny. She ate macaroni and cheese seven nights a week and weighed 110 pounds by the age of ten. At The Lake School, her classmates called her "The Blob." She was not smart enough for the overachievers, not pretty enough for the party crowd.

She spent most of her time alone in her room, reading serialized fantasy novels and filling notebooks with line drawings of airborne dragons. Bobby taught her to use a bong, and the two of them got high every night. She missed classes. Letters arrived from the Office of Thomas Lurie, expressing disappointment. The family doctor prescribed Elavil.

In 1980, at age twelve, Skye was quietly asked to leave Lake after she was arrested for buying a nickel bag from an undercover cop.

In the middle of a floor fight for a new transportation bill, Tom Lurie asked his senior advisor, Sawyer Stevenson, to arrange Skye's release. Sawyer was a Harvard legend. He had done his doctoral thesis on Hamiltonian monetary policies, and in the 1950s and 1960s, he taught economics and achieved notoriety through books and articles on innovative tax and welfare reform. By the 1970s, Sawyer was a behind-the-scenes strategist for liberal Democratic causes. Lurie hired him to advise his staff on fiscal matters when he was appointed to the Finance Subcommittee.

Sawyer was not well suited to the task of handling an errant teenager. He was a dry stick of a man, married to a North Shore matron named

Cecelia (Ceal) Prescott, and childless. But Lurie trusted Stevenson's Brahmin sense of discretion.

Sawyer met Skye at a juvenile hall lockup outside Hartford and oversaw her release with a stubborn determination to ignore reality. He called her by her given first name, which the family never used. "Katherine," he said, "I've brought an automobile to take you home."

The following week Sawyer drove Skye up the Maine coast to a boarding school called Bainbridge. He left her in the dean's office with a volume of Epictetus, who had helped Sawyer get out of a funk as a teenager, and who was famous for writing, "Control thy passions lest they take vengeance on thee."

For Skye, the move brought two differences. She was even more unpopular than at Lake, and an ounce of marijuana cost twice as much.

In 1981, Addie Huston married the rock producer Steve Bishop in a well-publicized ceremony in Carmel, California. Skye was not invited. Her mother sent her a letter, suggesting they meet during a Boston concert date but without providing details.

That April Skye was arrested in Cambridge, Massachusetts, during a pot bust. This time the family was unable to prevent press coverage. Skye's photo appeared in papers with the headline, "Skye High." Her face was captured full-on, her hair matted, her mouth drooping open.

Skye was expelled from Bainbridge and admitted to a live-in teen drug treatment in New Jersey called Promise House. She was thirteen.

During the day she participated in mandatory group therapy sessions, and at night her roommate showed her how to cook heroin with water and citric acid in a bottle cap over a cigarette lighter and inject it—"skin-pop" it— under the skin of the forearm. Once she was caught, the treatment center added a month of detox to her treatment regime.

Sawyer next arranged for Skye to attend a boarding school in Vermont called Plainfield Farm. The students performed farm chores and were assigned horses to care for. In her fourth month, Skye stole a car and drove north, where she was arrested at the Canadian border.

In November 1982, Tom Lurie was re-elected for a second term, and Addie Huston released her album "Falling Star," with that famous line in the title track "my love is like a light dying across a dark night." That same month, in a treatment center called Fresh Start in Wilmington, North Carolina, Skye set fire to a dormitory bathroom when she passed out while smoking heroin.

Over the years, Skye sampled every drug she could find, and like many addicts, had a working knowledge of pharmacology. She snorted coke and swallowed pills. She took downers—orange and red Seconal, red and ivory Dalmane, Miltown, Librium, Luminal, Nembutal, and Quaaludes. Blue devils, red birds, purple hearts. Enough of them sank her in a kind of coma, where she watched her own limbs suspended in front of her in syrup. For a party, there was Benzedrine, rushing in her veins and making her talk for an hour in one long sentence. Day to day, she carried yellow tablets loose in her pockets, Dilaudid and Percodan, and chewed them in the back of classrooms. But her favorite was the greatest pain reliever of them all, named for the German word for hero.

At Promise House, her first heroin high flooded her with euphoria—and for an instant, she floated above her heavy, over-stuffed body. She forgot who she was and how much she hated herself. After her first experience of skin popping, fear of needles kept her from injecting. She bought the purest white powder and snorted it or smoked it mixed with marijuana. When she couldn't find it, she bought oxycodone that she crushed and snorted.

If taking heroin was an act of extreme carelessness, her method of ingesting it involved a cautious calculus. She bought $10 bags in inch-square glassine envelopes. She tasted the powder on her tongue. Then she poured a pinch into a joint that she smoked and waited to feel the high. She had heard stories of dope so strong that it made you pass out on the first line and choke to death on your vomit or that made your breathing so slow you suffocated. She did one line and then another.

In her book, Skye described heroin as a snake. Its sinister chemistry wrapped around her, in the embrace of the memory of that wonderful first high and the despair that she would never find it again.

She went down a dark hole. In 1983, Skye was arrested when police responded to a fight in an apartment on Avenue B in New York's East Village, and discovered Skye with a loaded .22 caliber target pistol. Evidence showed that Skye had fired two rounds. There was blood on the carpet and the hallway, but a victim was never found. Sawyer arrived the day after the shooting and arranged for Skye to be released.

· · ·

When Skye and I worked together, most of the creative work was done late at night, when Skye sat in the living room, talking for hours on end, with a dozen candles burning and her cigarette smoke filling the air.

She had difficulty speaking coherently. She started a sentence on one subject and ended on another. All the school she had missed was apparent in her ignorance of the basic facts of history and current events. Her speech was careless, elided, and filled with obscenities. She used the word "fuck" so often that I once threatened to title her biography "Skye Fucking Lurie."

Skye woke most days around noon. Her face was puffy and white. Her skin had the look of a heroin user's "borrowed flesh" that William Burroughs describes, and her cheeks often had a fresh angry blemish.

For an hour, she sat alone in the kitchen drinking black coffee, smoking cigarettes, and coughing. The pages that I had written that morning were waiting in a pile. When the coffee had restored her, she slowly read the new material and summoned me to the table by yelling across the cottage.

Her voice was a husky masculine rasp. She was impulsive, impatient for the work to be done. She hated my attempts to add literary style. Whenever she came to a metaphor or an allusion to a poem or song lyric, she said, "What's that mean?" and blew cigarette smoke out of the side of her mouth to show her disdain. "You've got to be the only person in the world," she said, "who could make my life boring."

In the late afternoons, we walked on the beach near Siasconset. She walked with a crooked gait, her left foot pointed inward, her right leg rolling with each step, as if climbing over something. At the project's start, I had wondered whether a girl so young would really have a life-story to tell, but once I spent time with her, I had to keep reminding myself that she was only nineteen. In her hyped-up world, she seemed to have aged five years for every year of her life.

. . .

In 1984, Skye was living at the Kimball School for Girls in Newton, Massachusetts. The school was convenient for Sawyer Stevenson. He visited twice a week before going home to dinner.

By this time, Sawyer's life was laden with irony. He was one of a handful of men in the country who could speak intelligently about federal debt structure, but his energies were absorbed in escorting Tom Lurie's girlfriends out the back doors of hotels and in finding new refuges for Lurie's daughter.

On November 14, 1984, Sawyer stopped at Kimball and found Skye unconscious in her room. She had taped together two double-sided razor blades and cut across the wrist of her left arm, slicing through the ulnar artery but missing the larger radial. She lost enough blood to pass out but not enough to kill her.

The problem had been a young man. Skye thought he loved her, when in fact he wanted her heroin. It wasn't his fault he kissed her—he probably kissed other girls. How could he know this girl would register his casual attention like one of those seismic meters capable of sensing minute tremors thousands of miles away?

That night Skye woke in a bed at the Brigham and Womens Hospital. Beside her in a chair sat Sawyer, blood stains smeared across his suit and white shirt. His thin, patrician face gave no clue to his feelings, but she thought she saw his hand tremble slightly as it reached across the bed to touch her arm.

"It may be best, Katherine," he said, "if you would stay with Ceal and me for a few months. We have a guest room that might do."

After that, she went to live in the Stevensons' Back Bay townhouse, twelve rooms of hardwood floors, Persian carpets, and French antiques. At the start, with no child-rearing experience, the couple was as gentle and confused with her as they might have been with a large, unattractive dog left on their doorstep.

Skye accommodated herself to her new home. In the mornings, she attended methadone treatments at a drop-in center on Tremont Street. On her way home, she visited a 7-Eleven and paid a kid from the drop-in center to buy her the largest soda and two six packs of Pabst. Outside she poured the soda in the gutter and emptied two cans of beer into the cup and carried home the rest of the six packs in a brown bag. At the Stevensons' townhouse, she drank beer all day out of the soda cup. By evening she smelled of stale alcohol, and her eyes turned watery. Her guardians regarded her warily. The first time she vomited at the dinner table, Ceal looked down the table and said, "Good heavens, is there a problem with the soft shell?"

Once in the early morning hours, Ceal found Skye on the floor of the upstairs bathroom, vomiting into the bowl. Her face was suffused and sweating. Unsure, Ceal knelt behind her on the bathroom tiles and put her hands on Skye's shoulders. "My dear sweet girl," she said.

The dignified woman with her precise manners could not have known much about how to care for someone in drug withdrawal. But Ceal's menopause kept her awake, and she sat with Skye for an hour or two in the darkest part of the morning. She told Skye about the North Shore house where she grew up and the long sunroom where she sat reading the stories of Morte d'Arthur.

In March 1985, Ceal was diagnosed with stage-III breast cancer. Sawyer consulted Boston's leading oncologist, who ordered a mastectomy and an aggressive course of chemotherapy. Skye stayed with Ceal in the hospital. At the summer's end, Ceal asked to be allowed to die at home, and she passed away quietly the first week of October. Three days later Skye was arrested in the South End for smoking heroin in a parked car.

. . .

One week a month, while I wrote Skye's book, I flew back to Los Angeles to see Jill. We lived together in my house in Pacific Palisades. It was an odd, contrived arrangement. There was never enough time to stock the refrigerator and then eat the food before it was time to leave again.

I was consumed with work. The Ken Styles biography had set a sales record for paperback sports biographies. Before I finished Skye's book, my agent had four new projects waiting. The *Atlantic Monthly* commissioned articles, and I was invited to speak at writers' conferences. I wrote all day, every day—on planes, in waiting rooms, and during meals.

There was no longer time for my fiction, and I gave it up. But I had Jill now, and her presence was a wonderful respite from work. Three days a week, when we were together, she awoke early and drove to Fullerton, where she taught morning classes and brought home treasures—take-out barbecue from Koreatown and homemade ice cream from the Farmers Market.

On Thursday and Saturday afternoons, she met for rehearsals in my living room with the other members of the Toyon String Quartet. Toyon, Jill explained, is a California native shrub with red berries, commonly called the California holly. Because it covers the Hollywood Hills, Hollywood may have taken its name from the plant. "We call ourselves Toyon," Jill said, "because we're in opposition to the Hollywood institutions." Toyon played the usual repertoire—Haydn, Mozart, and Beethoven—but they also played more experimental twentieth-century pieces, including Bartók and Shostakovich. Their specialty was the playing of a pop song transcribed for string quartet.

The quartet's founder was the second violinist, Simone Solomon, a tightly wound woman with a face flushed from year-round allergies. The cellist was Arthur Howe, a cheerful, heavyset man in his fifties. The most outspoken member was its latest addition, the first violinist. The group's former lead violinist had left to have a baby. Her replacement was a Suzuki-trained prodigy named Eric Takahashi whom Jill had met at

Fullerton. Tak, as he liked to be called, was tall and thin and openly gay. He wore a uniform of tight jeans and precisely ironed white oxford button-down shirts. According to Jill, his playing had added a new energy to Toyon and expanded the group's repertoire, and his style had shaken up the quartet's staid presence.

After Saturday rehearsals, Simone, Arthur, and Tak stayed for dinner with Jill and me. Invariably, though, Simone ate only the crudités, and Arthur hurried home to his wife, leaving behind Tak.

Tak liked to tease Jill about her relationship with me. "You can't divide your affection, my dear," he said. "There's no room for Charlie. Your true relationship is with Toyon. A quartet's essentially a four-way."

"What I have with Charlie is different from what I have with you," Jill assured Tak solemnly.

"Impossible, Jilly," he said. "Charlie's words. We're music. What was it Walter Pater said? 'All art constantly aspires toward the condition of music.'"

For Jill and me, the one-week-a-month schedule gave our relationship built-in intensity. On Saturday nights, after the Toyon members left, we raced to the bedroom to make love. Two sides of the room were glass, with a view of the eucalyptus tops in the canyon behind the house, and in the distance, a thin line of the ocean where at night we could see the lights on passing boats. Our bed was a raised platform, and sometimes when we opened the curtains and held each other in the dark, we seemed to be joined with the fog floating in the night sky.

Night by night, we lay together in that incautious, youthful love, where every gesture—the strength of her arms around me, and the gentleness of my own hand on hers—was charged with desire and the sweet equality of holding on and letting go. We were happy to be alone together, as if for a little while only the two of us existed, but there were also hints of the fragility of our acts, of the delicate supports that held us aloft, high above the trees, and the lightness of all the air below.

"Have you ever thought about why some people fall in love and stay in love all their lives?" Jill asked one night. She had climbed out of bed, wearing only her panties, and stood with her back to me, looking out the window.

"Sure," I said. "It's the subject of half of literature. It's one of those imponderable questions."

"What if it's simpler? What if there are different kinds of hearts? Suppose it's just about finding someone with a heart like yours?"

"What's that mean?"

Jill turned around to face me, and I could see she was crying. She held her arms across her bare chest to shield her nakedness. "I like it when you come back to LA," she said. "And we spend these nights together. But you and I are so different."

"Wait a minute," I said. "Are you serious?" I climbed out of bed to join her, but she held up her hand against my embrace.

"It's not your fault. It's not anyone's fault." She wiped at the tears with her fingers. "You're right, it's complicated. There're a thousand things that bring two people together and drive two others apart. But maybe it's really one thing. Maybe it's the way we look at the world, what lies in our hearts."

"And you think you and I are different?"

"Look at us, Charlie. I've got four jobs, which don't pay anything, so I can play an instrument I love. You're writing books you don't care about because it pays well."

"That's what we do, not who we are. Besides, just because we've taken different paths doesn't mean we can't love each other. I don't think being in love means being the same. I can love you for what you've chosen without choosing it myself."

She turned back to face the window. "But what if that's wrong?" she said. "What if it's about that part deep inside us that we take for granted but that's not the same for everyone? Then no matter what we did, it wouldn't work."

That summer we attended a wedding of one of Jill's Fullerton colleagues. At the reception we sat at a round table with two other couples. Once, when the others had left to dance, Jill said, "If I were doing this, I'd have more fruit and less cake."

"Always a difficult balance," I said.

"And I'd have the band play only sixties pop and early Beatles."

'No Motown?"

"Maybe some, but nothing past 1970."

"You've thought about this. How do you see the groom?"

Jill looked at me and laughed. "Kind of like you," she said.

"*Like* me?" I asked.

"Yeah, you know, Charlie Teller-ish."

"You know who would be good for the bride?" I said. "I met this girl one time. It was at MacArthur's Books, and she had a ponytail and couldn't stop talking."

Jill laughed again. "I remember her," she said.

"My eager fan."

"Yeah, the one with the long fingers."

"Is this what you want?" I asked.

"Yes," she said and then she laughed. "No, I don't know."

"That's okay," I said. "I'm used to tepid endorsement."

"It's just we've never been together for more than a few days at one time."

"Someday we'll have that," I said.

"But we haven't yet," Jill said. "That's the thing."

"So you want to see a film of us twenty years from now, after we've spent time together?"

"Can you do that for me? I want to see if we're in love. I know it's crazy. I guess sometimes you just have to jump."

"Oh, great," I said. "We'll have that printed on the programs. Jill Bennett and Charles Teller invite you to share in the joy of their marriage ceremony. I guess sometimes you just have to jump."

Jill laughed. "I love being with you," she said.

"That's good," I said. "I think ninety percent of a marriage is sharing space."

Jill leaned forward and kissed me. "How can I say no when you make it sound so romantic," she said.

We were married the following spring. The ceremony, with sixty guests, was held in a chapel, built like a Spanish mission, outside Santa Barbara. The wedding reception had large bowls of fruit, and a band played oldies. The other three members of Toyon played a Mozart trio.

Among the photographs taken that day is one of Jill and me, in the dark cloisters behind the chapel. We're holding hands, two fingers hooked together, and looking out at the camera. She's wearing an ivory satin empire gown, and there's a ring of baby's breath in her hair. I'm wearing a dark suit and a mauve-colored silk tie that became a running joke among the wedding party. The expression on our faces combines tiredness and wonderment at how well everything has gone. Years later, it was hard to see it and not think how impossibly young we appear. We look, a friend once remarked, like we think we're going to be happy.

. . .

After her last heroin bust, Skye was committed to a treatment center in Westchester, New York. She arrived in time for an experimental care regime. Once a day she was given one tablet of buprenorphine, an opiate that had been shown to support withdrawal better than methadone, and an opiate antagonist called naltrexone that was being used as part of new rapid detox programs. Along with the medications, the center's director conducted daily one-on-one psychotherapy sessions with Skye. When she was released, she emerged without heroin dependency for the first time in three years.

The book that Skye and I wrote together, *Next Horizon*, told the story of a frightened girl's battle with addiction. The cover had a copy of the newspaper headline from her 1981 drug bust, with a pile of heroin powder and scattered pills in the foreground.

Readers and critics praised the book for its broader themes on the drug culture and the failure of sixties youth to become responsible parents. The book was particularly embraced by a generation of unhappy young girls, who saw it as their story. A year after publication, it was adapted to a cable film, and middle schools made the book assigned reading.

The book remade Skye. It helped people see her as something more than her trouble. She received hundreds of fan letters, stuffed with homemade drawings and photographs of teenage girls.

Following the book's release, Skye stayed true to her own daily version of sobriety—a six pack of beer and 30 milligrams of Valium—just enough, she said, to keep the lid on.

For a few years, we stayed in touch in a way that only Skye would conceive. Whenever the telephone rang at three am, I knew who was calling. Picking up the phone, I heard that raspy whisper. "Hey Charlie," the voice said. "It's Skye. How're you doing?"

"Guess what, man," she said. "This company said they'd pay me to give inspirational speeches. Can you imagine me in front of people? How sick is that? Maybe you could write something for me to say, like you used to."

Her voice sounded far away, almost not strong enough to reach me from wherever she lived. Holding the phone, I thought of the view from an airliner window on a late-night flight, when somewhere in the middle of the country, you look below and see a single light alone on a dark landscape.

In those three am calls, Skye did not trust me to keep up my end of the conversation. She took the lead, talking for hours, on and on through the morning, her mind stringing together subjects, faltering here and there, pausing sometimes, but always just managing to fill the emptiness between us.

CHAPTER 2 6

ABOUT FIVE, I left my apartment to drive to Jill's house for dinner. A storm had been forecast, and rain was already falling steadily as I drove up the freeway. Chandler Way was quiet when I pulled on to Jill's street. I imagined Raymond Chandler's description: The rain filled the street like the dark tears of a fallen angel.

A Dodge Ram sat in front of Jill's house. Dave's truck. Jill greeted me at the door. She was smiling in a broad, silly way I hadn't seen in years. She kissed my cheek. "C'mon in, Charlie," she said. "We're doing a vertical tasting."

Dave stood leaning against the kitchen counter. He was a large man, with a tanned face, brush moustache, and broad shoulders. He wore a western-style shirt, dress trousers, and cowboy boots. In greeting, his hand was strong and rough.

"It's a pleasure to meet you," he said. "I've heard so much about you from . . . well, Lucy."

"Yes, our little communicator," I said. "Where is she by the way?"

"Upstairs arranging her piercings," Jill said, giggling. "She'll be down in a second. Let's have some wine. Dave, tell Charlie what you were telling me."

Dave turned to the three bottles. "I thought it'd be fun to do a vertical tasting. You know, different vintages of the same wine. These are three vintages of our premium reserve pinot noir: 1999, 2000, and 2002."

He sliced off the foil, turned in the corkscrew, and pulled out the cork. "Do you like wine, Charlie?" he asked.

"Sure," I said. "But as a former substance abuser, I pretty much like anything."

Jill looked at me. The smile was gone.

"Pinot noir is challenging to make," Dave said. "The grape is the Holy Grail for most winemakers. Get it right, and you have ambrosia in your mouth. Get it wrong, and it tastes like rotten vegetables."

Dave poured three glasses of the 1999 vintage and began telling us about the weather that year and the vineyard lot. I watched Jill. She held her glass the way Dave had instructed and smelled across the top of the glass. She sipped some of the wine and smiled.

They've made love, I thought. Is that what all men think when they see their ex-wives with another man? I'd been unfaithful to Jill on one occasion during our marriage, and it had undermined our relationship. Had Jill wanted me to meet Dave as payback? I doubted it. Jill wasn't as petty as my own imagination.

I tipped my glass back, drank the wine in one gulp, and reached for the bottle to pour myself more. Before Dave could continue his lecture on the 2000 vintage, Lucy came down the stairs. She wore a top cut above her midriff, a miniskirt, and sandals. She hugged me and said hello to Dave.

"We're testing the boundaries this week," Jill said.

"I wish two of the boundaries were about five inches longer," I said.

Lucy ignored the comments. "Can I have some wine?" she asked.

"No," Jill said. "Have some juice."

Lucy slouched against the kitchen counter. She suddenly looked years older.

Dave opened the 2000 vintage and poured wine into our glasses.

"Do you want to tell daddy your big news?" Jill asked Lucy.

Lucy shrugged. "I got detention. For a week."

"What for?" I asked.

"Ditching."

"Ditching?"

"Yeah, me and Sage ditched a class and went to the mall. I don't see why it's such a big deal."

"It *is* a big deal. Your father and I'll talk about it later."

We moved to the dining room where place settings were already laid out around the table. Jill had made lamb, and she handed a knife to Dave and asked him to carve. They stood next to each other, grinning in that goofy new love way while my usurper cut perfect slices of the family roast.

"Dave read your baseball book," Jill said.

"Yeah," Dave said. "I don't read much, but I liked that one."

"Wasn't easy to write," I said. "Ken wasn't used to talking."

"Well, I thought you did a nice job of showing how one thing led to another, how things came apart for him."

"Speaking of one thing leading to another," I said. "Let's try a glass of that 2002 vintage."

Jill frowned at me. "Don't forget you're driving home," she said.

"Sure," I said. "Plenty of time."

"This is what she's like now," Lucy said, looking at her mother.

Dave poured the 2002 vintage in our glasses. "Can you taste the difference between this and the ninety-nine?" he asked.

"Absolutely," I said. "This is youthful by comparison. What's the word? Pubescent. Jejune."

Lucy giggled. I hated myself now.

Jill put down her glass and glared at me. "You two have something in common," she said. "You both know Rajiv Patel."

"I've managed vineyards for Rajiv's companies for years," Dave said. "Suncrest Vineyard in Forestville and his London Ranch Vineyard in Glen Ellen. Jill tells me you're helping him write his autobiography. I'll bet you're getting some good stories."

"Yeah, great stories," I said.

"Charlie doesn't like to talk about his books while he's writing, do you Charlie?" Jill said.

"Contractually I'm not supposed to."

"Did Rajiv invite you to his bud break party next week?" Dave asked. "It's always a huge deal. You'd get a real good picture of who Rajiv is in this community if you go."

"Yeah, I've been invited," I said. "I take it I'll see you there?"

"Actually both of us," Dave said. "Jill's coming as my guest, aren't you?"

"It sounds like fun," Jill said, smiling at him.

"Oh, boy, fun," I said.

·   ·   ·

It was after eleven when I left Jill's house and headed home. The storm had intensified. Heavy rain was falling and flooding the low-lying areas of the highways, and a gusty wind blew the rain against my car.

Reaching home, I dashed headlong from the car up the stairs and was already on the landing when I saw a shadow near the railing. The shadow rose toward me. I stood frozen for a moment, staring at the dark figure. Then a voice said, "Charlie, help me." I switched on the landing light, and in front of me stood Page.

Before I could say anything, she threw herself on me and held me. She laid her head on my shoulder, and I could feel her body shuddering as she cried. I held her and lay my hands across her back. We stood together for a few minutes, the rain pouring down on us. When I felt her crying subside, I opened the door and led her inside.

In the entranceway, she wouldn't let go of my arms and gripped my jacket with both hands. "It's Ray," she said. "He's dead."

"Ray Brenner?"

"Yeah, Ray. He's dead. It was awful. I'm . . . scared."

I held her in front of me to see her face, but she looked down at the floor. She was soaked through. Her long hair fell across her face and down her shoulders. Her jacket and jeans were dark and dripping. She began to shake again.

"What do you mean?" I asked. "How do you know he's dead?"

"He's on the sofa in my apartment," she said. "Someone shot him. There was all this blood." For the first time she looked at me. Her face was white.

"How did it happen?" I asked.

"I don't know. I came home and there he was. Sitting there."

"And no one else was there?"

"I don't think so. I just left. The place was torn apart."

"And you came straight here? Where's your car?"

"Behind the Mexican restaurant on the highway. I walked up."

I held her hands where they gripped my jacket. They felt like ice. "You need to get warm," I said.

"Wait," she said and went back outside. A minute later she reappeared carrying a plastic bag. She laid it on the counter and took out a laptop. "This is what they wanted," she said. "I had it in my car."

I held up my hand to stop her from speaking and led her to the bathroom. I ran hot water in the tub, laid a couple towels on the sink, and hung a terrycloth bathrobe on the hook behind the door. "Get warm," I said, "Then we'll talk."

In the kitchen I heated water for tea. I locked the door and switched off the landing light. I changed out of my wet clothes and put on a pair of khakis and a flannel shirt. As I finished, Page emerged from the bathroom. She wore my bathrobe, with a towel around her neck. Her hair was combed neatly back, and color had returned to her face. I pointed her to the sofa and gave her a cup of tea. I sat on a chair facing her. For a few minutes we both sat in silence, holding our cups of tea.

Finally I said, "We need to call the police."

"OK," she said.

"And tell them everything you know."

"Yeah sure."

She looked across the room at me. Her eyes filled with tears. "Paul told me if anything happened, you'd take care of it," she said.

"I don't know what I can do."

"Just come here for a second."

I set my teacup on the coffee table, sat next to her, and laid my arm around her shoulders. She leaned into me and rested her head on my chest. I'd like to say that warning bells went off in my brain, and I thought of the trouble that would come of this. But I didn't. Instead I sat there, smelling her hair and feeling the rhythm of her breathing and was lost.

CHAPTER 27

I GAVE PAGE a shirt and jeans to wear until her clothes dried, and we sat facing each other again.

"In ten minutes we're going to call Eddie Mahler," I said. "But first I need to understand some things. Let's start with Ray Brenner."

"Ray's been working for me since Paul was killed," she said. "I wanted someone strong around me. I was scared."

"Of what?"

"Whoever killed Paul. Someone's been following me. At first I thought it was you."

"So you had Brenner hire those kids?"

"They were just supposed to frighten you. I'm sorry you got hurt."

"You said at first you thought it was me following you. Did you see someone else?"

"Once at the club, and Ray saw somebody in a car outside my apartment."

"Do you know who it was?"

"Some guy."

"What did Ray want on Saturday in the parking lot of the club?"

"More money. Daryl and Mitch wanted him to buy them a new car. And he felt like he should be getting paid more for protecting me."

"What about Paul's laptop? Why're you hiding it?"

"I don't know. Paul told me to keep it. After Mahler came to my place looking for it, I put it in my car. Whoever killed Ray tore the place apart but didn't take anything."

"Paul didn't tell you what's on the laptop?"

"No. He just gave it to me before he was killed."

I checked my watch. "OK," I said. "You're going to call Mahler now. You're going to tell the truth about Ray and where you are. Tell him we'll come down to the police station."

I handed her a phone. "When you're finished, I'll call Molly Fryor. She's a lawyer. I'll ask her to meet us there."

Page began dialing. "One more thing," I said. "Let's leave the laptop out of this for the time being."

. . .

When we arrived at the police station, we were escorted to Mahler's office on the second floor. It was a large room with a desk and a conference table. Seated at the table were Mahler, Molly, and a young public defender named Ken Chan, who had been invited by Molly to represent Page.

Mahler said the conversation would be recorded and that Page's statement would become evidence in the murder investigation.

"We have a team at your apartment, and they've found Brenner," Mahler said. "So let's start there. What do you know about what happened?"

"I got home around nine-thirty. The front door was partway open. I saw Ray on the sofa."

"Did you go into your apartment?"

"No. I took off."

"Do you know if anyone was inside?"

"No."

"Where did you go?" Mahler asked. He was leaning forward, with both arms on the table in front of him.

"Nowhere. At first I just drove," Page said.

"You didn't call the police?"

"No. I freaked out."

"So you drove around?"

"I went to Charlie's place."

"Why?"

"I thought it'd be safe."

"What time was this?"

"I don't know."

Mahler looked at me. "I got home about eleven-thirty," I said. "She was waiting on the landing outside my door."

Mahler turned back to Page. "What did you do at Mr. Teller's house? Your call was logged here just after twelve-thirty."

"We talked. Charlie let me take a bath to get warm."

"Are these the clothes you were wearing tonight?"

"No. I borrowed these from Charlie."

"We'll need to see your clothes."

Page nodded.

"Why was Ray Brenner in your apartment?" Mahler asked.

"He probably came to ask for money. After Paul was killed, I hired Ray to look after me. I paid him, but he wanted more."

"Did he have a key to your apartment?"

"No. When I got home tonight, the door was broken."

"Why was Brenner working for you?"

"I thought someone was watching me."

"Who?"

Page looked at me. "I don't know. On Thursday I saw a guy in the hallway outside my class. He was just standing there. He had a tattoo of a face on his neck."

"You didn't mention this on Thursday night."

"I wasn't sure it meant anything. Then on Friday night Ray found a guy parked across the street from my apartment."

"The same guy?"

"Ray couldn't see the driver. The car was an old BMW. That's all I know."

"And why would someone be watching you?"

"I don't know. I thought it was the same person who killed Paul."

Mahler sat back in his chair. "All right," he said. "Let's talk about that. The last time we spoke, you said Paul wasn't selling coke. You still believe that?"

Page took a deep breath and let it out. "Paul sold coke for Kenny McDonald. For about a year and a half. It wasn't a big deal. A few thousand bucks a month. He sold to clients when he catered parties."

"So, earlier, when you said he wasn't selling, you were lying?"

"Is that necessary, detective?" Chan asked.

"It's not like he was selling street drugs," Page said. "These people could afford it. It was a convenience."

"Part of the menu," Mahler said.

"Hey, come on, Mahler," Chan said. "Give us a break."

Page ignored the comment. "About two months ago, something happened, and Paul stopped selling."

"What happened?" Mahler asked.

"I don't know. Maybe one of his regulars got sick, and he freaked. I don't know. He was working on something every night in his office."

"Did you ask him?"

"Yeah. He said he'd tell me when he was finished."

"But he didn't tell you?"

"No. But he started to act differently, saying unusual things. He said people weren't always who you thought they were."

"What do you think he meant?"

"I don't know."

"What did he tell you about the postponement of your wedding?"

"He said we'd have to wait. He said he knew you guys were watching him, that he was going to talk to a lawyer and try to make a deal."

"When Barkley was working on his computer, did he work at the restaurant, the club, or somewhere else?"

"At Galileo's. That's where he had all his records and his computer."

"What about his laptop? Did he ever use that?"

"Sure. Sometimes. And no, I don't know where it is."

Mahler stared at Page. "Has it occurred to you that someone besides me may be looking for that laptop and that you could be putting yourself at risk if you know anything about it?"

"I think she answered your question," Chan said.

Mahler's cell phone rang. He listened for a minute and hung up. "They found a shell casing the killer missed. The weapon used to kill Brenner was a Heckler and Koch 45-caliber Mark 23," he said. "Fired at close range. Someone wasn't taking any chances on missing." He looked at Page. "You have a gun, Ms Salinger?"

"You don't have to answer that," Chan said.

"I don't have a gun," Page said. "I didn't kill Ray Brenner."

"The killer also left a partial footprint and some dirt in the carpet near the body," Mahler said. "Someone wasn't as careful as they thought they were."

Chan turned to Mahler. "Are you finished, detective?" he asked. "I think we're all pretty tired."

Mahler switched off the tape recorder. Page asked if she could return to her apartment to pick up some clothes, and Mahler told her the crime scene unit would be finished by noon.

In the hallway, Molly pulled me aside. "Eddie found the guest lists on Paul's computer," she said. "He's going to show them to Stephen to identify the names that Paul added."

Then she added, "You need to find Page a place to stay. In the morning the press is going to be looking for her, and you don't want them coming to your apartment." She recommended a motel in Santa Rosa.

I caught up with Page in the lobby. She faced me and tried to smile. "All this part of what you owed Paul?" she asked.

CHAPTER 28

I FOUND THE motel Molly had recommended. It was a two-story building a block from the freeway. Page took a room in the front, on the ground floor.

Inside the room, Page turned to me. "Would you mind just staying here until the morning?"

I looked at her. She had washed off her makeup in the shower. Her face showed the lines of age and the stress of the past eight hours. Seeing me look at her, she pulled her hair away from her face, defying me to judge her.

"OK," I said.

Page turned away from me, took off the jeans I had loaned her, and still wearing my shirt, climbed into the king bed furthest from the door. I took the other bed and fell asleep in a few minutes.

When I awoke in the daylight, she was sitting cross-legged on the other bed, fully dressed. There was a tray of food in front of her, and she was holding a paper cup of coffee.

"They're serving breakfast in the lobby," she said. "Want something?" She handed me a cup of black coffee.

We sat for a few minutes in the quiet of the room, drinking coffee and eating pastries. Neither of us said anything. With the bright sun pouring through the curtains of the motel room, the events of the night before seemed unreal, like someone else's drama.

My cell phone rang, and it was Nico. She said Vincent had figured out something about the spreadsheet on the memory stick. They both had Mondays off and were on their way to a hot springs in Calistoga. She asked if they could come by my house on their way later that morning. I agreed.

I told her about Ray Brenner's murder. When I finished, there was silence on the other end of the line. Before Nico could speak, I said that I was with Page, that we had stayed in a motel, and that I would meet Vincent and her at my house in an hour.

I could hear Nico take a long breath. In a quiet voice, she said, "Hey, be careful, Charlie." I didn't know if she was referring to Brenner's killing or my being with Page.

I told Page I would drive her to the Mexican restaurant near my house so she could pick up her car. As she had agreed with Mahler, she would take the clothes she had worn the night before to the police station, and he would arrange for a police officer to escort her to her apartment to get what she needed.

On the drive, I tried several times to ask Page how she was feeling. She replied in one word answers, with an impatient tone, and looked out the window. She had turned tough again, and was eager to be away from me. I was starting to get used to these pendulum swings between hard-edged anger and the tender vulnerability.

* * *

I left Page beside her car at the Mexican restaurant and drove to my house. Nico and Vincent were waiting for me on the stair landing. Nico bounded down the steps and hugged me. "We're going to scare the tourists in Calistoga," she announced. "Want to come with us?"

"Love to," I said. "But I have to work."

Vincent nodded his head at me. "Mahler have any idea about Brenner?" he asked.

"All he would say was that it was a .45 caliber, unlike the gun used to kill Paul, and that the killer wasn't screwing around."

When Page drove up in her car, the three of them engaged in a series of uneasy greetings, and we all went inside. Page headed for the bathroom to get her clothes. Vincent sat in front of my computer, inserted the memory stick, and downloaded the file. He pointed to the column headings across the top of the spreadsheet. "See these units in each column?" he asked. "They're measurements. I saw one of these once when I was working construction in the summers as a kid. It's a civil engineering summary for a construction job. These columns are measurements for sidewalks, gutters, electric and gas lines."

He pointed to the cells across the left side the spreadsheet. "These are names of parts of the development. At first I thought they were streets, but I found out they're parts of a housing tract. I went to a government website where they list new building permits and plugged in these names. This is a building site near Sacramento."

Nico looked at me. "Cool, huh?"

"OK. I'm impressed you worked it out," I said. "But so what?"

"I don't know," Vincent said. "But Barkley must have seen something here, and he wanted to talk to you and Howard Miller about it."

"Why me?"

"The developer of the site is Rajiv Patel."

For a moment the three of us stared at each other. "All right," I said, "but this must be one of dozens of Patel's projects. Did Paul think I knew something about this spreadsheet because I'm doing the book?"

"Who knows," Vincent said. "What we know is Barkley wanted to talk to you and a lawyer who specializes in drug cases, and he gave you a copy of this. It must mean something."

"Maybe he didn't want to *ask* you about it," Nico said. "Maybe he wanted to *tell* you about it."

I looked back at the columns of numbers on the screen.

"You know what drives me crazy?" Nico said. "The way you men do everything. It's always indirect. If this had been a woman, she'd have walked up to you and said what she had to say—without all this mystery."

"I think Paul was trying to do that before he was killed," I said.

"I know, but he didn't, did he? Paul was a great guy. But he could never just tell me something. He always said one thing when he meant another. It was like way subtle. It was like interpreting smoke signals or something."

"Maybe you intimidated him."

"Me? What're you kidding? No, with you guys, it's about homophobia, fear of expressing yourselves because you're afraid someone will think you're gay."

"I'm a writer," I said. "I express myself for a living."

"But you express someone else's feelings, not your own. Look at the difference in the way we dress. Vincent, I love you sweetheart, but you dress like a stalker. And Charlie, you look like a lawyer on his day off. Both of you are shut down. Now look at me."

Vincent and I turned from the screen to face her. She was wearing a cut-off T-shirt, mini-skirt, athletic knee-socks, and red high-tops. "This is a woman's unafraid expression."

"Well, this is me dressed to interview an elderly woman in Oakmont this afternoon," I said.

Page came out of the bathroom and stood with us looking at the screen. "There's more of that stuff on Paul's laptop," she said. She picked up the laptop off the kitchen counter and handed it to Vincent.

Vincent looked at me. "Mahler know you have this?" he asked.

"No," I said. "We wanted to look at it before we gave it to him."

"Oh, that's OK then," Vincent said with a smile. "Haven't lost your touch for digging yourself into a hole."

Vincent opened the laptop, and Page typed in a passcode. Together they scanned the folders. Most were files for the club or the fitness center. Vincent opened several folders that turned out to be correspondence and personal accounts. Then he opened a folder called Sutter. It contained dozens of spreadsheets like the one on the memory stick.

"That's it," Page said. "These are the things I saw Paul working on."

Vincent opened up several files and scrolled across them. He pointed to the top left corner of the screen. "They all have the word 'Sutter' on this line," he said. He closed the file and switched off the computer.

"You shouldn't keep the computer here," Nico said, looking first at Page and then me.

"You think we should give it to Mahler?" I asked.

"I'm not giving it to him," Page said.

"Only a matter of time before someone comes to you to find it," Vincent said to Page.

"So what," Page said.

"Let us have it," Nico said. "No one knows us."

I watched Vincent's face for a reaction, but nothing changed in his expression.

"Someone should look through these spreadsheets and see what Barkley was looking at," Vincent said.

"You don't have to do this," I said.

Vincent stared at me. "I know what I don't have to do," he said.

CHAPTER 2 9

THAT AFTERNOON I drove across the valley to Oakmont Village for my meeting with Anita Kleinman. The development was built around a golf course, and the broad, gently curving streets were lined with custom homes and manicured lawns. It was quiet—the only sound in the mid-afternoon came from softly hissing lawn sprinklers. Kleinman's house lay at the end of a wide cul-de-sac.

Anita Kleinman was a slight woman in her seventies. Her hair was thinning and white with a touch of pink, and was swept back from her face in unbroken waves. She wore a full-length Chinese silk gown covered with bright gold dragons on a blue background. Her fingers were tipped with long red nails and heavy with gold rings. She held out her arms in an expression of welcome and perhaps to show me the full extent of her dragons.

"Charles Teller," she exclaimed in a high voice. "Come in. Come in."

The house's interior had a busy, cluttered look. The living room was filled with pastel furniture, and the walls were crowded with paintings, needlepoint, and photographs. We sat side by side on a long flowered sofa. On the coffee table beside us were a china tea set and piles of books.

She smiled at me and slowly shook her head. "Now that you're here, I can scarcely believe it," she said. "Oh, my. You'll have to excuse my incoherence. It's just that for so long you've been my absolute guide. And now you sit beside me." Her head was tilted to one side, and she spoke in an overly articulated way, as if she were performing in a drama.

"Yes, I understand from our phone conversation you're familiar with my books," I said.

"Familiar?" she said dismissively. "I'm an *aficionada*."

Looking at the books on the table, I recognized my own titles, neatly stacked together. On top sat the Virginia Hardy book.

Kleinman noticed where my attention had strayed. "My book club has read several of your books recently," she said. "My friends say, Anita, he sounds just like you. Can you imagine? Instead of the other way around."

I smiled. "I hope," I said, "you haven't also adopted my excesses."

She laughed as she handed me a cup of tea. She gestured toward the other books on the table. "I don't expect you've read any of my works," she said. "Celebrities of a distinctly more minor order—local figures. Politicians, wealthy ranchers, car dealers. Sometimes a combination of all three!" She rolled her eyes at the uncontrollable nature of celebrity stature. "Whoever can pay the tab."

I felt suddenly dizzy at the stark mimicking of my own life. I tried to change the subject. "As I mentioned on the phone," I said. "I'd like to talk to you about your book on Rajiv Patel."

"I wish it were otherwise. I've not had many failures. But that was undoubtedly one of them. An unpleasant episode."

"Tell me about Mrs. Patel. I haven't been able to find much information on her, except your manuscript."

"It's not surprising. Safia was abandoned by those who were supposed to care for her."

"I thought she was well cared for in her illness?"

"That's not what I meant. I meant earlier. Safia was from a traditional Gujarati family. She was a very inexperienced woman. Patel kept her hidden. She bore him children, but she was not a wife in any other sense."

"She told you this?"

"She didn't have to. It was clear from the way she lived. She had her own quarters. She ate alone. She didn't even know how to drive a car."

"What did she talk about when you interviewed her?"

"Her flowers. She kept a garden in the courtyard. Her children—she loved them. And God, she spoke about God a good deal. She was a simple woman, a child really. By the time I met her, she was dying, and she knew it."

"Why do you think Patel would not want me to include her in his own autobiography? He didn't even want me to ask any questions."

Kleinman put down her teacup. "As I say, he was uninterested in her. She was less important than many of the staff."

"What was that part of your manuscript where Safia described her husband and the devil?"

Kleinman narrowed her eyes. "That was probably what got me fired," she said. "Safia told me Rajiv had other women. She said they were whores, and he let her see them to show his lack of respect for her. This had been a long practice, and it no longer bothered her. She said God would punish him. But what frightened her, she said, was he carried the devil with him."

"Did she say what she meant by that?"

"Not really. She told me this after the nurse had left the room. But she said it several times. She said her husband had the devil, and it was killing people. She was a very traditional woman, and she spoke in a simple way."

"What did you think she meant?"

Kleinman raised her eyebrows. "Do you know what I thought? I really don't know why. It's such a silly idea. I thought it was drugs."

*   *   *

When I returned home about five, Page's car was parked beside the stairs to my house. I found her behind the kitchen counter, cooking at the stove. "You like fajitas?" she asked. "One of my specialties."

She held a piece of grilled steak to my mouth to taste. While I ate it, she turned back to the stove.

"It feels great to have my own clothes again," she said. "Mahler had one of his officers take me to my apartment and let me pick up some clothes."

She was wearing a white linen blouse and a short tan skirt. Her hair was pulled back in a ponytail. "You want a beer?" she asked.

She took a bottle from the refrigerator, opened it, and handed it to me.

"What're you doing here?" I asked.

"I was hungry," she said. "There's no place to cook at the motel. You don't mind, do you?"

"I wish you'd asked. I'm not sure this is the best thing right now."

Without speaking, she sliced a pepper and gathered the pieces in a pile. Then she looked up and said, "I've been scared for a week. Last night a guy was shot to death in my apartment, and if I'd been there, I'd be dead, too. I don't always know what the best thing is, do you?"

She put down the knife, wiped her hands on a towel, and came from behind the counter. She reached toward me with her left hand and held my shoulder. Then she leaned forward and kissed me slowly. When she finished, she left her hand on my shoulder. She smiled. "Don't make a judgment, Charlie," she said. "And, for once in your life, try not to say anything."

CHAPTER **30**

Tina Terrill

SOMETIMES, HOWEVER MUCH you plan, however many precautions you take, something happens, and in a minute the world is changed. After that, you're the person on the other side of that minute.

For Tina Terrill, the world changed at the 1984 Winter Olympic finals of the 500-meter long track speed skating. She was an odds-on favorite to win the event. Her time trials were five-tenths of a second ahead of the nearest rival—a large margin in the 500 meters.

But in the straightaway on the last 30 meters, for no apparent reason, her left skate turned too sharply and hit her right boot, and she fell, sliding across the ice, just ahead of the skater from China, into the barrier on the far side. There was no reason for the fall. Even the experts were at a loss to explain it.

She sat, legs crumpled, head bowed. The image would be shown on television for years to come. From then on, when you thought of Tina Terrill, you thought of that picture.

Following the Olympics, Tina declined interviews and disappeared. There were rumors she was being treated for depression, that she quit the sport. She resurfaced at the 1986 Nationals in Lake Placid and won. She trained for the 1988 Olympics in Calgary, where she dominated the spotlight again, but failed to win a gold medal. Still, there was something in her explosive, no-holds-barred style of skating that made crowds unable to take their eyes off her.

In 1990, during one of the weeks when I was on the West Coast, my agent Barry Carpenter invited me to meet Tina at her agent's office in Los Angeles. Tina was training for the 1992 Games, and there was talk she wanted to bring out a life story.

The agent's office was in a downtown glass tower. Tina sat at one end of a long table. She was thin and muscular, with the look of a twelve-year-old boy. She had short, bleached hair, combed straight back, and wore blue-tinted sunglasses. She nodded in greeting and sat staring out the window.

Her agent was Nancy Alden, a former professional tennis player. "I expect you're familiar with my client's story," she said.

"Sure," I said. "It's a good story."

"But we have an issue. Tina believes only someone with an athletic background can understand what makes her tick. I showed her your book, Charlie, on Ken Styles, which by the way, is a marvelous portrait of a professional baseball player from the inside out. But Tina's . . . not sure. She doesn't want to have to explain everything."

"We understand," Barry said. "It's a relationship, isn't it?"

I looked at Tina. She was still staring out the window.

"Well, as it turns out, there aren't any athlete slash autobiographers," Alden said, amused at herself. "So, as a compromise, we're bringing in talented writers, such as you, and asking them to make an offer, to . . ."

"Compete?" I said.

"Exactly."

Barry turned to me. "This is what's happening to the market," he said, as if he had seen this before. Turning to Alden, he said, "Who're we up against?"

"I suppose there's no harm in telling you," she said. "One is Arthur Salter."

"Artie, the footnote king," I said. "You'll get the biggest book ever written about a skater."

"Patricia Reynolds."

"Looks good on a press tour. Make sure you have someone to do the rewrite."

"Joe Gillis," Alden said, her voice less certain.

"Try to get a case discount on the vodka."

"David Sonnenshein," Alden said, making her last stand. "He co-wrote the autobiography of the actor Nessa Hamilton that won the National Book Award."

"That was 20 years ago. He must be 75."

Barry shifted uncomfortably in his seat.

Alden smiled at me. "Maybe you'd like to tell us how you'd approach the book," she said.

"I'm flattered you'd consider me," I said, pushing out my chair and standing up. "I'm not interested."

Barry held my arm. "What Charlie means," he said, "is that he wants to understand the terms of the competition."

For the first time Tina looked at me. "Why aren't you interested?" she asked. She tried to say this as a challenge but ran out of breath on the last word.

"I don't compete," I said. "I write books, and I'm good at it. Competing is your job, not mine. And if you don't want to explain what you do, you don't really want to tell your story."

Her blue sunglasses faced me. "If you did write the book, where would you start?" she asked. I couldn't see her eyes, but I saw her hands on the tabletop, the fingers interlocked, squeezed white.

"The fall," I said.

"Everyone's already read that."

"Not *your* version. Describe it in detail, what you saw, felt. The smell of the ice. Everything minute by minute, the way no one has read it before."

"Why?"

"You start with what the readers *think* they know, but you make it new. It's not like they expected. After that, you own the perspective. Besides, if you make it the beginning, it isn't the end."

The sunglasses continued to regard me. "You skate?" she asked.

"I hate being cold," I said.

Tina looked at Alden. "This is going to be fun," she said. Then she turned back to me and said, "By the way, ice doesn't smell like anything."

"There you go," I said.

"There I go what?" Tina asked.

"Your first sentence," I said. "There's your first sentence."

For a moment she stared at me without expression. Then she smiled a reluctant smile, and her fingers slightly unclenched. "All right," she said. "Let's try it."

. . .

She lived in Farmington Hills, Michigan, outside Detroit. Her father had bought her a two-story house on ten acres. Behind the house, in a corrugated steel half-shell, he built a full-size training rink, which the family called The Barn. Inside was a regulation oval track, 400 meters around. The interior temperature year-round was 28 degrees Fahrenheit. At one end were an exercise and weight room, a kitchen, and two rows of bleacher seating. Tina was the only person who ever skated on the track.

At the time of our book, Tina was twenty-two years old and in the best physical condition of her career. It was also obvious—although no one mentioned it—she was scared.

I lived in the guest bedroom and worked in an office down the hall. I adapted my schedule to Tina's training regimen. Her training was six days on, one day off. For the "on" days, Tina's coach, a former U.S. Olympic skater named Andy Waller, arrived at eight. They worked in the fitness room for a couple hours, or if it was warm enough, ran on an outdoor track. After lunch they skated and worked on technique. In the late afternoon, Tina read my drafts. In the evening, we conducted interviews.

On occasion, her boyfriend—a short track skater named Steve Pietronski—drove up from Chicago. Pietronski was a lifelong athlete like Tina. He averaged about 25 words per day, most of them related to the big screen television. Whenever he entered the room, he embraced Tina in a headlock and called her Tino.

For much of the time, though, after Waller had left, Tina and I were alone. She liked to cook, and we ate meals together. She knew what she wanted in her book, but she never let down her guard.

She had been born the youngest of four children. Her father, a college basketball star, encouraged his children's athletic interests. When Tina was three, an older sister taught her to skate. From the start, Tina wanted to get into races. Figure skating, she said, was a judgmental sport, where you were graded on your looks.

At six, she competed in and won midget-class races. At ten, her parents took her to regional competitions in Wisconsin and New York. At twelve, she had a national reputation in the racing community, and ranked in the top five of young girl skaters. But midway in her twelfth year, she came in third in a national final. Without telling her parents, she fired her own coach and hired a tough Minnesota skater named Betty Geist, who drilled her in a new lean, efficient glide technique. After that, for the next four years, Tina never lost a race.

In the year leading up to the 1984 Olympics, with each of the qualifying competitions, Tina seemed to grow stronger and to distance herself from the other competitors. She had a reputation for fierceness and drive. She wanted not just to win but to break records.

· · ·

Everything in long-track speed skating is sacrificed to one thing: speed.

The skates have sharp, 18-inch blades. The track ice is kept colder than figure skating rinks. Competitors wear suits known as "skins" so their bodies form drag-free profiles. When everything is working as it should, it is not uncommon for the best skaters to hit speeds of 35 miles per hour.

Skaters compete in pairs, but they're really racing against time. At the highest level, it is difficult to detect the winner by sight, and winning times are determined by electronic devices. In one Olympic competition, the winning skater won by the length of a skate blade. In another, the difference between first and second place was two-hundredths of a second—ten times faster than the blink of an eye.

Tina had looked forward to the Olympics from the time she was ten. For the 1984 Olympics, she trained for four years and competed in a dozen major qualifying races in cities around the world. The race itself was over in 39 seconds.

She sacrificed everything for speed skating—a normal childhood, neighborhood friends, schooling, a career. She pared it all away. Her training even shaped her body and her gender identity. She had small breasts and did not menstruate.

If she had a love, it was not Steve Pietronski but an enthrallment with that part of her life where all that mattered was going fast. In the evenings, she took me for rides on country roads in her Camaro, a bright yellow car with black racing stripes across the hood. She sat low in the seat, her eyes squinting in the sun, locked in a reverie as the car rocketed down the middle crown of the narrow road, always threatening but never quite sliding out of control.

• • •

When Tina stood on the 500-meter starting line at the 1984 Games, she was not thinking about falling. Speed skaters rarely fell. It was possible and spectacular when it occurred. But at that level of competition, skaters had ten years of training and technique behind them. Tina herself had never fallen in a major competition. Her quick, efficient style was designed to keep her center of gravity forward to prevent a spill.

She was thinking about the French skater Jean Meille, who had done better than expected. She was thinking about the strategy she and Andy had planned. Then she told herself not to think. She blocked out the crowd. She took a deep breath and felt the strength of her lungs.

Her break on the starting line was an explosion. Her legs dove at the ice, her arms pumped back and forth with each stride. In a dozen strides, she was ahead of the other skater, already out of her vision, and she was moving down the track. It was wonderful to be there at last. After all the preparation, traveling, and press conferences, she was on ice—at home. Each of her strides was just as she and Andy had planned. Ahead she could see the finish. Skate through it, not to it, said the voice in her head, a remnant of the coach she had had when she was twelve.

Then, as if in a dream, she felt her left leg and then her right fold under her and her hip hit the ice and she was sliding, it seemed forever, until she hit the soft barrier. She could get up, she thought, it wasn't too late. But a weight, as if the air itself were suddenly heavy, held her down.

Her head filled with a hollow roar. She could feel herself take a breath, but she couldn't hear it. The voices in the crowd, the announcements from the race officials were muffled. She stood and slowly skated across the track, uncertain of her feet. She saw Andy and skated toward him. He said something she couldn't hear.

The roar continued through the commiseration of her mother and father, her friends, and other skaters, through the media questions.

The next six months were a dream, someone else's life she pretended to live. She canceled appointments, stopped skating. For the first time in her memory, she had no plan or schedule. She woke each morning and waited to see what would happen.

Her father drove her to a psychiatrist in Detroit. The psychiatrist asked her what she saw, or heard, or tasted that very second. Name it, he said. Now what do you see? He was trying, she knew, to bring her back to the moment. Sometimes when she returned home, after her father had driven away, she sat alone in her living room, and said out loud, "Now I see the lamp. Now I see the TV. Now I see the window." When she heard her own voice, she laughed, and heard the laughter, and wondered at the woman living in her house.

In the end, she had no single moment of insight that restored her. Instead, one day she walked out to the Barn, put on her practice skates, and skated around the oval. She skated slowly, rocking back and forth. She put music on—the Blasters, a Detroit all-girl rock band, singing "Ain't I Cool." The voices and guitars blared across the empty dome. The rhythm faster and faster. Tina skated slowly round and round.

She did this a few times a day, without forethought. Early in the morning, in the middle of the night.

Once Tina stopped at the near-end curve in the oval, put her left skate sideways to the track, rose up on the toe of her right skate, and waited for the start. When it came, she bolted, and raced down the straightaway, ahead of Meille, Hingsson-Smyth, and Wu. She pumped her legs harder and harder and went through the finish line.

Days later, familiar objects and people began to appear, as if they had been there all along. She inhaled and felt the air fill her lungs.

Tina called Andy and went back to training. At the Lake Placid Nationals, she not only won but set a new world record. She was faster than everyone, even the eager new teenagers from China and Germany. But at the 1988 Olympics, she was afflicted with a last-minute bout of caution and ended up winning a bronze. The headline in one newspaper said, "Tina Doesn't Fall."

· · ·

Meanwhile I was on top.

I had written three best sellers in a row, and was working on what would be my biggest selling book. I had a nationally syndicated newspaper column and two monthly magazine columns.

When I complained to Skye about my workload, she sent me a packet of Dexedrine—capsules with orange-and-white granules "to keep your head above water." I threw them in a drawer and forgot them, but a few weeks later, trying to meet a deadline, I swallowed one, and after that, Skye gave me a phone number for more.

Jill was in the midst of conflicts with Toyon. Tak had found a record producer willing to record the quartet, but there were disagreements on the repertoire. The producer wanted Beethoven and Brahms. When she heard that, Simone said she would shoot herself before playing the Beethoven Opus 18 one more time. Tak suggested the Elliott Carter, but Arthur struggled with the cello cadenza.

On one of my stays in California, to distract Jill from the quartet's strife, I proposed we find a new house. I arranged with an agent to show us houses in Seal Beach, which was our favorite spot for weekend outings.

On our second trip, the agent showed us a three-story beachfront house. It was a square tower, with gleaming windows and panoramic views of ocean waves breaking two hundred yards away. The third floor had a guest bedroom that I could use for an office, and a family room large enough for rehearsal space.

Walking through the second floor, the agent pressed a wall button, which opened the curtains. With her back to the agent, Jill rolled her eyes at me. When the agent went outside, Jill said, "You're kidding, right?"

"You don't like this?" I asked.

"I'd be happy with a cottage."

"That'd be like where we are now. Let's try something different."

Realizing I was serious, Jill's smile disappeared. "It's way too much money," she said. "And it's all glass. It's like living in a display window."

I took one of her hands and led her out onto the second-floor deck. It was a crisp morning, with a few strands of pale fog floating above the ocean. We stood watching the breakers.

"Haven't you ever wanted to live like people who live like this?" I asked.

Jill laughed. "No," she said. "Do you really like this house, or is it the *idea* of having a house like this?"

"Is there a difference?"

"Of course. Charlie, you're almost never here. I'll be alone in this giant glass house."

"You'll have a shorter commute to Fullerton."

"You're not going to change your mind, are you?" Jill said. She looked at the beach. "All right," she said. "But don't try to pretend this was my idea."

We bought the house and moved, and two days later, I was back in Michigan with Tina. I came home twice a month for long weekends.

While I was out of town, Jill and I talked every other night by phone. One night, when she was telling me about a new class she was teaching on Mozart, she suddenly stopped.

"What's wrong?" I said.

"You're not interested," she said.

"What do you mean?" I asked. "I'm interested."

There was a long silence.

"No, you're not," she said. "You're drifting off, thinking about your book or something."

"That's not true," I said. "You were talking about the 'Queen of the Night' aria and how difficult it is to reach the F6."

"It's okay, Charlie," she said. "It doesn't matter." She hung up.

Two weeks later, when I was back in Los Angeles, Toyon came to our house for a rehearsal, and afterward, Tak stayed for dinner. "This is a wonderful place, *salut*," he said, raising his wine glass in a toast. "Every artist should live in a place like this. *I* should live in a place like this."

"You can't stay here, Tak," I said. "If that's where you're headed."

"Too bad," he said. "It's the quintessential house for you, Charlie. It's all glass. There and not there. Like you in your books."

After dinner, he coaxed Jill onto the third-floor deck with their instruments. They faced each other in the open air and played the Mozart duets. When they came inside, he proposed a new idea for Toyon: a newly written viola solo, to be composed by Jill, which would be inserted in the Haydn String Quartet no. 20, the so-called "Sun."

From across the room, I sat watching them, talking and laughing and picking up their instruments to play. They were like characters performing a play in my house.

That winter, I took more Dexedrine. What I liked best was the jolt in the first half hour, the gears shifting like a powerful engine in my central nervous system. It was the most definitive feeling of the day. I took the pills in the afternoon, but I began thinking of them when I woke up. I liked the feelings later, too, when I sat at my keyboard and was king in the land of words.

But, whatever the magic, I wasn't smarter than chemistry, and after a while, I heard two people talking in the empty room next door, their whispers coming out of the phone jack.

Later I could see Jill counting beats even when she wasn't playing her viola. One night in a booth of a Mexican restaurant, I watched her eating, and in the concentration behind her eyes, saw the music playing.

"Tell me where we are in the score," I said.

Jill looked at me.

"Tell me where we are in the score right now," I repeated.

Sometimes we do terrible things to the ones we love just to see what harm we can cause.

She leaned toward me. "I know about the things you're taking," she said. "I saw them in your kit. From now on, I don't want you taking them while you're with me."

"'No matter what disaster occurred,'" I said in a loud voice. "'She stood in desperate music wound.' Do you remember that? It's Yeats."

The couple in the next booth turned to watch us.

"Knock it off, Charlie," she said. "Or, I'll leave."

"'Wound, wound,'" I recited, "'and she made in her triumph, where the bales and baskets lay, no common intelligible sound, but sang O sea-starved, hungry sea.'"

She walked out and drove home. The terms for my returning were that I agree to therapy during my time back home, and I negotiate with Tina for a return to California earlier than planned. It was the therapist's idea that I enter a week-long amphetamine detox program in San Diego.

The therapist also suggested I return to writing fiction. "Find what feeds you," she said. I went back to my bankers' boxes of old stories, but they now seemed impossibly innocent and contrived. I started a science fiction novel about a spaceship, defending a twenty-second century Los

Angeles. I gave the heroic crew members the real names of editors in the major New York publishing houses, in the hopes of starting a bidding war.

"Have you lost your mind?" Barry said when he saw the sample chapters.

"I'm trying to find what feeds me," I said.

"What?" he screamed into the phone. "You don't piss off people like this. These people don't have a sense of humor about this stuff."

"Piss them off?" I said. "I made them heroes. Did you even read it? Some of them have super-human powers."

"Just finish the Terrill book."

I was back to where I started. What had Virginia Hardy said? Just finish the goddam book. If I ever wrote my autobiography, that would be the title: Just Finish the Goddam Book.

Jill and I got better slowly. We took long walks early in the morning before we worked, all the way to the southern edge of the beach and the end of the pier, often without speaking the whole way there and back.

Our love had grown different. We did not need each other as much. But we also found a new way of being together. Once I admitted my addiction, Jill treated me with tenderness, as if my admissions had earned me gentler handling. Having learned of the hurt I could cause, I pitied Jill for her vulnerabilities. At night we explored each other's body hesitantly and sweetly, like two teenagers unclothed for the first time. In this new solicitude, we surprised ourselves: near the end of that year, we found out Jill was pregnant.

. . .

The problem with paring everything away is that sometimes you're left with nothing.

In the first month I lived in Tina's house, I was awakened one night by a sound. It was four-thirty, still dark outside. Leaving my room, I found a light on in the kitchen. Tina was sitting in the nook, wrapped in a blanket. When she heard me, she raised her head, a look of terror in her eyes.

I stepped backward.

"I'm okay," she said. She was gulping air. "Making some tea."

I put the tea kettle on the stove and sat across from her.

"Sometimes I can't sleep," she said. "I have to get up."

She pulled the blanket tighter. "The doctor says they're panic attacks. You know anything about that?"

"No," I said.

"Neither did I," she said. "Something new." Her voice was wobbly.

I made two cups of chamomile tea and gave her one. She reached her hands out from the blanket and took the cup.

She had the attacks several times a week, early in the morning, and if I heard her moving about, I joined her in the kitchen. Her mind churned with fears: placing second, placing third, not placing, falling, and cracking up in front of an international audience.

The stoic face, the clockwork training, and the skins hid a frightened child. It was as though she awoke one morning and found the earth beneath her unreliable, as if she forgot how not to fall.

Deeper down, too, lay another monster. Past her rational mind, past the conscious part that she could argue with, in the viscera and fluids lived the unshakeable thought that if she lost the next race, she wouldn't exist.

When this demon ate its way out late at night, it woke her from a deep sleep, flooding her body in adrenalin and snatching the air from her lungs.

She ran into my room. "Charlie," she said in the dark. "I need to talk to you." She perched on the edge of my bed, gasping for air. "This's so weird. Shit. Shit. Shit."

If I reached toward her, she said, "Don't touch me. I just need to sit here."

Furious at her helplessness, she demanded conversation. "Tell me something," she said, and if I hesitated, she said, "Anything. Just talk."

I told her about Jill and her viola. I played an audiotape I carried with me when I traveled of Toyon playing Schubert's String Quartet in A Minor. Beside me, Tina listened, her eyes staring straight ahead, her lips white with the effort of breathing.

After a few minutes, Tina said, "Talk about something else. Make up a story." She concentrated on her breathing. I told her a story I had written years before about a singer who loses her voice.

When I finished, Tina said, "When I was a little girl, I made up my own story." She took a deep breath in and let it out to try to slow her breathing. "In the midget-class races, the coaches kept telling us we were racing against time, not the other girls. I hated it. Every day I got on the track and raced against time. Sometimes I hit a mark, but usually I lost." Tina's voice shook as she spoke, but her breathing was now more even.

"One day I made up a story about a teenage skater who makes a deal with Time. Time will give her a fraction of a second advantage in the race the next day, but she has to give Time something in return."

"Like what?" I asked.

"Oh, God," Tina said. "Some girls would have given up a family member for a tenth of a second."

"What was it for the girl in your story?"

Tina shrugged. "I could never decide," she said. "I was just a kid. It was part of that mental stuff the coaches did."

In the daylight, especially when she was with Andy Waller, Tina forgot her fear and wore a veneer of hardness.

When it came to her autobiography, she was ruled by her daylight self. Once, when we were going over drafts, I asked if she wanted to describe the panic attacks and how she was overcoming them. She stared at me coldly. "Why would I?" she asked.

"It's part of your life. It's what you've overcome."

"We've got enough of that overcome crap already."

She watched me. "You talk about this in an interview, and I'll sue you," she said.

I started to protest, and she said, "I'll say you came on to me. Who're they going to believe?"

After that, she became wary. She downloaded everything from my hard drive every two days.

. . .

She arrived at the 1992 Games out of the public spotlight. She refused pre-game interviews and kept her training secret. She stayed in her own RV away from the other competitors. Her qualifying races leading up to the games had been good but not spectacular.

Tina drew an early heat. Her time was the second fastest of her career. But the teenagers from China and Germany both set new world records, and another young American took third. Tina was shut out.

Two weeks later I met her at Nancy Alden's office to go over final plans for her book's launch. Tina looked stunned. Her face and voice had separated, like a film out of sync, and her voice came from some place behind her. On tour, she kept her answers short and wore a thin, strained smile.

The book, *On Ice*, had a cover photograph of Tina skating in the 1983 Nationals, her face tight with determination, her skates cutting a turn in the ice. In her acknowledgments, Tina thanked me for "helping a girl used to racing on a single track find a way to tell the story of my journey through life." The book started like this: "The ice of an Olympic speed track is hard and cold and gritty, but it has no smell. I know because in February 1984 I was lying on an Olympic track, my face two inches from the ice, taking my first breath as someone who would not win a gold medal."

The book sold out its first printing. The book was discussed on sports shows and women's programs. Skating clubs around the world reported increases in membership.

Tina's life went on. She became a skating coach and married a pro golfer. I saw her on TV, standing alongside him on a fairway.

Every few years a greeting card or poster company released another version of the classic photo of the crumpled skater. When she wasn't coaching, Tina earned a living on the corporate speaking circuit, touring boardrooms and giving talks on courage.

Five years or so after her autobiography was published, Tina wrote a second book, this time without me. It was a children's picture book that told the story of the young speed skater who Tina had first imagined when she was a teenager. The day before a race, Time appears to the skater and offers her the fraction of a second she'll need to win. But in return, Time tells her, sometime later in life, he'll take it back. Her life ahead of her, with millions of seconds to spare, the girl agrees.

That night the girl has a dream and sees all the moments she might be forced to surrender. The next day she declines Time's offer and loses by a thin margin. The book's power lay in the dream sequence. Only some-one like Tina, who knew time so intimately, could have named those imperiled seconds—the girl's foot reaching for a car brake, the touch of a boy's hand on her first dance, and the look in her lover's eyes when his heart melts—and made the subtraction of any one an unbearable loss.

CHAPTER **3 1**

AFTER DINNER I walked Page down the gravel road to the eucalyptus grove where she had parked her car. Self-conscious, neither of us spoke. At the car, I handed her a spare key to my apartment. For a moment she looked down at it in her hand as if it was a foreign object, and I said, "So you can cook."

The following morning I awoke thinking about the kiss. What I remembered was the feel of her hand on my shoulder. Despite the aggressiveness and bravado in Page's voice, that touch had been shy and tentative.

In my apartment I sat at my computer and began drafting the next chapter of Patel's book. It was a simple, straightforward account of his birth in Bombay. I described his maternal and paternal grandparents and his mother and father and included two stories from his childhood.

When I finished, I located the transcript of Anita Kleinman's interviews with Safia Patel. Although Patel and DeVries had requested that there be no inclusion of Safia, I decided to go ahead and write a chapter anyway. Without it, I would argue, the biography would become too dry and one-dimensional. From the transcript, I stitched together an account of the first meeting of Patel and Safia at the wedding of an acquaintance in Sacramento. Safia had given Kleinman a vivid description of the food, the clothing of the wedding party, and an improbable image of Patel dancing a traditional wedding dance.

It was noon by the time I had written the second chapter. I made copies of the two chapters that I had written on Saturday, and I put all four chapters in an envelope and took it to the estate compound, where I left it with DeVries' secretary. I ate a sandwich in the dining hall and got a call on my cell from Molly. She said Stephen had gone through guest lists for parties three months prior to January and identified the names Paul had added. Mahler was now reviewing the names.

At one o'clock I left for my appointment with Kenny McDonald.

* * *

Even in the middle of the day, the sky was dark and overcast, with thick, gray clouds low in the sky. On Kenny's private road, where it wound up through the dark cover, I turned on my headlights. When I arrived at Kenny's house, the door was open. I knocked and called into the house. No one answered.

I walked down the hallway. Music was coming from the speakers. It was a sixties pop song, with a woman's eerie, thin voice.

> *Why do the birds go on singing?*
> *Why do the stars glow above?*

There was something wrong with the recording, though. It sounded like a stretched tape or warped disk. The voice was abnormally slow, the words wobbly and off-key.

> *Don't they know it's the end of the world*
> *It ended when I lost your love.*

In the living room, I called Kenny's name. The drapes were closed, and I couldn't see anyone in the darkness. I crossed the room and opened the glass door to the patio. Kenny was sitting at his usual table. The song was playing on the outdoor speakers.

Kenny watched me approach. He sat slouched in a cast iron chair, dressed in a Hawaiian shirt splashed with yellow flowers. In front of him was a bottle of tequila, a half-filled glass, and the gun. I pulled out a chair across the table from him, and as I sat down, he said, "You know what your trouble is, Teller? You underestimate people. You think the rest of us are fucking idiots or too wasted to know what's going on."

His eyes seemed to swim in and out of focus. On the sound system the weird song started again.

"I made a few calls and found out who you really are," he said. "You're screwed up, man. You're not writing a profile on me. No one's going to publish anything you write. You're a down and outer."

"I'm a writer," I said. "I write profiles. That's what I do."

"You did, but you screwed up. You're here for something else. Don't shit me, man." He pushed back his chair and stood facing me. His pale, sagging torso was visible through his open shirt. For a moment he swayed on his feet.

"I was right the first time, wasn't I?" he said. "You're a fucking narc." Then he smiled as if he had thought of something amusing. He came toward me, and I rose abruptly, tipping over my chair, and backed away from him.

"Everybody in the pool," he shouted. He grabbed me by the shirt front, walked me quickly backward to the pool's edge, and hurled me in.

The water was cold. I sank to the bottom on my back and moved awkwardly in my clothes. My shoes felt like weights.

Coming to the surface in the deep end, I gasped for air. The fall had knocked off my glasses. I saw the sun and a blur of shapes. From above, something flew toward me, and I put up my right arm just as one of the cast-iron chairs crashed into the water. A chair leg hit square on my forearm, and the weight of the chair carried me under water.

I swam away from the chair and saw it sink below me. Underwater, I tugged at one shoe and pulled it off. A sharp piercing pain ran through my arm where the chair had hit. I came up for air.

Kenny's shape was at the edge of the pool. He was shouting something. The legs of another chair came at me. I turned too late and the base of the seat hit my head. I sank face down through the water, the chair behind me. The blow to my head had made a cut, and there was blood in the water.

At the bottom of the pool I kicked the chair away and swam upward, with my remaining shoe still dragging behind me like an anchor. Before I reached the surface, a dark shadow loomed above and grew larger as I came closer to the top of the water. I had to get air.

At the surface I saw the shadow was a cast iron table. Kenny had turned it upside down and was holding it over me. "Catch," he yelled.

I managed to lift up my left hand and break the table's fall, but it drove my hand into my face and plunged me to the bottom of the pool.

At the pool's floor, the table tipped slightly and I swung away from it and pulled with my left arm to the surface again. My right forearm was numb where the first chair had hit it. I sucked in air and water and tasted the blood that was running down my face.

I saw Kenny and swam away from him. But he was looking away from me to the other side of the pool. A sound was coming from there: a rhythmic slapping. I turned to see Kim-Ly walking slowly around the pool's perimeter. Her sandals flapped on the concrete as she walked. She was carrying something.

She turned the corner at the shallow end and walked toward me. She stared straight ahead without expression. In her hands was a towel. Kenny's gaze followed her, transfixed.

When she reached the deep end, she stopped and turned toward the water. I pulled myself toward the pool's edge at her feet. It took me several tries to maneuver myself out of the water with just one arm. I lay still for a minute on the deck. I could see Kenny on the other side of the pool, staring at the girl.

I coughed and then vomited. A bitter taste filled my mouth. I looked up at the girl. Her eyes were focused away from me on a middle distance. I took the towel from her. It was a soft beach towel, printed with bright tropical fish. I held it to my face and felt the sting of the cut on my forehead.

The girl turned without a word and walked back the way she had come, her sandals flapping on the concrete. When I looked across the pool, Kenny was gone.

I used the towel to dab at my shirt and jeans that still dripped with pool water. Taking off my right shoe, I let it fall into the pool. I stood stiffly, and with the pool skimmer fished out my glasses. Then I walked barefoot around the pool, through the house, to my car. Kenny was nowhere to be seen.

I drove slowly down the switch-backed road that dropped along the side of the hillside. On the valley floor, I drove past the vineyards to the edge of a housing development and a broad green playing field, where in the dark, overcast afternoon children were playing soccer.

CHAPTER 3 2

I ARRIVED HOME about four and changed out of my wet clothes and showered. My right arm was sore and stiff, and a dark bruise was already spreading down the inside forearm. I washed the cut on my forehead and covered it with a Band-Aid. I was about to call Vincent and tell him about my encounter with Kenny when the phone rang. It was Nico. She said Vincent wanted to show me something on the laptop, and invited me for dinner later that evening. I said okay and asked if Page could join us.

"Sure," Nico said. "What's the deal with you two anyway?"

"There's no deal. The cops won't let her back in her apartment, and she's afraid whoever killed Ray Brenner is coming after her. She doesn't want to be alone."

"Lucky you."

I started to protest, but I was still confused about the kiss the night before, and knew I wouldn't be convincing.

Page arrived at my house around five after her shift at the fitness center. She smiled but looked tired. She took a bottle of water from the refrigerator, and we sat on the deck. I told her about my encounter with Kenny. At the end she said, "Kenny's a maniac. Paul used to tell me stories. For a while Kenny had a cheetah in a caged run behind his house."

I watched Page as she talked. She looked different than she had a week earlier. The air of toughness was gone. I told her I was going to see Nico and Vincent and asked if she wanted to come along. She shook her head. "Vincent's too much for me," she said. "I'll hang out here."

I went to my closet and handed her a Ken Styles brand baseball bat. "Don't open the door," I said. "But if someone breaks in, use this."

Page held it reluctantly.

"It'll be okay," I said. "Anyone comes, you'll hear them on the stairs. Call 911."

* * *

During the forty-five-minute drive across the county, I went over Kenny's behavior in my mind. What had made him so much more paranoid in just three days? Was it just his phone calls to magazine editors to check up on me? Or did it have to do with Brenner's murder?

When I arrived at Nico and Vincent's house, Nico met me at the door and immediately asked about the cut on my forehead.

"I'll tell you both the whole story," I said.

"Where's your roommate?" Nico asked.

"Decided not to come."

"Yeah, somehow I didn't think she would." Nico hugged me and led inside.

Vincent was sitting in the living room. He looked up from his book and regarded me without a word.

"Something's wrong with Kenny," I said.

"You just figure that out?" Vincent said.

"No. I mean something different." I described my visit to Kenny's house. When I finished, Nico put her hand on my arm. "You okay?" she asked.

"Sure," I said. "The cut's stopped bleeding. I'm just sore."

"And you didn't see Kenny on your way out?"

"No. There was no one around. I just left."

Vincent still hadn't said anything. "What do you think?" I asked him.

Vincent shrugged. "He wanted to kill you, he would have shot you."

"He did a pretty good job with those chairs," I said. "What's odd is that the other two times he was suspicious. This time he was sure I was out to get him. It was like he knew something."

"I don't think he knows anything," Vincent said. "The guy's been snorting powder for thirty years."

We moved to the dining room, where Nico served us rice pilaf and steamed vegetables.

"Did you succeed in scaring the tourists in Calistoga yesterday?" I asked.

"It's getting harder to do," she said. "The average tourist has seen so much degradation on TV they're beyond noticing."

"Well I always notice you. Although I'm not always sure what I'm noticing. Last night you said you express yourself through your clothes, but what're you trying to say? Like tonight."

She was dressed in a lace camisole top and jeans with large tears in both knees. She put down her fork and spread out her arms. "These are our culture's dislocated values," she said. "The fashion industry designs our clothes to make us look like hookers. We're paraded for the pleasure of men. But some of us are saying, yeah, we're hot, but we can also kick some ass."

"I get that," I said. "But why do you *want* to kick anyone's ass?"

"I'm sorry, Charlie, but only a guy could ask that question. We live in a guy culture. It's all about guys. And men, wherever they are, are such subtracters. The more you're with them, the less you are."

"But look at your life. You have a job you like. You have a husband who loves you."

"Yeah, but you know what lives inside me? You know the history I had before Vincent? One loser after another. In middle school, I went out with this guy Wes, who got into fights all the time. He'd go up to someone and say, 'I'm calling you out, man.' He'd beat up some kid, and then he'd come over to my place and want to do me. And then there was Bobby. Caught him in bed with my roommate. He goes, 'What we were doing wasn't sex.' What is it with you guys, you're stupid enough to do it, and then suddenly you're like all like smart about what it's called. All the guys I went out with were such boys until I met Vincent."

She looked across the table and smiled at Vincent, who looked back without expression.

"But that's over, right?" I said.

"You think there's no residue from all that? You think I still don't see it every day? Besides, anger is part of my personal path. 'Anger is the first step towards courage.' That's St. Augustine."

"You've read St. Augustine?"

"I saw it in a magazine. Tell me, Charlie. I'm not an object of belittlement to you, am I?"

"No, of course not."

"I think of myself as a serious individual. Vincent sees me as a serious individual, don't you Vincent?"

Vincent looked up and nodded.

"I'd like to think you do too," she said.

"Sure," I said.

"I mean you two are the exceptions to everything I just said about men. You, Charlie, that whole thing with you and Susan Sparrow. You were like the ultimate schmo."

"The ultimate schmo?" I asked.

"And Vincent," she said, ignoring me, "has so much sensitivity it's not funny."

Vincent stopped eating for a moment and looked across the table at Nico.

"It means a lot to me that you take me seriously," Nico said.

When we finished eating, Vincent put Barkley's laptop on the table and opened a spreadsheet file. "This is the file we saw yesterday," he said. "There are a bunch of them, and they're all building specifications. This one is the specifications for a new state office building in Sacramento. The specs are dated two years ago. The building is under construction now."

With this knife, Vincent pointed to the spreadsheet cells that held the date and the name of the site.

"On the top left it says Torana Construction Company," I said.

"Yeah," Vincent said. He looked irritated at the interruption. "The specs were delivered to a company called Amtree down in San Jose. Their name's on a blind header. Amtree administers the bidding process for state building contracts. They post the state announcements, oversee applications, verify qualifications, analyze the bids, and make recommendations to the state.

"How do you know this?" I asked.

Vincent glared at me. "I looked them up on the web," he said.

"The important thing, and what Barkley must have discovered, is that Torana has more than one bid for the same job with different costs," Vincent said. He pointed to the columns in the middle of the spreadsheet. "Look at this. These columns are a breakdown of materials costs. The next set is labor. The subtotal of this column for precast is $1.6 million. But there's an identical file, with the same date, and different numbers."

Vincent opened another file and positioned it next to the first one. "Here the precast subtotal is $1.4 million."

"So Patel was submitting more than one bid for the same project?"

"Yeah, for these state projects, bidders were all pre-qualified. So low bid wins. In each of these cases, Patel's later bid is lower."

"How do you know which one's the later one?" Nico asked.

Vincent opened the directory of the files. "The date and time the files were created are shown in the directory," he said.

"But there must be some safeguards against this," I said.

"That's where Amtree comes in. They're supposed to certify the amount of each bid and the time it's received."

"So Amtree wasn't doing its job."

Vincent shook his head. "No, I think it had to be a little more active than that. This required some cooperation from Amtree, or at least someone at Amtree." Vincent enlarged the first file again and pointed to the top with his knife. "Yesterday I noticed that all the spreadsheets had the word 'Sutter' on this line," he said. "And Barkley named the whole folder Sutter."

"Someone working at Amtree?"

Vincent sat back in his chair. "I called the main number for Amtree's San Jose office this morning and asked to speak with Mr. Sutter," he said. "I was put on hold for a long time. Finally some head honcho came on the line and said Mr. Sutter was not in."

"So it *is* someone's name?" Nico said.

"Apparently," Vincent said. "He's Andrew A. Sutter. I looked him up in a database after I got off the phone."

"But we still don't know what any of this has to do with Paul and why he wanted to talk to me about it, right?" I said.

"No, but I think we can assume that Barkley saw the way the numbers in these files had been changed. Why else would he have copied them into this folder?"

"And maybe he knew something about this guy Sutter since he used his name for the folder," Nico said.

"Sounds like we should talk with Sutter," I said.

Vincent shrugged. "We'll have to find him," he said. "When I pressed the guy at Amtree, he said that Mr. Sutter no longer worked there, and he wouldn't give him any more information."

"You have any ideas where to start?"

"Already have. It'll take a few days."

"I better head home," I said. "It's been a long day." As I stood, I felt the pain in my right forearm.

I drove back east across the county. When I returned to my apartment, I found Page asleep on my sofa. *Next Horizon*, the Skye Lurie autobiography, lay open on her lap. The baseball bat was still propped beside the chair where I had left it. I took a down comforter from the closet and gently lay it over her. Then I switched out the lights and went to bed.

CHAPTER **3 3**

I WOKE UP late and discovered Page had already gone, leaving the comforter neatly folded on the couch and *Next Horizon* back on the bookshelf. I made a pot of coffee, and for half an hour I sat drinking it and looking out at the vineyard. The valley floor was still covered in fog.

I ate a couple pieces of toast in front of my computer. For the rest of the morning, I read through the interview transcripts on Patel's years just after his emigration to the United States and began outlining a chapter on the young Patel in America. I ate lunch in my room and spent the afternoon writing about Patel's years at Cornell and his first job out of college as a draftsman.

Around seven, my phone rang. It was Jill. Her voice sounded urgent. "Charlie," she said, "Something's happened. It's Lucy. She didn't come home this afternoon when she was supposed to. The police just called. She's been taken into custody. She was with another girl at the mall who was arrested for shoplifting."

I realized I had stopped breathing. I took a deep breath. "Wait a minute," I said. "Is Lucy okay?"

"Yes, they let me talk to her, and she's okay."

"Has she been arrested?"

"I don't know. It wasn't clear. I think just the other girl."

"Who was it?"

"I don't know, Charlie. Look, we have to pick her up at the downtown station. Can you meet me there?"

"Sure," I said. "Thirty minutes."

Jill hung up before I could say any more.

When I arrived at the police station, I found Jill already sitting in the waiting room. She looked up when I entered, but did not rise to meet me. She wore a trench coat over jeans and a blouse. Her hair was mussed and her eyes dark.

"She's okay," Jill said. "They're going to let us see her in a few minutes."

I stood in front of Jill for a moment, wanting to hug her, but when she didn't move, I took a seat beside her. At the other end of the room was a couple with a small child playing at their feet, and a few seats down from them two teenage girls dressed in goth outfits.

"What happened?" I asked.

"She was going shopping at the Plaza with her friend Sage," Jill said, looking straight ahead. "The arrangement was that Sage's mother would bring them home at four. At four-thirty, when she didn't arrive, I called Lucy's cell, but it was turned off. So I called Sage's mother, Karen, who's sitting over there." She gestured toward the couple across the room. "Karen didn't know anything about the arrangement. Sage had told her she was going to the school library and would be home at seven. Karen and I went to the library, which was closed and then to the Plaza, where we walked around for half an hour. That's when I got a call, telling me to come here."

Jill's voice sounded tired and angry. She turned and looked at me for the first time. "When I called your house last night," she said, "a woman answered the phone."

"It was Page," I said. I told Jill briefly about Brenner's murder. "The police won't let her back in her house, and the motel where she's staying doesn't have a kitchen," I said. "I've been letting her cook at my place. What'd you want to talk about?"

"Nothing. It doesn't matter," Jill said, turning away again.

A young female police officer entered the room and introduced herself as Officer Torres. A thin woman with an erect bearing and dressed in a perfectly pressed police uniform, she escorted us to a small office. Lucy was seated beside a desk in a molded plastic chair. She looked small. I noticed that the tips of her shoes just touched the floor. She regarded us with sullen, angry eyes.

Jill went to her first and bent down and hugged her where she sat in the chair. Lucy didn't move to put her arms around her mother. I reached across Jill and rested my hand on Lucy's shoulder.

For a moment no one spoke. Then Officer Torres said, "Your daughter hasn't been charged. She was a witness to a crime, and we needed to get her statement."

"Don't we have to be present for that since she's a minor?" I asked.

Officer Torres looked at me. "As I said, your daughter hasn't been charged," she said. "So, no, you don't have to be present for us to speak with her."

Jill took her arms from Lucy and stood up. "What was this all about?" she asked Officer Torres.

"Your daughter's friend stole a bracelet from Macy's. She was observed by a security guard, who apprehended her and turned her over to us to make the arrest. Your daughter has cooperated with us and made a statement. In most cases like this, it's not necessary for a witness to be involved any further. Sometimes there's a need for clarification. If that's the case, we'll contact you."

I looked at Lucy. She was staring down at her feet.

"So are we free to go?" I asked.

"You're free to go," Officer Torres said, stepping aside. As we neared the door, she said, "I'll tell you what I always tell parents. You were lucky. In my experience, something's going on here. I suggest you take a look at it sooner rather than later."

In the lobby Jill turned to Lucy and said, "Tell us what happened."

Lucy sighed with annoyance. "Me and Sage were looking at some jewelry, and this stupid clerk wouldn't help us. Sage took this bracelet to look at it, you know, in a different light. All of a sudden, this creep grabs Sage and starts saying all this stuff we couldn't understand. We didn't know who he was or anything, so we ran. Then all these cops showed up. It was so weird. We didn't do anything."

"Why didn't Sage's mother know where you were?" I asked.

"I guess Sage forgot to tell her."

"How were you going to get home?" Jill asked.

"We could call her mom or hitch or something. It was no big deal."

"You guys should head home," I said, looking around the lobby. "But, sweetheart," I said to Lucy, "we need to have a talk."

"You're never around," Lucy said.

"We'll set up a time," I said. "You could come out to my house one night for dinner."

"Actually, Charlie," Jill said. "I think it'd be better if I handle this. You're pretty busy right now. I don't want Lucy going to your place the way things are."

"What's that mean?" I asked.

Raising both arms, Lucy shouted, "Whatever!" and walked out of the station.

Jill turned to me and said, "Stay away from us for a while, okay, Charlie?"

*   *   *

When I returned home, I found Page in the kitchen. "There you are," she said. "I didn't know where you went. I made salmon steaks. I already ate, but I can reheat them, if you want."

"Sure, thanks," I said. I took a bottle of Dewars from the kitchen cabinet, filled a glass with ice, and poured scotch into the glass. I drank it and then poured another glassful and sat at the kitchen counter while Page worked at the stove. Neither of us spoke until she finished heating the salmon and some rice and handed me a plate. I ate at the counter, and as Page washed the rest of the dishes, I told her what happened with Lucy, omitting the part about Jill not wanting Lucy to visit while Page was in my house.

"Is it so unusual for a teenager to do something like that?" Page asked. "When I was that age, I got busted a few times."

"For what?"

"Smoking pot at school. Loud parties."

"Lucy hasn't been in trouble before. Until now, it seemed like the move from Southern California was good for her."

"Maybe it's just her choice of friends."

"I need to talk to Lucy. I'll see her tomorrow." Finishing the salmon, I drank the second scotch and crossed the room to sit on the sofa. For the first time, I felt how tired and sore I was and closed my eyes.

I heard Page follow me from the kitchen and felt her sit close to me on the sofa. I opened my eyes and looked at her. "So what's going on with us?" I asked.

"I don't know," she said. "Does it matter?" She smiled and kissed me on the cheek and then the lips. I felt her body pressed close to me. When the kiss ended, she looked into my eyes a moment. "Don't you ever do things and find out what they mean later?"

"That hasn't turned out so well for me," I said. "What about you? It's been a week and a half since your fiancé was killed."

"I loved Paul."

"Really?"

"Yeah, I did. And you don't know anything about it, so don't pretend you do. What's your problem, anyway? Is this too soon for expressions of intimacy? Is there some decent interval that I haven't observed?"

"I think it's a question of sincerity."

"You don't think I'm being sincere right here?"

"I don't know," I said. "This is a little sudden."

"Things don't just happen for you, do they?"

"Not usually. There's a reason somewhere."

Page sat back away from me. "You think I have some angle for coming on to you?" she asked.

"I didn't mean that," I said. "I just think it would be better if we got to know each other more before we . . . do this."

"Get to know each other?"

"Yeah."

Page smiled. "Sounds sweet," she said. "How about this? I just need some company for a few days. Think you can handle that?"

"Company?"

"Yeah, company," she said. "One thing at a time. That's what you want, right?"

"OK," I said. "One thing at a time."

CHAPTER 34

WHEN I AWOKE the following morning, Page was still asleep on the sofa. I dressed in the sitting area and walked down to the estate. At the pool, I swam laps for half an hour. Afterward I ate breakfast in the staff dining room. I checked the local paper, but there were no stories about the police investigations into either Paul's slaying or the Ray Brenner killing.

When I returned to my room, Page was gone. There was a note and half a cup of cold coffee on the kitchen counter. The note said, "Thanks for the sleepover."

I sat at my desk and read through what I had written the day before. I marked up places that I would need to rewrite. Then I pulled together my notes on the expansion of Torana Construction in the 1990s.

As I finished, Molly called. She said Mahler had reviewed the names that Paul had added to the guest lists and had identified most of them as known drug users. "The same names appeared on most of the lists," Molly said. "There were a few anomalies, and there was one name that appeared only once and that didn't match up with Eddie's list of users."

"What was it?" I asked.

"Sutter. Allen or Arthur."

"Andrew?"

"Yeah, I think so. How'd you know?"

"Long story. I'll tell you later. I have to see someone this morning, and I can't be late."

"One more thing. A county sheriff found a white pickup abandoned on a private road in the west county. Looks like it's been there a week."

"Does Eddie think it's the one I saw the night Paul was killed?"

"All I know is they found it," Molly said.

I drove to Windsor and found the deli near Lucy's school where she ate everyday. I was already sitting in a booth when she arrived with a group of her friends. She saw me and came over alone to my booth, carrying a large back-pack of books.

"Can we talk?" I asked.

"Mom said I shouldn't, but it's okay with me," she said. She threw her back-pack onto the seat across from me.

We ordered sandwiches and ate for a while in silence.

"I want to talk about last night," I said.

"I already told you everything there is," she said.

"How's school going?"

"It sort of sucks, but it's okay."

"You still glad you and mom moved up here?"

"Why? Are you feeling guilty or something?"

"Why should I feel guilty?"

"Isn't that the reason we moved up here? To get away after what happened to you in LA?"

"No. Your mother got a teaching job here."

"That pays way less."

"Where did you get all this?"

"Jesus, dad. I'm thirteen. I've got a brain."

"Well, it's not true. And I don't want to see you using something like that as an excuse for your behavior."

"I'm not. Are you listening to what I'm saying? And I'm not having prob-lems."

"Last night was a problem."

Lucy stared at me for a minute without speaking and shook her head. "You know what I hate?" she said. "The way you two are together. Can you hear your-selves? You weren't always that way. I remember when you weren't."

"A lot's happened."

"A lot happens to everybody. She's mad at you all the time, do you know that? And you, you say these things. They're like indirect. You're trying to talk to her, but it's not to her."

"You're right. We're not very good at communicating these days."

"I just wish you'd act like adults."

For a minute we ate in silence.

"Mom's got me a job a couple days after school," Lucy said. "At Myers Creek Winery where Dave works."

"What kind of work?" I asked.

"Just cleaning up in the lab and stuff. I think mom's trying to keep me away from Sage."

"All right, I just don't want . . ."

"Me hanging around with Dave?" Lucy asked with a smile.

"No, I wasn't going to say that. I was going to say I don't want you missing your homework."

"So what's the deal with you and Page Salinger?"

The question surprised me. "What do you mean?" I asked. "How do you know about Page?"

"Mom told me. She said Page's living with you."

"She's not living with me. She comes to my house for meals sometimes because she can't go back to her apartment."

"Mom doesn't want me to be there when Page is there. She thinks Page'll be a bad influence, or that you two are, you know, doing it." Lucy looked at me and smiled as she said this, enjoying its effect on me.

"That last part's not true, and even if it was, it wouldn't be any of your mother's or your business."

"It's not just that. Mom thinks you're close to the people involved in these two killings, and that it's dangerous."

"I do know them. But I'm being careful, too."

"Mom doesn't think so."

"Maybe you shouldn't come to my house right now," I said. "What's important is you know both your mother and I love you and care about you. We don't want you putting yourself and your schooling at risk by your behavior."

Lucy looked back at me with a bored expression. "I get that," she said.

"Need anything?"

She shook her head and looked across the deli to her friends' table.

"See you then," I said.

She looked once more at me, pulled her backpack off the booth seat, and joined her friends.

*   *   *

I returned to my house around one-thirty and found two police cruisers parked at the base of the stairs. A young, broad-shouldered officer emerged from one of the cruisers. He introduced himself as Officer Monroe and handed me a sheet of paper.

"We have a warrant to search your premises," he said. "We can legally enter without your permission, but we'd appreciate it if you'd let us in."

"What are you looking for?" I asked.

"As stated in the warrant, 'electronic media and other materials pertaining to the slaying of Paul Barkley and Ray Brenner.'"

I climbed the stairs ahead of Monroe and opened the door. As I let him in, he turned and said, "Also, Officer Reed down there is going to take you to see Detective Mahler."

"Can you tell me what it's about?"

"No, sir," he said. He stood in my doorway, waiting for me to walk back down the stairs.

Officer Reed was a balding, overweight man wearing aviator sunglasses. Without a word, he opened the rear door of his cruiser for me, and for the entire drive into Santa Rosa, I sat looking at the back of his head while he drove at a perfectly steady speed.

We drove to a residential neighborhood of Santa Rosa called Hidden Valley. The cruiser pulled into the drive of an L-shaped ranch house that I knew to be Mahler's by the sight of the black Mustang at the end of the turn-around.

Mahler met us at the door before we could ring. To me, he nodded silently in greeting but without the usual wise-guy grin. He thanked Reed and said he'd call him when he needed him.

Mahler's house was typical of a common style of late twentieth-century northern California homes. It had a cathedral ceiling in the entryway, an open kitchen bordered on one side by a dining nook, a couple of bedrooms off a hallway, and a large family room with glass doors that opened to a deck and pool. The house looked militarily neat and clean, and its surfaces were free of knick-knacks and personal items. The only hint of any exception to its bachelor status was a bikini drying on one of the pool chairs. Seeing me take in his house, Mahler mumbled something about never spending any time there.

Mahler led me through the family room to an office at the back of the house. The room held a desk with a laptop, two leather chairs, and a wall lined with books. Mounted on the wall opposite the bookshelves was a sound system with a stack of CDs and beside that, a small flat-screen TV.

Mahler gestured to me to sit in one of the leather chairs and said, "Like something to drink?" I looked back at him to see if he was kidding, and when I hesitated, he said, "Bottled water OK?" He disappeared for a few minutes.

While he was gone, I read the titles on the bookshelves. It was an eclectic but serious collection—modern fiction, poetry, Roman history, Kierkegaard, Sartre, and Greek philosophy. I even saw two of my own titles—the books on Virginia Hardy and Skye Lurie.

When Mahler returned, he handed me a glass of water and put the bottle between us.

I pointed to the bookshelves. "These from your college days?" I asked.

"Didn't go to college," he said. "A few classes at the JC. Just like to read, answer my own questions."

We both drank the water. "Before we become best buds, I want you to see something," he said. With a remote, he switched on the TV monitor. The screen glowed with a shaky color image that quickly came into focus. It was the back side of a house and swimming pool. In an instant I recognized it as Kenny McDonald's house. Kenny himself was visible in the center of the screen, seated at one of the poolside tables. A figure emerged from the house and walked across the deck. It was me.

I stared in fascination. Where, I wondered, was the camera mounted? I remembered Kenny's weird claim that a guy was watching him.

Mahler said, "Mr. McDonald has been under surveillance as part of joint state-local drug investigation."

On screen, Kenny and I sat at a poolside table. The sound quality was uneven, and it was difficult to tell what was being said. Abruptly Kenny and I stood, and Kenny heaved me backwards into the pool. I made an awkward splash. Kenny turned around, picked up the cast iron chair that I had tipped over, and threw it at me. I winced as the chair hit the figure struggling to the water's surface. For the next few minutes, I watched in fascination, for the first time seeing the scene from Kenny's point of view as he lumbered across the deck, first picking up another chair and then the table.

"Was the surveillance team ever moved to intervene on behalf of the guy in the pool?" I asked Mahler.

"What I heard was, they thought it was a lot of fun, and if the guy was one of the dirtbags in Kenny's drug crew, he probably deserved it."

When Kim-Ly entered the screen with the towel, I felt some relief. I watched myself crawl out of the pool and throw up. For the first time, I saw Kenny walk away from the pool and go into the house. I watched as my on-screen self dried off and walked across the deck into Kenny's house.

Mahler switched off the screen, picked up his glass, and took a drink. When he finished, he said, "Ever read the German philosopher Theodor Adorno?"

"Adorno?" I asked. "Sounds like a perfume."

Mahler shook his head. "That's the trouble with you, Teller," he said. "Your books always lacked any intellectual weight. There wasn't much there there."

"Some people thought there was too much there there."

Mahler ignored me. "Adorno was part of that German neo-Marxist crowd. Walter Benjamin, Georg Lukacs."

"OK. I heard of him."

"Adorno wrote a lot of crap about negative dialectics. But he also had this famous theory about popular music. He said popular music was stan-dardized, and as part of modern industrialized society, was all more or less the same. It was meant to serve the interests of the economic system by soothing and relaxing listeners, to keep them from thinking and from wanting what they were really denied, which was true freedom. Anyway, whenever I read Adorno, I think of Kenny McDonald and the Jays. Every one of their songs sounded exactly like every other one. I mean there was nothing original about any of them. It was like a junkie, trying to recapture that first high. Then what happens to Kenny? The guy's a pop icon in the sixties, and he literally becomes a cokehead. Spends thirty years shoving boatloads of coke up his nose, and he turns into a wack-job."

"What does any of this have to do with me?"

Mahler took another drink of his water. "We have another tape of you visiting Mr. McDonald's house," he said. "We want to know what you were doing there and what happened following the incident with the pool."

"Am I being charged with something?"

"Not yet. What we want is some information."

"If you have film of me coming and going, you know I left after I got out of the pool."

For the first time, Mahler's wise-guy grin returned. "Well, now, Teller," he said. "That's really the heart of the matter. You see, Kenny McDonald died yesterday of an apparent drug overdose, and the coroner puts the approximate time of death at about the time of this pool incident. Far as we can tell, you were the last person to see Mr. McDonald alive. You understand why we'd like to ask you some questions?"

CHAPTER **3 5**

Memory and Forgetting

IN THE WORLD of ghostwriting autobiographies, my niche lay in helping clients negotiate between the twin impulses of our time—memory and forgetting.

The people who hired me were masters of forgetting. They knew their pharmaceuticals and were familiar with the rich possibilities of alcohol. In that special poetry of addicts, they could describe each inch of their own surrender.

But my clients also knew the exact nature of what they were trying to forget—the hard little facts that pinched them: years, names, faces, rooms, and words. When we worked together, all those scraps returned with the unleashed energy of something long held down, and once on paper, they shone, as if polished by every effort to be rid of them.

"You know what you find when you get to know the biggest stars?" Paul Barkley asked me. We sat together late at night in his darkened café. "A hole at the center, an emptiness that they spend half their lives pouring drugs into. When you have everything, what you want is oblivion."

He told me about a recent catering assignment—a dinner party for thirty-five guests at a house in Dry Creek Valley. He had served mesquite-smoked squab on a bed of risotto. The hostess was the actress Alison McGuire, who had starred in two popular sitcoms in the nineties. She was forty but looked older, her beautiful face depleted by the rigors of cosmetic surgery. A five-year addiction to pain medication made her speech slow, and her friends inclined to congratulate her for the simplest expressions.

"What does it mean when the stars we hold in such high regard long for emptiness?" Barkley asked me. "It has to be a sign of something, doesn't it?"

This was the second of our two late-night talks. He had made gimlets again, but there was something darker and more serious about him this time. The light had gone out of his eyes. He had an old man's look, as if sad for the knowledge of the little time left to him.

"What spares us is memory," he said. "It's what makes us worth saving. However low we sink, whatever promise we no longer fulfill, we tell our stories. That's why you're so important, Charlie. You're a guardian of our national memory."

"Come on," I said. "Rich people pay me to write their books."

He looked at me and shook his head. "That's false modesty," he said. "Whenever I go on a binge of forgetting everything that's happened to me, I think of you, Charlie. You're what gives me hope. Maybe I should hire you to write my life. Would you do that? It would honest-to-god save me."

Embarrassed to be the focus of his attention, I said something trivial to deflect him, but he kept on.

"Tell me your methods," he said. "You're not like a magician, are you? Bound by a code of silence?" He stirred his drink. "You're the one who makes your books what they are, not your subjects," he said. "It's your voice on every page. You're not a real ghost, you know."

He saw how this unnerved me, but he pressed his point. "If I had to bet on something," he said. "If my life depended on it, I'd bet on you."

At that moment, all he might have told me, all the mystery I was to uncover, must have been arrayed in his mind, but something in his own sense of timing warned him away, and as suddenly as he had borne in on me, he backed off. His face relaxed, and he allowed himself a weary smile at his own change of heart. Then, sensing the debt he owed, he left me with this: "Life's a funny old dog, isn't it?" he said. "But I guess you already knew that."

Part III

CHAPTER 36

FOR THREE HOURS that afternoon, I sat in Eddie Mahler's home office while he asked questions about Kenny McDonald.

Mahler said Kim-Ly had discovered Kenny unconscious inside his home theater about three o'clock, soon after I left. When the EMTs arrived, they pronounced him dead. Prior to an autopsy, initial speculation was his death had been caused by an overdose. He also had a blunt force trauma to his head. The police were treating it as a homicide.

Because the surveillance team had only one camera at the rear of the house, the police were unable to tell if someone besides me had arrived and departed in front of the house.

"Where'd you go when you got out of the pool?" Mahler asked.

"Through the house to the front door."

"You see Kenny?"

"No."

"You see anyone else?"

"No, but what does Kim-Ly say? She'd know."

"Right now I'm asking you. Were there any cars parked out front, other than Kenny's?"

"There might have been. I didn't notice."

"Did you pass anyone coming toward you on your way down the hillside?"

"No."

"We also have you on tape last Wednesday at Kenny's house," Mahler said. He put another tape in the machine, and I saw the scene of Vincent and me sitting beside the pool.

"Who's your friend?" Mahler asked.

I thought of refusing to tell Mahler, but I knew he'd find out without me. "Vincent Ferreira," I said. "He's a friend. He went along to introduce me to Kenny."

"Is he a drug dealer?" Mahler wrote something in his notebook.

"No, he just knew Kenny."

"Anybody who knows Kenny is a drug dealer."

"Well, Vincent isn't. I told him I wanted to write a magazine profile of Kenny, and Vincent said he could introduce me."

"A profile of Kenny? You're kidding?"

"It was just a way to talk to him about Barkley. See if he knew anything."

"Did he?"

"Not then. I went back on Friday. It's not on tape because we met in the theater."

"What'd he say about Barkley?"

"Not much. But when I said that they worked together, Kenny got agitated."

"Agitated?"

"Freaked out. He didn't like me talking about it. He accused me of being a narc. It struck a nerve."

"How long were you there Friday?"

"About twenty minutes."

"See anyone else?"

"Just Kim-Ly."

Mahler turned off the video monitor and walked across the room to the CD player. He put in a CD, and the sound of an opera filled the room. "Sound familiar?" Mahler asked.

I listened for a minute. It was a soprano's voice. "Is that the thing Paul was listening to in his car?" I asked.

Mahler sat back in his chair. "Yeah," he said. "Donizetti's *Lucia di Lammermoor*. You know it?"

I shook my head.

"Interesting opera. It tells the story of Lucia, who is deceived by her brother and forced into a loveless marriage as a business arrangement."

"I know Paul had a few favorites. Sometimes at Galileo's, after the customers had left, he'd play recordings over the sound system."

"The night he was killed, he had this part on repeat," Mahler said. "It was playing over and over."

Mahler paused, and we both listened to the music. "Act One, Scene Two," he said. "Before the arranged marriage, Lucia is singing to her lover, telling him of her love. *Un più nobile, più santo, d'ogni voto è un puro amo.* A nobler, holier vow than any other is pure love."

Mahler looked at me. "That mean anything?" he asked.

I shrugged. "Paul didn't talk to me about his relationship with Page," I said. "I didn't even know he was engaged until after his death. You ask Page?"

"She's not very cooperative."

He switched off the music. "It doesn't matter," he said. "Once in a while you learn something from these little things."

Mahler poured the rest of the Pellegrino into our glasses. "You know, Teller," he said, "The thing that puzzles me most is not *what* you're doing in all this. We'll figure that out eventually. It's *why*. Why did you come out of the world of show business LA to Sonoma County and land yourself in the middle of a bunch of guys selling coke and killing each other? And, why do you need to go ask Kenny McDonald questions about Paul Barkley?"

"No disrespect, detective," I said. "But after Paul was killed, it seemed like the police weren't asking the right questions. Paul was a friend of mine. I thought I owed it to him."

"Doing the honorable thing?" Mahler gave me his wise-guy grin.

"Don't think I'm capable of it?"

"Let's just say it might be a new look for you."

Mahler flipped through his notebook and asked, "What do you know about Paul Barkley's business dealings with Rajiv Patel?"

"They knew each other. Paul catered parties for Patel. Paul made the contact for me to write the book."

"Did you ever see Barkley with Patel?"

"No."

"Did Barkley ever talk to you about Patel?"

I thought of the memory stick that Barkley had given me the night he was killed. "No," I said. "Why do you ask?"

Mahler shrugged. "There's some information about Patel on Barkley's computer. We're trying to understand why it's there."

He closed his notebook. "We're going to follow up on this," he said. "And we're going to want to talk to you again. Don't make any travel plans."

Mahler called Officer Reed and asked him to come pick me up. When Reed arrived, he handed me a form, indicating the police had conducted a search of my apartment and had downloaded files from my laptop. "The files will be returned to you at the end of our investigation," he said. Then he escorted me back outside to his car and drove me home.

It was after five when I walked into my apartment. There was a message on my answering machine from Page, saying she had to work late at the fitness club and would stay at the motel. I called Nico and Vincent. When Nico answered, I told her about Kenny's death.

"Someone must have thought Kenny knew too much," Nico said.

"Apparently," I said. "You should also know that the cops were watching Kenny, and they know about the meeting that Vincent and I had with Kenny.

They're going to ask Vincent some questions. You guys might want to put Paul's laptop somewhere out of sight and maybe clean out your garage."

"Oh good," she said. "This'll make Vincent happy."

I made myself a grilled cheese sandwich and finished a bottle of wine. After dinner I spent an hour re-reading the chapters I had delivered to DeVries in preparation for my meeting the following morning.

*   *   *

When I arrived at Patel's study at 10 am the next day, he was seated in his recliner, looking more awake and animated than usual. There were piles of paper spread across his lap. "Mr. Teller," he said. "I'd almost forgotten. You find us in the midst of party planning."

DeVries was at his desk, and Shawn waited at his post by the door, ready to break someone's nose. As I sat opposite Patel, he handed me a file. "There are some problems here we must discuss."

"Let's start with the easy ones," DeVries interrupted. "The two chapters on the growth of Torana are acceptable."

"And the chapter on my childhood is written well enough," Patel said.

"But, as Rajiv said, there are also serious problems," DeVries said. "Why did you feel it necessary to write a chapter on Safia and another on Rajiv's wedding when we had agreed it would not be necessary?"

"As I explained, I think readers will want to know something about Mr. Patel's private life. That's really the point of an autobiography. Not including his wife will leave a hole in the narrative."

Patel smiled. "Safia was a good woman," he said. "But she was not worldly. It's not necessary for this book to describe her in such detail."

"She may be mentioned, of course, but she doesn't require a complete chapter," DeVries said. "The point is, we're paying you to write this book, and we don't want you to waste time. It's important we move forward as quickly as possible."

"I thought you understood it would take some time to write a book like this."

"Mr. Teller, let me be frank. You've been with us for nearly two months. We provided you with a wealth of information and answered all your questions. And so far, you've only written a handful of chapters. To be honest, we're disappointed with your progress."

"I only received some of the materials two weeks ago. The writing's just getting started."

"But, according to your outline, there's much more to be done."

Patel sighed. "I don't have time to argue today," he said. "My staff has much to do in advance of our party tomorrow night. Now Whit and I have drawn up a schedule for you." DeVries handed me a sheet of paper with columns of dates and deliverables.

"This is how my business is run," Patel said. "If we didn't have schedules, we'd lose millions of dollars."

"Writing doesn't always fit into a schedule," I said.

"Why shouldn't it be like any other business?" Patel asked.

"Perhaps if you weren't preoccupied with other matters," DeVries said.

I looked at him.

"Yesterday, the police came to Rajiv's house looking for you," he said.

"In connection with the death of that drug dealer," Patel said.

"Didn't we make clear how your behavior in this community might reflect on Mr. Patel?" DeVries asked.

"I was not involved in . . . ," I said.

"What you did or didn't do is immaterial," DeVries said. "You'll be identi-fied in the papers as residing at *Shanti Bhavan*."

"Mr. Teller," Patel said. "You come to us with a . . . reputation. We've tried to make allowances. We'd hoped you wouldn't become a public figure once again."

"I didn't intend to."

"Nevertheless," Patel said.

"With this schedule, we're giving you notice," DeVries said. "If you don't meet these deadlines, and if you don't stay out of the public limelight, we'll ter-minate your contract and find another writer. Do you understand?"

I dropped the schedule and files in my briefcase. "Sure," I said. I looked at Patel. He was absorbed again in the papers on his lap. "Thank you, Mr. Teller," he said without looking up.

Back in my tower, I read through the schedule. It called for five chapters to be written per week for the next six weeks, and for revision and rewriting to be complete two weeks after that. The pace was twice as fast as my last few books.

When I wrote the books for Tina Terrill and Susan Sparrow, the schedule was part of my terms for accepting the project. The imposition of the schedule for the Patel book seemed another confirmation of my climb down the career ladder.

I ate lunch and spent the afternoon trying to write a chapter on Patel's building of a housing development in the San Fernando Valley. Around five, Page arrived. She had taught back-to-back aerobics classes and looked tired. I opened two bottles of beer, and we sat on the balcony.

"I got a call between classes on my cell," Page said. "It was a guy. He said he wanted Paul's laptop, and he knew where to find me. He said if I didn't give it to him, he'd do me like Ray." She drank from her bottle.

I stared at her. "You're kidding? Who was it? Did you recognize the voice?"

She shook her head.

"You call the police?"

"No, what're they going to do?"

I realized we hadn't seen each other since Thursday. She said she read a newspaper account of Kenny's death, but I told her about Mahler's interrogation and what the police knew about Kenny's overdose. I also gave a brief account of my meeting that morning with Patel and DeVries.

When I mentioned their preoccupation with the party, she asked, "Did they invite you?"

"It's all part of impressing the biographer," I said. "Jill's going to be there, too, with her new boyfriend, so I have to face seeing them again."

I looked at Page. "Why don't you come as my guest?" I said.

"Really?" Page said. "Are you sure we know each other well enough for that? Or, am I there just to even things up between you and Jill?"

"No, I don't think that's possible."

"Anyway, it doesn't matter. I can't go—Rajiv and I kind of have a history."

"A history?"

"I don't think I'd be welcome."

"It's going to a huge party. We'll probably never see either Jill or Rajiv. We'll hide in the sea of faces."

Page watched me. "If you say so," she said.

CHAPTER **3 7**

ON SATURDAY EVENING, the first sign of Patel's party was the filling of the field behind my tower with the cars of arriving guests. From the estate came the sound of giddy laughter and big band music. Strings of white lights glowed in the trees.

I dressed in a dark suit and white shirt without a tie. About seven Page appeared at the top of my stairs. She wore a long black dress, espadrilles, and a cashmere pashmina around her shoulders. We walked down the paved drive, first side by side and then arm in arm. At the gate we were met by a pair of barrel-chested security guards. One of them consulted my name on a clipboard. "Excuse me, sir," he said. "but I don't have a guest listed."

I leaned close to him and whispered, "Since her last film, my friend doesn't want the press to know she's in town," I said.

The guard studied Page's face and then nodded in recognition. "Nice to see you, ma'am," he said, as he unclipped the cable across the entranceway. "Welcome to Sonoma County."

The estate grounds were already busy with a couple hundred party-goers. The central plaza had been transformed for the occasion. At the eastern end, on a raised platform, was a 15-piece orchestra, and in front of it, a wooden dance floor, where a dozen couples were swirling in time with the music. Opposite it, across the yard, was a second, smaller raised stage, where a lone singer sat perched on a stool playing a guitar. Two sides of the courtyard were framed with white canopies. Here lines of guests surrounded long tables of buffet food platters, while an open grill piped a column of white smoke into the sky. Dotted around the yard were small booths draped in bunting, where attendants filled stemware with wine and explained the dark mysteries of *terroir*.

The rich and famous could be seen in every direction. Among the wine makers, I saw Matthew Nolan, Chris Maser, Marie Torterelli, and Lilly Hernandez. From Hollywood, there was the veteran TV star Bill Reed and Lisa Winslow, fresh off her latest HBO miniseries. Skip Brown was acting out a funny story for two couples—one of whom I recognized as the *Night Storm* actor Don Silver and his wife.

Page and I waded through the crowd toward one of the booths. In front of the winery table, I saw Molly talking with Eddie Mahler. They both noticed me and then saw Page and shuffled self-consciously.

"Everyone here tonight a potential life-story to you, Teller?" Mahler asked.

"I don't know," I said. "They all look like suspects to you?"

Molly was blushing, and I realized we'd interrupted a private conversation. I pulled Page toward the wine table.

We were tasting a Russian River old-vine zinfandel when a small clutch of people approached with our host, Rajiv Patel, at its center. He wore a black tuxedo with black shirt and black tie, and carried a half-filled champagne flute in his right hand. On his left arm was a famous lingerie model.

"Mister Teller," he said. "How are you enjoying my party?"

He introduced the model, who looked back at me with a hollow, drug-eyed stare.

I introduced Page, and for the first time Patel noticed her. His eyes traveled slowly down her body, and his expression darkened. "I'm acquainted with Miss Salinger," he said shortly.

Page tipped back her glass and drank the rest of the wine. "Hey Rajie," she said.

Without replying, he looked back at me. "You'll excuse me," he said. "I must welcome my other guests."

The entourage, with the little man at its forefront, shuffled off into the party crowd.

"Where do you know Patel from?" I asked Page.

"Through Paul," she said.

"Something going on with you two?"

"Something. I need a drink."

We found a booth, where a cheerful young woman filled our glasses with a cabernet. In the middle of the server's earnest description of malolactic fermentation, Page drank the wine in a single swallow and walked away. The young woman's mouth fell open in mid-sentence as she looked in the direction Page had gone. I smiled and tipped my glass to her. "Sometimes," I said, "you just want to experience it all at once."

I caught up with Page at the lines leading to the food tables. She already had another glass of wine in her hand.

"Having fun?" I asked.

"Barrel of laughs," she said.

We began filling our plates with grilled chicken and green salad. I felt a hand on my shoulder and turned to find DeVries and one of the monster security guards. DeVries wore a satin-lapelled tuxedo and red bow tie. He stood stiffly erect.

"Mister Teller," he said. "I'm afraid I need to ask you to leave, or at least to remove your guest. She's not on our security list." Having said this, he turned and looked at Page.

Page looked back at him. "Hi Whit," she said. "How's my favorite secretary?"

DeVries opened his mouth and seemed to choke on something.

"Rajie tell you to throw me out?" Page asked. "Is that what this is about?"

"As the host of this affair, Mister Patel has the right to . . ."

"Oh, fuck it," Page said. She drank down her wine, handed the empty glass to the security guard, and shoved the plate of food at DeVries. As he was trying to balance the plate and keep the chicken from falling onto his tuxedo, Page turned and in a moment had disappeared into the crowd.

"You'll be held responsible for this," DeVries said to me as he threw the plate into a trash bin and hurried off through the crowd after Page.

I stood for a few minutes by myself, eating the chicken and watching the crowd go by. Then a flash of light exploded in front of me. It was the photographer Bud Platt. "Charlie Teller," he boomed. "What a surprise."

"Leave me alone," I said.

"Oh, come on," he said. "It'll be a good story for tomorrow's paper: 'Famous Loser at Local Bash.'" Platt was wearing a plaid tux jacket and baggy trousers. In one hand was a camera and in the other, a glass of wine. He was perspiring heavily.

"Screw you," I said. A few minutes earlier the orchestra had taken a break, so our voices attracted the attention of half a dozen couples, who now turned to watch us.

"Whoa, tough guy," Platt said. "How's the scam going with Patel? About time for you to fuck up, isn't it?"

As he said this last part, his face swayed toward me. I pushed him away with the flat of my hand on his chest. "Knock it off," I said and turned to leave.

Platt caught me by the jacket sleeve, and I heard it tear. "Where's that piece of ass you came in with?" he asked.

I turned around and hit him hard in his mouth with my right fist. Already unsteady on his feet, he fell backward into the people who had gathered around us, tumbling onto his back and spilling several other guests over with him. As he fell, he dropped the camera, which shattered apart when it hit the gravel walkway. A woman screamed.

A man in the crowd grabbed me, although I had already backed away from the fallen photographer. Then one of the security guards appeared and took hold of me. "Let's go, pal," he said.

As the guard pushed me, the crowd parted to let us through. Suddenly in front of me were Jill and Dave, each holding a wine glass and food platter.

"Charlie," Jill said. She looked up at the security guard whose hand was clamped onto my shoulder.

"Yeah," I said. "Think I'll make it an early night."

The guard pushed me again, and we made our way across the crowded courtyard. Behind us, out of the quieted party, the night air was suddenly filled with the sound of a squealing microphone from the direction of the second stage. Then a woman's voice rose across the estate grounds. In the first few notes, I recognized Page's voice singing:

> *If I fell in love with you*
> *Would you promise to be true*
> *And help me understand*
> *'Cause I've been in love before*
> *And I found that love was more*
> *Than just . . .*

The voice stopped in mid-phrase, as the guard and I reached the entrance gate, and I imagined Page being pulled off stage.

The guard led me outside the fence perimeter, and I walked alone up the dark drive to my tower.

CHAPTER **38**

Susan Sparrow

SUSAN SPARROW'S LIFE story began with a box of audiotapes—in all, more than 200 of them. They sat in neat trays, numbered and labeled with the date of the recording. Each tape started the same way: "This is Susan Sparrow," the voice said. Then the voice announced that day's date.

If you picked a tape, you might hear Susan describing a 1984 radio interview with the director Ben Knight, who had directed a teenage slasher film starring Susan. In the interview, Knight had recounted an anecdote about Susan's shyness when performing in a brief nude scene. Now on the tape, Susan repeated Knight's account and then told the story from her own point of view—the activity on the set, comments made by one of the lighting technicians, and the drug addiction of her co-star. It lasted thirty minutes.

The stories were collected randomly, despite the chronological labeling on the cases. Following the description of the 1984 Ben Knight interview, Susan described a 1986 article in the *LA Times*, which in her view had misquoted her, and her own line-by-line recounting of what she had actually said.

Her recorded voice was quiet, almost furtive, as if she were concerned she might be overheard. There were frequent long pauses, when the listener heard Susan breathing or walking around the room. I say listener, but of course I was the only person who ever heard the tapes. Even Susan herself had never played them back. Before I opened the box, they had lain in a closet in her house, like a trapped and coiled embodiment of her inner life.

I first met Susan at a party in her Beverly Hills home. It was one of those massive old-Hollywood houses, built in the style of a French chateau, and later remodeled with a roman portico and antebellum columns. Downstairs was a dining room with seating for 30; upstairs enough bedrooms for a small hotel.

Jill and I had been invited as guests of the director Lyle Kennedy, who was making a film biography of Nick White. Our hostess greeted us in the library, a dim room lined with shelves of perfect leather spines. Here and there, amid the literary output, were small items of interest—a Fan Award for Susan's role in the film comedy *On Her Toes*, a letter from the Governor of Texas proclaiming February 2 Susan Sparrow Day, and a laminated and framed cover from the magazine *Show*, which featured a torso photograph of Susan in a low-cut gown and the headline "Sexiest Woman Alive!"

Standing beside this last display, Susan said every time she saw the cover, she imagined there were two categories of the award, and she was glad she had won the "alive" category. It was a tired joke, the kind of thing you could imagine her telling a hundred guests before you.

When she met us, Susan put her face close to Jill's and said in a mock grave tone, "I want to borrow your husband for about four months. I promise to return him in one piece."

Turning to me, she said, "Your book on Nick White blew me away—it like totally changed the way I look at spirituality."

I was transfixed by her lips, which were shimmering with a silvery metallic gloss.

"You have to write my story," she said. "I had my chart read the other day, and it said I should examine my life. When Lyle asked if he could bring you, I thought it must be a sign."

"Tell me how you work," she said. "I have a few audiotapes—just me talking into a microphone. You're welcome to listen to them."

She looked at Jill and laughed. "I'm sorry. I'm frightening you, aren't I? I do that sometimes." She held up her right hand as if she were swearing in court. "Trust me," she said. "This is going to be a great project for all of us."

I was between projects at the time and had promised Jill I would try to find clients in Los Angeles. Barry arranged a contract through Susan's management company. Two weeks later I was sitting in Susan's office in her home, opening the box of audiotapes.

"This one first," Susan said, handing me a tape from the top. "You've probably heard the story about when I first came to Los Angeles at sixteen to become a singer. My mom stayed back in Texas with my little sister, and I came with my Uncle Eugene. We lived in a motel in Eagle Rock. Gene was supposed to be my guardian, but he raped me."

"This is where I became the person I am," she said.

• • •

She was born in a small town in west Texas called Becker. Her father left home when she was two, and she lived with her mother and younger sister in a trailer parked behind a gas station. They were the poorest family in a bottom-rung town, where the other residents were grateful to have someone to look down on.

At twelve, she talked her mother into entering her in a beauty contest sponsored by the Farm Bureau. She lost but sang a song and fell in love with performing before an audience. Two years later she toured veterans' halls as the lead singer in a honky-tonk band.

When she turned sixteen, Susan announced her plans to go to Los Angeles to become a singer. Her mother acceded to the plan but insisted Susan be accompanied by her uncle.

Susan and Eugene found a cheap utility apartment in the town of Eagle Rock, just south of Glendale. On weekdays, Susan attended Eagle Rock High School, and in her spare time she made an audition tape and sent copies to record producers.

One night Eugene pulled back the covers of her bed, slid in beside her, and asked her to hold him. He had never been away from home for so long and was lonely, he said. He smelled like the cans of Budweiser piled around his chair in front of the television.

Susan was afraid to tell her mother for fear she'd be forced to give up her dream of becoming a singer and return to Texas. "I decided then," she said, "everything comes with a price."

In 1980, after two years in Los Angeles, she met a music producer named Steve Betts. Betts thought her singing voice was ordinary, but he liked her Texan accent and her confident style. He had a friend who was casting for an after-school television show—a comedy about an inner-city high school—and Betts arranged for an audition.

In the audition Susan read a page of dialogue with one of the producers. Never a strong reader, she stumbled over the words and laughed at herself in embarrassment. When she looked up, the producers were laughing too. At first she thought that they were making fun of her, but they told her to continue. In the next ten minutes, the producers found the actress for one of the parts of the show, and Susan discovered she could act.

The television show was *Monroe High*, and Susan played the part of Alice-Ann— the smart-aleck, white trash girl who steals every scene she appears in. Acting came easily to the young Susan Sparrow. She had been trained in the toughest of academies—Becker, Texas. From age three, she had been playing parts to survive, pretending not to be a little girl living in a crummy trailer, dressed in worn-out clothes, stuck in a town on the edge of nowhere.

Monroe High ran for two years and was known mainly as the spring-board for the teen actor Ronny Williams. But it also changed Susan's life. She made enough money to move out of Eugene's apartment, and to arrange for her mother and sister to come and live with her in Canoga Park. She hired an agent and found parts in television films. She played the younger sister in *Morningside* and the best friend in *Heart's Desire.*

In 1983, she made the leap to the big screen as one of the teenagers killed in the slasher film *Escape from Rosewood Lane.* Not long after the film's release, she married one of its producers, Craig Tremont.

Over the following five years, with Tremont's help, she appeared in half a dozen films whose creativity was limited to inventing opportunities for Susan to remove her clothes on screen. She divorced Tremont, and with a new manager, she appeared in more films, unconvincingly portraying a succession of professional women.

She dated actors and was photographed on the club scene. During a party at her house, a guest fell from a second-story window. She was arrested in Santa Barbara on a DUI. Her "secret" wedding with the actor Rey Sanchez made the cover of the major magazines, as did their divorce a year later.

At age 28, she had turned into a Hollywood joke, an actress known more for being in the tabloid press than for appearing in film. That was when I was hired.

· · ·

Writing Susan Sparrow's life was never intended to be a simple telling of her story. By the time she hired me, much had been written about her in the press, and Susan saw the main purpose of her autobiography as their refutation. On top of that, some of Susan's own accounts of events had already been disproved, so the book was also intended to clarify what she had meant on earlier occasions when she had been quoted. In the end, her biography was an amalgam of stories about her she denied, stories about her she had adopted, revised versions of earlier fabrications, and altogether new stories she made up.

Even had I wanted, it would have been difficult to find the truth. Her own fictions were tangled. Several versions existed of every anecdote, like different takes of a scene. Sometimes Susan had me write each one on a sheet of paper, and she spread them across the floor of her room to compare.

She had studied the lives of other great actresses and borrowed freely from them. Even her name—Susan Sparrow—was a complex creation. In her adolescence, she kept a notebook of names. When the *Monroe High* producers asked for her stage name, she opened her notebook and sat before a mirror, saying each name over and over and watching how her lips looked as she said the words. Susan Sparrow looked best.

• • •

Susan was, at least for one magazine, in one year, the "Sexiest Woman Alive!" Her sexual persona was powerful. While I worked with her, I watched men meet her for the first time. Most lost their bearings. Their smiles froze on their faces. They tried not to look at her lips or her breasts or her legs.

After Susan's film *Rapture* was released, a radio station asked men what they'd be willing to give in exchange for being alone for an hour with a nude Susan Sparrow. Offers included jewelry, cars, and airline tickets. More than two hundred men said that they'd be willing to give up their wives.

She crafted her seduction to meet men's expectations. She knew the meaning of each detail—a hemline inch, visible lingerie.

On screen, her confident control of her allure led her to believe she could inhabit any character. "I can *be* anything you want me to be," she once screamed at a director.

Still, after twenty years as the object of desire, she treated it with contempt. "Men are stupid," she said. "They're all fourteen-year-old boys, still surprised by their own erections. But once they have sex with you, most of them despise you for what they think you made them do. You ever notice, Charlie, how close sexual attraction and hate are? You arrange human feelings on a shelf, those two would be side by side."

• • •

While I worked on Susan's book, I arranged to stay overnight at her Beverly Hills home two nights a week. The rest of the week, I lived with Jill and Lucy in Seal Beach and worked in my office there.

Motherhood had forced Jill to take a leave of absence from her teaching position at Fullerton. She tried to stay on with the Toyon String Quartet, but the rehearsal and performance schedules were too rigorous.

Despite these sacrifices, Jill loved being a mother. She awoke with Lucy every morning at six and nursed her. In the middle of the morning, she took Lucy in a stroller to the end of the pier and back. The three of us ate lunch together on the second-floor deck. In the afternoon Jill and Lucy went for another walk, this time down to the main street shops.

My time with Lucy was in the evening after dinner. We sat together while I read her favorite story, Peter Rabbit. It was a small book with watercolors of the rabbit stealing carrots and being chased by a farmer named Mr. McGregor.

I had started taking amphetamines again, this time Benzedrine, which I kept out of sight in my briefcase. My routine was to take one after dinner to give me a few more hours of work time at night. Some evenings, as I sat with Lucy, the illustrations swirled in my head, and I found myself on the page, a crazed little junkie, scrambling just ahead of the farmer with his rake.

Later, after Jill and Lucy had gone to sleep, I sat at my desk and worked on one of several novels. My fiction motives were less pure than earlier in my career. I wrote what I called "unfinished novels," three-chapter setups I proposed to finish if a publisher was interested.

"Why're you doing this?" Barry asked.

"To spare everyone effort," I said. "If the publishers aren't interested in them, why should I go through all the trouble to make them longer? Besides most people don't finish the books they start. Publishers could sell these as partials. They end where the average reader stops reading."

"Do you want to get blacklisted?" Barry asked. "Do you want the New York houses to hate you?"

Of course I didn't want publishers to hate me. I wanted to be beloved. Charlie Teller, beloved author.

By this time, Jill had largely stopped talking to me about my work. In the evening, when I told Jill stories about Susan, Jill listened and nodded silently at the punch lines.

One night in the middle of a Susan anecdote, Jill suddenly said, "I don't want to hear this." She looked back at me and then continued eating.

"Why?" I asked. "It's OK. I'm sure Susan wouldn't mind."

"It's not that. I just don't think it's a good idea to talk about it in our home."

"Why not?"

"Just because," Jill said. "I don't want to hear it." She held Lucy in the crook of her arm while she ate.

"You don't want to hear that story, or you don't want me to talk about my book at all?"

"It's not your book, it's her book. And, no, if I don't have to, I don't want to hear about it at all."

"Why? Can you tell me that much?"

"Charlie, these stories are awful. I mean, I know people like to read that stuff, but it's awful." Jill looked down at Lucy's face. "We shouldn't even be having this conversation right now."

"This is what I do. This is what I have to talk about."

"Then let's not talk."

"You just want to sit here and eat?"

"If those are my choices, yes," Jill said.

"Maybe we be shouldn't be together," I said and left the room.

Charlie Teller, beloved husband.

·   ·   ·

Behind Susan's home were two acres of lawn and gardens and a large Italian marble pool. The pool had a rock grotto, two stone lions that spouted water out of their mouths, a waterfall, underwater lighting, and in one corner a raised hot tub whose water spilled down a flight of cascades into the pool. Around the pool were a redwood deck and a three-sided clubhouse. The clubhouse had changing rooms, a grill, refrigerator, and food pantry.

My work routine with Susan was to work every afternoon by the pool. I set up my laptop just inside the clubhouse, and Susan lay on a chaise a few feet away.

Susan liked to read pages as I printed them and suggested changes on the spot. When she was not reviewing drafts, she changed into a swimsuit and swam in the pool or tanned herself in the sun. When a few hours had gone by and she was bored, she coaxed me into the pool with her. We swam side by side underwater or played with a Frisbee. One of her favorite activities was to jump on my back and have me carry her up the steps to the hot tub.

In August of that year, there was a week of temperatures over 100. By noon, the clubhouse was baking. I worked in a swimsuit and jumped in the pool once an hour to cool off. On the heat wave's last day, Susan spent most of the afternoon in the comfort of her air-conditioned house. In my concentration, I didn't see her join me. When I looked up, she was lying on her chaise, without clothes. She saw me look at her and laughed. "My gosh, Charlie," she said. "I was wondering when you'd notice."

"Aren't you worried one of the gardeners is going to see you?" I asked.

"Day off," she said. "Besides, what're they going to do?"

I returned to my screen, but she called out, "Come on, Charlie. Let's go for a swim."

I pushed myself away from the desk and went to the pool. "No suit," she said. "Rules of the day."

I pulled off my trunks and dove into the pool. A minute later, she swam up to me and stood in waist-high water facing me. "This going to inspire you, Charlie?" she asked.

"I don't need inspiration," I said.

"Don't be grouchy," she said, splashing me.

Then it happened, as if it were nothing at all.

I started to swim away, but Susan took my left hand in hers and put her arms around me. I felt her breasts and her hips against my body. She kissed me, and the water from her hair ran down my face, and her tongue came into my mouth. I could have pulled away, but I let myself taste the kiss.

She ended the kiss and looked at me. "Oh, wow," she said.

We kissed again, this time longer. Then we shuffled together through the water still in the embrace to the low steps of the pool. She lay on her back on the first step and I lay on top of her. We kissed again, and she ran her fingers through my hair and pulled my head into the kiss.

When I was inside her, she suddenly propped herself up on her arms and said, "Wait a minute. Tell me you love me Charlie. Say 'I love you.'"

I stared at her, my mouth suddenly dry.

"Say it like this," she said. "I loooove you." Her voice elongated the second word.

I said, "I loooove you."

"No," she said. "You didn't close your eyes. Do it again and close your eyes."

I closed my eyes and said it again.

She laughed. "I loooove you, too," she said, this time imitating my own voice.

When it was over, I stood up first. In the shallow end, the water came to my knees. Around me was the stifling air of the heat wave. I felt as if I couldn't breathe. At the pool's edge, the stone lions continued to spout water from their mouths, in a mockery of our act.

I looked back at Susan. She was still lying on the pool step. "Well that was unexpected, wasn't it?" she said.

I swam across the pool to the clubhouse and put on my trunks. A few minutes later, she climbed out the pool. She stood facing me, still naked, pulling her hair together and squeezing out the water. "What's up with you?" she asked.

"Nothing," I said.

"Don't be stupid. What is it?"

"That shouldn't have happened. It was a mistake."

"There are no mistakes," she said.

"Yes, there are," I said. I wrapped a towel around my waist and dried myself.

She laughed. "Oh, for god sakes," she said. "We were in the pool. We were just playing around. It's not like we were in the bedroom or anything."

I stared at her.

"You weren't cheating on your wife," she said. "This is part of your work. We're working."

"You think that?" I said.

"Of course. Believe me, I know cheating. This is not cheating. If you like, I'll talk to Jill."

"Are you kidding?"

"No, really. If you want, I'll call her right now. It's no big deal."

"No," I said. "I'll talk to Jill. I'll tell her."

In the end, though, I didn't tell her that day—or ever. She found out another way.

. . .

Susan's book, *Sparrow's Song*, was a longer and more expensively produced book that any of my previous collaborations. It contained more than 400 pages, with twenty folios of color photographs bound into the book. The cover photograph was a closeup of Susan's face, her green eyes mischievously flirting with the camera and her lips glistening and slightly pursed. For the dust jacket, she re-shot my usual photograph and replaced it with a studio version of me in a tuxedo. In the acknowledgments, she wrote: "Most of all, I want to thank Charlie Teller, who helped me find the voice I thought I lost, the song that's in this book. I love you, Charlie."

The critics were unanimous in their dislike. The *New York Times* wrote: "Rarely have so many words been expended on someone who appears on screen with so little talent and so few clothes." *Vanity Fair* even singled me out: "Ghostwriter Charlie Teller, who previously helped Ken

Styles and Tina Terrill explain their falls from grace, is taking a vacation, this time in BimboLand."

The book was published as part of a national media campaign. The press tour was larger than for any of the other books that I had co-written. At every signing, long lines of autograph seekers formed outside the stores. I accompanied Susan for the signings but stayed in the background.

In the first three weeks, Susan also did more than twenty TV and radio interviews. One of the interviews was on a women's daytime TV show with a live audience and a hostess known for her bawdy style. When Susan sat beside her on the set, the hostess started by saying, "All right, Susan, let's talk sex."

The audience roared.

"OK," Susan said. "What'd you want to know?"

"Rey Sanchez. Honeymoon night. And don't skimp on the details."

The audience laughed and clapped.

Susan repeated the story from the book about her night of passionate love-making with Sanchez on the lanai of their private house in Hawaii.

The hostess pretended to wipe the perspiration from her brow. "Wow," she said. "And you told all this to ..." She consulted the book's cover. "Charlie Teller?"

"Charlie and I had a *special* relationship," Susan said.

The audience hooted.

"How special?"

"Sometimes we worked in the nude."

"Now that *is* special."

"There were no secrets between us. Charlie helped me find my voice."

"And what'd you help *him* find?"

Susan feigned modesty. "Let's just say, you can't write about it, if you haven't done it."

The audience roared.

The hostess looked at the camera. "Charlie Teller, wherever you are, you're one lucky man."

The next day an account of the interview appeared in a couple newspapers. The following day, it was picked up by the wire services and TV talk shows. Reporters called my house, and when I wasn't home, Jill took the calls. The first two asked for me and left a message. The third said, "I understand your husband had sex with Susan Sparrow. Would you like to comment?"

As revelations go in twenty-first century America, it wasn't much of a story: a famous actress making love with her ghostwriter. There were no disgraced politicians, no fortunes squandered. It involved Susan Sparrow, already known for public indiscretions. Still there was an irony to the circumstances—a biography writer, caught in the act—which appealed to the editorial writers anxious to make a larger point. And it was about sex, and therefore impossible to ignore.

There were jokes about me on late-night television. "Hey, have you heard about this ghostwriter Charlie Teller?" the host asked in his monologue. "Does it in a swimming pool with Susan Sparrow while he's writing her memoirs. How's that for a cure for writer's block?" (*Laughter*) "Talk about wet dreams!" (*More laughter and applause*).

After that, the digging started: past TV interviews, book deals, rejected book deals, traffic tickets, drug prescriptions. Details spilled out and collected themselves into a pattern. For a while, I became that classic public figure in our late modern age: the Worst Human Being on Earth This Week.

Like most stories, mine had its own life. There were apparent revelations, followed by denials from Barry. Then new revelations appeared, and I participated in a clear-the-air live TV interview. Then came more damning revelations, and news footage of my image fleeing reporters.

A week later, the daughter of a famous record producer was killed, and her body found in the trunk of a car in New York City. From then on, the public lost interest in my sordid story.

But lives are easily unraveled, and like that, mine had come undone.

"It's not how they're saying it was," I told Jill. "I'm not sure how it happened." We were standing in the kitchen of the Seal Beach house. Jill had her back to me and was looking through the floor-to-ceiling glass toward the expanse of white sand and blue ocean. The million-dollar view, the real estate agent had called it. A hundred yards away, a couple in swimsuits ran on the beach, the guy chasing the girl, both of them laughing.

"But you *do* know, Charlie," Jill said without turning around. "You probably have five different versions in your head, and you're editing them right now, trying to decide which one works best."

"You don't really think that, do you?" I said.

Jill turned and faced me. Her eyes stared at mine as if I were suddenly far away, and she was having trouble recognizing me. "Of course I do," she said. "Why else would I say it? I want you to understand something. I don't want to know what happened. I don't want to know what really happened, and I especially don't want to know what you say really happened. And I won't use Lucy as an excuse. I don't want to be with you anymore, Charlie. It's not even that I don't love you anymore. I—just—don't—want-to—be—with—you."

She turned and looked back outside. The guy on the beach caught the girl, and the girl closed her eyes and raised her head to be kissed.

Jill and I stood there for a minute in silence, both of us watching the sand and the waves and the couple who were now kissing. I thought of five things to say and didn't say any of them. After a minute I left.

On the professional side, two book contracts were canceled. Barry had difficulty packaging me, and suggested I find other representation.

Susan's book, of course, sold well; later editions carried a dust jacket chevron that read "As Seen on TV!"

I never saw or spoke to Susan again. She went back to starring in sex kitten comedies. Somewhere, though, I imagine there's an audiotape. It starts with that day's date, and then Susan's whispery voice can be heard saying, "That year, I met a writer named Charlie Teller, and I asked him to write the story of my life. Later the media distorted the things I said about Charlie. The truth is this."

CHAPTER 3 9

BACK IN MY tower, I poured some scotch into a tumbler and found Van Morrison on my MP3 player. After about 20 minutes, I heard footsteps on the stairs, and Page walked in. Her hair was loose over her shoulders. She was carrying her shoes. Her mascara was smeared. She looked at me with dark, angry eyes, but did not say anything. She sat on the sofa and put her bare feet on the coffee table.

I went to the kitchen and made her a drink. She accepted it without looking at me and swallowed it slowly. For a few minutes, neither of us talked.

Then she said, "Before I was old enough to drive, every Saturday my friends and I took the bus to the mall. We wore our hottest outfits and sat on the same bench and watched the guys."

"The weird ones were the married guys—young husbands with their wives and two little kids in strollers, out of the house for the evening. They walked by, and after they passed, the husband looked back at me. Right there, with his wife beside him. He looked at me, not even trying to be subtle about it."

"When I was in my twenties, older guys in their forties and fifties asked me out. Sometimes they were married. They always had plenty of money. At the start, I remember thinking it was going to be different: these guys could have anything they wanted. We went to great restaurants. They told me about their businesses, how tough they had to be, where they traveled, their cars, their houses."

"But after a while it felt like a drama. The dark restaurant, the food, and the wine were all part of the drama. They intended it to be sophisticated and subtle. We both acted as if it were real, as if the whole evening were spontaneous, and we were just getting to know each other. But none of it was real."

"When the food was gone, and we were finishing the wine, the same thing always happened. He put his hand on mine, and his voice changed, as if he were being serious for the first time. Then he told me something private that he'd never told anyone. I suppose, in his mind, it was a sort of gift, an opening of his heart in a way that was unusual for him. But after a while, I found out what it really was. It was a key that he thought was going to let him inside me."

She started to cry. Tears ran down her face. She put up her palms to wipe at the streams coming down her cheeks. I stood up to join her on the sofa, but she shook her head, and I sat back down on the recliner.

"Paul wasn't like that," she said. "We talked for hours about our families and growing up. He told stories. He was a great storyteller—I think that's why he liked you. And sometimes he asked me a few questions, and then he just sat there and listened."

"He didn't want anything. We were friends. I'd been with him for a couple of weeks before we even kissed. The sex was okay, but it was never that important. We just liked being with each other. For me, all that was new."

For a moment she sat crying silently.

"I miss him," she said. "Especially when something like tonight happens."

"What did happen tonight?" I asked. "What was that with you and Patel?"

"I told you we had a history. A couple months ago, he came on to me. It was awful. The guy's a creep. I know he's a big deal, but he's a creep."

"Patel came on to you?"

"Yeah. It's a long story. I shouldn't have gone there tonight. I knew something was going to happen."

She wiped her face with hands again. "Look, I'm tired," she said. "I really need to sleep."

I gave her a pair of my pajamas. We re-made the sofa into a bed, and she lay under the comforter. I switched off the lights and went to my bed. As I lay waiting to sleep, the lights from Patel's party glowed through my window, and the orchestra music floated across the night sky.

* * *

I awoke early Sunday morning. Not wanting to wake Page, I took a cup of coffee and the telephone out to the balcony and watched the early morning sun spread across the other side of the valley.

About nine, the phone rang, and it was Vincent. "Hey Teller," he said. "I found a few more things. You remember those specifications I showed you Tuesday night for the building in Sacramento? Patel's company won the bid. The building's under construction right now."

"So whatever arrangement Patel had with Amtree, it worked in this case?"

"I guess so. Your friend Barkley didn't seem to have anything else."

"Maybe he spoke with the guy at Amtree, that guy Sutter." I told Vincent about Andrew Sutter's name turning up in a list of names added to guest lists for a party catered by Paul Barkley.

"Sutter's a minor-level pencil pusher in San Jose," Vincent said. "What the hell's he doing at an exclusive party with a bunch of show business cokeheads two hours away in Sonoma County?"

"Maybe the same question occurred to Paul."

"Well if it did, he didn't write it down. And I'm not sure what good it's going to do us."

"Why's that?"

"On Friday, I finally got through to someone else at Amtree. I said I'd submitted a bid and needed to talk with Sutter. The guy on the other end of the line hemmed and hawed, but he finally said Sutter hasn't been in the office in three weeks. Amtree's trying to keep it low key so as not to alarm any clients, but it's clear they don't know where Sutter is. His wife hasn't seen him. The San Jose police are treating it as a missing person."

"What does that mean?"

"I don't know. Could be Sutter had some scam going with Patel, got spooked and decided to take off. I'll make a few calls and see if I can find out anything else."

Twenty minutes later, on my second cup of coffee, the phone rang again. This time it was Jill. Her voice was barely audible. "Charlie," she said. "I've spoken with Richard Mansfield. I've asked him to file a petition for a change in our custody agreement for Lucy."

There was silence on the phone.

"What're you talking about?" I said.

"Lucy told me you went to her school on Thursday."

"So what? I wanted to talk to her about the shoplifting incident."

"I told you I didn't want you seeing her."

"Oh, come on . . ."

"Charlie, I don't want to argue about it. I'm tired of arguing."

"Me too."

"This just isn't working out."

"What isn't working out?"

"For you to be here, to be around us. I thought when you moved up here and took that job, that things were going to change. But they haven't. I mean, look at you. Look what happened last night, what's happened the past three weeks."

"You think it's my fault?"

"I don't know whose fault it is or what you're doing. All I know is, it's not a good thing for you to be around Lucy right now. I've got my hands full trying to help her grow up, and you're just making it harder. You're not around, and when you are, you're doing something crazy. I don't need this."

"You don't need this?"

"No, I don't."

"Listen, I just want . . ."

"No, I'm not going to listen. I called to tell you about the petition. That's all." She hung up.

I sat for a while, staring down at the trellised rows of grapes. Behind me, I heard sounds coming from inside my apartment. Page was sitting at the kitchen counter drinking a cup of coffee. She was wearing her black dress. She had washed off her makeup, and her face looked pale and tired.

"I've got to go," she said. "I have a morning class." She put her arms around me and kissed me lightly on the cheek. From my western window, I watched her walk down the driveway to her car.

I took a shower and straightened up the apartment. At noon there was a knock at my door. It was DeVries in a white tennis sweater and white slacks. Behind him was Shawn Lawrence.

DeVries handed me a sheet of paper. "That's a notice of eviction," he said. "Effective immediately. You have one hour to vacate. If you're not gone in an hour, Shawn has the authority to escort you off the property or to contact the police and have you arrested for noncompliance. Anything you leave will be destroyed. Do you understand?"

"No, could you repeat it?"

DeVries's face tightened in anger. "All of the electronic files and hardcopy on Mr. Patel's autobiography are the property of Mr. Patel. If they're not delivered to his office or left here, you'll be charged with theft."

"Are you going to ask me if I understand that?"

DeVries looked at his watch. "You've got an hour," he said. He turned and walked down the stairs, with Shawn behind him.

CHAPTER 4 0

THE THING ABOUT hitting bottom is that, in the middle of it, sometimes you don't know if you're really hitting bottom or just bouncing off ledges on your way further down.

After DeVries left, I packed my clothes in two suitcases and piled my books back in the boxes in which they had been shipped three months earlier. I downloaded Patel's files onto a DVD and printed out a clean hardcopy of the latest drafts. I closed up my computer and took three pictures off the walls. The rest belonged to the apartment. In forty-five minutes, my car was filled, and I was driving away. As I drove, I wasn't sure which was more disturbing—being fired from a job and thrown out of an apartment, or realizing that, at age fifty-two, everything I owned fit in a mid-size car.

Once on the highway, I considered where I ought to go. I could call Nico and Vincent, but having dinner with them was tense enough without my living in their house.

I thought of Molly. I called her office, but there was no answer. I tried her cell, and she picked up on the first ring.

"Interesting scene last night," she said. "You and your date created quite a stir. Have you seen today's paper?"

"No, I haven't seen it. Where are you?"

"I'm at home, Charlie. It's Sunday, remember?"

"Oh sure. Where do you live anyway?"

"Montecito Heights. Why this interest in my house? Is something wrong?" In the background I could hear a man's voice.

"No, I just need to . . . talk to you sometime." I suddenly realized I didn't know Molly very well and felt awkward asking for a place to stay.

There was a pause, and again I heard someone speaking in the background. "What about?" Molly asked. "Is that jerk Platt suing you for assault?"

"No, it's nothing like that. It's Jill and a custody thing. I need some advice."

"Could it wait, Charlie? I'll be in my office tomorrow. Say eleven?"

"Sure. See you at eleven."

I drove to the freeway, and tried three motels near the downtown off-ramp. They were all full. After twenty minutes, I found myself in the parking lot of the Redwood Lodge, where Page was staying. The front desk said they had no availability for the next week. Across the street I bought a cup of coffee at a coffee shop and took it back to my car.

I turned on the radio. Otis Redding was singing "I've Been Loving You Too Long." I drank the coffee and listened to the music.

I looked at the backseat and thought about living in my car. In my twenties, I had once driven alone from Los Angeles to Baja in an old Mercury Montego. At night I parked on the beach and slept in the backseat.

As I finished my coffee, it started to rain. Then it poured. Huge sheets of water beat on the car. The parking lot filled with water, and streams gushed through the gutters. I looked at the motel windows. A light was on in Page's room. At several other windows, I could see the glow of television sets. A man appeared at a window on the second floor and looked down at me. He was holding a drink in one hand. I felt as if I were in a boat in a storm.

My cell phone rang. "Charlie, where are you?" Page asked. "I went to your place. There were a couple of maids cleaning, and they said you moved out."

"I got fired and asked to leave," I said. "I wasn't given an official reason, but it was either my punching Bud Platt or your murdering the Beatles."

"What're you going to do?"

"I'm considering other properties. But it's the same old problem. You can hardly find a house these days with a decent wine cellar."

"You can stay with me," Page said

"Really?" I said.

"Are you far from here?"

"Not that far."

"I'll see you then."

"Okay, I'll see you."

"Charlie," Page said. "I'm glad you're coming."

"Yeah, me too," I said.

*   *   *

We bought take-out sandwiches and ate in Page's room. She wore a cashmere sweater and jeans, and looked recovered from the night before.

"I'm sorry about the way I behaved," she said. "I hope I wasn't the cause of your being fired."

I shook my head. "There were plenty of reasons," I said. "I should never have been there in the first place."

"But I owe you an explanation," Page said. She went to the bed and sat cross-legged facing me. "Rajiv was giving Paul a lot of gigs for his catering business—his own parties and his friends' parties. Other things were going on between Rajiv and Paul, too, drug stuff. I never knew exactly what it all was. All I know is Paul was getting a lot of money from Rajiv, and they were spending time together three, four times a week."

"In January, just after Paul and I started going out together, Rajiv invited Paul to a small dinner party at *Shanti Bhavan*. He wanted to introduce Paul to some friends as a caterer, and he told Paul to bring a date."

"Paul invited me. I bought a new dress and shoes. It was pretty exciting. Pete Tru was there with his wife—remember, he was the drummer in Heart. The actress Melissa Fortune was there, too. We were in a small room sitting around a table, and Rajiv couldn't keep his eyes off me. He had this weird smile, like he knew something and was happy about it. Afterward, when we were standing in the hallway to say goodnight, I could tell he was going to put his hand on me, and he did. It was very polite, but he did it."

"The next day Rajiv asked Paul to come out to *Shanti Bhavan* to talk about a catering event, and while they were talking, out of the blue, he asked Paul what my story was. Paul was a little surprised, but he thought that Rajiv had a job for me. He told him I'm an instructor at the fitness club, and we've just started dating."

"Paul could see that Rajiv was only half paying attention, and then Rajiv asked what he really wanted to ask. He asked how much Paul thought I would charge to spend the night with him." Page smiled and shook her head.

"You're kidding," I said.

"No," Page said. "And he asked just like that. It wasn't *if* I'd do it, but *how much* I'd charge. Like he already knew I'd do it, but it was only a question of cost."

"What'd Paul say?"

"At first he couldn't believe it. He thought he misunderstood Rajiv—you know how Rajiv talks in that soft voice. But Rajiv repeated it. It wasn't a joke. And he got explicit about what he wanted. Paul told him he'd gotten the wrong impression. He acted as if it were some cultural misunderstanding on Rajiv's part. Missed signals. He was diplomatic, polite. You know how good Paul was at something like that?"

"Yeah, I remember," I said.

"Rajiv wouldn't let go of it, and he told Paul to pass along the offer to me. Paul saw that nothing he said was getting through, so he left. But afterward,

Paul thought about it, and he got more pissed. He told me, expecting me to be shocked, but I wasn't. I've known a hundred jerks like that."

"Paul decided to make an issue of it. He sent Rajiv a letter, demanding an apology. Rajiv never replied. But their relationship changed. The catering gigs dried up. Paul wasn't invited to *Shanti Bhavan*."

As Page told the story, I remembered the opera excerpt that Mahler had played for me at his house, the music that Paul had been listening to the night he was killed.

Page stood up and cleared away the take-out.

"All this happened at the end of January?" I asked.

"About then, yeah," she said.

"Which is about the time that Paul began to look into Patel's bidding scam."

"He started to see Rajiv in a new light," Page said. "I think the information about the rigged bidding just fell into his lap. He was fascinated with it. He wanted to see where it would lead."

"Why?"

"I don't know. When Paul was killed, at first I thought it was all my fault. If Rajiv hadn't come on to me and Paul hadn't reacted the way he did, he wouldn't have been killed. But I think Paul did what he did because he saw this chance, this opening, to change his own life. He told me he wanted to start over."

"To stop selling coke?"

"Yeah. He said you'd understand."

"*I* would?"

"He said that's what your books are all about—starting over."

I smiled and shook my head.

"I'm just telling you what he said," Page said.

I went out to my car to get my bag. When I returned, Page was dressed in a bathrobe and standing in front of a mirror combing her hair. I went into the bathroom and put on my pajamas. When I emerged, she was standing in front of me.

Without saying anything, we put our arms around each other and kissed. She spread her hands at the small of my back. I held her head and slowly kissed her. She looked at me and smiled. "Hey, Charlie," she said. Then we silently looked at each other, surprised at what we had done.

In bed, Page unbuttoned my pajamas and slipped out of her robe. With her right hand, she explored my chest and arms and smiled. "You need to work out, Charlie," she said.

"I don't think so," I said.

"Really. You should come to the club."

"Take one of your classes?"

"Think you could keep up?"

She ran her hand down my leg, and her fingers traced a line on the inside of my thigh. She kissed me again, and her hair fell across my face. We tested each other, slowly finding our way. At first I felt Page's clenched energy against me, each of her movements aimed like a challenge. Then she softened and gently drew me toward her. Time slowed, and we moved without hurry, feeling here and there a long minute lengthen between us.

The room's curtains had parted slightly in the middle, letting a thin column of white light from the parking lot fall across the bed. As we made love, Page and I moved in and out of the light. For one moment, we were fully caught in it, so we could look into each other's eyes. In the next moment, we were back in the darkness, discovering each other, slowly and blindly, by touch.

Afterward we lay together without speaking for a few minutes.

"Are we still taking one thing at a time?" I finally asked.

"I think we just went beyond one thing."

"Well right now I'm trying to get used to the idea that the woman beside me is the same one who two weeks ago called me a fucking writer guy."

Page laughed. "Paul called that my street voice," she said. "He thought I overdid it sometimes."

"I'd say so."

"I've always had to take care of myself. Sometimes it means being tough."

I sat up beside her. "And then here you are," I said.

She smiled. "People are complicated," she said. "Didn't they teach you that in biography school?"

"I'm just a ghostwriter," I said. "I only know what someone tells me."

CHAPTER 4 1

THE FOLLOWING MORNING Page woke me with a cup of takeout coffee. Through a space in the room's curtains, I could see the pale orange of the sunrise. Page was already dressed in her aerobics outfit and sweatshirt. Her hair was pulled back in a ponytail.

"I've got to go," she said. "Early class." She bent down and kissed me on the lips.

In the motel lobby I found a copy of the previous day's newspaper. The front page of the B section carried a short article on Patel's party. There was a photograph of Patel arm in arm with his lingerie model and standing next to Skip Brown and Jessica Walker. The party was described as a "glittering gathering of local winemakers and entertainers." Near the bottom was a reference to a scuffle, described by an unnamed source as a misunderstanding between "former celebrity writer Charles Teller and a photographer."

About ten-thirty I drove downtown to Molly's office. Her admin announced me, and I found Molly with her reading glasses on, bent over a pile of manila folders on her desk. "Good news," she said before I could speak. "The police have dropped the charges against Stephen. They're releasing him this afternoon."

"What happened?" I asked.

"Couple things. The parking lot footprint was not Stephen's. The pickup they found last Thursday matches your description of the one leaving the parking lot after Paul was killed. The techs found traces of Paul's blood on the inside. The shooter must have gotten it on him from blowback. The VIN number for the truck was filed off the primary location on the frame. But forensics found the number on another location. It belongs to a contractor who works at *Shanti Bhavan*—of all places."

"Also," Molly said. "They've turned up something more on those guest lists on Paul's computer. They were emailed to Paul. The forensics guys are tracing the source."

"They have a suspect?"

"I don't know. But, as they say, the investigation is taking a different direction."

"So that's great for Stephen."

"You want to come with me? I'm meeting him at two when he's released, to give him a ride home." Molly began looking through the papers in one of the folders on her desk.

"I can't," I said. "I'm busy."

"Deadline on the book?" She asked without looking up.

"No, actually I won't be finishing the book."

Molly looked up. "They canned you for taking a swing at Platt?"

"Something like that." I told her the story of my firing.

"That was yesterday? Is that what you wanted to talk about when you called me? Wow, I feel bad now. If you had told me then what happened, we could have talked."

"It sounded like you had guests. I didn't want to interrupt you."

Molly blushed and went back to the folders in front of her. "I had a friend over," she said.

"Really? It's good to have a friend over."

"Yeah, it was."

"I know some of your friends."

Molly took a deep breath and let it out. "Okay, let's not make a big deal out of it. It was Eddie."

"Eddie Mahler?"

"Yeah, Eddie Mahler. We're sort of seeing each other." She was blushing more deeply now.

"Good for you."

"But let's get back to you," Molly said, serious again. "Where are you staying?"

"I have a room at the Redwood Lodge until I can find a place."

Molly looked at me. "Are you staying with Page?"

"Just for the time being."

She shook her head. "Oh man, Charlie," she said.

"Didn't we just agree it's good to have a friend over?"

"Yes, it's just that some friends involve more trouble than others. Speaking of which, what's this custody thing you wanted to talk to me about?"

I told Molly what Jill had said the day before about filing for a change in the custody agreement.

When I finished, Molly said, "So you thought a good first step would be to move in with Page?"

"I needed a place to stay. I tried other places. You were having a friend over, remember? Anyway, talk to me like a lawyer. What should I do?"

"Not much. Her lawyer, Mansfield, is a shark. She's probably got a pretty good case, too. I mean, look at you. You're a mess. You're involved in a murder investigation. No, correction, you're a suspect in a murder investigation. There've been two attempts on your life in the past two weeks. You've been fired from your job for assaulting a man. You're hanging around the fiancée of the murder victim, who also, by the way, found a dead guy in her apartment. Now you're sleeping with that woman. Did I leave anything out?"

"You make it all sound so negative."

"Okay. Tell me something that qualifies you to share the custody of your daughter."

"I'm not actually in jail."

"Very funny. She can take Lucy away from you, Charlie."

"I moved up here to be near Lucy."

"They'll make the case that that was not in Lucy's best interest."

"I love my daughter."

Molly took off her glasses. "I know, Charlie," she said. "But it's not enough."

"What should I do?"

"Talk to Jill."

"I don't know if she'll talk to me."

"Talk to her," Molly said. "Tell her you want to be a part of Lucy's life, that Lucy needs her father. Tell her . . . I don't know. That you'll do better, that you'll start over."

"Start over?"

"Yes, from where you are now, that might be the best thing, to start over."

*   *   *

Outside in my car, I called Jill on my cell phone. I was expecting to leave a message, but she answered.

"Hey," I said. "It's me."

There was a long silence.

"Could we just talk before we go down this road?" I said. "I know I haven't had a great couple of weeks, but I love our daughter, and I don't want to lose her. I just want to talk to you."

The line was silent. Then Jill said, "When?"

"Tonight. We could have dinner. Or a drink. Could we meet at Tadeo's?"

"All right. I'll be there at seven." The line went dead.

I drove across town to the fitness club. As I pulled into the parking lot, my cell phone rang. It was Vincent.

"We need to talk," he said.

"We can talk now," I said. "I'm parked."

"Not over the phone."

"Okay. Whenever you want. I could come out to your place tonight."

"Not here. Denny's downtown. Tomorrow morning at seven."

I went into the fitness club and found Page on the second floor aerobics room, where a class had just ended. She was standing in the middle of the room talking to two young women. She demonstrated a dance move, and one of the students copied her. Then she saw me and waved.

I waited outside the room until the students had finished. "Welcome to my office," Page said. She dried her face with a towel.

"How many classes have you taught today?" I asked.

"That was my third. Post-partum moms."

I picked up a set of hand weights.

"You need to work on those abs," she said, rubbing a hand across my stomach. "Want me to show you an exercise?"

"No, I think I can imagine it."

She laughed and put her hands on my hips and kissed me. I looked back through the glass walls at the hallway.

"Self-conscious?" she asked. She let go of me and walked around the room picking up the hand weights.

"What time do you finish?" I asked.

"Four."

"Long day."

She put the last set of weights on the shelves and looked at me. "What's up?" she asked.

"Nothing," I said. "I'm unemployed, remember? I had some time on my hands."

"So you came to see me?"

"Yeah. That all right?"

Page watched me.

"I wanted to tell you that I won't be back at the room for dinner tonight."

"Oh, no," Page said. "I was planning to make your favorite pot roast."

"I'm having dinner with Jill to talk about Lucy and the custody arrangement."

She turned and began putting a pile of CDs back in their cases.

"I didn't want you to wonder where I was," I said. "Considering what's going on."

"Considering what's going on?" she asked.

"With the threats you've received. And you and me."

Page turned and looked at me. "You spent a night in a motel with me, Charlie. You don't have to act all weird."

"I didn't realize I was."

She turned her back to me again.

"I'll see you around nine," I said.

She didn't say anything.

I walked out of the room and down the hallway. About halfway, I turned around and looked back. She was gone.

CHAPTER 42

Leslie Hartford

AFTER THE NEWS of my relationship with Susan Sparrow was made public, I didn't work for a few years. For the first year, I lived off savings and stayed home, pretending it was not unusual that I had nothing to do all day. It took most of that year to wean myself off Benzedrine.

Jill and I signed divorce papers, and made an effort to be polite to each other. She went back to work teaching. The following year we sold the house in Seal Beach. Jill rented a small place in Santa Monica, and I rented an apartment a few miles away. I saw Lucy on Tuesdays and Saturdays.

After that I ran out of money. I took freelance jobs—short-term, fixed-fee projects to revise manuscripts, ghostwriting for other ghostwriters.

At the end of the third year, I was approached by a small press publisher called Northwood House Press in Berkeley, California, to write the autobiography of the classical pianist Leslie Hartford. Hartford had been the *wunderkind* of his generation. At nineteen, he made a controversial and best-selling recording of Bach. He was known, too, for his eccentric behavior. He had long hair, and wore his tuxedo open-collared with beads around his neck. He toured the world in the late 1960s and early 1970s, and then suddenly stopped performing. He hadn't been seen in public in more than twenty-five years.

The autobiography was intended to bring Hartford out of seclusion. The publisher was a boutique house, with a staff of two, which published half a dozen books a year. They had no experience with biographies, but the owner knew someone who knew someone who knew Hartford, and had arranged with Hartford and his old recording company to publish the autobiography in conjunction with a reissuing of his original landmark Bach recording.

The offer came to me from the other member of the two-person Northwood House staff—a woman named Reggie Walworth, whom I had known at Princeton in the sixties. Reggie's family was East Coast old wealth and was descended from the Rhode Island Walworths, who were famous for being the first in the American Colonies to have made and sold some particular item of household utility. I've forgotten exactly what it was, although I knew at one time, and I remember thinking that, of course, someone would have had to have been the first, and how unfailing our history was that, after more than 200 years, we still knew who it was. The family lost its fortune in the 1929 crash, and the contemporary Walworths lived an ordinary existence. But they were still remembered for having descended from those who had been the first to have made that thing, and were regarded with esteem appropriate to original sources. Buildings and streets in Providence were named after them, and the endorsement of an elder Walworth still carried weight in some regional political campaigns. At Princeton, where there was no shortage of famous progeny, Reggie enjoyed a minor notoriety. Students pointed her out across a quad and took pleasure in repeating the story of her colonial family, and I believe she used her heritage to be first in line whenever nickel bags went on sale.

Reggie and I had kept up an occasional correspondence since college and had met once at a reunion. Even so, her call came out of the blue. She said she thought of me first when the opportunity presented itself. We both knew this wasn't true, and that her prime motivation was that she could hire me for almost nothing. But what is all that East Coast propriety for if not for a circumstance such as this? I let myself be guided by her good manners. In exchange for my usual fee, I took an advance to pay off bills.

Reggie was vague about what Hartford had been doing since he left the concert world. She would only say that he had agreed to the book and that she had already talked to him and he was super. He lived in Berkeley, not far from her office, and she suggested that I fly up to the Bay Area to meet him. Our first meeting was in a Berkeley coffee shop, a busy student hangout on Telegraph Avenue. Reggie and Hartford were already seated at a table when I arrived. Reggie was dressed in jeans and an expensive shirt. She greeted me with nervous good humor.

Across the table sat Hartford. He was a tall man with babyish features—a pale, fleshy face and slightly balding scalp—like an unfinished child grown large. He wore a bowling shirt from the 1950s and baggy khakis. When we were introduced, he shook my hand. Then he put his hands in his pockets, thought better of it and cupped his hands in front of him on the table, and changed his mind and let his arms swing at his sides. He looked down at his arms and watched them swing.

The waitress came to take our order. I ordered coffee, Reggie a complicated latte. Hartford asked for meatloaf. The waitress, who looked like a veteran of wise-ass students and homeless panhandlers, gave Hartford a take-no-crap look and waited. Reggie intervened and explained the nature of the coffee shop and coaxed Hartford into ordering a coffee and biscotti.

"Charlie specializes in helping people write their autobiographies," Reggie said. "He's already worked with another musician—Nick White, the British rock star. You remember him, Les? He was in Circle of White."

Hartford looked blankly at us.

"And athletes," Reggie continued. "Who was that baseball player, Charlie, whose book you helped write?"

"Ken Styles," I said.

"Styles, that's right," Reggie said. "He was a famous player back in the seventies. Ever go to a baseball game, Les?"

"Take me out to the ballgame," Hartford said, cheerfully.

"Yeah," Reggie said. "The seventh inning stretch song."

"Take me out to the crowd," Hartford said. He looked more serious now. "Buy me some peanuts and cracker jacks. I don't care if we never come back."

"There you go," Reggie said.

Hartford looked down at his arms again and watched them swinging at his side. "Oh, do not ask, What is it?" he said. "Let us go and make our visit."

Reggie waited for a moment to see if he was finished. Then she turned to me with a stiff smile and explained my payment schedule.

The coffee arrived, and Reggie looked relieved to turn her attention to it. Across the table, Hartford sat looking into his cup. He tested its temperature with his right index finger. Then he dipped the finger into the coffee up to the first knuckle, and looking up, painted his lips with the dark liquid. He did this several times, pursing his lips slightly as if applying lipstick, and taking care not to let the coffee spread outside the edges of his lips.

Reggie watched him, her determined smile now glued in place. When she reached into her purse to pay for the coffee, I saw her hands shaking.

"So Charlie," she said. "Are we good?"

. . .

He was born Leslie Allen Hartford in the Philadelphia suburbs. For the boy's fifth birthday, Hartford's father bought him a quarter-size violin and intended to teach him scales on the piano, but within a month, the young boy had abandoned the little violin for the keyboard.

Over the next half dozen years, Hartford outgrew his teachers—first his father, then a local music teacher, and finally a Philadelphia impresario. When Hartford was twelve, a wealthy aunt gave the family money to send Hartford to Paris to study with the renowned pianist Jose-Antonio Alvarez.

In his eighties and no longer able to play himself, Alvarez taught a generation of students. His lessons were legendary: in one, he made them stand in front of him, the score in their hands, and sing the notes out loud. "Listen," he told them, "until you hear the sounds the composer heard in his dreams."

Alvarez taught the young Hartford to play the romantic masters—Liszt, Chopin, and Rachmaninoff—and allowed him to grow his hair until it fell down across his face as he played. By fourteen, Hartford was touring Europe—the mop-topped boy from Philadelphia with his repertoire of "money pieces." Two years later, he released a recording of Chopin interpretations. On the cover photo, he looked like a rock star. He returned to the United States and played with orchestras in five American cities.

At seventeen, Hartford stopped touring. A year later, when he returned to the public appearances, he revealed he had spent the year studying Bach's *Well-Tempered Clavier*—two books, each with 24 pairs of preludes and fugues, for solo keyboard, composed as a kind of perfectly symmetrical piano lesson. The pairs of preludes and fugues were written in all 24 major and minor keys in a rising chromatic pattern.

For Hartford, Bach was a transformative experience. In 1968, he released his recording of the Clavier Book I, which critics found to be a powerful new interpretation. The record was also a commercial success; it broke through the niche classical music market and became a popular best seller.

His concerts were like long meditations, attended by serious concertgoers and stoned hippies. Hartford himself adopted the persona of a music guru and played as if in a trance.

I saw him at the Hollywood Bowl. He played for ninety minutes without an intermission, his head nearly touching the keys as he played.

In 1976, there were signs of trouble. He canceled concerts. He was arrested for disorderly conduct. In 1977, his long-awaited new recording was devoted to an obscure twentieth-century American composer named Kenneth Holliday.

The following year, he declined to commit to a concert schedule. Then he simply vanished. He was captured once in a newspaper photograph, walking in Berkeley, disheveled and a look of confusion on his face.

· · ·

My contract for the Hartford book included the provision for me to live with him for the project's duration. Hartford's "house," located a few blocks east of the university campus, was a six-story dormitory tower that had once been part of student housing. Hartford lived on the south side of the fourth floor, which had been redesigned as an apartment. The living space included a living room, kitchen, bedroom, and a small studio with a Steinway D-274 and shelves crammed with hundreds of phonograph records.

The rest of the building was empty and a preserve of 1960s-era student life. Thirty-year-old trash lay in the hallways, graffiti covered the bathrooms, and brittle paper posters advertised concerts of long-dead rock musicians. At night, the wind blowing through the cracked windows and banging the Venetian blinds sounded like the rough-housing of freshmen, back from a late-night kegger.

I staked out two rooms on the first floor, making one an office and the other my bedroom. Reggie outfitted them with furniture from a month-to-month rental store, and I cooked and ate my meals in a common room.

I arranged to meet Hartford every morning from 10 to noon to conduct interviews. We sat in his studio, each of us sunk deep in identical facing slingback chairs.

The interviews varied, but I never learned anything useable about Hartford in any of them. They went like this:

TELLER: You grew up outside Philadelphia. Can you tell me about your childhood there?

HARTFORD: I was a boy, of course, with torso and limbs in proportion to my age.

TELLER: I understand your father introduced you to the piano. Do you remember that?

HARTFORD: My father or the piano?

TELLER: Your father introducing you to the piano.

HARTFORD: What about it?

TELLER: What do you remember about your father introducing you to the piano?

HARTFORD: Nothing.

TELLER: Let's talk about Bach.

HARTFORD: The Kapellmeister of Leipzig.

TELLER: Yes, what is it about his music that attracted you?

HARTFORD: What is it?

TELLER: Bach's music.

HARTFORD: What is it?

TELLER: Wasn't it a departure from your earlier romantic repertoire?
HARTFORD: It?

I rarely saw Hartford outside these interviews. He was like a spirit haunting the building. I could hear him late at night, riding the groaning elevator between floors.

After two weeks, I called Reggie and threatened to quit. She was unsympathetic.

"Come on, Charlie," she said. "You're getting paid. I shouldn't have to babysit you."

"That's not what I'm asking for," I said. "If he doesn't cooperate, I can't write the book. I'm not even sure if he knows I'm writing a book. What exactly did he say when he agreed to this project?"

Reggie ignored me. "If it was easy," she said. "I would've hired a graduate student. You must've had difficulties with other clients. I don't imagine Ken Styles and Skye Lurie were very articulate."

"Yeah, but they spoke a version of English I understood. What's that thing he keeps saying about 'Don't ask, What is it?'"

"T. S. Eliot's Prufrock. Jesus, didn't you read anything at Princeton?"

"But why's he saying it all the time?"

"How should I know? Look, just talk to him. Tell him you won't write his book if he isn't forthcoming."

In my next session with Hartford, I remained standing behind the slingback chair. "My job here, Leslie," I said, "is to help you write your life story. But you need to give me the information."

Hartford looked up at me like an attentive child and laughed out loud. "Of course, it's already written down," he said. Searching through his shelves, he pulled out a book and handed it to me. "My life story," he said. "I wrote it a few years ago."

It was an inexpensive bound journal with lined pages. On the first page in clear script handwriting were the words: In Memoriam by Leslie Allen Hartford. I flipped through the book. The pages, more than 200 of them, were filled with the dense scrawl.

"Take it," Hartford said, waving his arms at me. "Use whatever you need."

I was stunned. Why hadn't he said anything earlier? Why had we wasted all that time?

Back on the first floor, I sat at my desk to read the notebook. The first page began: "Of my origin, let me say my wellspring was of an ordinary kind. I put my toes on the starting line, like many before me, and embarked on my journey. As mortals, we are bound by the ineluctable circumstances of our existence, and we spring from this or that source, like so many blind fledglings. If we could but know the weave and warp of reality that contains the patterns—the very threads—of the life before us, would we choose one path over another? All beginnings are blessed, the poet said. The blessing is in the seed."

Turning a few pages, I read: "This particular passage occurred during the reign of the one whom I shall call the Sun King. It was with his beneficence that I was to succeed. Can you conceive of the splendor of the palaces? There was always, of course, obeisance to be paid. I dropped my shekels in the offering like all the others. Afterward came dinner. Then conveyances, one more wondrous than another: into the night, destination unknown. No matter, what was of import was the alacrity with which it was achieved."

A dozen pages further on was this: "Take the great works of Mister Bach or Mister Mozart. Or, for that matter, the Bard of Stratford. Here one finds the search for the meaning of life. Each note—or, in the latter case, word—has the power to affect the heart in a way that allows us to descry our innermost conscience. Agenbite of inwit, the again biting of the inner wit—what is the answer to that question?"

I scanned twenty-five pages before I closed the notebook. I felt sick. I looked up from my desk. Outside was an ordinary spring morning. I thought of the advice of Tina Terrill's therapist, who had sought to coax her back to reality: name the reality before you. "I see a student carrying books," I said out loud. "I see three parked cars."

The next morning I found Hartford sitting in his slingback chair. I handed the notebook back to him. "This is very creative," I said. "But what I really need are the facts of your life—dates and places."

He looked down at the notebook in his lap without recognition, as if it had fallen out of the sky. "Dates and places," he said, considering the words. "An accounting, as it were. On this year, such and such. On that year, such and such."

"Yes," I said. "Something like that."

He stood up and put the notebook back in his shelf. "Perhaps someone has been keeping notes," he said happily.

He grabbed my right hand and led me to his piano. "Do you know what the essential problem of the piano is?" he asked. He held me so his head was a few inches from my own. His eyes darted back and forth. "It is impossible to play continuously on a piano string like a violin. The problem is to *sustain* a note."

He let go of my hand and went to the keyboard. "A piano is stored vibration," he said. "The strings are stretched to over 200 pounds of tension. Imagine it!"

He pressed a key. "A hammer hits a string, and it vibrates. But the tone begins and decays. Every note you play on the piano, no matter what you do, will decay and die." He looked at me solemnly and then grinned.

"But the problem has a solution," Hartford said, sitting on the piano bench and reaching with his foot to depress the right pedal. "*Senza sordini*—the damper pedal. *Molte grazie* Cristofori!"

He jumped up and laid a heavy book on the pedal. "Come, come," he said. He pulled me next to him and held my arm tightly in his right hand. Then he bent his head into the piano, above the strings, and shouted "Wahoo." The sound made the piano strings vibrate and echo.

"Say something," he said. "Anything."

"Hello," I said.

"Louder. Say 'Woo.'"

"Woo," I called down onto the strings. The sound reverberated back to me.

"Louder," Hartford said, squeezing my arm.

"WOO," I shouted at the strings and sound blared back. Hartford laughed.

"Again," he said, and this time he joined me. "WOO," we shouted together into the piano, the sound from the strings filling our heads.

. . .

Every two weeks, on Friday afternoons, I drove eight hours from Berkeley to Santa Monica, down Interstate 5, to see Jill and Lucy for a long weekend. I stayed in their apartment's spare room, where Jill set up a futon beside the bicycles and toy boxes. When I woke each morning, the first thing I saw was Lucy's chalk easel, where she wrote messages to me: "Lets Hav Pancakes."

On these visits, I spent all day Saturday with Lucy. We made father-daughter excursions to the beach, the Farmers Market, and Palisades Park.

On Saturday evenings, we did something special for dinner, going to a favorite restaurant or inviting a friend for dinner. One Saturday, Jill invited Tak to join us, and the two of them reminisced about the Toyon String Quartet while I put Lucy to sleep. When I returned, I said, "All those years of listening to the four of you rehearsing taught me a few things about music that're useful for the Hartford biography."

"Like what?" Jill asked. "Hartford's not a quartet musician, and his repertoire was very different."

"Tempi," I said. "One of you was always complaining that the other was misinterpreting the time signatures."

"Really?" Tak said. "I can't imagine who did that?"

Jill smiled at him. "So what's that have to do with Hartford?" she asked me.

"The tempo is very controversial in the Well-Tempered Clavier," I said. "For one thing, most critics agree that Bach notated tempo differently than we do today, and that he may have meant something different when he wrote *andante*. For another, there're only nine tempo words in the entire Clavier, whereas today they'd be in every section. Hartford's performance and recording of Book I were controversial because he never romanticized the tempo."

Jill and Tak were both watching me and were silent for a moment. Then Tak said, "He's right about the Bach. And the Hartford recording. It's very moving. It made people listen to all of Bach differently."

Jill stood to clear the table.

"OK," Tak said. "Why's tempo important?"

Jill watched me. "It's the music's heartbeat," I said. "The source of feeling that the player gives the music."

"Not bad," Tak said. "You're like a sponge, Charlie. You know, your books have more to them than you were given credit for. I re-read the Virginia Hardy book earlier this year, and it's pretty good. I always thought you got a bum rap."

Jill and I looked at each other.

"In the press, I mean," Tak said.

Sundays were reserved for the three of us to spend time together. Lucy was interested in the monuments of her own short history. We drove down to Pacific Palisades where Jill and I had lived before we were married or to Seal Beach to show Lucy the house where she had been born.

One Sunday, as we drove home in the late afternoon freeway traffic after seeing a Dodgers game with Ken Styles, Lucy turned on the cassette player and played the tape inside. It was the tape that Jill had given me years earlier of Toyon playing Schubert's String Quartet in A Minor. Lucy asked what it was, and I told her.

"The music's named after a woman," I said. "Rosamunde."

"Did you know her, mommy?" Lucy asked.

"No, it was a long time ago," Jill said.

"Which one's you?" Lucy asked.

Jill rewound the tape to the beginning of the first movement. "Now listen," she said. "That first sound is me."

Lucy listened. "I can hear you and then the others and then you again," she said.

"That's right," Jill said. "The four of us play together, and sometimes one or two of us stops, and the others continue to play. Some people say it's like people talking and listening."

"Do you play this while you're driving to see us?" Lucy asked me.

"Sometimes," I said.

"So it's like having people talking even when you're alone?"

"Yeah. Except it's not just people talking. It's old friends talking, and it's a beautiful talk."

Lucy fell asleep in the back seat. I looked beside me at Jill's face, still bright from the excitement of the baseball game, squinting into the sun at the highway ahead of us.

"There are times," I said, "when I want to tell you something."

"Let's not spoil this," Jill said.

"I want to tell you I'm sorry. I don't think I ever said that."

"Charlie, don't."

"But I just want . . ."

"Don't, Charlie," Jill said. "We can't do this now. Let's just drive. Let's just go home."

.   .   .

My circumstances were these: I had accepted two payments totaling $10,000 from Northwood House Press and had already spent most of it. I had signed a contract, agreeing to deliver, in three months, a book manuscript, to be no less than 200 pages, comprising a memoir (what the contract referred to as "the first intimate portrait") of the pianist Leslie Hartford. After six weeks on the job, I had no useable information from Hartford and no prospects of getting any information. I was not a musician; I could not read music or play an instrument. The only book I had written about a musician was about a rock star who found Jesus.

There's an old adage: the sensation of drowning reminds you of everything you ever knew about swimming.

My twenty-five years of co-writing autobiographies had taught me to swim. I downloaded pages off the Internet on Hartford and Alvarez, and after two days, had enough to fill a banker's box. I boiled down everything in the box to notes that I stored in my computer in folders labeled for separate decades of Hartford's life. For another three days, I sat in the university library, reading old microfilm reviews of Hartford's concerts and recordings. I read Wolff on Bach, Walker on Liszt, and Huneker on Chopin.

Then I started writing. My schedule was five pages a day, six days a week. I took off one day a week to rest my fevered brain and to contemplate the special place in hell where I was going to spend eternity.

I described childhood scenes, lessons with Alvarez, the first public concert, and the Chopin recording. After a few days, a strange thing happened. I could hear his voice in my ears, the languid, childish voice telling me stories.

After that, for two months, sitting at my computer, I became that great baby-man. I was gentle with my father, who had already passed away, and generous toward Maestro Jose-Antonio, who had taught me to use my fingers in the service of art. I remembered my discovery of Chopin's nocturnes, how the notes sang to me. I saw the audiences in Prague, St. Louis, and Tokyo.

I wrote faster and faster, trying to keep up with his voice. Some days I wrote 10 and 15 pages. I wrote with everything that Virginia Hardy, Nick White, and Skye Lurie had taught me about how to tell one individual's life. As a piece of pure writing, Hartford's book was the best thing I had ever done.

In the end, the final manuscript was more than 300 pages. I called Reggie and let her know of my progress, and then I called Hartford and arranged to deliver a copy to him for review. At the agreed time, I rode the elevator to his apartment and presented him with the book in loose pages.

He sat in his slingback chair and held the pile of pages. "Well, this is something," he said.

"It's all there," I said. I pointed to the title page, which read "Sustaining the Note: My Life by Leslie Hartford."

Hartford looked up at me. "Exactly right," he said. "What's the next step?"

"We'd like you to read it. Make any corrections that are necessary."

"Of course. Standard procedure."

We agreed I would check back with him in a week. I spent the week in my office preparing my own version of author's corrections. First, I went through the manuscript, page by page, and made handwritten corrections to the text and wrote comments in the margins. Then I used those markings to prepare a new corrected copy.

At the end of the week, I met Hartford to pick up the manuscript. He greeted me warmly. "Top notch," he said, handing me the manuscript. I flipped through the pages, and as I expected, there was not a mark on any page. I gave Hartford a copy of Northwood House's author release form and waited while he signed it.

The following week I delivered the author's corrections, the clean copy, and Hartford's release to Reggie. She read through a dozen pages of the author's corrections.

"So in the end, you guys figured out a way of making it work?" she asked.

"Something like that," I said.

"Well, whatever it was, there's some good stuff in here," she said. "You couldn't make these things up."

. . .

Six weeks later, when the book was in galleys, Reggie called me. By this time, I had moved out of Hartford's dormitory and was living in an apartment in North Berkeley and writing ad copy as a freelancer. "We've got a problem," she said.

I was invited to attend a meeting at the Northwood House Press offices. When I arrived, a small group was already gathered around the company's conference room table. Reggie sat on one side, her face white and stiff. Across from her was Hartford, wearing a mussed dark suit and white shirt without tie. Beside him was an attorney named Jonathan Miles. On the tabletop was a galley proof of the book.

Miles spoke first. "I've been retained by Mr. Hartford," he said, "to bring suit against Northwood House to stop publication of this book."

"The book," he continued, "which is intended to be my client's autobiography, and which is purported to have been co-written by Mr. Hartford and Mr. Teller, was in fact, written without my client's participation."

Hartford sat silently and conducted another version of his arm-swinging experiment.

"Your client signed the author's release," Reggie said. "He approved the book's contents, subject to his corrections being made, which they were."

"Those corrections are not my client's," Miles said. "Mr. Hartford did not read the book until last week, at which time he discovered the book's fraudulent nature."

"What do you mean fraudulent?"

"It's our contention that Mr. Teller alone, or acting with you, created this book out of whole cloth. Because the information contained in the book was not provided by Mr. Hartford, it includes many falsehoods and inventions, which would be harmful to his reputation and professional stature."

Miles took some papers from his briefcase and slid them across the table to Reggie and me. They were copies of an affidavit, signed by Hartford, stating that the autobiography had been written without his consent. "Apparently," Miles said. "Mister Teller did not actually conduct any fruitful interviews with Mr. Hartford. The resulting book, therefore, constitutes a fraud. We're bringing suit against Northwood House Press and Mr. Teller personally for defamation and are seeking damages."

After that, Reggie tried again to assert the legal authority of the release form and said she would contact the law firm representing Northwood, but really it was all over.

In the end, Northwood House's insurance company settled with Hartford. Northwood House sued me for breach of contract, then dropped the suit when it became clear that I had no assets to claim. Hartford's book—my longest work of fiction to date—was never published.

All of this back and forth was handled out of court, through a private exchange of letters. At one point, though, a nationally syndicated columnist got wind of it and wrote a witty column about the nature of pseudo-biography at the start of the new century. Then a young *Wall Street Journal* reporter launched his own career by writing about my life in an award-winning, three-part series that portrayed me as a Shakespearean figure and ennobled my fate in elegiac prose that reminded me of passages of my own writing that I had used years earlier to encase the life of Virginia Hardy.

CHAPTER 43

OF COURSE, WHEN you fall out of love, it's rarely about just one failure or one betrayal, is it? For Jill and me, it wasn't only about my moment with Susan Sparrow—although that would have been enough. In our marriage, we had quarreled over a hundred things, until we couldn't hear each other and stopped talking and endured silent evenings. Over time, those quarrels worked with the abrasion of a geologic force that wore away, without our noticing, the invisible bonds that hold two people together.

How does it happen? All those things you once loved about each other are replaced by other things that remind you of something you hate until you're always setting each other off, and what you share is a battleground. In the end, the failure turns out to be less about sex—which surprises most men—and more about loss of respect. One morning your partner looks at you across the bed and wonders at the waywardness of her own heart—how, she asks herself, can she feel such disdain for someone she once felt such love?

I arrived at Tadeo's at seven, and a few minutes later, Jill came in. She was grim-faced and sat down without saying a word. When the waiter came over and began to describe the night's specials, she said in a quiet voice, "I'm not having anything."

I asked the waiter to give us a few minutes, and he left.

Jill took a drink of water and looked at me. "I'm trying," she said, "I mean really trying, not to think about you or me or the problems that you've got, but about Lucy and what's best for her, and what she needs right now."

"That's what I . . . "

"Charlie," she said, "if you say anything right now, I'm going to leave."

I held up my hands in surrender.

"I don't know what's happening to you," she said. "It's like you're in some other world, all by yourself, with your own set of rules. You keep throwing things away—your money, your work, who you are. Where are you going, Charlie, do you even know?"

She sat back in her seat, inhaled a deep breath and let it out. "Lucy's going through a difficult time for a girl. She has these feelings, and she doesn't know what to do with them. One minute she wants to yell and scream, and the next minute she wants to cry. She's a bundle of emotions."

"She seemed fine a month ago," I said.

"She was fine. She still is fine. You don't see her every day, so you don't see this stuff. A lot of it's normal for her age, and what's happening to her body. She's going through changes, and she doesn't understand them."

"Does she talk to you about it?"

"Sometimes. Mostly not. She doesn't know how to, and she probably can't imagine that her mother knows anything about it." Jill took a roll from the basket, pulled it apart, and ate a piece.

"Then there's our move up here," she said. "And her having to start over and meet all new friends. And in that process, she met Sage. She's probably an okay kid, but together they do the dumbest things, like the other day in the store."

"Lucy told me you're trying to keep her away from Sage by making her take a job at a winery," I said.

"I found her an after-school job, working in the cellar at Myers Creek Winery."

"Where Dave works."

"Yes, where Dave works. It's just a few hours, three days a week. She helps out the cellarmaster, cleaning the cellar or working in the lab. I take her there and pick her. She probably won't admit it, but she likes it. Anyway it's an experiment."

"And how are things with you and Dave?"

"He's a friend, Charlie. We enjoy each other's company. You and I are divorced, remember?"

"If I forgot, I'm sure you'd remind me."

"Charlie, part of what's going on with our daughter is this, right here. She's old enough now to feel the tension between us, and she doesn't want it to be there, but she's powerless to do anything about it. It makes her angry. It makes her want to do things to make us see her."

"Doesn't she know we see her?"

"Do we? Really? I think she's balancing on this edge. I've seen other kids like this. The years between middle school and high school are the time for it. Kids come up to this point, and one or two things can send them in one direction or another."

"And you think that it'll help to have me out of the picture? Is that part of the experiment?"

Jill looked at me. "I don't know what I think. All I know is that every time I turn around, you're caught up in something. Ever since your friend Paul was killed, it doesn't seem safe with you. Is Page living with you on Patel's estate?"

"No," I said. "She's not."

"All right. Here's my suggestion. I'll hold off for the time being on amending the custody agreement. But I want you to take some time—a week, two weeks, whatever your need—and disentangle yourself from all this stuff that's going on with the police. And in that time, you don't see Lucy. I'm saying this, Charlie, because I need to know our daughter is safe."

"You must know I want her to be safe, too," I said.

"I'm sure you do, Charlie," Jill said. "But I don't think you're in a position to promise it right now."

*   *   *

I drove back to the Redwood Lodge. When I arrived at Page's room, she was sitting on the bed, drying her hair.

"You're early," she said.

"We finished early," I said. I told Page what Jill had said. When I described Jill's request that I disengage myself from the murder investigation, I said Jill had set conditions to my seeing Lucy.

Page put the towel around her neck. "Like not being with me?" she asked.

"She doesn't know I'm with you."

"Because you didn't tell her?"

"Because I told her that I wasn't with you."

Page stared at me.

"I didn't know what to say," I said.

"I think you knew exactly what to say," Page said.

I looked away from her.

"Why don't you want your ex-wife to know we're together?" she asked.

"Jill thinks it's dangerous because of what happened to Paul and Ray Brenner."

"Is that it? Or, are you ashamed of me?"

"No, of course not."

"No? This afternoon at the club you stumbled around trying to describe what's happening between us. What does this relationship mean to you?"

"I haven't felt this way in a long time."

"Really?"

"Yes. Why are we doing this?"

"Because I want to know why you're lying about me to your ex-wife."

For a moment neither of us spoke. Then Page's cell phone rang, and she stood up to answer it. As she spoke, broken glass flew through the window, cracking sounds whistled into the room, and two bullets hit the back wall.

I jumped across the room and pulled Page with me to the floor.

"Are you hurt?" I asked as we lay tangled together.

Page was shivering. "I don't think so," she said.

"Call 911."

I crawled to the door and threw the deadbolt and turned out the overhead light. Then I pulled a couch in front of the door. Behind me, I could hear Page talking to the 911 operator.

After that we lay on the floor waiting.

CHAPTER **44**

TWO POLICE CARS screeched to a stop outside our motel room. The first officer was Monroe, the one who had searched my apartment at *Shanti Bhavan*. He checked that we were uninjured and took charge of the scene, directing the officers from the other car to search the motel premises for the shooter and then interview the other motel occupants, who were spilling out of their rooms into the parking lot. Monroe himself followed us into our room and sat at the table with a small notebook in front of him. For the next few minutes, Page and I told him what we knew about the shooting.

A crime tech photographed the room and measured the floor with a metal tape. At the back wall, he photographed where the bullets had entered the sheetrock and used some tools to extract the bullets.

The motel night clerk taped a large sheet of cardboard over the broken window and vacuumed the broken glass on the carpet.

Among the people coming in and out, I saw Eddie Mahler. Glancing at Page and me without speaking, he walked across the room and looked at the bullet holes on the back wall. Then he huddled in the back corner with Monroe and the crime scene tech, the three of them talking in low voices and staring at their feet.

When the other two men left, Mahler came to us and sat at the table. "This is pretty cozy, isn't it?" he said. He slouched in his chair and played with the salt and pepper shakers.

"So Teller," he said. "Are you just visiting or staying here?"

"I'm staying here," I said.

He nodded his head. "Get laid off after your little ruckus at the party Saturday night?"

"Something like that."

"Yeah. I imagine it's something like that." He lined up the shakers. Taking Monroe's notebook out of his jacket pocket, he spread it in front of him on the tabletop. He looked at Page. "Somebody must not like you very much, Ms.

Salinger," he said. "Those are some serious holes in the wall. My tech tells me they're .45 caliber. We'll look at them in the lab, but I'm willing to bet they're from a Heckler and Koch, like the one used to kill Ray Brenner."

"I told your officer I've been getting threatening calls on my cell," Page said. "The same guy called tonight just before the shooting."

Mahler looked down at the notebook. "He says the same thing each time?" he asked.

"Yeah. That he's going to kill me like Ray Brenner."

"You don't recognize the voice?"

"No."

Mahler turned the pages of the notebook. "You know," he said. "It takes a lot of trouble to shoot a .45 into a motel room. More than you might think. Usually when someone does it, he has a good reason. Maybe he wishes you harm, or maybe he thinks you know something or have something he wants."

"I guess he thinks I know something about Paul," Page said.

"Which," Mahler said, "We know you don't."

"Just what I've already told you," Page said.

"How about you, Teller?" Mahler said turning to me. "I don't suppose you have any insight into this shooting? Now that you're a free agent and not bound by any client-biographer privilege?"

"No," I said. "I don't."

"No, neither of you knows anything. Well, shall we talk about what we *do* know? The shooter parked his car in the parking lot outside your room. He—we're assuming it was a male, since it was a male voice that you heard on the phone. He got out of his car and stood about 20 feet from your window. He dialed your cell phone. When you answered, he fired two rounds into your room. He got back in his car—two of your fellow guests heard a door slam—and drove around the back of the motel and out to Cleveland Avenue. A guy on the second floor saw a car leave the lot at a high rate of speed. Might have been a Mazda."

Mahler closed the notebook. "Not much. But it's something. Each little bit—pretty soon we have a story."

"Speaking of which," he continued. "Remember the dirt in the carpet that we found in your apartment, Ms. Salinger?"

Mahler looked at me. "You'll find this interesting, Boswell. Turns out we know a lot about local soils. The character of wine is shaped by the vineyard soil, so geologists have studied and mapped it throughout the county. Our lab told us the soil in Ms. Salinger's carpet could be a type found in the Sonoma Valley, called Sonoma volcanics. Contains more volcanic ash than other local dirt. So whoever popped Ray Brenner had spent some time recently walking around in some dirt in the Valley of the Moon. Isn't that interesting?"

"Sure," I said.

"We also found the guy who was watching you, Ms. Salinger," Mahler said. "The one with the tattoo of a face on his neck. Name's Dennis Harper. One of Kenny's crew. We're holding him for questioning."

"It's like I told you when we first met, Teller," Mahler said. "You and I, we both put together pieces of information. In the beginning they may not mean anything. But eventually they fit together to tell a story. Right now we have a lot of little pieces, and we can't tell exactly how they'll come together, but we're starting to get an idea. You know what that's like, Teller?"

"I did," I said.

"Ah yes, sore subject," Mahler said. "You're unemployed. Well, there'll be others to tell their stories."

Mahler stood and said, "One other thing, Teller. I want you to come to the station tomorrow to look at something we found. My forensics guys looked closer at that videotape at Kenny's house the day he was killed and they found something. I'd like you to see it. Come in around eight tomorrow morning."

* * *

After Mahler left, Page and I undressed to go to sleep. We sat for a few minutes in bed, neither of us wanting to return to our earlier conversation.

"What'd you mean last night when you said Paul was unhappy and wanted to start over?" I asked.

"He was looking at his life in a new way," she said. "The crowd that supported his businesses never really accepted him as an equal. They hired him and complimented him. But they never wanted him around unless they needed him for something—to run their parties and bring their drugs. He was hired help."

"He didn't realize that before?" I asked.

"No, that's just it. You know those people. They don't associate with anyone—my god, they practically live in their own solar system. But they talked to Paul, they hugged him, they confided their little problems. So it seemed like he was special."

"Last year Maria Craig was here on hiatus from her TV show. Paul did a little party for her, and her ten-year-old son attached himself to Paul. Paul taught him to make a sauce. Maria loved it—thought he needed a man in his life or something. Anyway Maria invited Paul to her house by himself. So here's this caterer hanging out with one of the hottest TV stars. Just the two of them."

"Then he didn't hear from her for a month. He decided she must have gone back to LA, but then he saw her at the symphony. She was interested in Paul for that week, and then she wasn't. Short attention span. He thought he was on the inside, but he was just the guy who cooks the food. He was like the other guy who fixes their car or does their taxes."

"Or writes their life stories," I said.

"Yeah, but I'm guessing they needed you a little longer than for lunch," Page said. "Paul was thin-skinned. A couple of months ago, he was doing a birthday party for Skip Brown. Skip was in his element, life of the party. He was also drinking Grey Goose martinis. At one point he ran out of goat cheese or some damn thing and started yelling for that 'pufta caterer.' Everybody laughed. But Paul was across the room and heard it. The thing with Patel wanting to pay for me was just the last straw. It sent him over the top. He wanted out."

"What was he going to do?"

"I don't think he knew. I guess he was going to confess to the cops on the dealing. Knowing Paul, he probably thought he was cleansing himself."

She lay on her back and looked up at the ceiling. Then she turned toward me. "Can we go back to where we were last night Charlie?" she asked.

I smiled. I put my arms around her and kissed her. She pulled herself close to me, and she brushed her hair away from her face with the back of her hand, and in that instant I saw her as I had seen her two weeks earlier in her apartment when I pushed her down and she backed me against the wall.

I heard Page say, "Where'd you just go?"

"What do you mean?" I asked.

Page sat up in bed, facing me. "Come on, Charlie. I could feel it. You went away. What were you thinking about?"

"I don't know. You, when we had that thing in your apartment."

"You were thinking about that *now*?"

"You told me to make up my mind."

"I was trying to push your buttons."

"No, you were right."

Page looked at me, and anger filled her eyes. "You probably think you're different from other men," she said. "You're smarter, and you know how to talk. But it just takes you longer to get to the same place."

We looked at each other for a minute, and neither of us said anything. Page turned away, switched out the light, and lay down in the bed, and I sat in the dark beside her.

CHAPTER 45

I GOT OUT of bed at six-thirty and dressed in the dark. I closed the door softly so as not to wake Page.

When I arrived at Denny's, the restaurant was bustling. Nico and Vincent sat in the same booth where we had had lunch a week earlier. Nico called my name across the room. Vincent looked at me without speaking.

"I hear you got fired," Nico said. She wore a white blouse and plaid miniskirt with suspenders. She was eating a large platter of biscuits and gravy.

"Who told you that?" I asked.

"Molly. She said you're staying with Page at a motel." She smiled.

"Until I find a place."

Nico shook her head. "You're full of surprises."

The waitress came and took my order for coffee.

Vincent looked at us impatiently. "What is it, Vincent?" I asked.

"I found Sutter," he said.

"Andrew Sutter? The guy who was helping Patel run the bidding scam? Where is he?"

"In the desert, about 20 miles outside Las Vegas."

"What's he doing?"

"Not a lot. He's dead. Clark County sheriffs found him about a week ago."

"How'd you find out?"

Vincent stared at me.

"I don't suppose he died of natural causes," I said.

"Depends what you consider natural. He was shot twice in the head. The gun was a . . ."

"Heckler and Koch," I said. "Forty-five caliber."

Vincent looked at me, surprised, or Vincent's version of surprised. "That's right," he said.

"Coincidence," I said. "Same kind of gun used to kill Ray Brenner."

"Yeah, same kind of gun."

"Another coincidence. Last night someone used the same kind of gun to fire two rounds into our motel room."

"Holy shit," Nico said loudly.

A woman leaned over the back of the adjoining booth and frowned at Nico, who mouthed an apology.

Vincent watched me. "You're going to want to be careful," he said.

From the booth beside us came the sound of a small child saying holy shit over and over. Nico put on her sunglasses.

"How'd the shooter find you?" Vincent asked.

"He must have followed Page from the fitness center. He called her cell so he could see her."

"All right," Vincent said. "So Barkley sees Andrew Sutter's name added to a guest list at a party he's catering."

"And this guy Sutter's way out of place," Nico said. "Since Paul knows everybody, he wonders who this guy is."

"Yeah," I said. "My guess is, Sutter made some kind of deal with Patel to let him go to the parties so he could mingle with a few movie stars. Paul got curious, poked around, and stumbled on this bidding scam."

"You've still got a problem with the shooter," Vincent said.

"Yeah," I said. "Any suggestions?"

"Somebody's unhappy," Vincent said.

"Is it time to turn over the laptop?" I asked.

"Who are you going to give it to?"

"The unhappy person."

"Might be more complicated now."

"So what do you suggest?"

"Next time he calls, say you want to meet," Vincent said. "Then call me."

* * *

When I left Denny's, I drove up Sonoma Avenue to the police station. Eddie Mahler met me in the lobby. "I want you to look at something," he said. He led me to a second-floor meeting room and motioned for me to sit in front of a video monitor.

He pressed a button, and the screen lit up with the surveillance video of Kenny's house. This time, the video started later in the sequence. In the video I had already pulled myself out of the pool and was staggering across Kenny's deck.

"You look a mess, Teller," Mahler said.

"You wanted me to see that again?" I asked.

"Hang on," he said. I watched myself on screen enter the back of the house and disappear. A moment later, Mahler said, "There." He stopped the tape and pointed to a shadow in the lower right of the screen. It was the image of a man. "See that?" he asked. "This is a minute and a half after you left."

Mahler pressed a button. The image grew clearer. It was a young man in his twenties.

"Let me zoom it," Mahler said.

The focus sharpened on the man's upper body to reveal a broad chest and a shaved head.

"You know this guy?" Mahler asked.

"Yeah," I said. "Name's Shawn Lawrence. Works for Rajiv Patel."

"What's he do?"

"Bodyguard. Follows Patel around everywhere. Breaks people's noses. You think he killed Kenny?"

"I don't know. But if I had to guess, I'd say this Shawn Lawrence is the guy who Ray Brenner saw outside Ms. Salinger's apartment, and who put the two rounds in your motel room last night."

"And killed Paul."

"Maybe," Mahler said. "We know the pickup truck we recovered last week is registered to someone at *Shanti Bhavan*. The forensic accountant hired by John Coffey says Barkley's books have all the classic signs of money laundering. Huge amounts of cash in and out. Someone around Barkley had a lot of money."

"Patel?"

Mahler shrugged. "We don't know. There's another interesting thing. After the shooting at your motel last night, we ran the ballistics on that H&K .45 caliber through our system and turned up something. About a year ago, a young woman, named Anna Sinclair, was killed in a motel down in Petaluma. The weapon was the same H&K. The Petaluma cops never solved that killing. But there was one item in the file. The woman had been driving a stolen car, a late-model platinum-silver Jaguar. Belonged to Rajiv Patel."

I smiled.

"You know something about this?" Mahler asked.

"A little," I said. "Rumor at the estate was that the young lady was Patel's mistress."

"Maybe we need to check into that."

I stood to leave.

"Listen," Mahler said, "We're going to be looking for this guy Lawrence, but if you see or hear from him, stay away from him and call us."

CHAPTER 46

RETURNING TO THE motel after my meeting with Mahler, I found Page had already gone to work. I spent the day running errands. While I sat in the laundromat, I looked at my bank balance and calculated I could only afford another two weeks before I'd need to find a paying job.

Page returned at seven, and we shared a dinner of Thai take-out. She was quiet, and neither of us mentioned our conversation of the night before. When we finished eating, we cleared the table together. Once as we passed by each other, I felt her hand rest for a moment on my back.

We spent the evening reading on separate beds, like fighters in neutral corners. About nine, Page's cell phone rang. For a moment she hesitated, remembering the last time. Then she picked it up, listened for a few seconds, and handed it to me.

It was Shawn. "Hey man," he said. "I'm at Myers Creek Winery. I've got your ex-wife and kid. Bring the laptop. Don't take all night." He hung up.

I felt panic rising in my throat. How had he known who Jill and Lucy were and where they'd be? I called Jill at her home number and on her cell, but there was no answer.

I turned to Page and told her what Shawn said. "He's not going to hurt them, Charlie," she said. "He wants that computer."

I called Vincent. "He's probably telling the truth," Vincent said. "We need to do what he says."

"Should I call Mahler?" I asked.

"No," Vincent said. "I'll be right there."

I told Page to lock the motel room door after me and to call 911 if anyone tried to get in.

When Vincent's pickup pulled up outside our room, I climbed in next to Nico. None of us said anything. Ten minutes later we were driving up the long curving driveway that led to the Myers Creek tasting room.

A few hundred yards from the gate, Vincent stopped the truck and turned to Nico. "There's probably a camera at the gates, and he could be watching it," Vincent said. "I want you to get out here and wait for us. You have your cell?"

Nico felt in her pocket and nodded.

"Something funny happens," Vincent said, "I'm going to press my cell to send you a text message. I won't have time to say anything. But you see that, you call the police."

Nico leaned over and kissed Vincent's cheek and climbed over me to the door.

We drove to the gates and pressed the security call button. A few seconds later the gates opened. Vincent parked the pickup at the base of the entrance stairs. He reached under the front seat and handed me the laptop. "We get inside, stay calm. This guy's killed a couple people already, so he's got nothing to lose. He'll be wired tighter than shit. Don't argue with him."

The door at the top of the stairs was partway open. Inside, the tasting room was brightly lighted. Across the room, at the small bar, stood Shawn. In one hand he held a glass of red wine, in the other a handgun—what I assumed to be the H&K. A few feet further on the floor was the figure of a man lying motionless.

Shawn watched us come in. "Who's this?" he asked, waving the gun toward Vincent.

"A friend," I said.

"You shouldn't come." He tipped back the glass and drank the wine.

"Where are my wife and daughter?" I asked.

"They had to leave with Rajiv," Shawn said.

"The deal was, I bring the laptop, you let them go."

Shawn shrugged. "Guess you got fucked," he said. He put down the wine glass and held out his hand for the laptop.

I walked across the room and handed it to him. Closer, I could see the figure on the floor was Dave Reynolds.

"You kill him?" I asked.

Shawn put the laptop on the bar without taking his eyes from us.

"I hit him on the head," Shawn said with a smile. "He's just sleeping."

Shawn looked at Vincent. "What's your friend's name?" he asked me.

When I told him, Shawn said, "What's he? Like your man? Tell him to say something."

For a minute the two men looked at each other in silence. Then Vincent said, "You have what you wanted, we're walking out of here."

"That's not going to happen."

He came close to Vincent. "You bring something with you?" he asked. Pointing his gun at Vincent, he patted his other hand against Vincent's waist and legs.

In Vincent's right pocket, Shawn found Vincent's cell phone. He looked at it and handed it back to Vincent. "Call your girlfriend," he said, "and tell her there'll be no bone tonight."

Stepping away from Vincent, Shawn said, "Time to go to the cellar."

"What's in the cellar?" I asked.

"Where they make the wine," Shawn said. He nodded his head toward the other side of the room, to an arched entrance to the cellar.

I went first, followed by Vincent and Shawn. The stairs were narrow and dark. For the first third of the way, there was no railing. Instead, lining the walls on both sides were shelves, filled with cellar supplies. As we descended, each of us took hold of the shelves to brace ourselves. Looking for handholds on the shelves, I spotted a pile of grape knives—wood-handled, three-inch blades that pickers use to cut grape clusters at harvest. As my hand reached the shelf, I palmed a knife and slid it up my sleeve.

At the base of the stairs, we reached a concrete floor and a long, broad aisle of racks, thirty feet high and filled with stacked oak barrels. Above us hanging lights cast dim pools of light. The air was cool and damp.

Shawn walked past Vincent and me and led us down the aisle. Smaller corridors branched away from us on either side. Shawn walked backward, alternately watching us and glancing down the side corridors.

Each time he looked back at us, Shawn waved the gun, like a workman proud of a strong tool and the way it felt in his hand.

Shawn watched Vincent carefully, wary of his presence. But when he looked at me, he wore an expression of confident recognition. He had known other men like me, the expression said, weak men who spent their life indoors and who didn't know how to fight. He was comfortable dealing with such men. As far as I was concerned, his job this night would be simple. Shawn was right, of course. I was like the other men he had known. But like many generalizations, it was right only in a general sense and failed to allow for exceptions.

As Shawn turned again to check on Vincent, I let the small grape knife slide down my wrist until I held the barrel of the handle. Then I stepped closer and shoved the blade into his left side under the ribcage. The sharp steel went into his body easily, and I pushed it to the hilt of the handle.

Shawn jumped away from me and looked down at the knife handle. "What'd you do, man?" he said. As he watched, a circle of blood began to pool around the handle. His right hand dropped the gun, and he reached with both hands to touch the handle end.

He looked up at me. His eyes now filled with deep sadness and disappointment. This was wrong, his eyes said. Here was another thing he had to fix.

Then, in the same instant, Vincent leapt toward the fallen gun, and Shawn dropped to floor where the gun lay. Shawn reached it first and fired it into Vincent, who was nearly on top of him. The shot hit Vincent but did not slow his forward motion. In one movement, he grabbed Shawn's wrist and caught the H&K. As Shawn got to his feet, and staggered toward him, Vincent fired two rounds into his mid-section until Shawn fell face forward onto the concrete floor.

Vincent crawled across the floor to where Shawn lay. "He's dead," Vincent said.

"You OK?" I asked.

"What'd you think?" he said.

I knelt next to him and helped him pull off his T-shirt. The bullet had entered his right side above his waist. We doubled over the shirt and pressed it against the wound.

Vincent called Nico on his cell phone and told her what had happened. He told her to call 911 and to check on Dave Reynolds.

Then he turned back to me. "Jesus, Teller," he said. "That was the smallest fucking knife I've ever seen."

"It's what I had," I said. "You going to tell me you had another plan I was supposed to know?"

"I was going to take the gun away him. Nothing too complicated."

"Well, I didn't know that. Look, I need to go to Patel."

"We'll call Mahler and tell him to go. Just wait for him."

"I don't think I can wait."

Vincent looked at me. He dug in his pocket and handed me his truck keys. "Go upstairs and take the laptop," he said. "I don't know if it'll make a difference at this point, but it might."

Then Vincent picked up the H&K and pulled out the clip. "You've got three left," he said. "You ever fire a gun?"

"No," I said.

Vincent handed me the gun. "It's got a safety that needs to be taken off," he said. "The barrel comes up a little when it fires. Hold it with both hands or brace it as best you can. Aim for the torso."

I stood to leave.

"You'll have one chance," Vincent said. "You'll know when it is."

CHAPTER 47

WHEN I ARRIVED at *Shanti Bhavan*, I drove straight through the grounds to the main house. No lights were visible in the windows. I grabbed the laptop and the H&K from the front seat and ran to the back of the house.

I found a spot against the wall, near the back entrance, and waited for Eddie Mahler. I looked at my watch. It had taken me ten minutes to drive from the winery. If Mahler left as soon as Vincent called, he would still have at least another ten minutes to drive from Santa Rosa.

The night was quiet—the only sound came from the wind blowing through the leaves of the live oak trees above me. Then I heard a woman crying, and I recognized Jill's voice.

The door to the back entrance was unlocked. I shoved the gun in my jacket pocket and ran down the dark hall to the lighted doorway of Patel's study.

Patel saw me at the door. "Charlie," he said. "Come join us. You're just in time."

He was seated, as always, in the black leather recliner. He wore his silk dressing gown and dark trousers. On his lap was a large automatic pistol. The two Irish wolfhounds lay behind his chair, tethered to the chair's base. Their large heads followed me as I entered.

On the sofa, to Patel's right side, were Jill and Lucy, sitting close together and holding hands. They both looked at me. Jill's face was red and wet from crying.

Patel picked up the pistol in his right hand and gestured with it toward the chair facing him. "Take a seat, Charlie," he said. "I'll kill you in a few minutes. It'll be good for you."

I sat in the chair and laid the laptop on the coffee table between us. "You can have the computer," I said.

Patel smiled. "Computer!" he said contemptuously. "Why would I want the computer?"

"The police don't have this."

"I imagine they have other things," Patel said in a weary voice.

He laid the pistol back down in his lap. "Tell me, how was Shawn when you saw him?" he asked.

"Dead."

"Is he? That's a pity. He was a good boy. Did you kill him yourself?"

"I helped."

Patel laughed. "Now that's you, Charlie, isn't it? Always the helper, never the doer."

"He's still dead."

"Yes, well, we'll all be dead one day, won't we?" He looked over at Jill and Lucy.

"Why don't you let them leave," I said. "They're not involved in this."

"Of course they are," Patel said. "They're part of your little world."

He picked up the pistol again. "You see these people?" he asked, waving the tip of the pistol in a circle to indicate the photographs on the wall—the actors, singers, and politicians, each captured in a single moment, shaking Patel's hand.

"They're people who achieved things in their lives," Patel said. "Big things. They lived on the stage of life, not behind the scenes." He looked admiringly at the photographs.

There was a grimness to the images now. Their frozen smiles looked down on our sad little party.

"They took risks," he said. "Sometimes they failed, fell on their faces. That's one of the consequences of taking chances."

His gaze returned to me. "What did you do? Copied their petty stories. Followed their ups and downs. What were their consequences to you? Nothing. The more sordid the tale, the better the sales of your books."

"Until you stumbled and fell," he said. "Then you came to me, your tail between your legs. All you had to do was to write my book. But you didn't do that, did you? Your generation never does the job you're paid to do. You're easily distracted. Saving the world."

His face reddened, and he gripped the pistol tightly in his hand.

"You spent your time, which I was paying for, asking questions, causing problems. In the end it was all a waste of time."

"Not all of it," I said. "I found out who killed my friend."

"Your friend? Barkley?"

"You underestimated him, didn't you?"

"A drug dealer. A party giver. Someone else who didn't do his job."

He gazed across the room, lost for a moment in thought.

"Let's get to the good stuff," Patel said, becoming alert again. He pointed the gun carelessly at Jill and Lucy.

"I want you to see the consequences, this time. Which one of them should we kill first?" he asked me. "Come on, Charlie, participate in life. Pick one!"

Jill was crying again. Lucy squeezed her mother's hand and closed her eyes.

Patel fired the gun a few inches to the right side of Jill's head. The sudden explosion made all of us jump. The bullet crashed into the wall behind Jill and Lucy, into the photograph of the nightclub singer Frank Almateri, shattering the glass and spraying shards across the floor. The dogs leaped up, pulling at their leashes and digging at the carpet. One of them howled.

"Pick!" Patel screamed at me.

"Stop it!" I yelled.

Patel looked at me, his eyes shining. He swung the pistol around again and fired without aiming. This time, the shot went to the left of Jill, the bullet smashing the frame of the photograph of the comedienne Melissa Martin.

"Pick!" Patel screamed again. The room was ringing with the gun's explosion. The dogs gagged and choked as their collars tightened around their necks. I was half out of my chair, reaching in my pocket for the H&K.

"I want to say something to my father," Lucy suddenly said.

The room fell silent. I sat back in my seat.

Lucy looked at Patel. It took a moment for him to notice her. She stood up, still holding Jill's hand. Patel watched her.

"This is for you, daddy," she said, turning to face me. She straightened her posture. "I learned it in school. It's called a Poet to his Beloved. By William Butler Yeats."

She took a breath and said,

> *I bring you with reverent hands*
> *The books of my numberless dreams*

She spoke the words slowly and clearly, as if wanting to be certain of each one. Patel stared at her.

> *White woman that passion has worn*
> *As the tide wears the dove-grey sands,*

Lucy paused. Jill stopped crying and looked up at her. The stillness of the room seemed to slow time.

> *And with heart more old than the horn*
> *That is brimmed from the pale fire of time*

I reached my hand into my jacket pocket again and felt the H&K. Without removing the gun from my pocket, I clicked off the safety and pointed the barrel toward Patel. He was still watching Lucy.

> *White woman with numberless dreams*
> *I bring you my passionate rhyme.*

I pulled the trigger. The shot went past Patel and into the back wall, just above the wolfhounds. One of them broke free of the leash but tangled itself with the other dog, and the two of them growled and fought on the floor.

Patel turned toward me, awakened. I fired again, and this time hit him in the left shoulder. He flinched at the impact but raised his pistol and shot. The bullet hit my left thigh. The impact felt like my leg had been struck by a rock. I fell backward onto the carpet and dropped my gun.

Jill pulled Lucy onto the sofa and covered her.

I sat up. My thigh was numb, but there was a sticky wet spot on my trousers. I looked for the gun. It was out of sight, under the coffee table or sofa.

Patel came toward me, his arm fully extended and hanging stiffly at his side, the gun still in his hand.

There was a sound at the door that I thought was the dogs. Then I saw Eddie Mahler standing a few feet away, pointing a gun. "Police," he yelled.

Patel laughed. He slowly raised his gun and aimed it at my head. "Goodbye," he said.

Then I heard Mahler's gun, and something exploded from Patel's chest, and he was thrown forward across the table toward me, his dressing gown billowing as he fell.

The dogs broke free and charged out of the room, their claws skittering across the stone tiles in the hallway.

Mahler stood over Patel. Still aiming his gun at the prone figure with one hand, he felt for a pulse with his other hand. Satisfied, he shoved his gun in his holster and knelt next to me.

"He the only shooter?" Mahler asked.

I nodded.

"I miss anything?" he asked.

"You were here for the important part," I said.

I looked across the room. Jill was holding Lucy in her arms on the sofa.

Mahler quickly lowered me on my back. Where the bullet had torn a hole in my trousers, he ripped the cloth open. He pulled off his jacket, folded one sleeve in half, and pressed it down on the wound with his left hand.

With his right hand, Mahler opened and yanked off my belt. He slid it under my leg and tightened it above the wound. Then, still holding his jacket sleeve in place, he said, "I have to turn you over." He gently eased me on my side and looked at the backside of my thigh.

"How's it look?" I asked.

Mahler shrugged. "My rule of thumb," he said. "Don't get shot."

"So that's what I did wrong."

Mahler helped me onto my back again. "Looks like the bullet went right through," he said. "Which means the surgeon's not going to have to dig it out. Judging by the small amount of blood, I'd guess it didn't hit the femoral artery. How do you feel?"

"Not much," I said. "It's numb."

"That's good. If the bullet hit a bone, you'd be screaming by now."

He looked back at Jill and Lucy. "How're you two doing?" he asked.

"OK," Jill said softly.

Mahler pulled out his cell phone and pressed a speed dial button. When someone answered, he said, "We've got a DOA and a gunshot wound to the leg and stabilized." He gave directions through the estate to the house. "They'll be here in a few minutes," he said.

Mahler looked around the room at the broken photographs. "Looks like a tough night for the rich and famous," he said. "How'd you three manage to keep from being killed?"

"Yeats," I said.

"Yeats? The poet?"

I watched Jill holding Lucy. Jill looked at me, and raised her hand in a single silent wave.

"Yeah," I said. "My rule of thumb. Sometimes the best thing in the world is a love poem."

CHAPTER 4 8

FOR THE NEXT four hours, every one who examined me told me how lucky I was. If I was going to be shot, apparently I had chosen a good way to do it. The bullet had entered the front of my leg and exited the back without striking a large artery or bone. The wound itself was about the size of a dime and left a small crescent-shaped tear in the skin.

In the ER, the trauma team cleaned and examined the wound, injected painkillers, started an IV, and ordered X-rays and arteriograms. All the while, like a crazed version of myself, they asked hundreds of questions.

Later a surgeon did what he called "small artery repair," cleaned and irrigated the entry site, and ordered me filled with antibiotics. I ended up with a five-inch bandage wrapped around my thigh and a tube in my forearm.

That morning I awoke in a room on the hospital's top floor. Nico sat in the chair beside my bed. Her hair was dyed brown and combed straight across her head from a part on the left side. She wore a blue oxford shirt with a button-down collar and khaki trousers.

"Hey, Charlie," she said. "How's the leg?"

"I don't feel anything," I said. "Which is a good thing for now."

"That's what Vincent says. Thank God for drugs."

"Where is he? How is he?"

"Two doors down. Room 808. He's going to be all right. The bullet went through his side, where I guess there aren't any major organs. Anyway Vincent said if the bullet hit lower, you know, into his equipment, it would have been a different story."

"More serious injury."

"Yeah, and he'd want to kill you more than he does."

"Vincent wants to kill me?"

"Not so much. He asked how you were, and I said you were alive and stuff, and he was happy."

"What'd he say?"

"He didn't actually say anything, but I could tell he was happy. I was going to see if I could have you guys moved into the same room, but I think I'll wait until, you know . . ."

"He wants to kill me less?"

"Yeah."

"So what's with this outfit?" I asked. "I'm trying to figure out if you're real or a product of my meds."

"It's a new look," Nico said.

"You look somehow oddly familiar."

"I should. This is you. It's my 'homage to Charlie Teller.'"

"What brought this on?"

"I wanted to celebrate you, Charlie," she said. "These last couple weeks, what you've done has meant a lot to me."

"Investigating Paul's murder?"

"No. The way you've listened to me and taken me seriously."

"Is that so unusual?"

"What're you kidding? No one takes me seriously. Except Vincent, but then he takes everyone seriously."

After a few minutes, Nico looked around and saw the bouquet of bird of paradise on the bedside table behind her. "Hey, who're the weird flowers from?" she asked. Removing the card from the plant, she read: "'To the speedy recovery of our local Tolstoy. Anita Kleinman.' Who's Anita Kleinman?"

"An ardent admirer," I said.

Nico touched one flower with an index finger. "I guess this means she's happy," she said.

There was a knock on my door, and Page came in. Nico and Page silently nodded at each other. "I was just leaving," Nico said, edging around the end of the bed. "I'll go check on Vincent."

Page came to the bedside and kissed me on the forehead. "The nurse at the station said you're going to be all right," she said.

"Yeah," I said. "The surgeon called it a 'through and through.'"

Neither of us said anything for a minute. Then Page said, "When you're ready for it, John has a class that can help with your rehab."

I nodded. We looked at each other without speaking. She wore jeans and a long-sleeved flannel shirt. She looked more beautiful than I remembered.

"I went back to my apartment," Page said. She sat on the chair beside my bed. "I cleaned up everything. Put it all back together. It doesn't look so bad."

"There's an extra room if you need a place to stay when you get out of here," Page said. "It's set up as an office. Paul worked there sometimes when he stayed over."

"I remember," I said.

"Do you know what you're going to do?"

"I don't know. Maybe I'll write something. I think I can still write."

Page looked at me.

"That's not what you meant, is it?" I said. "Are you asking me to move in with you?"

"I was offering you a place to stay," she said. "Are you planning on moving back to the motel?"

"I hadn't gotten that far."

She shook her head. "It's okay if you don't want to live with me, Charlie," she said.

"I hadn't made any decision."

"Yes, you did. The minute I asked you, you decided. It's okay."

"I don't know what I want. Everything's up in the air. I have to take some time to . . ."

"You can stop, Charlie. I know you're a writer, and you think it helps, but explaining it doesn't change it."

"We're not going to go back to being hard asses with each other, are we? You're not going to say fuck all the time again? We're past that, aren't we?"

"Are we? I don't know where we are."

"Two people who like each other."

"Sounds like something Paul would say," she said. "When we first started going out, he said he liked hanging out with me."

"Not a bad thing," I said.

"No," Page said. "I guess not."

She looked at me again. "I was just getting used to being Paul's girlfriend when he was killed," she said. "You probably think Paul didn't introduce me to you and his friends because he was ashamed of me. But that wasn't it. I wasn't ready. Did you ever have someone see you in a certain way, and it's not really true? But you like being seen that way, and you think you can change and be the person they see?"

"And you wanted to be that person with me?" I said.

"When I first came to you after the thing with Ray, all I could think about was keeping everything the way it was. Then you were there, and you were sweet like Paul, and you took care of me the way he did. I wanted you to love me the way he did."

"And I just asked you a lot of questions."

Page smiled. "Some of them were good questions."

"You can still be the person Paul saw," I said. "Even without him. I don't think Paul was fantasizing it. I think he saw it was who you are."

"You think so?"

"Yeah, it was that hopeful side of him that made things possible."

She stood to leave but paused, as if not knowing what to do. Finally she looked at me with a new shyness and smiled. "Can I practice with you?" she asked.

"Sure," I said. "I'll be the one you tell everything to. I'm used to that."

* * *

My nurse had warned me that the pain medication would make me sleep, and after Page left, I drifted off. I dreamed, at first, of being chased by a faceless assailant, always a step behind, sometimes holding a knife, other times a gun. I ran down long corridors, my legs in slow motion.

Then the threat was gone, and I dreamed of Paul, the one who had set off the chain of events in this story. In those last months of his life, my friend must have known how difficult it would be to expose Patel, how entangled his own affairs were with Kenny McDonald and Patel himself. He had already tried once to remake himself, to escape from his own past, and now he was on the run from the very man he had become in flight. Had he really thought he could succeed? Perhaps the night he was killed, when he came to talk to me, he had wanted to ask what I thought of his chances, given what I knew of the arc of life. What would I have said? Would I have told him that if we survive long enough, sometimes we reach a point where the ironies of our life pile up, and however hard we try, we end up fulfilling them? Or, would I have been infected by his own high hopes and said that anything is possible?

In my dream that day, Paul did not look as he had in the late-night meetings in his café. Instead he was the man I had seen that last night. He was dancing, and there was a lightness about him, as if of something unburdened. He was in love with a beautiful woman, who loved him in return. And, as happened so often in his life, he was on the brink of a new deal that was going to transform everything. He had decided how to start over, and he had given the means of it to the best person he knew for the job, a washed-up writer who could not resist telling another story.

That afternoon one of the nurses helped me into a wheelchair and took me to the solarium on the second floor, where I could sit and look at the vineyard on the hillside behind the hospital.

After I had been there a while, I heard someone approach behind me, and when I looked, I saw Eddie Mahler, standing a few feet away, his hands in his pockets.

"I hear you're going to make it," he said.

"The surgeon told me whoever stopped the bleeding knew what he was doing," I said.

Mahler shrugged. "Just trying to keep down the local death toll," he said. "Maybe now you're in the hospital, we won't have so many dead bodies turning up. You know, Teller, this isn't LA. We're not used to people shooting each other." He sat on the sofa beside my wheelchair.

"You fitting together all the pieces of the puzzle?" I asked.

"Most of them," he said. "We can tie Shawn Lawrence to the murders of Ray Brenner, Andrew Sutter, and the young woman down in Petaluma with the Jaguar, Anna Sinclair. There's enough circumstantial evidence to tie him to the shooting of Paul Barkley and the overdose of Kenny McDonald."

"What about Patel?"

Mahler shook his head. "Too early to say if we can find any real evidence that Patel ordered the hits, but that's not out of the question. There's going to be a state investigation of Patel's bid-rigging scheme. And the state drug task force that's been looking at Kenny McDonald will widen their investigation to include Patel."

"I assume you've looked at Paul's laptop and memory stick?"

"Yeah, and we've talked to your friend Vincent. You two could've saved yourselves a lot of trouble by turning those things in. Molly's trying hard to keep the district attorney from charging both of you with withholding evidence and obstruction."

"I'll have to thank her."

Neither of us said anything for a minute. Then Mahler asked, "So what's next?"

"I don't know," I said. "I think I'll stick around here. Try to write something. Patel didn't deserve an autobiography, but there's probably an article in there. Maybe do something on Kenny McDonald. Work in that whole Theodor Adorno angle of yours."

"Yeah," Mahler said, smiling. "I bet *Rolling Stone* eats that up."

"Or, I'll go back to fiction, write a novel. I've always wanted to write a story about two people falling in love."

"What's the first lesson of writing? Write what you know or what you want to learn."

"In my case, it could be some of each," I said.

At the end of the hallway, I saw Jill and Lucy approaching. When they got closer, Lucy broke into a run. "Daddy!" she cried, as she reached my wheelchair and put her arms out to hug me. Jill bent down and kissed me on the cheek.

"I assume you've already met Detective Mahler," I said.

"Yes," Jill said. "He took our stories this morning."

Mahler looked at Jill. "I meant to tell you," he said, "You did a great job of keeping Shawn and Patel occupied before we arrived," Mahler said. "I know it wasn't easy."

I took Lucy's hand. "And thank you for your poem, sweetheart," I said. "You were very brave."

Lucy blushed. "I just wanted you to hear it before . . . he did something," she said.

Mahler turned to me. "When you get out of here, come by the house," he said. "We'll drink some wine and talk about Thomas Hardy and your own novel."

After Mahler had gone, I asked Jill and Lucy to wheel me back to my room and help me into bed. Lucy walked around the room, looking out the window. "This is the greatest room," she said. "It's like the penthouse."

"Yeah, except they wake you up every two hours," I said.

"Can I see your leg?" she asked.

"Not much to see," I said, pulling aside the covers. "It's all bandaged."

Lucy stared at the wrapping around my leg. "You're going to be okay, right?" she said.

"Sure. Might take me a while to get back to normal. You can help—we'll go for walks."

"I have a job for you right now," I said. "See these flowers? Take them over to Room 808. A friend of mine, named Vincent, is there. Give the flowers to him, and say they're from the local office of the DEA."

"D-E-A?" Lucy asked.

"Yeah. He'll know what it means."

When Lucy had gone, Jill took my hand and squeezed it. "We were lucky," she said.

"I know," I said. "I never intended for you and Lucy to be involved. I'm sorry. I was trying to help a friend. I guess I didn't really do a good job of it. How's Dave?"

"He had a concussion," Jill said. She let go of my hand. "He's okay. Awful bruise on his face."

"I'm sorry he got caught up in this."

"I'm not seeing him, Charlie. He's just a friend."

Jill looked out the window. "I met Page," she said. "Last night in the ER. We were both there. She was . . . worried about you."

Jill looked back at me. "She's a beautiful woman," she said. "She loves you, you know that?"

"Maybe," I said.

"Not maybe, she does. You never know when someone loves you."

"Don't I?"

"Do you love her?"

"I don't know. No."

Jill studied my face.

"I slept with her," I said.

"Charlie, we're divorced," Jill said. "You can do what you want."

"I know, but there's . . ."

Jill waited for me to finish, and when I didn't, she reached into her purse and pulled out an iPod. "I brought you some music," she said. "It's a recording of me playing Bach's Three Suites for the Cello, transcribed for the viola. Maybe you can replace that old tape you're always carrying around."

"Thanks," I said. "But I liked carrying around that old tape."

Jill smiled. "My loyal fan," she said.

"I wanted to tell you I see how moving up here has changed you," I said. "You seem like you've found what you want."

"It's a challenge. Sometimes I wish I had a more ordinary way of making a living."

"A more ordinary husband might've helped."

"I'm sorry I said that thing about your throwing things away. I know it's not true. And I've called Richard Mansfield and told him that I won't be filing a petition for change of custody."

"Thank you for that. It's been wonderful to spend time with Lucy these past couple months."

"I'm going to need all the help I can get with her," Jill said.

"I miss you, you know that?" I said, taking Jill's hand. "I miss talking to you."

Jill looked down at my hand holding hers and took a deep breath and let it out. "You know what it is about you, Charlie, that makes it so hard?" she asked.

"It?" I said. "You mean there's just one thing?"

"You *think* you want to be one of the good guys, but you're not sure. You have to look on the other side, to see what it's like."

"Curiosity. Occupational hazard."

"The problem is, you know what a good guy is, and you know everything it takes to be one. You're more conscious than most of the men I know. You're *this* close."

"But not really there?" I asked. I looked at her face and knew her eyes well enough to see that they were softer. I hadn't saved everything in Rajiv Patel's study. No single act is entirely redemptive, but all a fallen man has is the first step back.

Jill squeezed my hand. "No," she said, smiling. "Not really there. But what was it Nick White told you? No one in this world is without hope."

She laid her hand on the side of my face and leaned down and kissed me slowly on the lips. "We could always try it again," she said.

"Yeah," I said, smiling back. "We could always do that."

An Excerpt from *Elise: A Novel*, the next Frederick Weisel novel, featuring police detective Eddie Mahler:

Chapter 1

(Tuesday, 6:10 am)

THACKREY HAD BEEN awake for three days—or, was it four? He couldn't remember. When he had been taking Adderall, it had been easier to tell. Thirty milligrams of extended release in the morning, another sixty in the afternoon. But since he had been doing stacks of Provigil and ephedrine and crushing Ritalin, the hours and days blurred together. Now he dried a wooden coffee stirrer on his sleeve, poked it into the plastic bag on his lap, and balanced a tiny pile of powder on the end. He sniffed it.

He was in the front seat of the Mercedes in the parking lot of an all-night Circle K in Santa Rosa. At this hour, the customers were mostly admins and techs on the morning shift at the hospital and medical building on the other side of the lot. Thing One and Thing Two were in the back seat. They had started out drinking coffee to get their hands warm, but now they were bored and were playing rounds of Cell Phone Invader.

They watched a silver Jetta roar into the lot, swerve toward a spot, and park with two wheels over the line. The driver emerged, a young woman in black slacks and jacket, a paisley scarf knotted at her neck. She pressed a remote lock, and the car blared. Her boots clicked across the lot toward the entrance.

"My turn," Thackrey said. "Her name's Leslie. She's in Sterile Processing, and she's just had an all-nighter with the new urology resident."

He passed the plastic bag to the back seat and picked up his phone. Holding it in his right hand, he used his thumb to scroll through the menu until he came to the jailbreak app he and the boys had made for getting through the DMV firewall. He tapped it open and looked across the lot and typed in the

Jetta plate. While the phone did its job, he licked the rest of the powder off the stirrer.

A file opened: Stacie Singer. "God, what an awful name," Thackrey said.

"Minus five points," said Russell, who had leaned forward from the back seat to see the screen. He wore earbuds and bobbed his head in time with a faint, tinny beat.

"Shouldn't I get something for guessing a name ending in 'e'?" Thackrey asked. He opened Facebook and typed in the name. As the search ran, Thackrey turned in his seat and said, "So, Terence, my faithful Hadji, have we thought about how to remove the blood from the trunk liner?"

"All the perfumes in Arabia will not sweeten this little hand," Terence said.

"No hurry, of course," Thackrey said. "But eventually something will need to be done."

"Too bad we didn't put down plastic," Russell said.

"What's done cannot be undone," said Terence.

"OK, Macbeth, we get it, Terry," Thackrey said. "Now focus."

"Two options," Terence said. "One, I remove the liner and wash it in a laundromat, in one of those large-capacity machines."

"That's going to attract a lot of attention and be remembered later," Russell said. "Besides the blood's in the fibers now."

"Or, two, I replace the liner with a new one," Terence said. "I can order one online, and request overnight shipment. We'd have it by tomorrow."

"You always were the smart one," Thackrey said.

"Thank you, sahib," Terence said.

Thackrey lowered the car's side window and looked outside. The sky was black and starless, and along the rim, the coastal fog had blown inland and covered the lower reaches like the thick folds of a shroud.

He looked back at his phone. "Stacie only shares some of her profile information with everyone," he read out loud.

"How ungenerous of you, Stacie," he said. He opened a new window on the screen, scrolled to a key app, and tapped it. "In we go," he said.

Thackrey watched the cell phone screen open. "Ouch," he said. "Someone needs new friends."

"Minus five more," Russell said, looking over Thackrey's shoulder at the cell phone. "She's a business manager at Brookside."

"I'll make it up in the call round," Thackrey said, scrolling through the profile. "In a relationship with Brian Conover. Look at the ears. Interests: pop tarts. Quotations: Cyndi Lauper: 'God loves all the flowers, even the wild ones that grow on the side of the highway.' Could anything be sadder than this?"

The last hit of Ritalin scratched and burned in Thackrey's nostrils. Now he felt a popping rush. His hearing burst open: the East Asian techno pop inside Russell's earbuds, Terence drumming his fingers on his empty coffee cup, and outside, the sizzle of the mercury vapor lamps in the parking lot. He caught himself. "Where's the phone with spoofing?" he asked.

Russell handed Thackrey a phone.

"Am I old boyfriend or eager suitor?" Thackrey asked.

"Old boyfriend," Russell said.

"Do I need to enter one of your Hong Kong prep school passwords?" Thackrey asked. "Which one was it? The King George School?"

"Give it a rest, Ben," Russell said.

Thackrey typed Stacie's number on the keypad and tapped Call. The call was picked up on the third ring. Thackrey put it on speaker.

"Hello?" The voice was high and impatient.

"Hey, Stacie," Thackrey said. "How's it going?"

"I'm sorry," she said. "Who's this?"

"It's me," Thackrey said. "The one who was shtupping you before Brian."

"What'd you say? Jerry?"

"I miss our nights listening to Chris Brown and watching Sandra Bullock movies."

"Do I know you?" Stacie asked.

"How's Mister Tingles?" Thackrey asked.

"Is that a pet or part of her body?" Terence asked.

"What is this?" Stacie asked. "Who else is there?"

"You look great, by the way," Thackrey said. "That scarf looks like a Fendi."

"In her dreams," Russell said.

There was silence on the other end. "If this is supposed to be a joke, it's not funny," Stacie said after a few seconds.

"No joke," Terence said. "Five points."

"But you really should take better care of yourself, Stacie," Thackrey said. "You drive that little Jetta way too fast."

Across the parking lot, they could see the young woman come out the front door of the Circle K. "Where are you?" she asked, looking at the lot.

"And how safe are River View Apartments?" Thackrey said. "Every time I was there, I worried about the deadbolt. Come on—all it takes is a couple of tweekers following you home one night. With a tension wrench, they'd be inside. I could be in there right now, for all you know."

"Listen, you sick jerk," Stacie said, her voice rising. "I'm going to call the police and have them trace this call."

"Police," said Russell. "Ten points."

"Do you still look under the bed before you go to sleep?" Thackrey asked. "You really should from now on. We'll be there next time."

"Fuck you," Stacie said.

"F-word," Russell said. "Five points."

"The problem is, you need to be less stupid if you're not going to get hurt. That's going to be a problem for you, isn't it, Stacie?"

"Fuck you," she said, hanging up and shoving the phone in her pocket.

"Five more," Terence said.

The young woman pointed a remote at her car, and the horn blared again. She jumped in and gunned the car out of the lot.

"Fifteen, love, front seat," Thackrey said. "Second set."

He held up the phone for Russell and exchanged it for the plastic bag. "Let's order that trunk liner," he said.

Frederick Weisel has been a writer and editor for more than 30 years.
He lives with his wife in Santa Rosa, California.

CPSIA information can be obtained at www.ICGtesting.com
Printed in the USA
BVOW070008281111

276952BV00002B/100/P